WHITE

RIVER

RED

A NOVEL

BECKY MARIETTA

Relax. Read. Repeat.

WHITE RIVER RED
By Becky Marietta
Published by TouchPoint Press
Brookland, AR 72417
www.touchpointpress.com

ISBN-13: 978-1-952816-14-7

Editor: Jenn Haskin
Cover Design: Hannah Linder Designs

Visit the author's website at http://beckymarietta.com

First Edition

Printed in the United States of America.

For Molly, the bravest girl I know, who read this story in its infancy and decorated the pages with hearts; for Casey, in whose arms I am always safe; and for Colin, my mirth-maker. You'll have to read the book now that your name is in it, Son.

CHAPTER ONE

Fayetteville, 1972

WHEN SHE WAS TWENTY-THREE years old, Betty McLaughlin met her first real-life hero, and, as is so often the case when heroes are involved, she didn't realize how important the moment was until much, much later. In truth, she was just trying to get out of writing obituaries.

Betty had landed a job at *The Springdale Times* a week after graduating with a degree in English from the University of Arkansas, and in the year that followed, her job had consisted of writing the weekly "What's About Town" announcement column (garage sales, fairs, church rummage sales, Little Miss Sweet Pea results) and obituaries. She'd gained a certain amount of popularity when she first penned an obituary for a Mrs. Fredericka Hammond, 73, opening with the lines, "It is with great joy and humble acceptance that we release our beloved Fredericka into the Lord's loving arms." People really liked the shift from the typical "It is with great sorrow" intro of most obits; soon they were calling in to *The Times* regularly, telling whoever was answering phones that day that they needed an obituary written, and they'd sure like the "humble joy" writer to do it.

At first, Betty had been flattered, feeling as if she'd already begun making her mark as a writer and a journalist, a dream she'd had since childhood. After a while, though, the shine began to rub off the penny. She'd been the first person in her family to graduate college, and trying to convince her father, who'd paid for that college, that the money had been well spent was getting harder as each month passed. He'd wondered, more than once, if anyone with a pencil and a grasp of basic English grammar could do Betty's job without the expense of school. Betty hated to admit that lately she'd been wondering if maybe her dad was right.

One day as Betty sat wearily at her desk, trying to come up with ten different ways to say the same thing, she decided it was time to, as Dr. Jeffries, her favorite English professor at the U of A, loved to say, "effect radical change." She shoved herself out of her chair, sending it squealing behind her as she stood. Kevin Ash, in charge of sales and ads for the paper, glanced up at the sound, squinted at her for a moment, then settled back into trying to solve last week's Sunday crossword puzzle.

Before she could lose her resolve, Betty marched in her clunky leather clogs to the door of Murray Jackson, editor-in-chief and boss-man extraordinaire, and rapped on the wooden door loudly. Her knock was answered by a low, weary voice saying, "Come."

Betty opened the door and stepped in, pulling the door shut behind her. Murray was, as usual, half-hidden behind several disheveled piles of papers, his eyes down on whatever he was reading, his bald pate pointed at her like a pale pink stop sign. Now she was there, she found she was too afraid to speak. Maybe tomorrow would be a better time to effect some change, and less than radical would be fine.

Murray barked, "Well?" and Betty jumped a little. He looked up. "What do you want? I'm drowning in next week's deadlines already." His eyes, behind the rimless glasses perched precariously on the end of his nose, were about as welcoming as a drink of unsweetened tea. Betty swallowed hard and thought of her favorite line from *Pride and Prejudice*: "My courage always rises at every attempt to intimidate me." Surely Murray could be no worse than Lady Catherine de Bourgh.

"Murray," she said, then stopped, gathering herself. She'd always been slightly terrified of him, not only because he was her first boss, but also because he'd never seemed charmed by her youth and prettiness. It was what she liked best about him, too—when he hired her, she knew it was because he believed she could do the job, not because he hoped for a little tussle on the desk with a sweet young dolly. In the busy world of journalism, as much as she'd seen of it anyway, Murray was unique in this. He'd never asked her to make coffee for him, never dropped a pen so he could make her pick it up in order to admire her shapely derriere, never once called her "honey" or "sweetie." He was a good boss—but he was scary.

"Good grief, Betty, speak," Murray snapped. "Did you finish the Clark woman's obit? The family wants it in this weekend's paper because the funeral is Monday."

"Yes, sir," Betty said. "I finished it—it's probably in that pile there." She pointed to a half-foot high stack of papers on the right edge of Murray's desk.

"So?"

Courage, Betty told herself again. She realized she was twisting her hands together in front of her and forced herself to quit fidgeting. "Murray, you know how much I like working here, and honestly, I don't mind the obits and local happenings, but. . . ." She took a deep breath and put her hands on her hips. "Well, isn't it time I get to do something else? I mean, Carson has been here six months and you've already got him writing headlines. He's not a better writer than me." Actually, she thought Carson was barely literate, but she wisely kept that to herself. Bad-mouthing others to push herself forward was not her way.

Murray sighed. "I suppose you are going to bleat at me until I give you something," he grumbled. "That's usually how it works with you young folks. You're never happy where you are. Lucky for you, I've learned that it isn't worth the aggravation to say no." He shook his head, and then began rummaging around in his nest. He finally pulled out a yellow sheet of lined legal paper and held it out to her. "Sunday special story insert—one of those 'where-are-they-now, pull-the-heart-strings deals.'"

Betty took the paper from him and looked at the scribbled writing on it: *White River Red, aka Forrestina Campbell. Fayetteville Oaks Nursing Home.* "White River Red?" she asked.

"You don't know about her?" Murray said. "I'm surprised—though I guess you're a little young to have seen her around. There was once a time when she was a pretty common sight, especially during fair season. She ran a betting game that used real, live rats at the annual carnival." He shook his head. "As a kid, I heard more wild stories about that old bird than you can shake a stick at. You never did see such a fiery-haired, fiery-tempered crone in your whole life. I remember her stomping all around town dressed in old denim overalls, her hair cut short, wearing an old leather hat and boots, swearing at any man who got in her way, including the sheriff. *Especially* the sheriff." He laughed. "I tell you, I think some of the first dirty words I ever heard came out of that woman's mouth."

Betty watched in astonishment as a wry smile appeared on Murray's normally sour face. "She didn't act that way around other women, though. The minute another female her age or older entered the scene, Red would suddenly become like a lady born and bred, complimenting the other woman on her dress or hair, talking about fine weather and flower gardens, like she was on her way to a cotillion and butter wouldn't melt in her mouth. And though she always looked as poor as a preacher's pocket, everybody knew somebody she'd helped out in some way—she'd pay doctors' bills in secret or leave sacks of vegetables or piles of wood on the porches of people down on their luck." He shook his head, still smiling. "I didn't know she was still alive until someone called the other day to ask if you'd had to write an obit for her. I was curious, so I dug around and found out that she's still with us on this mortal coil. I figured it might be good to see how many of those tall tales are really true before she finally does kick the bucket." He leaned back into the wooden slats of his chair, lacing his hands behind his head. "So what do you think? You up for the job? I warn you, it's not going to be easy—Red can be meaner than a molting rattler if you aren't careful, and she isn't as dainty with young ladies as she is with old."

"I can handle it," Betty said, nodding. "I've always wanted to practice my snake-charming skills."

"Famous last words," Murray snorted. "In fact, you may want to go ahead and write up your own obituary to have on hand, just in case." He returned to the pile of papers in front of him. "I'll give you three weeks for interviews and a week to get it polished," he said. "Now, get."

"Thank you, Murray," Betty said. "You won't be sorry, I promise."

"Yeah, yeah," Murray said as Betty turned to leave. "You still have to keep up with the obits and town happenings. On time and with all that humble joy."

On her way back to her desk, Betty nabbed a dog-eared, coffee-ring-stained Yellow Pages from a battered table where general reference material was stacked haphazardly. She settled into her chair and, searching the yellow page listings, found the number and ad for Fayetteville Oaks Nursing Home. She read through the description of the listing and frowned. Fayetteville Oaks was a government-funded institute. She remembered her Grandma Mary extracting a promise from Betty's mother to never put her in a government place, claiming that it was like an orphanage for old folks with no money. "Destitute and alone—that's who gets stuck in there," Grandma Mary had said. "You've read *Oliver Twist*, Jean. You want your momma begging for a little more gruel?"

"Poor Red," Betty muttered, staring at the listing. Picking up the phone's receiver and holding it to her ear with her shoulder, she punched in the number. The phone rang twice, and then a clipped voice said, "Fayetteville Oaks Nursing Home."

"Hello," Betty said, "This is Betty McLaughlin from *The Springdale Times*. I believe you have a resident there, a Mrs. Forrestina Campbell, and I'd like to set up an interview with her at her earliest convenience. Do you think she is—"

"Is she what? Crazy? Lucid? Yes to both—and with a mouth that spits acid. More's the pity," the woman on the other end of the line said. Betty,

5

feeling strangely defensive of the supposed legend she'd never met, decided she didn't like this person on the phone at all.

"Available, was what I was going to ask," she said coldly. "Do you think she'd be willing to talk to me?"

"She'd talk the leg off a kitchen table because it couldn't run away," the no-nonsense voice replied. "As far as available, I'm pretty sure she's got nothing on her busy calendar. No one ever visits the old coot, though she does get a letter every couple of weeks or so from some place up north. I'll tell her to expect you tomorrow at 1:00; after lunch she is usually in a more amiable mood. Since we're having beans and weenies, which I believe is a particular favorite of hers, she may not even take your hide off." The attendant paused, then said, "What do you want to talk to her about, anyway?"

Betty did not feel like engaging in a cozy conversation, but she knew that reporters who burned bridges early on were usually stuck on the wrong side of the bank. She replied, "Well, ma'am, if all goes well, you'll be able to read about it in our paper in a few weeks. I'll give you a free copy for your help. Thank you, and goodbye."

After hanging up the phone, Betty rose and grabbed her tan windbreaker from the back of her chair. Kevin glanced up and said, "Geez, Betty. You're not quitting for the day already, are you?"

Betty patted the edges of her shoulder-length, feathered-cut hair. "Go back to your puzzles, ad-man," she said airily, pushing her arms through her jacket sleeves. "I've got to do an interview for my feature, and I need to go home to prepare some questions. It's too noisy to think in this place."

Kevin whistled low. "Get a load of Dorothy Parker," he said to no one listening. He picked his pencil back up. "You know a four-letter word for shark food that starts with a 'c,' Dorothy?"

"Chum, chum," she said, slipping the long leather strap of her purse over her shoulder.

Kevin traced the letters in the squares and grinned. "Go get 'em, kid," he hollered after her as she left the office. She tossed him a wave with the back of her hand and hurried out the door. She'd told Kevin a fib—she didn't have a problem with the staccato clacking of typewriters and murmurs of telephone calls in the office; in fact, she found the din comforting. The truth was, she wanted to get out before Murray had a chance to change his mind.

Betty spent a feverish evening writing up a list of questions. The next day, after a bologna-on-white-bread lunch at her desk, she hopped in her light blue Volkswagen Beetle and drove to Fayetteville Oaks, glancing down at the handwritten directions on the seat next to her. What she saw when she arrived filled her with dismay—the nursing home was a series of rectangular yellow-bricked buildings with absolutely no oaks in sight. In fact, there weren't any trees near the premises at all. Betty pulled into the asphalt parking lot in the front and clucked disapprovingly. Instead of a lawn, there were half-moon shaped spaces along both sides of the glass-paned entrance filled with glaringly white gravel, presumably to keep ground-care to a minimum. How awful it would be to have to spend one's last days in such an ugly, disheartening place.

Betty walked up to the front desk just inside the automatic sliding doors of the main building. "Hello. . ." she said cheerfully. She leaned forward a bit and read the nametag of the woman behind the laminate counter. ". . . Sue."

Sue, thin and pinched-faced, barely looked up from the *National Enquirer* magazine spread out in front of her. Betty could see the article that claimed the woman's attention was about an alien's love child with a farmer's wife in Idaho. Betty tried again. "I'm Betty McLaughlin from *The Springdale Times*. I have an interview with one of your residents—Mrs. Forrestina Campbell."

Sue flipped the page. "Down the hall on your left, all the way t' the end, door on the right," she droned. "Hope you've had your shots."

Betty resisted all her Southern instincts to be polite and say thank you. Instead, she turned on her heel and stalked off down the hallway.

"You're welcome," Sue called after her, sounding irritated.

"Kiss my Bundt cake," Betty muttered under her breath. She wondered why everyone in this place was so hateful about Forrestina. She refused to believe the woman could be so bad—Murray's brief wander down memory lane in his office had been tinged with grudging admiration and a little affection. But then, he'd also made that comment about rattlers, so maybe there was a good reason for all the snide remarks she'd heard from the staff. Still, Betty was resolved to give Forrestina a fair shake and make up her own mind.

At the very end of the narrow hallway, she found a door with a faded purple construction-paper sign taped to it. On the paper, written in blocky black marker letters, were the names "Campbell and Lyons." She knocked tentatively. Nervousness, combined with the overwhelming smell of the Pine-Sol used to wash the cheap vinyl floors, made her feel a little sick to her stomach.

"Enter!" a gravelly voice called out. Betty pushed the door open and stuck her head into the room. "Ms. Campbell?" she said. "I'm Betty McLaughlin, from the paper, and—"

"I know, I know. You're here to do a story about me. Well, come in. You're letting all the air conditioning out." The woman cackled at a joke Betty didn't get; it was artificially freezing in the hall. She wondered why the AC was on so high in April. It was just starting to warm up outside, and every elderly person she'd known was always colder rather than warmer. She stepped into the room and noted a diminutive woman in the single bed closest to the door lying curled on her side under a thin beige cotton blanket, her body barely substantial enough to make a shape under the covers. She did not react to Betty's presence but simply stared with blank, faded eyes. Another woman, obviously the one who had invited her in, said, "Don't mind Ethel. She's out of it most of the time."

A little unnerved, Betty moved forward and got her first real look at the infamous White River Red. Forrestina Campbell, as vibrant and hearty as her roommate was pale and still, was sitting in a mustard-colored vinyl easy chair in the sunlight near the large double-paned window that took up most of one wall of the room. Betty was gratified to see that she was wearing the famed overalls, faded and patched on the knee with a bright red-and-white paisley kerchief. Under the overalls, she wore a plaid flannel shirt rolled up to the elbows. Her feet, clad in weathered, scuffed leather work-boots, were kicked up on a neatly made bed covered in the same beige cotton bedspread as Ethel's. When Betty walked towards her, Forrestina pulled her feet down and gestured to an identical chair set up across from her.

Betty sat down, carefully smoothing the hem of her mini-dress, wincing a little as the sun-warmed vinyl touched her bare legs. She was keenly aware of Forrestina squinting at her, saying nothing. She took a deep breath, remembered her Lizzie Bennet mantra, then smiled broadly, extending her right hand. "Ms. Campbell, thank you for agreeing to talk to me," she said. "I've heard so many nice things about you."

"Bull hockey," Forrestina said flatly, gripping Betty's hand in her own strong, callused old paw and pumping it emphatically. "You may have heard things about me, girlie, but I bet they weren't nice."

Her habitual Southern good manners kicked in again and caused Betty to begin the requisite protestations, but Forrestina stopped her mid-protest. "No, ma'am," she said, shaking her head. "If you're going to ask me questions, I'm going to tell you the truth. That means I expect you to give me the same courtesy. Don't you worry about my feelings, honey. I'm no delicate flower, and I won't wilt if you say something mean."

Betty bit back a smile at the understatement of the century. She imagined "delicate" and "flower-like" were two descriptions that had never been used to describe Forrestina. Besides her men's clothing and old leather hat, Forrestina's red hair, faded to a pale orange by time, was cropped in a ragged blunt bob that landed between her stooped shoulders and sharp chin. She was thin and rangy and surprisingly shorter than Betty had expected; her sonorous voice made her sound like a giantess, but when she got up to find Betty a glass of water, Betty noticed that she was just a couple inches taller than five feet. She handed Betty the water and then returned to her chair.

Betty took a sip. "Thanks," she said.

"Pleasure," Forrestina replied automatically. A robin hopped onto the concrete slab outside the window and trilled obnoxiously, and when Forrestina cocked her head to the side slightly to the left at the sound, Betty noticed a flash of white light resting for a moment on the old lady's jawline. A pair of lovely teardrop diamond earrings shone in the unlikely earlobes of the elderly woman. Betty made a mental note to ask about those, then placed the glass beside her on the nubby avocado-green carpet. It was time. "So," she said, a dime-store notebook balanced on her thighs, her pen poised in the air, "where shall we begin?"

Forrestina leaned forward, resting her elbows on her knees. "How about the day I up and run away from home to join the Ringling Brothers Circus?" she asked. "Isn't that where all the best stories start? *Once upon a time, a foolish child left home and hearth for the great unknown, hoping to find something better.*" A natural storyteller and true showman, Forrestina had Betty hooked; Betty found herself leaning in as well, eager for the tale that was about to unfold.

Forrestina closed her eyes, and Betty watched a smile as sweet and young as new peas drift over the old woman's face. It lasted just a moment, a flash of sunlight on the surface of a gray lake, then Forrestina opened her eyes, fixed Betty in her fierce gaze, and began to speak.

CHAPTER TWO

The Circus Years, 1906

FORRESTINA SAT WITH HER PARENTS and two younger sisters at dinner, her eyes cast down as she sipped potato soup from a silver spoon. She was trying not to slurp, to clink her spoon against the china bowl, to do *anything* that might annoy Mother, who was silently glaring in her direction. She was obviously still in trouble; the scolding she'd endured last week had apparently not been the end of the matter. Best to wait out the storm as meekly as possible.

After many porridge-thick, excruciating minutes, her mother, a tiny, plump woman with a rapier tongue, pushed her untouched dinner away, wiped the corners of her downturned mouth with a linen napkin, and announced to the table at large, "In a month, Forrestina is to be sent away."

Everyone in the room froze, some in the act of scooping, others with their spoons midair. Forrestina's own spoon went clattering into her bowl. Desperately she looked over at her father, willing him to dispute her mother's statement. Papa was gazing deep into his soup as if trying to divine an escape therein. No help for her there, then. She dropped her hands into her lap, clenching her fingers together tightly. "Mother. . ." she began, trying to keep calm and speak respectfully.

Mother Bradley raised her right hand in the universal "cease" sign. "No, no. I won't brook a word of argument. After your escapade with Petey in the elm tree, it has become abundantly clear that you need to learn what it is to be

11

a young lady of society. We have neglected your education entirely too long."
She turned to her husband for affirmation. "Papa?"

Papa sighed and dragged his gaze from the soup bowl. "Your mother is
right," he muttered. He cleared his throat. "High time you begin acting like a
young lady." He reached for a sourdough roll and tore it in half. "High time,"
he repeated, and returned to the solace of his dinner.

Coward, Forrestina thought fiercely. Her mind raced as she tried to figure
out how this situation had careened out of her control. Yes, her tree
"escapade" had been pretty bad, and Mother had been right to be furious, but
was it really terrible enough to send her away? Surely she'd done worse
before. She glanced over at her father again and scowled. If anything, this was
partly his fault. Sending her to the circus is what had inspired her to climb out
on the roof in the first place—that wonderful, perfect, birthday gift, when, a
week and a half ago, John Bradley had handed two silver dollars to Tilly, the
girls' colored nanny, and said, "Forrestina's given me no peace since she
heard the Ringling Brothers pulled in to Hannibal, and now she's got Beatrice
and Genevieve all riled up too. I can't get away from the bank, but I want you
to take all three girls and your boy. I imagine Mrs. Bradley will be happy for
some peace and quiet. This fourth pregnancy has been hard on her." He looked
over Tilly's head at Forrestina, who stood nearby dancing on her toes in
excitement, and grinned.

"Yes, sir," Tilly said, dutifully wrapping the coins into a worn
handkerchief with purple peonies embroidered on the hem, "the Missus does
look like she needs some extra rest. And when the baby gets here, she'll need
even more. We'll have us a good day, don't you fret." Tilly tucked the bundle
into her ancient black leather pocketbook. "Kiss your Pa thanks," she said.
Forrestina happily obeyed, throwing her arms around her father's neck and
covering his bearded cheek with kisses.

"Now, now," Father said, patting her on the back, embarrassed but
obviously pleased. "You all go on now and have a good time."

It'd been a perfect day—the mid-April sun was bright and just warm enough for comfort, and there was not a cloud to be found in the big, deep, pale blue sky. Once they'd finished gazing in wonder at the fantastically strange animals in the menagerie wagons and gorging themselves on salted peanuts, buttery popcorn, and air-fluffed cotton candy, the lucky party made their way into the dark cavern of the Big Top for the main show. Beatrice and Genevieve, eleven and eight, were mesmerized by the elephants, and Petey, who'd beaten Forrestina to fifteen two months earlier, laughed until he almost split at the clowns, but it was the trapeze act that reached down and stole Forrestina's heart right from her chest. She sat dazzled, stock-still, captivated by the heat of the lights and a hundred bodies pressed together in collective wonder, inhaling the smell of manure, animal flesh, and human sweat. She watched as the two trapeze artists, a slender, dark-haired man dressed in a silky white body-suit, and a reed-like woman, also dressed in filmy white silk that drifted like feathers around her, threw themselves into the air with abandon, catching the bars that hung from the Big Top's ceilings carelessly, almost as afterthoughts. They were like wild doves all alone, seeming not to notice or care about the crowd of people watching them from below. As she stared at them, Forrestina felt something unnamable shift in her young bones. She suddenly pictured herself soaring up there with them, far away from the restrictive rules and plain ordinary sameness of her life, and began to shiver with desire. Tilly reached over and hugged her close. "You cold, baby?" she asked, her smooth forehead creasing in worry. "You getting sick? Had we better leave?"

Forrestina shook her head. "I'm fine," she whispered. She laid her right temple on Tilly's soft, substantial shoulder, her eyes still fixed upward. "I don't ever want to leave."

The next day, still flushed with excitement and unable to clear her mind of the images of the flying trapeze artists, Forrestina decided to try her hand at tight-rope walking. She'd always loved heights, climbing trees to their very tips, or slipping out onto the roof that spanned her bedroom window so she could tiptoe along the shingled ridge and pretend that she was a squirrel. Later in the morning, as soon as she was able to get away from her mother's watchful gaze, she sought out Petey, who was sitting on the back steps and shucking corn for his mother. "Meet me at the climbing elm round back," she told him. "And bring some rope—about twenty feet oughta do it."

Petey, who was used to Forrestina's impulsive whims and always game for an adventure, agreed at once, and in a few minutes Forrestina spotted him at the foot of the tree, a massive elm rumored to be a hundred and fifty years old. The ancient behemoth's trunk was at least six feet around and had tangles of thick branches that reached thirty feet into the air. It had patiently welcomed the nimble feet and hands of generations of children, including Forrestina, who'd spent hours in the crook of its wooden embrace as she hid from inevitable and constant scoldings, piano lessons, and dreary comportment lectures.

"Petey! Up here!" she called, waving her arm. She was standing on the roof outside her bedroom window, shed of her button-up shoes and white stockings, her bare toes curled into the warm shingles. She lifted her face, feeling as if she could reach up and dip her hand in the golden mid-morning sunlight, then shook herself back to reality. Time was a'wasting, and she didn't want her mother to start looking for her. She hollered to Petey, "Climb up to that big branch across from here," then watched as he obeyed, the rope looped around his shoulder and waist. Once he was in place, Forrestina said, "Good! Now tie one end of that rope to the branch, about a foot away from the trunk. There, where it's the sturdiest."

Petey tied the rope, knotting it expertly, then looked to Forrestina for more instructions. She clapped her hands, giddy with anticipation. Despite all her climbing here and there, she'd never yet tried to walk on the air. Petey heaved the other end of the rope to her, which she caught deftly. She carried the rope to her window and climbed inside. Her four-poster bed, a heavy mahogany beast that had been in the family for decades, was set against the wall nearest the window. She tied the rope to the closest post of the bed, tugging at the knot forcefully to make sure it was fastened tight, then stuck her head out of the window to check her work. The rope, a mere inch in diameter, stretched taut between the house and the elm, a yellow thread of glorious possibility hanging fifteen feet above the ground. She climbed back outside and stood again at the edge of the roof, this time straddling the new line she and Petey had just created.

She inhaled, exhaled slowly through rounded lips, opened her arms straight out from her sides, and took one pointed step onto the rope. She paused, and after a moment, when she was sure that she was not about to plummet to her death, she lifted her chin high and began to walk carefully between the shingled roof corner and the elm tree. Sounds of a southern spring hummed and buzzed and clicked dimly around her, but the loudest sound was the quick thrumming of her heart as she moved further and further along the rope. She allowed herself a quick glance across the chasm and saw Petey's face, a perfect "O" of dismay forming his mouth. This made her wobble a bit. "Stop looking at me like that," she hissed at him. "You're throwing off my concentration."

Petey slumped against the trunk, burying his hands in his face. "I can't look," he moaned. "Crazy white girl."

Forrestina continued along the rope, sliding first one foot forward carefully, and then the other. She felt so light and airy, she thought she might just float up off the rope and drift along with the wind like a dandelion's wish. As she neared the tree branch, however, a banshee shriek woke her from her reverie: "Forrestina Bridgette Magdalena Bradley, what in our Good Lord's and Holy Mary, our Mother's name are you doing up there?"

Startled, Forrestina lost her balance and began to slide sideways, fighting to right herself. As she beat the air with her arms, desperately trying to gain control, she felt Petey's strong hand clamp onto her left wrist. He yanked her forward to the safety of the thick branch he was standing on, as below her a cacophony of female screams crested and then wound down. Forrestina extracted herself from Petey's steel grip. The boy was trembling and had turned a queer ashy color. "Thanks, Pete," she gasped. She looked down at a group of young women dressed in the season's finest whites and pinks and pale greens, all standing aghast with her mother. Mother Bradley's horrified face suggested murder. "Oh, hell," Forrestina muttered. "I forgot about my birthday luncheon."

Petey, who was still shaking, barked out a little laugh. He slapped Forrestina on the back. "Tina, I wouldn't be you right now for all the gold bars in Fort Knox," he said. His expression quickly changed to one of misery. "I guess I wouldn't wanna be *me* either," he said glumly. "My momma will tan my hide for this when your momma tells her I was a part of it."

"Yeah, sorry about that," Forrestina said absently, peering down again at the group whirring around on the ground like fashionable ants. "You can tell her I made you do it, but it probably won't stop you from getting a whipping. I'll figure out how to make it up to you, I promise." She sighed. "Well, I better go down and make myself presentable."

By the time her bare feet hit the grass of the lawn, Mother Bradley had succeeded in ushering the other girls into the parlor, where an array of white-bread encased cucumber sandwiches, cream buns, early strawberries, and other assorted goodies were spread out for them on a long table. As Forrestina slouched into the room, Mrs. Bradley glared at her eldest daughter and said, through gritted teeth, "Go up to your room and change your clothes. We will speak about this later."

And they did, though it was Mother Bradley who did all the speaking, shouting at Forrestina in a tone and timbre that dogs for miles around heard and cowered at. After Mother had exhausted herself and left the room in a hoarse rage, Forrestina gratefully stepped out of her flounced skirt, unbuttoned her matching flounced blouse, and undid her corset, sighing at the exquisite deliciousness of unbinding herself. She pulled a white cotton nightgown over her head and padded over to the bedroom window, pushing it open and breathing in the fragrant-heavy smell of early honeysuckle. She sat in the windowsill, her feet pulled up, her chin resting on her knees, and gazed out at the rope that still remained taut between the roof and the tree. She thought again of the circus and imagined herself in all that black quietness, sailing through the air to the roar of the admiring crowd below. She regretted nothing she'd done today. She left the windowsill and climbed into bed, falling asleep almost instantly, her mother's fiery words extinguished in the sweet drowsy oblivion of her dreams.

And so, the night that Mother issued her dinner proclamation that Forrestina would be sent to Boston, Massachusetts, in order to attend the prestigious Brown's Finishing School for Young Ladies, Forrestina decided to run away from home and join the circus. She waited until everyone was asleep, then packed her father's cardboard valise, which she'd retrieved from a high shelf in the upstairs hall closet. She folded two dresses, two pairs of stockings, a few unmentionables, a boar-bristle brush, necessary toiletries, and a much-read copy of *Treasure Island* into the case, pulled it closed tightly by its two leather straps, then scribbled out a note she left on her pillow. It read, "Father and Mother, I'm going to find my own way in the world. I'm sorry I'm not a proper lady, and that I don't care to ever be one. Perhaps someday you can forgive me for this. Until then, know that I am always Fondly Yours, Forrestina." She tiptoed into her little sisters' room and risked kissing their sleep-warmed cheeks, then slipped out of the house in the middle of the night. She walked two miles to the nearest train stop and hopped unseen aboard a waiting freight car headed for Kansas City. She never once had the good sense to be afraid; the world was open to her like a star-filled night, and she was ready to fly through it.

Chapter Three

WHEN THE KANSAS CITY SOUTHERN pulled into its hometown, Forrestina was waiting at the open door of the freight train, anxious to disembark. Her bladder was full and her stomach was empty; the jolting six-hour train ride atop a stack of wooden crates had not been comfortable, but that no longer mattered because she had finally arrived. She jumped from the train car as it slowed, holding her skirts high in one hand, the other gripping the handle of her suitcase. Her feet hit the gravel running as she dashed to the public outhouse she'd spotted adjacent to the depot. After relieving herself, she set out towards what she figured was downtown, following the bustle of men in their round black hats and women in their warm-weather cotton dresses. Once in town, she spied a bakery and slipped inside. The smell of fresh rolls and bread baked that morning caused her stomach to let out a lionesque growl.

The portly man behind the counter, his apron and arms white with flour, grinned at her. "Well, I won't ask if you're hungry," he said amiably. He put his hands atop the glass counter, his plump fingers spread spider-leg wide, and said, "What'll it be, Miss?"

Forrestina leaned down and examined the wares in the case. Sticky caramel buns glistening with frosting, donuts topped with powdered sugar and oozing red jam, and perfectly browned loaves of bread, stacked one atop another, beckoned her eyes and assaulted her nose with delicious smells. After a moment's consideration, she pointed to a round loaf of sourdough the size of a dinner plate. She longed for a donut, but she only had one dollar from her savings. She must economize, and a loaf would go further than a donut, she decided with regret.

The man lifted the loaf from the case and wrapped it in white waxed paper, tying it up with a bit of string. "That'll be a nickel," he said. Forrestina pulled her change purse from where it was tied to her waist by a stout red ribbon, and handed the clerk five pennies, thanking him as he passed the warm loaf of bread to her. He dropped the coins in the register at the end of the counter, and then, as she started to leave, he said, "Here, Miss." She turned back and saw a jam donut in his outstretched hand. She hesitated. Did he think that she was a poor charity case? Mother had drummed it in her to *never* accept charity. Still, the smell was irresistible.

The baker waggled the donut back and forth. "It's on the house—a gift for a new customer. Call it an investment in our future partnership; you just make sure you come back here for all your baked goods." He smiled broadly at her and she smiled back, taking the donut from him gratefully, then, because she could not wait one minute more, she sank her teeth into the soft dough, relishing the sweetness of the sugar and the tartness of the cherry jam. In three bites, she had devoured the donut and was licking the remnant sugar and jam off her fingers.

"Thank you," she said through her last muffled bite.

The baker laughed and flapped his hand at her. "It's nothing," he said.

Forrestina walked to the door and was just pushing it open when the back side of a poster fixed in the window caught her eye. She stepped outside to have a better look. "Ringling Bros. Circus Troupe," the sign blared out at her in bold red letters. "A Menagerie of Animals Most Exotical! Death-Defying Flights of Wonder! Beautiful Dancing Girls! Clowns! Do Not Be Left Out— In Town for Two Weeks Only!" Forrestina leaned in to fully examine the black ink figures illustrating the poster, her nose almost touching the glass, her breath creating a ghostly fog that pulsed with every exhale. She continued reading until she found the part she was looking for: the circus was staked out in some area north of town called "Johnson's Field."

She pushed the door of the bakery back open. "Excuse me, sir," she said to the baker, "I was wondering if you could tell me how far Johnson's Field is, and perhaps point me in the direction I should go."

"Wanting to go see the circus, huh?" the baker said. "My kids have already made me swear a solemn oath to take them as soon as possible. It's set up about five miles that way"—he pointed to his right—"but I don't think they're open yet. A fella came in about a week ago and tacked posters up all over town, but their trains just pulled in yesterday. You missed the big parade down Main Street. They like to do that—get folk all hyped up and impatient. Makes for bigger crowds, I suppose. I believe they said they would be starting things up officially on Saturday."

Forrestina thanked him again and left the shop, fortified with sugar and hope. She walked briskly along the bustling sidewalks, nimbly dodging those who were ambling along and enjoying the bright morning. As the sidewalk ended at an adjoining road, Forrestina, distracted by trying to keep her long skirt from dragging in the mud, stepped off the curb and directly in front of a horse and carriage. The huge rusty-brown gelding swerved, rearing slightly, flinging mud in all directions—including all over Forrestina. The driver of the carriage pulled the reins sharply and jumped down from his seat. "Girl, what the hell is wrong with you?" he bellowed. "Are you blind?"

Shaken, Forrestina looked down at her cream skirt and blouse set, which was now dotted with splotches of dirt. "What the hell is wrong with YOU?" she roared back, balling up her fists and shaking them at the man. "Why were you driving so fast? And will you just look at my dress? What an awful mess!" With that, she burst into furious tears.

The man whipped out a bright orange kerchief from the front pocket of his faded bib overalls and began trying to dab the mud from her face and shoulders, succeeding only in smearing the grime into streaks. "Come on now, hush that," he murmured, his broad forehead puckered with despair. He was a giant—over six and a half feet tall, and stout. The sleeves of his red checkered shirt were rolled past his meaty freckled forearms, and he wore a jaunty brown bowler hat pushed back on his head. Forrestina noticed that there seemed to be no hair under that hat; however, a thick ginger beard on his face more than made up for the lack of hair on his head.

"There now, see?" he crooned. "You're all right." Forrestina's sniffles began to cease, and the man nodded, relieved. She dried her eyes with the back of her hand and swiped at her wet nose with her forearm. Now that her heartbeat was no longer racing, she was feeling ashamed for losing her temper; she *had* been the one at fault, after all. Still, a secret part of her thrilled at having used a swear word in public to a stranger. What would Mother say? She could only imagine. She pulled her features into an appropriately contrite expression and said, "I'm very sorry I stepped out in front of you, sir. Is your horse all right?"

"Aw, Baxter is fine—it would take a lot more than a little bit of a thing like you to hurt this old horse." The bearded giant patted the gelding on its velvet nose affectionately. The horse, now entirely serene, shifted the bit in his mouth and waited patiently for whatever was coming next.

Forrestina reached up and stroked the horse's side. "My apologies, Baxter," she murmured. Her gaze shifted to the carriage that Baxter was pulling. Behind the planked, open air seat was a garish enclosed blue and green box, gilded in gold paint, with the words "Ringling Bros." emblazoned in cursive writing on the side. "Oh!" she gasped, not believing her luck.

The man stepped back and looked at her, startled. "What's wrong? Does something pain you?"

Forrestina clutched at his arm. "Sir, you are from the circus?"

"The name's Jonas,'" he said, "and yeah, I'm from the circus. I'm a roustabout." Catching Forrestina's puzzled look, he explained, "I drive tent posts into the ground and haul and lift and fix whatever needs fixing. I came into town to get some grease for these carriage wheels."

Thrilled, Forrestina gripped Jonas's arm tighter. "Do you suppose I could ride with you to the circus? The very reason I am here in Kansas City is to join the Ringling Brothers' show."

"You don't say?" Jonas replied. He bent down and looked her fully in the face, his hands on his thighs. "And what might you be wanting to do in the circus? With that temper of yours, maybe you plan on taming the tigers." He threw his head back and laughed, slapping his ample mid-section as he did so. "I swear, I ain't never seen such a little girl get so mad so quick!" He reached out and tugged at a lock of Forrestina's hair, which had come loose from her bun. "Must be that red hair," he said. "I'm afflicted with the same problem." He lifted his hat and rubbed at his bald head. "Well, I *used* to be able to blame my red head. The hair's gone but the temper's still there sometimes."

Forrestina blushed, pushing the stray curl back into place. "Well, for your information," she replied primly, "I want to walk the tightrope—maybe perform in the trapeze someday."

Jonas whistled low. "Brave girl. I can't stand being higher than a stepstool, myself." He gestured to the carriage. "Well, then. I guess we'd better get you to the boss and see what he has to say, huh?" He climbed onto the bench seat and held out his huge hand. Forrestina accepted it, and soon she was settled next to him, her valise at her feet. With a snap of the reins, they were off.

As they entered the circus site, a vast, treeless, open field of brush-hogged clumps of grass and hard-packed dirt, Forrestina was overwhelmed by the bustle of activity. Men in garb similar to Jonas's were everywhere, busily driving stakes and tugging at ropes, hollering encouragement to each other as huge canvas tents were hauled into the sky and then secured by massive steel stakes. Parked along the outside of the tented circus area were the menagerie caravans, and Forrestina could smell the alien wildness of the jungle and hear snorts and growls, though she could not yet make out which animals were inside the brightly painted cages. After a moment, Jonas stopped the carriage and jumped down from his seat. He lifted Forrestina down as well, picking her up by the waist as if she weighed nothing but air, before handing her suitcase to her. "Yonder is the manager's office—he's the one you need to speak to about employment." He pinched the edge of his bowler hat. "Good luck to you, little missy. I hope it works out the way you want." He dropped her a wink. "And if you do get a job taming the tigers, well, I feel sorry for them cats. They don't know who they're tangling with."

Forrestina looked towards the tent Jonas had indicated with a jerk of his head. It was small compared to the show tent—a faded white canvas, its right-side door flap held open by a rope tied to a stake. Forrestina swallowed hard. "So, Jonas," she said, "which of the Mr. Ringlings is inside? I mean, which brother?"

Jonas stared at her for moment, dumbfounded. "Which of the—?" He snorted out a laugh. "Girl, the 'Mister Ringlings,' as you put it, don't deal with the common circus folk. They stay at the finest hotels during the stops—if they come along at all—and leave the hiring and firing to their manager, Mr. William Stone. He's the one in that tent you need to talk to."

Mr. Stone. Forrestina hoped his name wasn't an indication of his character. After a moment's hesitation, she stepped forward, and then stopped, suddenly very nervous. What was she doing in this unfamiliar place, so unlike the gentle plantation of her youth? And what had made her suppose anyone would hire her to do anything? She turned back to Jonas, thinking she might stall by asking him some more questions, but he was already busy unloading the drums of grease he had purchased in town. "All right then, Forrestina," she muttered, setting her jaw. "I dare you to go in there and get a job." She had never, never backed down on a dare, and she wasn't going to start today. She took a deep breath, squared her shoulders, and marched to the tent's opening. There she paused for a moment, unsure of what to do next—there was no actual door upon which to knock, after all. Instead, she poked her head in and was momentarily blinded, unable to focus her eyes after going from the bright April sunshine to the dim interior of the tent.

"May I help you?" a dry voice intoned.

Forrestina stepped fully inside and set her case at her feet. She was thankful when her eyes adjusted and she could see a man sitting ramrod-backed behind a plain wooden desk. The surface of his desk was meticulous in chaos—papers were everywhere but arranged in neat little piles that crossed each other horizontally and then vertically, six inches high. She cleared her throat and crossed her arms behind her, standing tall, trying to mask her nervousness. "Sir," she said, her tone sure, her voice strong, "My name is Forrestina Bradley, and I would very much like to join your circus."

William Stone leaned forward, his thin elbows resting on the table, his clean-shaven chin resting on his knuckles. He peered at her from behind a pair of silver-rimmed, circle-lensed spectacles, saying nothing. Forrestina willed herself not to fidget under his scrutiny, focusing her eyes on his forehead. She knew what he was seeing—like most girls of a certain age, she had spent a fair amount of her time at the looking glass—a small young woman, five feet, two inches tall, thin, small-breasted and fair-skinned, save a spattering of light freckles dusted across her slightly hooked but not offensively large nose. She had a tumble of red hair (her mother called it "apple red" because it was a true, startlingly deep red) bound up in a soft bun. A few stubborn curls that never stayed put had escaped and framed the sides of her oval face. Her eyes were aquamarine, a bright, light blue speckled with large dark hazel and brown spots; her sister Beatrice always claimed Forrestina's eyes were "polka-dotted" because of those spots. After her hair, it was the feature people mentioned the most upon meeting her. She was painfully aware that she did not look her best at this moment—the mud from her escapade with Jonas had smudged her clothes, and the hem of her long skirt was banded with dirt. Still, she was not there for her looks but for her talent. Just wait until Mr. Stone saw her up on the wire.

"Turn around," Mr. Stone said, finally breaking his speculative silence. Forrestina obeyed, slowly turning in a circle, her arms lifted slightly from her sides. After another long moment, Mr. Stone said flatly, "Okay."

Forrestina was sure she had misheard. "Okay?" she squeaked, dropping her arms.

"Okay," Mr. Stone repeated. He pulled a sheet of paper from one of the stacks on his desk and began filling it out, dipping his pen in ink and scratching down pertinent information. After a moment, he pushed the paper forward. "This is your contract," he said. "You will want to read it over carefully before you sign."

Forrestina stepped forward and took the paper. On it she read *Contract for Employment: Ringling Bros., 1906 Summer Season.* Under that she saw, *Position: Generally Useful. Payment: Room and board plus $5.00 a week for rehearsals and two performances per day, Monday-Saturday. NO EXCEPTIONS.* She looked up, alarmed. "Excuse me, sir. I am here to work as an aerialist—perhaps on the tightrope?"

Stone squinted at her over his glasses. His eyes were a hard grey. *Maybe his name* did *reflect his character*, Forrestina thought. "Do you have references?" he asked.

"References, sir?"

Stone sighed. "From other circuses where you performed."

"I've never performed in a circus before, sir. But I've always been good with heights."

William Stone shook his head. "Here's the thing, girl. Every young man or woman who comes into my tent has plans to be a star, yet only a half dozen truly ever achieve stardom. If you want to be a part of the Ringling Brothers Circus, you will perform in whatever capacity you are needed—most likely as a ballet girl with seventy other girls just as beautiful and ambitious as yourself. If that doesn't suit you, you may certainly show yourself out." He picked up a ledger from his desk and began flipping through it.

Forrestina reached for the pen and dipped the nib into the ink, then signed her full name in a dainty, precise cursive. She had no intentions of staying a ballet girl for long, but if this was how she had to start, then so be it. She handed the signed document to Mr. Stone. He took it from her, blew on it briefly to dry the ink, and then placed it atop one of the stacks of paper. "Fine, Miss . . ." He glanced down at her contract. ". . . Bradley. Once you leave this tent, go and find Mrs. Hayes. She is the matron of your troupe. There she will apprise you of the rules that you have agreed to follow and explain the terms of your employment in detail. Goodbye." He bent again over his ledger dismissively.

"Thank you, Mr. Stone," Forrestina said to the crown of his head, then she picked up her case and walked back out into the bright sunlight. She wanted to whoop and sing. Clear of the tent, she spun around, drinking in the sights and sounds of a circus before it puts its finery on—everyone in everyday work clothes, not a spangle or feather to be seen. She wandered to her left, towards a large rectangular tent where a group of women were sunning themselves like hound dogs, leaning back on their squat wooden stools with their legs straight out in front of them, ankles crossed, their somber-colored skirts fashioning curtains to the ground. One of the drowsing young ladies, dark-haired and long-limbed, spotted Forrestina and sat up. "Say," she called out, "you look lost."

Forrestina hurried forward gratefully. "I am," she admitted. "I am supposed to find a Mrs. Hayes, but I have no idea where to start looking." She swept her hands out and wailed, "This place is like a maze!"

The dark-haired girl stood, and Forrestina gaped at her; she was easily six feet tall and as thin as a wash-line. She was also luminously beautiful—her marble skin, white and smooth and completely blemish-free, seemed to glow from the inside. In her perfectly-shaped earlobes, a pair of diamond tear-drop earrings sparkled like white fire and cast sparks of light on her cheeks. Forrestina had never met anyone with pierced ears before, and she wondered if the diamonds were real. The girl smiled at Forrestina. "I'm Sarah Walker," she said. "I'm one of the ballet girls, and if you're looking for Mrs. Hayes, you're about to be one of my tribe. I'll take you to her." She swept off and Forrestina trotted along beside her, having to take three steps for every one of Sarah's.

"I wasn't planning on being a ballet girl," Forrestina panted. "I don't know the first thing about dancing. Mr. Stone didn't really give me much of a choice."

Sarah looked down at her, that cool, easy smile still on her lovely face. "Let me guess—trapeze?" she asked. "You look like the brave type." When Forrestina nodded, Sarah nodded as well. "All the pretty ones start as ballet girls, and all of them wanted to be something different to begin with. Most learn to like their jobs, though, so don't worry. After all, we are the beauties that attract the beasts." She laughed merrily, showing even white teeth.

Forrestina remembered watching the tableau of the ballet girls when she'd attended the circus before. She, along with the rest of the crowd, had admired the beautiful young women who played out various exotic scenes in different parts of the ring between the larger acts—glossy black-haired slave girls from Egypt, jingling the gold coins fastened around their tiny waists; Greek goddesses in their snow-white tunics who strummed golden lyres, their elaborately braided hair piled atop their graceful heads; Japanese geishas with white painted faces and silk kimonos the colors of the rainbow. As much as she'd enjoyed watching them, however, not one of the lovely women had stuck out in her memory, unlike the acrobats, whose soaring figures nestled like a burr in her brain. She wanted to be remembered long after the show was over and had no intention of remaining a common rose in the circus garden.

She kept this reflection to herself, however. The gravity of what she'd done by running away from home was starting to sink in as she gazed at the bustle of strangers around her. For the first time in her life, she was very much alone. This Sarah, who seemed kind and cheerful and above all things, *helpful,* was a possible friend, and she had no wish to offend her. So instead she replied, "I don't even have the title of 'ballet girl' on my contract. Apparently I am to be 'generally useful.' Does that mean I have to wash dishes and mend costumes?"

Sarah laughed again. "No. 'Generally Useful' is Ringling's way of getting as much bang for their buck as they can. You'll be a ballet girl during the shows, dance and wave in the parades, and act as background for some of the other acts as needed." Without breaking stride, she swiftly began to braid her damp, waist-length, unbound hair, which she'd said she'd been letting dry in the sunshine when Forrestina had come along. "As to the washing and mending, we all wash up our own dishes and are in charge of mending our own costumes. There are women here who do the cooking and cleaning up, but they are older. There's no way Mr. Stone would let that face and figure of yours go to waste in the cook-tent, and dish-pan hands are not attractive on a goddess." She waggled her own long, shapely fingers for emphasis.

Forrestina was gratified by Sarah's praise. She'd never considered herself particularly attractive; truly, the slight hook in her nose was the sorrow of her young life. Her own mother had been a great beauty in her youth, delicately blond and honey-colored, and Forrestina had grown up in her shadow, painfully aware that she took after her awkward red-haired, freckled, pale-skinned father. To hear someone as heart-stoppingly lovely as Sarah compliment her on her looks was a revelation.

After a few minutes winding through tents and people, Forrestina and Sarah arrived at Mrs. Hayes's office tent. Sarah thrust her head inside and called out, "Mrs. Hayes, we've got a new one for you." She stood back and motioned for Forrestina to enter ahead of her.

A narrow woman, all angles and no curves, was bent over a trunk, rummaging through it impatiently. When Sarah spoke, she turned, balancing on her heels. She glared wordlessly at Forrestina for a good twenty seconds before emitting a "hmph" sound. She placed one hand on the opened lid of the trunk and the other on a nearby chair and heaved herself into a standing position. She smoothed back non-existent stray hairs from her forehead, her hands skimming the smooth brown hair pulled back into a tightly coiled bun. She reached into a pocket of her navy-blue skirt and pulled out a pair of rimless, armless spectacles and jammed them onto her blade of a nose. "Pull the tent flaps back wider, Sarah. I can barely see either of you," she said.

Sarah obeyed and Mrs. Hayes walked forward, looking Forrestina up and down. "Name?" she snapped.

Forrestina looked directly into the older woman's eyes. "Forrestina Bradley, Ma'am," she said, slowly and clearly. She'd thought Mr. Stone nerve-wracking, but he suddenly seemed a kitten compared to the formidable creature examining her so critically now.

Mrs. Hayes's eyes narrowed a bit. "Judging by that hair and skin, I'd wager your people are from the Old Country, right? Irish to the hilt. Catholic?"

Forrestina opened her mouth to affirm that yes, her father's family had immigrated from Ireland, and yes, the Bradleys were casual Catholics—they attended Holy Day masses but rarely any others—but Mrs. Hayes cut her off. "It makes no difference to me, mind. We have all sorts and creeds in this place. Your new religion will be circus life, and your people will be circus people. Just don't let me catch you tipping the bottle—I realize that's a problem for your kind."

Forrestina flushed, furious. Her parents were strict teetotalers, and she'd never sipped even a drop of alcohol. Who exactly did this woman think she was, with her crude accusations? Before she could offer a sharp retort, however, Mrs. Hayes turned to a small desk in the right corner of the tent and began again searching for something. "Easy, girl," Sarah whispered in her ear, her breath warm and smelling of peppermints. "Don't let her get to you. Just say 'Yes, Ma'am.'"

"Sound advice, Miss Walker," Mrs. Hayes said, finding what she'd been looking for and turning back to the two girls. She smiled, a hard, brittle expression that looked as if it pained her. "That's right, I heard. I hear all and see all. I am like God in that way, and don't you forget it." She handed a booklet to Forrestina. "Your first job is to read this. It is the rules of conduct for the single female employees of the Ringling Brothers Circus. Read it, memorize it, follow every word." She leaned forward, her pale eyes shards of flint. "We brook no deviance to the rules—one mistake and you are out with no pay."

Forrestina took the booklet and bobbed a curtsey. "Yes, Ma'am," she said, swallowing her anger, which slid down like a pebble in an ostrich's throat.

"Well, la-dee-da," sniffed Mrs. Hayes. "Get a load of the Duchess of Kildare, will ya?" She shrugged. "Better than no manners at all, I guess." She walked over to her desk and sank into a chair behind it. "Sit," she said, gesturing to another chair in front of the desk. "And Sarah, that will be all."

"Yes, Mrs. Hayes," Sarah said. She winked at Forrestina and mouthed "Good luck." After she left, Forrestina suddenly felt very lonely again.

"So, Miss Bradley," Mrs. Hayes said. "How old are you?" Before Forrestina could reply, Mrs. Hayes held up her palm. "And don't lie to me," she said. "It makes no matter to me if you're fourteen or eighteen, as long as you are past puberty and unmarried."

"I am fifteen, Ma'am," Forrestina replied, and then added wryly, "and unmarried."

"Good to know," Mrs. Hayes commented, writing Forrestina's answer down on a sheet of paper on the desk in front of her. "Will anyone be missing you?"

Forrestina chewed her lower lip, trying to think of an answer. Would anyone at home miss her? She supposed Petey would, and Papa and the girls, maybe. Tilly, most certainly. Her mother? Probably not; after all, she still had two good little girls—maybe three, soon, if the baby turned out to be another girl—to mold into perfect ladies. Forrestina felt the unexpected sting of tears at the rim of her lower lashes, and she closed her eyes tight for a moment, willing them to retreat. She opened her eyes again when Mrs. Hayes said impatiently, "Oh good grief, girl. What I mean is, did you run off in such a way that the law will be looking for you? We don't need any trouble from the police. This is a respectable establishment."

Forrestina exhaled. She hadn't realized she'd been holding her breath. "Oh no, Ma'am," she said. "I've never been in trouble before and I didn't take off with anything that didn't belong to me."

Mrs. Hayes nodded, scratched a few more words onto her paper, then said, "Right. Your duties are as follows: You will dance in the ballet, perform in the tableau during the pre-shows, and do whatever is required as a background performer during specific acts." She glanced up. "You don't have a problem showing some skin, do you? Some of the outfits are designed to titillate the imagination—nothing tawdry, mind you. We are not that sort of show. It's just that some of the classical or exotic costumes, which are crafted to be as historically accurate as possible, are somewhat less *Victorian* than our present-day garb."

"I'm not shy, Ma'am," Forrestina said. "In fact, I like being bare-footed better than anything."

Mrs. Hayes pursed her thin lips. "Mind you," she said, "when you're *not* performing, you will be expected to dress modestly and behave yourself accordingly. That includes wearing shoes and stockings. The Ringling Brothers Circus has a very strict morality clause, which you signed before you came in here. Let's go ahead and talk about rules." She pulled out another booklet exactly the same as the one she'd handed Forrestina earlier and opened it. "First," she said, "you may not be seen using any type of intoxicant, either in your sleeping tent, dressing room, or during the shows. Some girls like to have a drink with the circus men, but I caution you against becoming too friendly with them; they are not bound by the same rules as you girls, and there is nothing like the Devil's own drink to make a woman forget her duties.

"Second, you are to be in your bed at 10:00 p.m. sharp on the nights before a performance; on performance nights, you are to be in the sleeping tent no later than two hours after the show ends. You were hired to be your perkiest and most lovely—tired girls who have not had adequate sleep do not tend to shine with beauty. Your looks are part of your job, Miss Bradley, so do what you can to keep them. A regimented skin care routine and careful diet and exercise are imperative." She paused, her finger marking her place in the book. "I advise the regular application of Nivea cream. Do you have any?"

Forrestina shook her head and Mrs. Hayes frowned. "You will need to make a list of necessary items and go into town with Sarah to purchase them as soon as possible. Make sure you remember the Nivea cream." She lifted the booklet up towards her nose and continued to read:

"Third: Men are not allowed in your sleeping tent or your dressing room. You are to conduct yourself with decorum and grace, and must not, under any circumstances, allow yourself to be deemed 'fast.' Your reputation should be as pure as your body. Do not be excessively loud in speech, flirtatious, or a gum-chewer; at all times behave like a lady, regardless of your costume or the comments of others around you. And keep your temper." Mrs. Hayes paused and pointed at Forrestina's blazing hair. "I mean it, child—hot-heads do not last very long around here. Practice checking yourself before you respond, no matter how crude or unkind men may be. The world is full of cruelty, but you must rise above."

She continued. "Fourth: when we move along, you may not stay at a hotel. You may not visit relatives if we land in your hometown—your relatives can come visit you here. You may not visit any male members of the circus in their private quarters. This includes performers, gamers, freaks, roustabouts, or management. If you have an issue with any of the men in the circus, you must report it to me immediately. Do not bother Mr. Stone with complaints; as General Keeper for the unmarried females of the circus, I am your advocate and your warden, and my aim is to protect both your reputation and that of the circus. You will be assigned a trunk for your belongings; you may not have any other luggage, and all your personal items must be stored in that trunk. You may not carry along with you the following: pets of any kinds, cigarettes, or alcohol. Do you have any questions?"

"No, Ma'am."

Mrs. Hayes snapped her booklet shut and rose to her feet. "Then welcome to the Ringling Brothers Circus, Miss Bradley," she said. "Allow me to show you around your new home."

CHAPTER FOUR

MORNING CAME EARLY FOR circus folks, big and small, furry and smooth. Before the sun had a chance to raise its lemon-gold arms and yawn, Mrs. Hayes made the rounds in the sleeping tents of the ballet girls—eleven tents that housed seven bunks each—calling out, "Wake up, girls. Breakfast in thirty minutes." Forrestina—never one for early rising—added her groans to the others in the tent. "Lord," she said, sitting up and stretching her arms out wide, "I feel like I just went to sleep a minute ago." She peered at the tin-hatted alarm clock sitting on her trunk. "Is five o'clock even considered daytime?"

Sarah, who had sweet-talked Mrs. Hayes into putting Forrestina in her tent so that she could "show her the ropes easier," reached over and patted Forrestina's wild mane. "Miss Bradley, you should've woken up at four—your hair is going to take an hour to comb out. Those gorgeous red curls of yours have turned into a rag-rug of knots."

Forrestina felt the top and back of her head, her fingers snagging in twists of hair. She groaned again. She envied Sarah's string-straight hair, which hung down the older girl's back in a black shining sheet with nary a knot in sight. Sighing, she reached under her narrow cot, which was covered by a thin blue-and-white striped mattress, and pulled out her regulation-sized metal trunk. Lifting the lid, she rummaged around until she found her soft-bristled brush, then she set about torturing the tangles from her hair. It took her ages to finish the painful task, but finally securing her now-tamed hair into a loose bun, she buttoned herself into her plain light blue cotton "everyday" dress and stepped outside. The sun had finally begun to peep over the edge of darkness, and the colors on the horizon were magnificent, rosy red fading into blushing peach.

Carrying a face-towel, her toothbrush, and a tin of tooth powder, Forrestina waited her turn at the wash basin, which was set up under a hand-pump. She noticed that the circus was also taking its time waking up—men who would soon be hollering commands or jokes at one another were subdued, murmuring short, one-word sentences; horses stamped their feet, while the more exotic animals were stretching or snorting, anticipating their breakfast. Instead of the ringing echo of stakes being pounded into dirt, the sound of sizzling bacon and eggs frying in the cook tent filled the quiet air. Forrestina closed her eyes, inhaled deeply, and smiled. She still couldn't believe that this was now her life.

She washed up quickly and took her turn at the outhouse, then returned her toiletries to her trunk and headed for the cook tent, her stomach clanging. Ringling believed in feeding their employees well, and the cooks they hired were excellent at whipping up massive quantities of hearty meals. Sarah caught up with her and slipped her arm through Forrestina's. "We have a lot to do today," she said as they made their way into the cook tent and found space on a bench at one of the long plank tables. "Our director, Mr. Wilson, designed a new tableau for us. We will be the wives of King Solomon's harem, chosen from all the kingdoms of the world to please him. I imagine I will be Egyptian, Indian, or Oriental; those are usually my roles because of my hair." She squinted at Forrestina. "I have no IDEA what they will do with you. You'll probably get a wig."

Forrestina frowned, thinking of the long summer ahead of her. A wig in June and July would be extra hot and itchy. Sarah, reading her expression, nodded in sympathy and said, "Cheer up. Maybe you can be the Queen of Sheba—she stays cool by wearing a thin skirt and nothing on top but a thick gold necklace that *almost* covers her breasts."

Forrestina blushed in horror at the thought and Sarah dissolved into peals of laughter. "Your face just went as red as your hair," she declared. "Don't worry; I'm just teasing. The ballet girl 'stars' get the big roles—you won't actually have to be Sheba."

"Who's going to be Sheba?" A young man Forrestina guessed to be about twenty sat down on the bench beside her. He placed his tin plate and coffee cup on the wooden table in front of him. A stack of hotcakes, golden-crisp and drowning in thick maple syrup, was on his plate, along with two sunny-side up eggs and several pieces of bacon. Forrestina's stomach rumbled loudly. The man laughed and pushed his plate over to her. "Here," he said. "I'll go get another plate for myself and Sarah. You sound like you need this now."

"Thank you," Forrestina said, feeling her face grow hot again. A side-effect of being red-haired was having skin that so easily broadcasted her every emotion. She loathed it. "Mister . . .?"

"Carl," he said. He stuck his hand out and Forrestina shook it. She could not help noticing how strong the fingers were that held her own. "Carl Jenkins. No 'mister' to it." He stood up and made his way to the front of the tent where the cook was laying out plates of food. Forrestina watched him go, noting his short, strong legs and the muscles that moved easily beneath his chambray work shirt.

Sarah shoved her. "Knock it off, Miss," she said. "Carl is just one of the many handsome fellows who work the circus route—you can't be giving your heart away to every boy you see." She followed Forrestina's gaze. "Though Carl is one of the good ones."

"I am not about to give my heart away to anyone," Forrestina replied tartly, shoving Sarah back. She picked up a fork and began devouring her breakfast. By the time Carl returned, she'd finished eating, scraped the plate clean, and was sipping the strong black coffee he'd left behind. He sat down next to her again and eyed her empty plate. "Well done," he said, "I do like a woman with a big appetite." He winked at her and Forrestina fought another blush.

Sarah came to her rescue. "Oh please," the dark-haired girl said, "name one thing about any woman that you *don't* like, Carl Jenkins."

"I don't like women who use my first and last name, *Sarah Walker*," Carl retorted.

"Yeah, yeah," Sarah said, crunching into a crispy piece of bacon. "Carl here is a groom," she told Forrestina. "Takes care of the horses. That's why he smells so bad."

"She means that's why I am so good for a roll in the hay," Carl said, grinning wickedly around a mouthful of food. Forrestina gasped, and Sarah broke into more raucous laughter. "Just look at that face! Carl, you should be ashamed of yourself, shocking our new innocent." She patted Forrestina's arm. "Don't worry, honey. Carl is all talk. He knows better than to mess with us ballet girls. We are prized property," she turned to address Carl, "and you're not even supposed to be talking to us. So go away before you get us in trouble."

Carl nodded forlornly. "It's true," he said. "You are all but dreams to me. It's why I can't wait for bed every night."

Forrestina couldn't resist smiling, though she was still shocked. She imagined what their parish priest back home, Father Christopher, would say about this, and then stopped herself. Catholic guilt was part of her past—she was here to live a new life. She sipped her coffee and tried to look worldly and unimpressed and succeeded only in blushing again. Carl chuckled and picked up his plate and mug. "See you around, Red," he drawled. He winked at Sarah. "Take care of our new flower." He sauntered outside of the tent to the water pump, and Forrestina studied him as he began washing his dishes. She was sorry that he had gone.

"Oh, Lord," Sarah said. "I see that I'm going to have to acquaint you with the ways of the world real quick to keep you out of trouble. But I don't have time right now. Drink up, Missy. Mrs. Hayes wants you ready for the show by tomorrow. You won't have to do much this time—a little shimmy and shake until we see where your special talents lie."

Forrestina followed her friend outside. They washed their dishes quickly, placing them on a wood-slatted table to dry in the warming sunshine. As they walked towards the Big Top, Sarah explained the basic plan of the circus, which tended to be the same no matter what field they set down in. "It's easier on the roustabouts if everything is always in roughly the same place, and easier for us too," Sarah said. She gestured to the right. "You have already entered through the gates and probably saw that big tent when you came in. That is the side-show tent—the freak show."

"Freaks? What are they like?" Forrestina glanced around worriedly. "I've always been a little afraid of the freak show tent," she confessed. "Tilly wouldn't let us go in and look, said it was a sin to profit on the sufferings of God's own creation. The advertisements painted on the tents were enough to keep me out, anyway. Some of them were pretty gruesome."

Sarah shrugged. "You will get used to them—they're just people inside, same as you and me. Not all of them are deformed; some can do weird stuff with their bodies, like Miko, who can bend herself into a pretzel, or Franz Rhodes, who is tattooed like a lizard and spits fire. And there is Darling Dorine—she is just the tiniest, cutest little thing you've ever seen, but she's really pretty old. In her thirties, I think. She's a hoot. You'll like her— everybody does." She sighed. "It's a living, I guess. Besides, you'll not meet a more cheerful bunch, honestly." She pointed to the manager's office tent. "Behind that is Mr. Miles's tent—he's the press agent. He is in charge of promoting the circus, getting the word out, arranging interviews for the stars with local papers. In front of that is the menagerie tent, where the animals are displayed preshow and where they are taken between performances."

The girls arrived at the edge of a tent so enormous that Forrestina could not see around it or over it. "Holy smokes," she said, craning her neck.

"One thousand feet long, forty feet high," Sarah trilled in a barker's voice. "Three rings and two stages of mag-ni-ficent wonder, all for your thrilled consideration. Come one, come all." They walked around the oblong edge and entered an adjacent smaller tent. The walls were lined on both sides with metal racks, which were stuffed with clothes. Below the racks were black trunks, their lids bolted shut, "Property of Ringling Bros. Circus" stenciled in white along the tops. In the center of the tent were wooden benches and foldable chairs. Forrestina saw that the back half of the tent was divided by thick green velvet curtains attached to the tent's ceiling.

"And THIS," Sarah said, pushing one of the curtains to the side, "is our dressing room. Women on the right, men on the left, common waiting area and costumes where we came in." She pointed to a narrow canvas tunnel. "That connects us to the Big Top—you must never let the plebeians see you walking around in costume unless it's in a show or a parade. Spoils the magical effect."

Forrestina didn't know what a "plebian" was, but she was grateful not to be one; *she* was a circus girl. Smiling at the thought, she reached out and ran her fingers over the shoulder of one of the spangled orange leotards hanging on a metal rack, then brushed her palm along the feathery plume of the pink dress next to it.

Sarah said, "Come on. We'll get a chance to dress later this evening. First we learn our characters and moves, *then* we practice in costumes. Let's go introduce you to Mr. Wilson."

Forrestina slipped through the canvas tunnel and emerged into a cacophony of sound and movement that was swallowed up in the enormity of the tent. *This must be what Jonah felt like in the belly of the whale*, she thought. She paused, looking up, and her heart flipped over. There they were: the trapeze artists, busy practicing their spins and turns on the hoops and rings hanging from the tent's roof. Below them, a net was waiting like a web.

"They didn't use nets when I came to watch the show," Forrestina remarked.

"They don't for shows," Sarah said. "Only in practice because they're constantly trying to do something more dangerous." She shuddered. "I don't know why anyone would risk their necks like that—I hate heights."

Forrestina gazed at the whirling, muscular figures above her, then spotted a wire thirty feet up, stretched from one side of the tent to the other, connecting two slender wooden beams and two square platforms. She felt an urge to run to the rungs that jutted all the way up the beams and start climbing, but Sarah tugged her along.

"Hurry," Sarah said. "There's Mr. Wilson, and he's lining the girls up, giving them their orders. He hates when we're late."

In the throng of young women (sixty-eight if Mr. Stone was to be believed), a diminutive man was holding court. He was tiny, shorter than Forrestina, and round as an apple. His blue-black hair was parted severely down the middle and shone with some sort of hair tonic. A moustache so thin it could have been drawn on with a grease pencil overshadowed his top lip, and his bottom lip, as if to compensate for its lack of décor, plumped out wet and pink. He was wearing a suit, his spats a brilliant white, his shoes polished to a mirror. Instead of a coattail, he wore a swirling red cape. He was what Forrestina's papa would have derisively called a "dandy," but Forrestina thought he was wonderful. He was shouting instructions in a squeaky voice, pointing with one beringed pudgy index finger for emphasis.

"This is our new girl, Mr. Wilson," Sarah called out, pulling Forrestina forward. Forrestina smiled, clasping her hands in front of her as her new boss looked her over.

"Lovely figure," he said. "And that hair!" He reached forward and gently loosed a strand from Forrestina's carefully coiled bun, rubbing it between his fingers. "What a color! And all natural—I can tell. I can spot a dye job a mile away. I may have to construct a whole show on the fairy isle of Ireland next time, just so we can showcase your hair." He slipped an arm around Forrestina's waist, the top of his head just reaching her shoulder. "Did you know that people once thought that red-haired women were witches? It was good Queen Bess of England and her orange locks that forced them to change their minds." He leaned forward a little and said, "Thank you, Sarah. I will take it from here. You run along to the Egyptian troupe over there with the rest of wise King Solomon's far-eastern and African wives."

Sarah flashed an "I-told-you-so" grin at Forrestina and obeyed. Mr. Wilson led Forrestina to the center of the bustling crowd of young women. "What's your name, dear?" he asked.

"Forrestina Bradley," she replied, her head swiveling from side to side, her eyes trying to drink in all the sights and sounds of the ring at once.

"Forrestina? What a splendidly old-fashioned name! Though alas a name that will not work for our purposes—you shall be one of our Jewish lasses, I think. You will have to wear a wig and bronzing makeup on that pale skin of yours. King Solomon's kingdom never quite reached the Gaelic islands, you know. Come, come," he said. "We will soon have you perfecting the dance of the Hebrews in no time." With that, Mr. Wilson swept Forrestina over to a group of blondes and other less vivid redheads. "Welcome to the troupe," he said. "Girls, let's try it again. From the top!"

CHAPTER FIVE

THREE MONTHS SPED BY, and Forrestina changed from a starry-eyed, easily-embarrassed girl to a confident young woman who reveled in her ability to become someone else every night in a different town every few weeks. Though the wig she wore, black as night and cascading down her back in loose curls, was indeed hot and itchy, and her outfit so skimpy that at first she thought there was no way she'd be able to exit the dressing tent, she soon became used to both. The animal smell of the ring, the gasoline lights, the roar of the crowd—it was addictive, and she soon forgot all discomfort. Night after night, beaming beatifically, she followed the other girls out into the ring, swaying to the Middle-Eastern pipe music, waving her indigo-blue feathered plume as she approached the enormous throne of their King Solomon, a stage-actor-handsome, dark-haired, chiseled young man named John Logan who was as crushingly boring and aloof as he was good looking. Sarah said he was never interested in any girl as much as he was in himself, though Forrestina had seen his eyes rest on her for a moment before moving on as he surveyed all of the female forms that belonged to him—at least for the show. He ruled on a gold painted throne, tall and proud in his deep purple royal robes, his fingers bejeweled in fake gems, a short, pointed beard emphasizing his strong jawline. After his nightly duties, he always instantly disappeared; Forrestina had heard rumors about trips into town to carouse and frequent the local cat-houses. Mrs. Hayes had been right; the rules for the men of the circus were definitely different than the rules for the women. Forrestina wasn't even allowed out of her tent past midnight.

Forrestina's place was directly behind the king, so while she did not have to dance the entire time, she did have to fan John with the plume, being careful to blend into the background. "You are scenery, my dear," Mr. Wilson told her during practice. "You are something lovely to look at but not to command attention—we must allow the focus to shift to the various wives of Solomon and the arrival of Sheba and her entourage. And for heaven's sake" (grabbing the plume from her and demonstrating), "slow and steady! Do not blind our king by hitting him in his exquisite brown eyes with a feather! It is very hard to look princely with tears running down one's face."

Today as she fanned at exactly the right tempo, she stole glances at the crowd. As usual, the lights made it impossible for her to make out individual faces, but she could hear their cheers and whistles, especially wolfish as the men in the audience reacted to the stunning women in the ring. She tried to imagine what they saw when they looked at her—foreign, because of her false hair, her legs bare beneath a clinging white sleeveless silk dress that was split up one leg to the top of her thigh, a red jeweled sash banded around her small waist, her bare upper arms circled in thin copper bands, her feet in leather sandals.

Ten trumpets sounded, and "Sheba" entered on an elephant, her gorgeous chocolate skin gleaming under the gaslights, her neck swan-like as she calmly presided over the thirty dancing girls that came before her. Forrestina hid a smile; that beautiful African princess entrancing the crowd was really named Agnes March, the daughter of a sharecropping family from Jackson, Mississippi. Agnes, a practical girl, had decided that if she was going to be stared at everywhere she went because of her beauty and her color, she would darn well make it worth her while. Forrestina had discovered that the circus was a great equalizer—ballet girls and animal trainers made a decent living, trapeze artists made an even *better* living, roustabouts and cooks made a fair wage, and it didn't matter if you were male or female, black or white: working hard and doing what you were supposed to do was all that counted. It was certainly different from the way things were in Hannibal, Missouri.

Sheba rode in regal silence, her thick black hair pulled up in an impossibly complicated coif of braids that emphasized her slender neck. Below that neck, she wore nothing but a huge golden (golden-*looking*—nothing was real in the circus) necklace that covered her chest, allowing only a glimpse of the underside of her large, firm breasts. Her skirt was leopard print, slit up both sides so that her shapely legs, crossed at the ankles, could be displayed to their best effect. The crowd held their breath, momentarily stunned into silence by all the sensual nakedness that was not allowed in any public place *but* the circus, and Forrestina felt their thrill as if she were seeing the show for the first time. These simple people—farmers and shopkeepers and housewives and children—were able to glimpse, for just a moment, worlds they'd never conceived of as they trudged through their dreary lives. It was powerful enchantment.

After the final act had ended and the tent emptied of all save the cleaning crew, Forrestina wearily sat down at a mirrored table in the women's dressing room. She was exhausted; it'd been her turn to collect and organize the props from their show that night, and that added a good thirty minutes to her workload. She pulled her heavy wig from her head, sighing in relief and scratching at her itchy scalp furiously. She longed for her bed. As she sat scrabbling at her head, Luciana Portechov, a trapeze ring artist and Forrestina's hero, strode into the dressing room and began peeling off her pink-hued stockings.

Luciana (called "Lucy" by the circus folk) glanced over her shoulder at Forrestina. "Some show, eh?" she said, stretching her arms over her head. She had a thick eastern European accent—Sarah'd said that Lucy and her family, all trapeze artists, were from Russia.

Forrestina nodded dumbly in response to Lucy's question, thrilled at having been spoken to. *Say something back, you dope,* she thought desperately. She cleared her throat. "I saw most of your act tonight. You were wonderful," she said. She paused, then added, "You're always wonderful." She snapped her mouth shut, horrified that Lucy might think she was gushing.

Lucy, who'd sat down at the dressing table next to her and was busy unpinning her midnight hair, met Forrestina's eyes in their shared mirror. "Thank you," she said. Her slow smile was a cat-twitch of lips, a small curl on either side of her mouth.

Forrestina plowed on. In for a penny, in for a pound, Tilly always said. "It must be wonderful to spend so much time up there, off the ground," she stammered. She dropped her eyes, feeling her face flush in her embarrassment. She *was* a dope.

"Huh. There's that word 'wonderful' again," Lucy said musingly, freeing the last of her pinned curls, which bounced down her shoulders to the middle of her back, tiny lustrous acrobats all themselves. She reached out a tiny hand, the pointed nails a sharp and glossy red, and turned Forrestina's chin so that they were face-to-face. Now that she could see her up close, Forrestina realized that Lucy was not the young girl she'd first supposed her to be because of the woman's small frame and the infantile flouncy pale-pink, poufy thigh-skimming skirt she wore over her matching pink leotard. Her dark hair had threads of grey in it, and fine wrinkles creased the skin beside her coal-black eyes. Mrs. Portechov was more forty than fifteen, yet she crackled with an energy that made her seem ageless. "What's your name?" she demanded.

"It's Forrestina, ma'am," Forrestina stammered.

Lucy cocked her head. "Polite girl. I like that. For-ess-teee-nah?" she said. "That's almost as hard to say as Luciana, no? I think 'Lollo' is better for me." She stood and belted her silk kimono-style dressing gown tightly around her waist. "Come, Lollo," she said, holding her hand out. "You want to play in the 'wonderful' rafters? We'll see how you do. Mind," she warned, "we will have to check to see if they have put the practice net back up. I'll not be responsible to Mr. Wilson for killing one of his girls."

They stepped together out of the tented corridor that connected the dressing room with the Big Top into the ring. It was dark; the cleaning crew had extinguished the lights after shoveling up the animal waste from the ring and sweeping up popcorn and sticky caramel apple sticks from the stands. Forrestina followed Lucy as if she were in a dream to the pole that stretched into the blackness near the top of the tent. About eight feet from the ground, a thick rope net had indeed been fastened in a square. Lucy began nimbly climbing the slats fastened to the back of the pole, her bare legs flashing in and out of her dressing gown as she rose higher and higher. She paused, looking down, and said, "Well? Come along!"

Forrestina obeyed, moving rapidly up the pole. Soon the ground was far, far below her, a dark expanse illuminated only by the dim light coming through the dressing tent corridor. About ten feet from the tent's top, a simple wooden platform had been erected, and a wire extended horizontally to another platform and pole across the ring. Forrestina joined Lucy on the platform, which was hardly big enough for the two of them. She looked down and swallowed hard. In the darkness, it seemed as if there was no ground at all, only space.

Lucy smacked her lightly on the shoulder. "Never look down," she commanded. "First rule. If you look down—if you even *think* about looking down—you will fall." She gestured to the rope. "So? Go on. Walk that rope. Let's see if it is as marvelous as you imagine." She eyed Forrestina's feet. "You should take your shoes off first, I think."

Forrestina obeyed, her fingers trembling as she bent down to slip off her leather "Hebrew" sandals. It was not fear that caused her to tremble, but excitement. She put her bare right foot on the taut wire and began to slide forward, carefully moving one foot along, and then the other. She extended her arms out to the side, her back straight, her eyes fixed on the platform across from her, and felt that old familiar thrill of no longer being earth-bound. She couldn't help herself; she began to laugh aloud from the pure joy of it, and behind her, she heard Lucy's tinkling laughter joining her own. "You were right. Lollo," Lucy called. "It *is* wonderful."

A sharp male voice from below thundered, "What are you doing up there, you fool girl? You're going to break your damn neck. Get down here right now!"

Alarmed, Forrestina started to wobble on the tight rope. She tried desperately to catch her balance, leaning too far one way and then the other, but she was not able to regain that solid middle. After a moment's struggle, she toppled over, the ground rushing at her. Instinctively she curled up like a sow bug, her hands wrapped around her knees, her head tucked in, and when she hit the net, she bounced around like a rubber ball, unharmed, her heart beating wildly.

"Joseph, for shame! You scared her," she heard Lucy's scolding voice say above her. With a whoosh, Lucy plummeted off the platform and into the net like the angel of death, and then, with a graceful turn, she flipped herself out of the net, dragging it down so that it was only a couple feet from the ground. She let go, and the net sprang back up, cradling the still-stunned Forrestina, who uncurled herself and peered over the edge.

Joseph, a slender man with oily black hair and an impressive handle-bar moustache, gestured in Forrestina's direction wildly. "Luciana, what?" he cried. "If you kill ballet girls, we will surely be driven from the circus."

"Pah," Lucy said dismissively, apparently forgetting that this had been her exact worry a few minutes ago. "She is not dead, as you can see. In fact, she would've made it to the other side if you'd not interrupted her with your bellowing." She turned to Forrestina, who was still caught in the net. "Wad up some of the rope in your right hand, bounce a bit, then do a somersault, throwing your weight forward. This will stretch you closer to the ground— once you get there, release the net. And be careful to land with your knees bent."

Forrestina obeyed, making sure her wrist was not tangled in the net when she let go. She landed on the soft packed dirt with a *flumph*. She was shaken, though not as much by the actual fall as by disappointment that Joseph, Lucy's husband and partner on the trapeze, had seen her ungraceful tumble towards earth. So much for her idea that she was some sort of special tight-rope prodigy.

Lucy was busy arguing with Joseph, her feet planted apart in an aggressive stance, her hands on her hips. "She did well, Joseph," Lucy said. "She is a natural. She had no fear of the fall—when she began to wobble, she did not fight but let herself go. That takes most years to learn—and you know that when the fear is gone, the fall doesn't happen." She looked over her shoulder at Forrestina. "We need new blood now that Carlita has run off with that no-good salesman," she said. "I promised Mr. Stone I would be on the lookout for new talent." She gestured with one hand at Forrestina. "Why not try her?"

"But she's not one of us," Joseph argued. "She's not our people. Who is she? A ballet girl from Nowhere, America? She's going to join generations of family trapeze artists because she knows how to fall?" He glared at his wife, and she glared back, not giving an inch. Finally, Joseph heaved a sigh of resignation. He obviously knew when he was beat. "Come," he snapped, beckoning Forrestina with his hand. "Let's have a look at you then." He was much taller than she was, so Forrestina found herself craning her neck a little in order to look directly into his sharp black gypsy eyes. She forced herself to stare him down, not blinking, wrapping Lucy's words about having no fear around her heart like armor. He held her gaze for a moment, then walked in a small circle around her, rubbing his chin. Finally he declared, "Well, if my Lucy thinks you should have a chance to learn to walk the wires, then you should have a chance to walk the wires. What say you? Would you like to try?"

"Yes sir, I would love nothing more in this world," Forrestina said, fighting the urge to whoop aloud, or worse, throw her arms around Joseph in a victory hug. A sudden thought made her heart sink. "But I can't. I am contracted as a ballet girl for the entire season. I signed an agreement."

"That's not a problem," Joseph said. "I'll speak to Mr. Stone about you beginning your training with Lucy and me. We will work around your dance practice and performances, and he can relieve you of the other general duties so that you may train. After the season ends, depending on your progress, you may be signed on as a rope walker for the next season, and you'll spend the winter preparing for your debut." Joseph turned from her and raised an eyebrow at Lucy. "Are you sure about this?" he said. "She's awfully scrawny."

Lucy shrugged. "Muscles grow," she said. "Besides, she thinks this job is wonderful. I remember thinking that, too." She reached out and took Forrestina's hand, squeezing it tightly—tight enough to be just a little painful. "You will not let me down," she said.

It was not a question.

CHAPTER SIX

Postcard: To Mr. and Mrs. John Bradley
1735 Sweet Briar Street
Hannibal, MO

July 15, 1906

Dear Father and Mother,

I am writing to tell you that I am alive and well. I hope you are also all in fine health. I think of you often and with fondness. Please do not fret over me; I am working and I keep myself respectable. I promise that I have not forgotten the "paths in the way I should go." Kiss the girls for me, and the new baby, and please pass along my good wishes to Petey and Tilly.

Your Daughter Ever,

Forrestina

CHAPTER SEVEN

The Circus Years, 1909

"MOVE YOUR FOOT FURTHER BEFORE that step! Further! You cannot lift your back leg in that stance!"

Forrestina gritted her teeth and obeyed the commands thrown at her, sliding her right leg along the ½-inch-thick cable, pivoting her right foot so that it cupped the wire in her instep. Slowly she leaned forward, arms extended over her head, and brought her left foot up and back, bending until her face was parallel with the ground. Far below her, through the squares of the safety net, she could see Joseph pacing as he watched her. Lucy sat off to the side on a low stool; every once in a while she would murmur something, and Joseph would bark out a new order or critique. It had been three years since Forrestina joined the circus, and over two since she'd begun exclusively working as Ringling Brothers' featured tightrope walker, yet under the hawkish eyes of Lucy and Joseph, she still felt as if she were that girl trying to walk the rope between her roof and tree.

Lucy never raised her voice; she left that job to Joseph—*who*, Forrestina thought bitterly, *seems to relish it.* Yet there was no doubt that she was the boss of their part of the show. She'd been in the circus business since birth; her immigrant acrobatic parents had taught her to contort and tumble as soon as she was able to take her first toddling steps, and they cemented her future by encouraging her to join forces with Joseph, a ring trapeze artist from the same Ruska Roma gypsy tribe as theirs. Lucy and Joseph's act had resulted in marriage and a top spot with Ringling, where they'd been for over fifteen years. As with many immigrants, they both had a punishing work ethic, rising well before dawn to spend hours in the ring perfecting their ever-increasingly difficult and dangerous act. They ignored sprains, muscle soreness, and bleeding, blistered palms, and they expected no less from Forrestina. "You want, you work," was Lucy's oft-repeated motto, delivered dryly in her husky, brook-no-argument voice.

And so Forrestina swallowed her whimpers when the wire cut into her tender bare feet, pausing only long enough to swipe the blood away when it made the wire too slippery for her to continue. Soon her straining leg and arm muscles were strong instead of sore, the bottoms of her feet calloused over (as Lucy had promised they would), and her bruises from falls into the net faded. She doggedly endured the physical pain and verbal abuse because when the season began and the spotlights trained on her high above the darkened ring, she'd have the chance to dazzle the combined thousands of people taking in her weightless splendor night after night. It was for them that she worked until she wanted to weep, though they'd never know how much it took for her to be there. They would only see a petite, fire-haired nymph who danced along the air, the wire she moved on painted black so that it was invisible to their wondering eyes, *Forrestina, Fairy Princess of the Irish Woodlands, Sprite of the Air and Wonder of the Big Top.* Every time she saw her title and likeness on a poster, she had to pinch herself to make sure it was all real. She thought back to her first performance—her heart galloping both in fear and excitement, the knife-sharp silver light that blinded her for a moment before she stepped into the utter blackness, aware that below her was nothing but space and a hard ground if she fell. She could sense the hundreds of people transfixed by her, holding their breaths as she shook herself, lifted her chin, and smiled. She stepped out onto the wire, and then remembered nothing else until her feet touched the other platform and the roar of the appreciative crowd rushed over her. She'd waved until her arm ached, tears pouring down her cheeks. *That* part, she'd never forget; the joy she'd felt knowing she'd touched others with something she had to give was worth all the weariness and pain.

She lifted her left leg back up, slowly brought it around, and with a tiny hop, turned to face the other direction, her left leg down, her right leg extended. It was a solid movement with hardly a quiver, and she heard Lucy call, "Good. That was good, Lollo. Now come down. I am tired of watching you and I need a drink. Tomorrow you will do better."

"I did fine today," Forrestina muttered. She pushed off the wire with both legs, executing a quick forward spin as she fell towards the net. She landed easily and bounced out. Once on earth again, she strode over to Lucy's chair and knelt beside the older woman. "Lucy, I think perhaps I should make that leap larger—land more in the middle so that I have room to tiptoe to the right before spinning again." She adjusted the black silk shawl, embroidered all over with rich red and pink roses, around Lucy's thin shoulders. The thick black fringe sewn into the edges pattered the back of her hands like raindrops. "What do you think?"

Lucy reached out a dry little claw, which had just started to bow up from years of gripping Joseph's muscular forearms or a steel ring, and patted Forrestina's curls. "What do I think?" Lucy asked. "I think you will do better tomorrow." She grasped a strand of Forrestina's hair and tugged sharply, the sting of it making Forrestina's eyes water. "You did 'fine,' yes, but you can do better, and for that sly little comment you mumbled up there, you get to stay here and work for another hour." She released Forrestina's hair. "Chit," she said smugly.

Forrestina rubbed her sore scalp; she'd forgotten that Lucy had ears like a bat. Lucy gestured wordlessly to Joseph, who moved forward. "I will see you again in the morning," she said to Forrestina, standing. "Joseph, you stay here and remind our Lollo that she is not weightless. Make her work." She strode out of the ring, her head lifted like a tiny dark queen, and Joseph and Forrestina, both aggrieved, watched her go.

Joseph heaved a sigh. "So what are you waiting for—an engraved invitation? You heard her—go," he said crossly.

Stalling, wishing for a reprieve, Forrestina swung up on the first rung of her ladder and said, "Joseph, why does Lucy call me 'Lollo'?"

"You never asked yourself?"

"I have—lots of times—but she always just cocks her head and says, in a deep, mysterious growl, 'Eets a gypsy seecret.' I think she just likes to aggravate me."

"Psh. Some secret. It's the Romany word for 'red,'" Joseph said. "Because of your hair. She thinks your hair is lucky for us, though if I were to give you a name, I'd call you 'kolyuchka.'"

Forrestina didn't want to ask but couldn't help herself. "What is that?" she asked.

Joseph bared his white teeth, his version of a smile. It was mildly terrifying. "It's Russian for 'thorn.' Which you are—a thorn in my damn flesh."

"Well, I'll stick with Lollo, then. Thanks all the same," Forrestina replied tartly.

Joseph snorted. "Fine, *Lollo-kolyuchka*." He bent down and rubbed at a spot on his black boot and said, without looking at her, "Now get back to work."

Forrestina stuck her tongue out at his back, and began to climb the ladder to her tightrope platform. Below, Joseph was pacing again, craning his neck to look up at her. She stepped to the edge of the platform and then, taking a deep breath, she flung her arms to the side, pointing the bare toes of her right foot at the wire. She lifted her left leg in an exaggerated step and began her air dance once again. She swung her right leg around in a pirouette, her body now facing the platform, before slowly bending backwards until her hands were both gripping the wire. Snapping her legs over, she lifted her body upright again. This was when she usually fell; the split second between letting go of the wire with her hands and gripping the wire again with her feet was when gravity tried its best to exert its natural law on her. She fought to keep her balance, gritting her teeth, grimly resisting the pull of her body as it teetered back and forth. She pictured gravity as her stern-faced mother, always trying to force Forrestina to bend to her will. She flailed her arms and below heard Joseph shout, "Stop resisting! Stand tall and center yourself. You are in charge! And don't look down, for God's sake. Keep your damn face lifted!"

She hadn't even thought of looking down until now. "Thanks heaps, Joe, you Ruskie bastard," she grumbled. Fortunately Joe did not have the sonar hearing of his wife. She forced her gaze up and fixed her eyes on a small tear in the red canvas top above her. The wind blew the flap of torn fabric open and shut, and sunlight winked off and on as it moved. *Someone had better fix that before it rains,* she thought. She stretched an arm out over her head and covered the tear's light with her palm, no longer fighting for balance. Her mind emptied itself of thought, funneling like clear water disappearing down a drain. She took one, two, three tiny jumps forward, one foot at a time, like a child creeping up to frighten an unsuspecting adult, then finished with three rapid flips forward, her hands catching and then releasing the wire as she allowed the momentum to propel her up and down.

After her last flip, she regarded the platform in front of her, and then, extending one leg in front and bending the other deeply, she bowed, her left arm at her stomach, her right straight out from her shoulder, her chin tucked into her chest. She stepped daintily onto the platform and waited for Joseph's inevitable criticisms. All was silent—Joseph had gone, probably off to find a drink before joining his wife in their shared tent. He'd always said he never could stand being in the ring for long without his Lucy.

Now unfettered by criticism, Forrestina took a deep breath and turned, eager to walk the wire again. She listened to no sound other than her own heartbeat, which slowed and quickened, slowed and quickened. There was no one yelling at her, no bright lights, no cheers or gasps; she was solitary in the vast space of her own air, a mote of dust floating in a strip of sunlight. Flip, turn, lift; flip, turn, lift: the repetitive movements were soothing, her mind a careful blank.

Her trance was broken by Sarah's voice far below her. "Tina, are you ever coming down? The food from dinner will be cleared away if you don't hurry."

"Is it really dinner-time already?" Forrestina asked, surprised as always at how quickly time sped by when she was practicing. Her stomach, finally able to make itself known now that it was not in competition with her brain and legs and arms, grumbled noisily. She said, "Yes, I'm coming—hold on!" She caught a glimpse of Sarah's oval face looking anxiously up at her. Dear, worried Sarah. She pretended to wobble dangerously on the wire, batting the air with her arms, trying to look alarmed, even giving out a little shriek of terror for effect. She heard Sarah's frightened cry as she allowed herself to tumble backwards.

Sarah ran over just in time to see Forrestina's mischievous grin as she rolled out of the net and onto the ground, which gave a soft *whoof* as it exhaled powdery dust clouds around them both. Sarah swatted at her friend. "Don't *do* that!" she cried. "You know how afraid of heights I am—it makes me dizzy just to look at you."

Forrestina brushed the dust from her feet and then reached over to shake dust from Sarah's pale ankle-length, canary-yellow skirt. "I'm sorry—I just couldn't resist," she said. "Joseph never lets me fall just for fun."

Sarah sniffed. "I don't think Joseph knows the word 'fun.' In Russian, *fun* is probably translated to mean *work harder*."

Forrestina laughed. It was true that Joseph went about his business doggedly, his shoulders hunched, disdain for frivolity evident in every step, every move, every word. Odd for a circus man, she thought. Weren't they all supposed to be a jolly bunch? The only time she spotted any sort of weakness in him was when he was with Lucy. With her, he rarely raised his voice, and never criticized or complained. His eyes followed her diminutive figure everywhere, an unexpected gentleness in his expression. That momentary softness vanished as soon as he turned his eyes away from Lucy, and his face settled back into its sharp, dangerous angles: his nose, blade-straight; his cheekbones and square jaw as prominent and unforgiving as granite; his black eyes set deep in his head and sparking. Joseph reminded Forrestina of the black panther in the menagerie, an angry, sleek cat who paced the length of his cage day and night, glowing eyes seeing and not seeing the world behind his bars, his rage rippling just under the surface of his fur. *If that panther ever escapes*, she often thought as she watched him wearing grooves into the wooden-planked floor, *he'll tear the very limbs off of the world before he is put down.* She wondered what would happen if Joseph ever escaped his cage and Lucy wasn't there to tame him.

In the dressing tent, Forrestina slipped out of her practice tights and leotard. She tugged a moss-green skirt on and then turned her back. "Help me," she said to Sarah, who had followed her in. Sarah gathered the laces of Forrestina's beige corset in both hands and pulled, binding her friend's slim figure into the fabric cage. Forrestina shrugged her matching green blouse on over the corset, buttoning up the gold buttons that ran along her right side, curved around the outside of her right breast, and ended in three more buttons up her neck. She peered into the looking glass and disconsolately reached for a brush on the table.

"Oh, let me," Sarah said. "Otherwise we will be here forever. Sit." Forrestina obeyed, watching in the mirror as her friend's deft fingers removed the string Forrestina used to tie her hair up and out of her face. Sarah untangled the multiple knots of curls, and then, with a swoop of the brush, puffed and poofed until she had Forrestina's hair in a neat Gibson-girl pompadour bun. She jabbed a couple of bone hairpins in to hold everything in place, then, using her index fingers, she hooked two shining curlicues out on either side of Forrestina's temple. "There," she said. She stepped back and surveyed her handiwork, nodding her head in satisfaction.

Forrestina turned her head this way and that admiringly. "You are a miracle worker," she said, patting her hair, softer now that it was no longer wild with tangles.

"I know," Sarah chirped. She handed Forrestina a pair of black button-up boots. "When I am too old to make men's mouths water, maybe I'll do their wives' hair."

"And I guess I'll just come along to be your 'before-and-after' model," Forrestina said, fastening the last button on her shoe. She sprang from her seat and leapt onto a nearby tent-post, which jutted out two feet from the ground. She balanced on her right instep, leaning forward slightly. "By then I will obviously be too old to climb up a ladder, and what job can an elderly tightrope-walker get?"

Sarah laughed and pulled her down. "You can always put on a monkey suit when the chimp dies," she said. "Though I imagine Jack Ape would be perturbed at seeing his old pal so lively. I don't know which of the two is lazier."

"Jack Ape" was what everyone called the monkey handler, and Sarah was right—an idler man was hard to find. He and his chimp spent their days asleep in whatever shade was available—the monkey under his platform, Jack Ape under his battered straw hat. Forrestina had once heard someone say that people began to look like their pets if they were together long enough; this was certainly true for Jack Ape and his monkey.

"Jack Ape's monkey. . ." she mused. She shook her head. "No, when I'm done with the circus, I don't want any more jobs where I have to wear a costume." She threaded her arm through her friend's. "So I reckon you'll just have to settle down and marry well, and I will come along and be a nursemaid for your fifteen children."

"Married? Settled down? FIFTEEN CHILDREN? Perish the thought," Sarah gasped. They made their way to the cook tent, their laughter trailing behind them like the perfumed scent of dogwood blossoms in the night air.

Later, after sopping up a supper of brown beans with yellow cornbread, Forrestina and Sarah sat outside in the darkness, watching the roustabouts roll things up for the night. A breeze, mercifully cool, lifted Forrestina's now-damp curls from her cheeks, and she sighed. Listening to the low murmurs of the other circus folk as they went about their after-hours business—some of them playing poker on a makeshift tree-stump table, others mending costumes by soft lantern light, still others telling stories and jokes—Forrestina's thoughts drifted, not for the first time, back to the folks at home in Missouri. Though she'd dutifully sent her mother and father postcards every few months to let them know that she was still alive, she'd never once told them about her job in the circus. She didn't imagine they would ever try to track her down— she was eighteen now and plenty old enough to make her own way in the world—but just in case, she waited until she was on her way out of whatever town the circus was playing in before mailing her letters. It was better that they never know the truth. Forrestina missed her sisters, though, and Petey and Tilly, and she longed to swap news with them. What were the girls doing now? Did she have a new baby brother or another baby sister? Where was Petey—did he have a job somewhere else? Did Tilly still pray for her every night as she had done when Forrestina was a child, kneeling beside Forrestina's bed, her rough hands folded as she whispered soft words about peace and care?

"Penny for 'em, doll?" Sarah asked, interrupting her from her lonely thoughts.

Forrestina reached over to steal the cigarette Sarah held between her fingers and took a long drag. Immediately she began to choke and cough, and Sarah laughed, taking the cigarette back. Forrestina watched in envy as her friend pulled in the smoke expertly and then released it into the air in lazy ovals, her mouth opening and closing like a gasping, albeit elegant, dying goldfish. "My thoughts aren't worth a penny," she said. "You can have them for free." She leaned forward on the log stump where she was sitting and drew patterns in the loose dry dirt with the pointed toe of her boot. "I was thinking about home, wondering if my people ever miss me." She squinted at her friend. "What about you? Do you ever get to wondering about the family you left behind?" It occurred to her, as she asked the question, that in all their years of friendship she and Sarah had never discussed their families. She wasn't sure why. Maybe they were always too busy for a long heart-to-heart, or maybe they'd always just tried to stay on the lighter side of life. It was safer there. Now, though, she was honestly curious.

Sarah snorted, flicking her cigarette to the ground and crushing it out with her heel. "I don't have a family," she said flatly. "My momma died when I was ten, and Daddy married the first lady crazy enough to take on his six children. She was a mean, spiteful woman who'd smack you twice before you had a chance to get your breakfast in you—she always said that we'd mess up soon enough, so she might as well get a head start on the whipping. The minute I turned fourteen, I was out of there, carrying with me the only thing of value my momma ever had." She touched her left earlobe with an index finger. "These earrings were a wedding gift from my Spanish grandmother. When Momma died, I took them out of her ears while everyone was busy grieving, and I hid them in a tin can I buried in the back yard under the maple tree." She examined the tips of her fingernails, her palms facing up. "After I left home, I worked for a few smaller circus outfits before finding my way into the Big Show. Boy, that was a nightmare time, let me tell you. The things they expected me to do." She shuddered, her expression turning hard. "I plan on staying here as long as they'll have me," she said. She fingered an earring in her lobe absently, "So I guess the Ringling folk are my family now." She turned to look at Forrestina. "What about you—why'd you leave home?"

Forrestina closed her eyes. "My reasons weren't as good as yours," she said. "It's just that my mother was so cold, I liked to get frostbite every time I was in the same room as her. I don't think she ever liked me that much." She shivered, and Sarah wrapped her arms around her. Forrestina leaned her head on her friend's shoulder. "Aren't you supposed to love your kids, even if they aren't exactly what you hoped they'd be? Lord, I never knew if I was alive or dead in that house, you know?"

"And so some of God's misfits packed up and headed off for the glamour of the circus life," Sarah said, as if she were finishing a sermon, her breath warm on Forrestina's scalp. "Here we wear our scars as brightly colored cloaks, paint happy faces on our sorrows, and we never look behind us." She kissed the crown of Forrestina's head. "Hear me?" she whispered. "We never look back."

Forrestina shifted so that her head was now in Sarah's lap. She stared into the sky above her, at the black velvet scattered with chips of diamond starlight, listening to the non-silence of the quietly busy night, coming to terms with her past, thinking hard thoughts, growing up. Unloved by her mother or not, she wasn't a ghost in her own skin anymore, and that had to count for something. Yes sir, it had to count for something.

CHAPTER EIGHT

"LADIES AAAAAND GENTLEMAN! Welcome to the most magnificent, the most stupendous, the grrreatest show on eaaarth!" Bob Mack, Ringmaster General of the Ringling Bros. Circus, strode around the ring in his thigh-high black leather boots, his top hat Lincoln-esque and adding a good foot to his already impressive six-foot-three frame. He was as thin as Honest Abe too, but "honest" was not a word anyone would ascribe to him; indeed, if Bob was breathing, he was lying. He'd once told Forrestina, in his booming theatrical bass, "There's truth and then there's the show, and Lamb-chop, it's the show what pays my salary. The truth just makes a man sad and poor."

He was right. The circus was all about lies (though the performers all preferred to use the more polite term "illusion" to describe what they did). Hardly anyone ever used his or her real name in the ring; from Sheba, the Queen of the Ballet Girls, to Oscar, the clown, to Nina, the Fat Lady from Bombay, they all carried a different name and a different story in their purses or pockets, and they sold their "illusions" to the rubes who paid to see them night after night. Forrestina was an anomaly in that she was billed by her real name, but the back-story created for her—that of a fairy sprite captured and sent over from the Green Isle to work off a debt owed by her leprechaun father—was laughably absurd. Besides being 100% human, before running away to join Ringling Brothers Forrestina had never been north of St. Louis, and Ireland might as well have been the moon in her imagination. Still, she happily played along, pulling on the emerald-green tutu-style dress that molded against her body and flowed to the mid-point of her thighs. The tiny gossamer cellophane wings affixed to her back shimmered ethereally in the spotlight, as did the crystals sewn into her dress, which sparkled like star-chips as she danced the wire. She was less happy with her hair, which was a source of contention between her and Mr. Wilson, who designed the costumes for all the girls, ballet or not. "Unbind!" he'd cried. "There is no one in this world who has such exquisitely crimson hair." He unpinned her bun and set her curls free. "You should look like a mermaid."

"Yes, but a mermaid just has to swim," Forrestina replied crossly, pulling her thick hair from his hands and gathering it back up. "Mr. Wilson, I simply cannot see the wire with all this mess in my face!"

"But my dear," Mr. Wilson protested, wringing his hands, his saucer-round face creased in dismay. "What price fame? What price beauty?"

"Fame and beauty mean nothing if Lollo is lying dead in the dirt," Lucy said, walking in on their conversation. She reached out and began to deftly braid Forrestina's hair into several plaits along her head. "We will compromise," she said soothingly. "If she wears her hair like this, she can still see what she is doing, and the crowd can get a glimpse of her hair." She stepped back and surveyed her work. "We can braid some flowers and more crystals in the plaits so that she looks suitably wild and fairy-like."

"I'd like to just chop it all off," Forrestina grumbled, and Mr. Wilson gasped in horror, his pudgy fingers splayed on his chest. Yes, illusions for the rubes took work.

Tonight as she waited in the wings for Bob Mack to introduce her, she felt the old familiar jittering of her nerves winging around her tummy. "Easy, girl," she heard Lucy say at her shoulder. Forrestina nodded without turning her head. When she heard her cue—Bob Mack saying, "And from the fairy kingdom of the Emerald Isle, her mother a fairy queen, her father a leprechaun captured in a teapot, brought all the way here for your wondrous beholding, I turn your attention to our very own air-dancer, Forrestina of the Forest!"— Forrestina stepped out of the darkness and into the blinding light. She stood tall, her back overextended and slightly curved as she waved to all sides of the tent. She sprang lightly on her toes, tripping daintily to the beam where her ladder steps were attached, and began her climb as Bob continued to spin the origin tale Mr. Wilson had written especially for her. Thank goodness it didn't contain any mention of mermaids.

"Do not be afraid, gentle ladies," Bob cried as she stepped onto the platform. "Though a fall from such a height would surely kill her, our fairy princess has conquered gravity. Why, look! She waltzes upon the very air we breathe!"

At that Forrestina took her first step onto the black wire and began her routine, prancing and flipping, disguising her necessary steadying motions with dramatic arm and leg gestures, extending her limbs out to either side gracefully. She ignored the gasps and small shrieks from below and let all the hours of practice guide her movements, her mind focused only on executing whatever trick came next. Before she knew it, the performance was over and it was time for her dramatic descent. Stepping onto the opposite platform, both arms lifted, she turned and bowed with one arm out to the side. With the other hand, she swiftly clipped a metal clasp to a ring connected to her fabric "ivy" belt. The clasp was tied to a cable set in a pulley, and she took one calm step off of the platform, being very careful to extend her arms overhead. She straightened one leg, her other leg bent so that her foot touched her opposite knee, and in this way, she gracefully "flew" to the ground while cheers and whistles filled the big top. As she neared earth, Bob Mack strode over to her and affected a one-arm embrace; he was in fact unclipping her from the clasp. The rope was pulled up and away by an unseen roustabout in the shadows, and Forrestina twirled on her toes, bowing several times before heading back into the dark cave of the dressing tent.

Sarah was waiting for her, her hands clasped to her heart. "Oh, Forrestina," she breathed. "You were magnificent! I swear, no matter how many times I see you perform, I can't stop being awestruck. It really looks like you're up there jumping around on nothing but air." She looked up at the platform and then back to the ground. "But I can't breathe until you're safely down again. What if you fell? You'd be dashed to pieces."

"Not a chance," Forrestina said, giving her friend's arm a squeeze. She tossed her head. "I'm the master of gravity, remember?"

"I remember a certain verse in the Bible that says 'pride goeth before a fall,'" a deep voice growled behind them. Joseph, every bulge of muscle evident in his satin shimmering white leotard, glared at the two girls. He and Lucy stood at the Big Top's entrance waiting for Bob Mack to spin his tale of these two Romanian gypsies who used rings and bars to fly through the air into the arms of love, or some such nonsense. It was a story both Joseph and Lucy despised but, as Mr. Wilson pointed out many times, there was no magic in a story about hard-working Russian immigrants who practiced hours a day.

Forrestina crossed her eyes as she swept past Joseph. "Have a good show, *Lucy*," she said deliberately.

Lucy, eyes twinkling, nodded. "Thank you, Lollo," she said. She paused, then commented casually, "Hey Lollo, didn't your mother ever tell you if you cross your eyes like that, they will stay that way forever?" Joseph turned swiftly, and Forrestina and Sarah dashed away from his murderous look, giggling wildly.

Once they were back in the ladies' dressing area, they were accosted by Darling Dorine, the three-foot-tall midget from the side-show. Her short arms were brimming with wildflowers: purple hydrangeas, gerbera daisies of red, orange, pink, and yellow, sweet pea blossoms, and three huge sunflowers, all tied up with a thin filmy ribbon the color of lilacs. The bouquet was so large that Dorine's face was invisible behind it; all Forrestina could see of her was the top of the little woman's dark head.

"Here," Dorine gasped, tottering blindly forward. "These are for you, Red."

Forrestina lifted the bouquet from Dorine's arms, holding the flowers to her nose and inhaling deeply. Behind her, Sarah whistled.

"Where did these come from, Dorine?" Forrestina asked.

Dorine made her way to a small folding chair and hopped up onto it, her legs dangling down like a child's. "From some dark, handsome devil. He cornered me outside the tent—said he'd seen your show every night this week and wanted you to know how much he admired"—here she pressed her hands to her heart and intoned—"your talent and your beeyouootee." She folded her hands in her lap. "He wanted to give them to you himself but I informed him of the rules forbidding strange men fraternizing with the single circus girls in their dressing tent."

Sarah perched her hip on the edge of the dressing table next to where Dorine sat. "I'd say the flowers do enough talking," she said. She leaned forward. "Hey, there's a card next to the biggest sunflower."

Forrestina parted the blossoms and found the plain white square of cardboard nestled in the bouquet. It read simply: *You are a marvel to behold. Signed, M. Keyes.* She read the message aloud, and Dorine slapped her own forehead with the palm of her hand.

"Come to think of it, I *do* know that fella," she said. "Works for the Shell & Sons circus. They call him 'Big Broad Tosser,' I think." She kicked her heels back and forth in the air. "He looks like trouble—what my mother would call original sin in a suit. Best throw those flowers in the trash and forget you ever saw them."

"You will do no such thing," Sarah said pertly. "Just because you keep the flowers doesn't mean you have to keep the man." She stood and pressed her face into the bouquet in Forrestina's arms. "They smell heavenly."

"Well, don't say I didn't warn you," said Dorine, shrugging. She clumsily rolled herself from her chair. "I've got to scoot. I promised Rotunda I would help her with her stockings. I swear, that girl can't keep stockings darned to save her five-hundred-pound life." Dorine gestured to her own tiny shoes. "I don't think she's even seen her feet in fifteen years. But friends do for friends, and freaks take care of each other." She waggled her short stumpy fingers as she made her way out of the tent. "Toodles, Miss 'Marvel' and Miss Marvel's friend."

"Bye, Darling Dorine," Forrestina called after her as Sarah blew the little woman an air kiss. "Thanks for the delivery." She looked over the flowers once more and then gently set the bouquet down on the dressing table. "Shell & Sons," she said glumly. "Drats."

Everywhere Ringling stopped to perform, some other show (called "grafters" by the Ringling folk because they tried to graft themselves onto the lucrative branch of Ringling's fame), would set up tents and unfurl their greasier, more sinister wares as close to the Big Show as they could. The titles of the grafter circuses were always respectable, familial names—Jones & Sons, Rogers & Co., The Beal Family Circus—but the circuses themselves were decidedly not family-oriented. Run by mean little men who'd stab their own mothers if they thought she held an extra dime, they exploited the most desperate, performers *and* rubes, and never lost a wink of sleep over it. Ringling tried its best to keep the competition away, implementing strict legal parameters for each site by requiring a quarter-acre buffer all the way around their grounds, and hiring lawmen to prosecute any trespassers who tried to breach their protective moat, but every shady circus knew exactly what they could get away with. They'd set up shop right at the boundary line across from the entrance/exit of Ringling, erecting their own rigged games of chance, burlesque tents, and freak and side-show exhibits, which housed underfed, sullen, bruised, unhappy souls who'd already been dealt a rough hand in life and were now often literally kicked while they were down.

Those smaller circus were a far cry from Ringling Brothers, where Otto, Al, Charles, Alf T, and John Ringling, the brothers themselves, demanded propriety in all things—no card hustling and no girlie tents. They insisted on the utmost respect for all the employees of the circus as well; this included the freaks, whose inclusion in the show had lately caused the brothers a certain amount of moral angst. They'd actually discussed dropping the freaks from their circus because Al believed it was inhumane to encourage people to gawk at what he deemed the "less fortunate" for a price. "Should we profit from their suffering?" he'd asked. "Our midget, our fat lady, our seven-foot-tall giant, our armless man—isn't this adding to their pain? Shouldn't we divest ourselves from the guilt?"

Of course, the Ringling Brothers' freaks, seeing no other means of income and despairing at the idea of being forced to leave their gentle employers, objected loudly to Al's concerns, and so far, the other four brothers had managed to convince him that the real cruelty was to deprive the freaks of a livelihood. Besides, the brothers argued, they could not afford the loss of income—their human oddities brought in a tidy sum of cash. For now, Al had been appeased with the promise that the freaks would be afforded the same dignity and honor as the trapeze artists. "They make us almost as much money," the others pointed out to Al, "so we will compensate them handsomely. As long as people are interested in paying to look at them, we will continue to keep them working."

The smaller circuses suffered no such bouts of conscience, of course. Along with their mistreated freaks, their corpse-inhabited "menageries" were sorry affairs housing a few sickly, starved, threadbare animals and were supplemented with taxidermy grotesques that they had created themselves: calves with extra heads sewn on, a twelve-legged lamb, a snake body attached to the head of a snarling dog. The smell of formaldehyde, urine, and excrement from filthy cages permeated the air around them. Their circus clowns were bitter drunks who hated children, and they had no trapeze acts because no one would work the wires for them (too many falls and breaks and occasional deaths due to faulty riggings and nets), so it was their naked girlie shows and crooked games of "chance" that drew in the cash. Theirs was the circus of the dark, attended by the men who'd spotted them on their way out of the Big Show with their families. Those men would invariably sneak back later to gamble, drink, dream, and sometimes, if the price was right, fornicate with some of the more capitalistic performers from the burlesque tent. Now in El Paso, Texas, where Ringling was currently set up, the leech extending towards the Big Show was called Shell & Sons, Esquire (though the circus actually belonged to a man named Mister Groves). As soon as the Ringling train had pulled into the station and began to set up in its rented field, Groves had sprung into action, hauling his own pitiful wagons out and hoisting his ragged tents.

Forrestina hated grafters, as did all the girls of Ringling. Though she often chafed at the strict rules and hawk-eyes of Mrs. Hayes, when she passed over the line from the safety of her circus into the dismal territory of the flesh circuses and saw the tired, heavily made-up faces of the burlesque dancers as they stood outside their tents, smoking and swilling whiskey from the bottles of admiring customers, she was grateful for the protection of her "Sunday School" circus. Being admired by a mysterious stranger was gratifying, but Dorine was right—no good could come of being tangled up with anyone from Shell & Sons. She gathered the flowers in her arms, took one last, lingering inhale of the perfumed petals, and deposited them in the trash. Upon Sarah's loud protest, she faked a big sneeze. "Allergies," she said, wiping her eyes. She hurried to change from her costume to her everyday clothes. "Come on, Sarah; let's go find something to eat. I heard the cook was making apricot fried pies, and I asked her to set some aside for us. Pies are better than flowers any day." Sarah cast a reluctant look over her shoulder at the stalks of flowers just visible at the trashcan rim but allowed herself to be led away, still lamenting their loss as the girls moved towards the food tent.

The flowers were all but forgotten until a few days later when, during a performance, Forrestina's flesh-colored tights snagged on a splintered edge of her ladder and ripped along the calf. She took the stockings to Donna, the circus seamstress, to see if they could be repaired. The seamstress took one look at the flapping fabric and promptly proclaimed the stockings a lost cause. "Here," she said, scribbling a name and some figures on a scrap of paper.

"This is the hosier in El Paso. Give him these measurements and tell him to add the tights to the Ringling bill. Lord knows we've already given him plenty of business—Mr. Wilson's 'French Revolution' story meant the ballet girls all needed new stockings—so you shouldn't hear a word of complaint from him."

Forrestina thanked Donna, taking the scrap of paper and tucking it into her pocket. After breakfast the next morning she set out towards El Paso to find the hosier. She'd been feeling cooped up and restless lately, and the two-mile walk into town would be a welcome respite from circus life. She tied a straw sun bonnet on her head to protect her fair skin, laced up her boots, and began her journey. Her only sorrow on this fine summer morning was that Sarah couldn't go with her. Mr. Wilson was in crisis mode; his "Marie Antoinette" had mysteriously snuck off in the dead of night—whispers were that she had met herself a handsome cowboy—and he had to scramble up a new show. Of course, that meant extra practice for all the ballet girls, which also meant Sarah wouldn't have a moment to herself all day.

Forrestina briefly considered asking Carl to come with her, but after her recent rejection of him (they'd kissed and canoodled a few times, but when he tried to see what was under her skirts behind the dressing tent a few weeks ago, he'd received a good smack on the ear for his troubles), he'd stayed away from her, his normally friendly grin disappearing whenever she caught his eye. "He'll recover," Sarah told her as Forrestina fretted over it. "Just wait until the next batch of girls are hired—he will fall in love all over again, and you'll be just another pretty face in the scenery." Forrestina hoped Sarah was right; she liked Carl and his frank, off-color jokes, and though she had no interest in him as a serious beau, she hated to think they could no longer be friends. She couldn't wait for him to thaw out before going to purchase her new tights, however—fluttering, torn stockings would simply not work up on the wire. So she steeled herself against the inevitable cat-calls of the Shell & Sons employees as she crossed into their territory and set out alone.

Thankfully the flesh circus, a prowling night animal that grew indolent as dawn broke, slept late, so even though it was coming on eleven, Forrestina was able to pass through the mostly silent tents unmolested and uncommented on. Once in town, she relaxed and took her time, drinking in the sights of a new place. This was just one of the many things she liked about her new life, moving from town to town, seeing new sights and meeting new people, listening to accents change, sampling different types of foods. She strolled along the sidewalk, peering into shop windows as she passed. El Paso was not a very grand town—certainly not as impressive as some of the places she'd seen in her time with the circus, such as San Francisco, California, or Boston, Massachusetts—but it had its charms. She did sometimes still miss her cozy little hometown in Missouri, and this big sprawling state, with its friendly, smiling citizens in cowboy hats and boots, felt oddly familiar to her. She began to hum "The Yellow Rose of Texas" loudly to herself, pausing a moment to admire a royal-blue, feather-trimmed hat displayed in the window of the local milliners. As she gazed at the hat, her stomach growled, and she decided that later she'd stop by the small café she'd spotted coming into town and try one of those "taco" things she'd seen advertised in soap-lettering on the big glass window.

"You'd look good in that hat," a man's deep voice said next to her, startling her out of her reverie. "Better'n that old straw bonnet you're wearing. Did you steal that thing from a scarecrow?"

Offended, she turned towards the speaker, ready to give him a piece of her mind, and paused when she saw that he was very handsome. Though he was not particularly tall—probably only about 5'10—he was broad shouldered and slim-waisted, dark-haired and dark-eyed, and dressed in a fine deep blue suit. He was what Sarah, a great admirer of tormented literary poets, would most likely deem "Byronesque." After a dumbstruck moment, Forrestina gathered herself; Byron be damned, this fellow had tweaked the wrong girl's nose. She opened her mouth to really let him have it, to tell him to mind his own business and then question him about his mother's lack of ability in raising children, but before she could form a scathingly tart retort, the man wrapped his strong hand around her waist and ushered her into the shop. She was so stunned by the sudden movement that she was unable to recover her ability to speak until she was actually standing face-to-face with the shop-girl behind the counter. The man asked to see the hat, and as the shop-girl turned to remove it from the stand in the window, Forrestina bleated loudly, "No!" She shoved the man's hand, which was still gripping her waist, away. The clerk, a prim-looking girl of about twenty, turned to her, eyes widened. "I mean, no, thank you," Forrestina stammered. She took a deep breath to calm herself, smoothed her hands along her skirt, and said, "I am not in the market for a new hat today."

"Oh, nonsense," the man scoffed. He placed two shiny quarters on the glass counter and took the hat in his hands. "We don't need it wrapped," he said over his shoulder to the shop-girl, who had dropped the quarters into the till and was reaching for a sheet of thin white tissue paper, "she'll wear it out." With that, he snatched the sun bonnet from Forrestina's head and replaced it with the new hat. He stood back a little, surveying his work, and then with a grunt, adjusted it so that it sat better on her head. "There we go," he said, satisfied. "That's better." Furiously, Forrestina reached up to remove the hat, and he stopped her, wrapping his steel fingers around her own.

"Really, Mister," Forrestina said, trying to sound haughty, uncomfortably aware of the heat from his fingers burning a path down her arms and up her throat, "I cannot accept a gift from a stranger."

"Then let's get acquainted," he said, ushering her out of the shop. "The name's Maxwell Keyes—Max for short." He released her and swept his own hat, a black bowler, from his head, bowing exaggeratedly. "And you must be Aphrodite, goddess of the morning." He grabbed her right hand with his left and kissed it, letting his lips linger on her skin. Forrestina's heart began to beat as if she were stepping out on the tightrope.

"Please," she said, "this is too much." She tried to pull her hand free but Max tightened his grip. A dark shadow flickered behind his eyes for just a moment, and then he chased it away with a smile, his teeth strong and white against the dark tan of his clean-shaven face.

"Come on, now," he said, "don't deny me the pleasure of giving a pretty girl a pretty hat on such a pretty morning. And would you stop looking so alarmed? All I ask in return is that I may escort you around town and perhaps walk you back to the circus when you're done with your errands."

"So you've seen the show," Forrestina said, finally extracting her hand from his. She was used to admiration from the rubes, though Mrs. Hayes usually ran the more arduous ones off before they could become a bother. There was no Mrs. Hayes to protect her now, though thinking of Carl and his boxed ear, she inadvertently flexed her fingers and suppressed a smile. She didn't think she really needed protection.

"I have seen the show," Max agreed. "You are Forrestina of the Fairie Isles, the result of a passionate night between a leprechaun and a fairy queen, gifted with the enchanting ability to dance on air with only your wings to support you."

Forrestina laughed. His tale was very close to the one Mr. Wilson had created, though the Ballet Master would *never* have come right out and suggested copulation in such bold terms. For a man who did not like to leave much to the imagination in terms of the human female form, he was surprisingly prudish when it came to acknowledging the lust his costumes and stories inevitably created. Sarah said it was because he was more fascinated with the male of the species and that lust for a woman was as foreign to him as a cat being in love with a dog. He had a remarkable eye for what made a woman look her most sensual, though, so Forrestina wasn't sure if Sarah was right.

Max grinned down at her and jutted his left elbow out, indicating that she should slip her arm through his. After a minute she obeyed. She was enjoying herself and not quite ready to part from this man whose kiss on her hand still burned. Besides, they were in public view, surrounded by shops and people. What could be the harm? Together they headed down the sidewalk, deeper into town. "So what's your real name?" Max asked.

"It really is Forrestina," she said. "Forrestina Magdalena Bradley."

"Irish-Catholic girl," Max said. He placed his free hand over his heart and intoned, "Hail Mary, full of grace. The Lord is with thee. Blessed art thou amongst women and blessed is the fruit of thy womb, Jesus." Forrestina automatically crossed herself, then realized that Max was watching her with amusement, the corners of his mouth crooked in a smile. She noticed, too, that he did not make the sign of the cross. "I'm half-Wop, and that half is Catholic, too," he said. "Even though I'm not religious now, I was raised with that ever-present sense that I should always be confessing, whether I'd done something wrong or not. One day I just decided, 'Hell, if I'm always apologizing, I may as well do something to feel sorry for.' So I ran off and joined the circus, and now I sin to my little black heart's content." He dropped his voice confidingly. "Thing is, now that I'm a real sinner, I just can't seem to make myself go to confession."

Forrestina could believe it; Max had a positively wicked smile. "You're in the circus?" she asked. "I have never seen you. Are you a roustabout? I thought I knew everyone, at least by sight, but—"

"Oh, I'm not in the BIG circus," Max said. "I've floated around in several little outfits. Currently, I am with Shell & Sons. You probably passed through our camp on your way to town."

Forrestina stopped walking, and Max, still entangled in her arm, stopped too. "What's wrong?" he asked.

"M. Keyes. You were the one who sent me flowers a few days ago," she said. Flowers she'd thrown in the trash because he was from that horrible little grafter circus. What was this self-proclaimed "sinner's" job there, she wondered. Barker for the flesh tent? Procurer of base delights for the strippers? Beater of the poor mistreated freaks? What had Dorine called him—"Big Broad Tosser"? What exactly did he toss?

"Yes, that was me," Max drawled. "And you're welcome, by the way." He glanced at her. "Hey, now," he said. "I can see what you're thinking, plain as if you were spitting in my face. Get this straight: I do work for Shell & Sons, but I'm a free agent. I work the card table in the game-of-chance section; Three-Card Monte is my game. Don't you begrudge a man his living—after all, what would *your* people say about what you do, tiptoeing around in next to nothing for all the world to see? When's the last time you visited Father O'Whatsits to confess *that?*"

Stung, Forrestina pulled her arm from his and strode away. She was furious with herself—how could she have been so careless, allowing a strange man to buy her a hat and then sashay her down the street in broad daylight? What if someone had seen her and reported her to Mrs. Hayes? When Max caught up with her, she pulled the hat from her head and handed it to him, looking straight ahead as she did. "I appreciate the kind gift and the flowers, Mr. Keyes," she said, "but it was wrong for me to accept them. We have strict rules concerning our conduct at Ringling—rules designed to protect our reputations, both as employees and as ambassadors for our circus. I am sure you will have no problem finding some other grateful female to bestow this on."

"For pity's sake," Max exclaimed. He grabbed her by the elbow and whirled her around to face him. She expected him to be angry and was astonished to see that Max was grinning. "Will you get a load of this?" he hooted to no one in particular. "Listen, darlin'. I get it—you're the princess and I am the frog here, but I gotta say, you take your role more serious than anyone I ever met." He spun the brim of the new hat on his long index finger, the blue feather flashing like a streak of sky. "Just let me ask you one thing: Why'd you join the circus?" He stopped spinning the hat and tucked it under his arm, then leaned down, his face close to hers. His eyes were so deeply brown they were almost as black as their irises. "I'll tell you why I joined," he said confidingly. "So I didn't have to follow anyone else's rules. So I could be free to do as I pleased, when I pleased, and no one could tell me otherwise."

He straightened and touched his index finger and thumb to his hat brim lightly. "But that's just me. You enjoy your ambassadorship, my lady." He thrust his hands in his trouser pockets and walked away, whistling as he went.

Forrestina watched him go, her heart in her throat. He was right. Though she loved the pageantry and glitter of performing, the real reason she'd run away from home three years ago was to escape her mother's ever-present, unending list of dos and don'ts for a lady. Yet Mrs. Hayes was just as bad as Mother—maybe worse because she was always around. Forrestina suddenly recalled a story Carl had told her about a tawny mountain lion the circus had once owned, a beautiful female cat who, when the circus had first obtained her, sat very still in the corner of her cage, her eyes mere slits in her lovely face. Every day, she'd rise to eat and drink, and then she'd go back to sitting with those golden eyes of hers covered by her dark lids. She sat that way, eyes half-closed, for years, and then one ordinary day, for no reason that anyone could figure, she suddenly opened her eyes wide and dashed full speed into the metal bars. She crashed backwards, blood pouring from a gash in her head, and then went into a wild panic, yowling and clawing at the air, running into the bars over and over and over. Before anyone could get in to stop her, she'd crushed her own skull. Carl said that it was as if the lion had just woken up one day and for the first time noticed the bars around her world. As she watched Max striding away, Forrestina suddenly saw the bars of her own cage, and she picked up her skirts and ran. When she caught up with him, Max slowed his pace and, without looking at her, handed her the new hat. She pinned it back onto her head and took his elbow again. "I need to go to the hosier," she said, panting. "Then perhaps later you can show me how to play cards."

Max grinned down at her. "Darlin'," he said, "any old fool can play cards. I will show you how to *win*."

CHAPTER NINE

ONCE UPON A TIME, Forrestina Bradley thought the most daring, adventurous thing she could do was run away from home and join the circus. Then Max ripped the hidden possibilities of life open even more, and Forrestina found herself tumbling into a world truly outside rules and regulations. In her nightly escapes to Max's circus, she learned how to be crafty and stealthy, creeping soundlessly through the acrobats' sleeping tent, grateful that she no longer bunked with the ballet girls. No matter how light-footed she thought she was, she was certain Mrs. Hayes, with her sonar-hearing, would have discovered her. Holding her breath, she listened to the heavy sounds of sleep escaping from her tent-mates (Chinese identical twin sisters Ming Su and Ming Lu, whose act consisted of aerial feats involving long crimson ribbons), then tiptoed to the door, lifting the canvas open just enough for her slender figure to slip through into the night air.

Once she reached the menagerie, she was almost free; many of the caged animals were nocturnal, and their prowling masked any sound she might make. Some of the animals eyed her with curiosity, seeming to wonder why she was moving about in their world when all the other oddities that walked on two legs were fast asleep, but most ignored her and let her pass by with nary a warning sound. When she was finally past the menagerie, she pressed herself against the plank wall that had been erected around the circus property and pushed aside a board that Max had loosened for her. After that, it was just a short walk across an empty ditch, and then she was in the middle of the blazing and noisy world of the grafter circus.

Tonight as Forrestina climbed up the side of the scrubby-grassed ditch, she heard someone holler out to her, "Hey there, Red." Al, a burly barker at the bottle-toss, waved at her as she stepped from behind his tent and into the main carnival path.

She returned his greeting with a smile. "You seen Max tonight?" she asked, watching as Al lined up a crowd of teen-age boys who wanted to show off for their girls. He was busy collecting coins and handing out rings, but at her question, he paused. "He's set up near the girlie tent tonight," he said, and Forrestina didn't like the trace of pity she saw in the look he gave her with his answer.

Her lips turned downwards and her smile dropped away like spilled marbles. "Thanks, Al," she muttered. She made her way through the shabby tents, the gruff call of the barkers filling her ears as she passed: *Bottle Toss, four shots a penny. Win a big prize for your lady. Test your strength—impress your girl! Darts, darts, throw some darts. Everyone's a winner, guaranteed.* She only half-listened, consumed by the familiar burn of jealousy. It seemed to her that Max too often set up shop near the naked young women who were the lifeblood of the seedy circus—women who called to him in a cloying, knowing way that boiled Forrestina's blood and made her itch to rip their hair out at their painted roots.

She had to seethe in silence, though. "You know I go where the money is, honey," Max said to her when she greeted him with a complaint. He smoothed the black velvet that covered his high collapsible tray table with his palms. "There is no better place for fools to be parted with their money than outside yon Forbidden Gardens. The rubes come outta there full of piss and vinegar, and that's when I hook 'em, give 'em a chance to win big so they can tell themselves that they are still real men before they trudge home to their fat wives and passels of snot-nosed brats." He tipped her a wink. "Some play in the hopes that they can win enough to secure a quick minute with one of the dream-girls in the tent." He drew out his cards and began to shuffle, moving so fast that the cards streamed out as one long chain, and then he snapped them face down, one after another. "Of course, they don't ever win, so they go home broke and more frustrated than before. If they still have any gumption left, I imagine their wives either get tumbled before those fine ladies have a chance to wake up—maybe make yet another little mouth to feed—or they spend the night in the barn with just the cows for company."

Forrestina winced. Despite the nickname, she'd always thought of the "rubes" as friends; after all, with no audience, there was no circus. Those faded men and women in their Sunday best warmed her with their applause, their expressions youthful and delighted, full of hope and expectation. She loved their children even more—the "brats" Max referred to—loved the way their eyes lit up at every little thing, from the animals to the acrobats, to the salted peanuts and caramel apples. The tots still believed in magic, and seeing their entranced faces, Forrestina remembered to believe too. What right did Max have to make something so precious ugly?

Max noticed her cross expression and pulled her to him. "Oh, did I offend Her Ladyship? My apologies." His voice turned husky as he kissed her jawline, and she shivered at the light touch of his lips on her skin. "Would you like me to stop talking about such naughty things?" he murmured. "How about I show you instead?" He began unfastening the tiny pearl buttons at her neck and she soon forgot her anger. She let him kiss her just a minute more before pushing him away. "Max," she said, refastening her buttons reluctantly, "we're in public."

He dropped his hand and sighed exaggeratedly, but she could tell he wasn't really upset. That was good; when Max got angry, he could be mean. "True enough," he said. He pointed to a squat wooden bench set at an angle behind him. "If you're going to deny me a little loving, then would you mind moving over? I'm working, you know."

Forrestina obeyed, positioning herself so that she could watch the proceedings better. Max tapped the cards on his table and began his bark at the passersby in a booming, authoritative voice: "Three Card Monte—step right up. Big wins, easy money—all you have to do is find Her Majesty, the Red Queen. Yes sir, that darling Queen of Hearts." He shot Forrestina an air kiss with his lips and she shook her head at him, smiling. Oh, but she did love him.

A fat man dressed in plaid trousers and a white button-up shirt that was so soaked through with sweat it was almost clear walked by, and Max called out to him, "You, sir!" When the man turned, Max beckoned him with his hand. "You look like a fella who knows his way around a card table. Forget the kiddie games—this is where the men come to try their luck. Hell, luck doesn't have anything to do with it. This here is a game of skill!" He brought out that slow, carnal smile of his and directed it to the dolly clinging to the fat man's pork-loin forearm. "And I bet he's quite a skillful man, isn't he, miss? He must be, to have a looker like you."

The woman, Trixie (who, Forrestina knew, also worked for Shell & Sons), trilled, "What fun, Tommy! I want to see you try!"

"Waste of time," the rube grumbled. Trixie giggled. She reached up, purred something that Forrestina could not hear into Tommy's ear, then caught his earlobe in her teeth gently. Tommy groaned, a noise that sounded to Forrestina an awful lot like a hop-toad during mating season. It made her vaguely sick to her stomach, but that was the way these circuses worked— everyone pulled together, and everyone got a piece of the pie. Max would get his money, and Trixie would too.

"Come on, Tom. Listen to your girl there. It's only a nickel for one try; two for a dime." Max smiled widely at the small crowd that had gathered, letting them know that *he* knew how clever he was being. There was no doubt that he was charming—and out of all the girls warming under that handsome grin, only Forrestina got to claim him as her own. She still couldn't believe her luck.

Trixie fluttered her eyelashes and looked beseechingly at Tom, who, after a few seconds, reluctantly laid out a nickel. Max made the coin disappear into his pants pocket, then he extracted three cards from the top of the deck.

"Observe," he said, showing the man and the crowd the cards, "a ten of spades, a five of clubs, and voila!" He flipped the last card like he was flipping a coin and displayed it for all to see. "Her Highness, the Queen of Hearts." He held the card aloft while affecting a deep, reverential bow. Cupping the cards in his left hand and then folding them lengthwise, he created a shallow crease in all three. He began to toss the cards with both hands like he was juggling, extending his long fingers as the cards shifted in space, and then he threw the cards into the air one more time, flipping his wrists downward, letting them drop face down in a perfect line back onto the table. It was like watching a magic trick.

Max gestured to the line of cards. "All right, good sir," he said. "This game—a game of skill for a man with sharp eyes, as I'm sure you have—is simple. Merely tell me where the queen hides her pretty face and you win triple your money." He winked at Trixie. "Or would you like your lucky lady to do the guessing?"

Tom grinned, slipped his fat hand onto Trixie's ample bottom, and gave it a good squeeze. She gasped theatrically and slapped at him, then snuggled in closer. "Go ahead," Tom told her magnanimously. "I know which one it is, but let's see how you do."

Trixie leaned forward, tapping her teeth with a polished scarlet nail. "Um," she said in a high-pitched, little-girl voice, "I think it's right there." She pointed to the card in the middle. Max flipped it over and, to the applause of the crowd, showed the red queen. He handed Trixie back the nickel plus one dime. Trixie bounced up and down, allowing Tom a chance to appreciate what the movement did to her generous bosom. "I want to try again," she squealed, laying down one of her coins. Max touched the top of his hat to her with his index finger and began his magic tossing, ending with the same flourish and the same neat line of facedown cards. Trixie leaned in again, biting her lip in mock concentration, then straightened and said, "There! It's there!" She pointed to the card on the left, and again squealed with happiness when it turned up red.

"Mercy," Max said. "You sure are lucky, miss. How about we raise the stakes?" He laid out a dollar—half a week's wages for most of the people watching. "You put in twenty-five cents and I'll put in a whole buck."

"That's just foolish," Tom said. "You've come out all right, Trixie. Let's go."

Trixie pulled the rube aside and said, in a whisper loud enough for Forrestina to hear, "I have his trick, Tom. The corner on the queen is bent—I spotted it the first time and made sure the second. I don't think he knows I know. We have a chance to make some real money here." She rubbed his belly with her palm and cooed, "And with that extra money, we could maybe find us a nice hotel room for the night."

Tom almost knocked the table over in his hurry to get back to it. "I'll have a go," he said. "Two to your six." He plonked two dollars down and watched as Max tossed the cards. When they landed, Tom squinted at the backs of the cards for a moment, then triumphantly pointed to the left card. "She's there." He reached for the six dollar bills on the table eagerly.

Max flipped the card Tom had chosen over and frowned. "Damn it," he said. "You have her." Tom preened as Trixie clapped and bounced some more. "You're so smart," she exclaimed. "Why, I bet you could clean house if you placed a really big bet—I mean a really big one. Ten dollars to his thirty!" Tom shifted his ponderous weight from one foot to the other, caught up in the excitement, and pulled out his wallet. He paused for just a second before beginning to count out his money.

"Oh, no," Max said, holding his palms out in front of him. "I don't think—" He was interrupted by Tom slamming down the six dollars he had won and adding four to it.

"Triple or nothing," Tom demanded, and Forrestina could see the sweat trickling down his boiled-lobster forehead. "It's all I got in my pocket."

"Really, sir," Max argued. "I don't think I can take a bet like this. Especially not when you and your lady friend are on such a hot streak."

"Chicken" Trixie called out. She clucked, and the crowd, which had grown larger as the winnings increased, hooted with laughter.

Max glared at them all, but Forrestina recognized the sparkle in his eyes. It was the gleam of triumph. "Fine," he said morosely. "But this is the last bet of the night. Anyone want to jump in on ol' Lucky's winnings here?" Several people pushed forward and threw dollars and quarters onto the table. Max noted their names and bet amounts on a scratch-pad of paper, stacking the money in neat piles as he did so. Finally he picked up the cards, careful to show them to the crowd before shuffling, tossing, and letting them fall. Tom pulled Trixie in with him to watch, and when the cards settled, they pointed in unison to the card on the right, cackling wildly. Max let out an exaggerated, forlorn exhale, flipped the card over, and then stepped back to sudden silence.

It was a black ten of spades.

After a beat, the crowd groaned aloud. Tom's face went from white to crimson to eggplant in a matter of seconds. "How—what—" he sputtered. "That's not possible. That's—" he brought both his meaty hands to his forehead "—impossible!" He looked around at the crowd like a dumb bear caught in a trap. "It's rigged," he shouted. "It must be!"

Max, who was busy stuffing his earnings into his pockets, said smoothly, "Now, sir. Fair is fair. You and your girl beat me three times—your luck just ran out. There's no rigging here. I run an honest game." He looked at the silver-toned watch on his wrist. "And that's it for me. Have a grand night, folks, and enjoy your time at Shell & Sons Circus." He tucked his cards in his vest pocket, folded the piece of velvet up into a square, and snapped his extendable table closed like an umbrella. "Quickly, my love," he whispered to Forrestina, pulling her from her perch. "You're in show biz; you know the first rule: always leave them wanting more." And with that, he hurried her along through the stupefied crowd. Forrestina, running to keep up with Max's long stride, her arm yanked to its full extension, saw Trixie beating a hasty retreat in the other direction.

"You conned him," she panted. "How?"

Max grinned over his shoulder at her. "It's all in the thumbs, my dear. I put a bend in the red queen and let Trixie help me convince poor fat Tom that she had spotted my secret. After we got him and the rest of the rubes nice and secure, I smoothed the queen out and bent the same corner on the ten of spades." He swept her into the gin tent and pushed her into a chair. "Usually I keep the bets small and save the big finale for my last performance of the town—otherwise the rubes get wise and try to string me up." He snapped his fingers and a woman in a tight red dress brought over a bottle and two glasses. "Leave the bottle, Clare," he said, and handed her a dollar.

"Wow. You must've had a good night, Max," Clare said. She trailed her hand down his arm with her fingertips, then narrowed her eyes at Forrestina before meandering off, flicking her backside right and left as she went. Forrestina watched her go and saw that Max was also watching the cat-twitch movement of her rear-end. Irritated, she reached over and pulled his chin— and his gaze—back to her. She saw a flash of annoyance in his eyes, then he smiled at her coolly.

"Yes?" he said. There was a warning under the word.

Forrestina heard it and retreated. "So, Trixie?" she asked, as Max poured them both half-glasses of the gin.

"Trixie works in the nudie tent and makes extra money by helping me," Max said. He downed his drink and gestured for Forrestina to do the same. She took a few sips and then coughed as the liquid made its burning trail down her throat. She still didn't like spirits of any kind. Max poured himself another drink. "She is getting older and not as welcome on the stage these days, so she works the crowd while the men get revved up by the younger models. To make ends meet, she will sometimes keep a man entertained for the evening—if the price is right—and other times she just *says* 'yes' and then brings him on over to see 'Big Broad Tosser' Keyes." Max pulled his cards from the pocket inside his jacket lapel and began shuffling them in that mesmerizing way of his. Forrestina watched, entranced, and when he flicked one card high, she extended her hand and let the card settle face-up on her palm. It was the red queen of hearts.

Max took it from her and kissed the card theatrically. "There she is," he said. "My favorite broad." He leaned over and kissed Forrestina full on the mouth. "Well," he amended, "she's now my *second* favorite broad." He lifted his glass and clinked it against Forrestina's, then swallowed the gin in one gulp. "Let's get out of here," he said. He pulled Forrestina up and wrapped his arm around her waist. "I know a dark tent with a dark cot that has your name on it, sweetheart."

Forrestina, tipsy and experiencing warmth in all sorts of places, allowed him to lead her away. After only a month of sneaking around, she'd given herself to him, and each time she ended up in his bed she was able to banish her feelings of guilt and shame when he held her afterwards, murmuring his assurances that he loved her and only her. "One day," he told her that night as she laid drowsy and flushed next to him, her face pressed into his bare chest, "we will leave this wandering life and settle down—have a couple of kids, grow vegetables."

Forrestina rolled up onto her elbow, her curls tumbling over her breasts, and regarded him seriously. "You really want that?" she asked. She couldn't picture Max grubbing in the dirt.

He stroked her hair. "Don't you?" he asked.

She laid back down, silent. She'd never imagined herself settling down; she loved the ever-moving, ever-changing circus scene. Of course, she had never imagined Max either. Maybe for her second act, being a little wife and mother wouldn't be so bad, really. Wouldn't it be funny if they became those rubes Max disdained so very much? "I suppose I do. Someday," she said, speaking into the quiet darkness. They'd only been together for four months, and though she loved Max desperately, his short temper sometimes scared her.

Max interrupted her thoughts. "So what are we waiting for?" he asked. "Life's short, so we may as well get to it, don't you think?"

When she didn't answer right away, Max sat up and grabbed her wrist tightly, twisting it a little. Forrestina cried out in pain. "Max, stop," she said.

He tightened his grip. "Do you want to marry me or don't you?" he asked, his teeth gritted. "It's a simple question. Because if you don't, then get out. Stop wasting my time, Miss High-and-Mighty. Go find some other peasant to roll around in the dirt with."

"I'm not high and mighty, Max," Forrestina said. "Of course I'll marry you. Tomorrow, if you want." She was desperate for him to let her go and even more desperate that he understand that she loved him just as he was, something he never seemed able to believe. He stared at her for a moment then released her. Folding her back in his arms, he said, "Good." He kissed the top of her head. "Good." He fell promptly asleep, but Forrestina stayed awake and tried to convince herself that once they were married, everything would be all right.

When Forrestina told Sarah her news the next morning, her friend gazed at her seriously. "Are you sure, Tina?" she said. She reached out and touched the fresh bruise that circled Forrestina's wrist like a bracelet. "What's your hurry?"

Forrestina pulled her hand away and covered the bruise with the sleeve of her dress. "I'm sure I love him," she snapped. "And I expected you to be happy for me."

Sarah sighed. "I just wish I knew more about him," she said. "You've kept him a secret from us all." She reached over and hugged her friend. "Still, if you're happy, I'm happy."

"I am," Forrestina said, and ignored how the words felt like a lie in her mouth.

She and Max were married a week later. Forrestina wore a simple dove-grey blouse and skirt set with cream-colored lace trim at the neck and wrists. Max wore a new black suit. Their wedding was a small affair, performed at the only Catholic church in town. The priest, a wizened, tortoise-featured man who was at least eighty years old, scolded them both for their lack of attendance at Mass and required a confession from each of them before he would agree to marry them. Forrestina was waiting in the pews when Max emerged from the confessional booth. The priest stumbled out a few seconds later and Forrestina saw that his hands were shaking. He threw Forrestina a pitying look, glared at Max, and tottered back to his quarters in the rectory.

"What was that all about?" she asked, standing up and following Max out of the church.

"Bit off more than he could chew when he demanded I share all my sins, I reckon. I haven't been to confession in fifteen years and honey, they had piled up." He laughed and waggled his eyebrows at her.

Forrestina shook her head, trying to smile, ignoring the clang of alarm bells going off in her heart. Max was just Max, and she loved him. She was sure the rest would work itself out.

Though the wedding had been small, the reception was not. Both circuses put their differences aside for the afternoon and laid out tables of food and drink for the occasion. Bright balloons were tied to the outside of the three open tents designated for the wedding, and fresh flowers in mason jars were set on the long wooden tables inside. The circus people toasted the happy couple with red punch spiked with whiskey and enjoyed plates of barbeque pulled-pork sandwiches, deviled eggs, baked beans, crisp dill pickles, and tangy mustard potato salad. Iced cakes were sliced and served, and Max and Forrestina accepted the congratulations of so many people, they became hoarse from saying "Thank you." Forrestina's cheeks actually began to ache from smiling and laughing so much.

After the food, Johnny Two-Shoes, the vaudeville ivory-tickler from the Shell & Sons girlie tent, sat down at his piano (which he had hauled out for the occasion), and began to play. Max led Forrestina to a clearing in the center of the tent and held her close in his arms as they danced, singing softly into her hair: "*I've taken quite a fancy to you, dear; I'd like to paddle your canoe. And I fancy you could like me too, dear, or you wouldn't act the way you do.*" He twirled her around and continued to sing, "*There's no one in this wide, wide world, dear, whose tootsie-wootsie I would be. If you'd only take a fancy, dearie, to a fancy little boy like me.*" He dipped her dramatically to the applause of the watching crowd.

Forrestina and Max bowed together, and when Johnny began to play "Cuddle up a Little Closer, Lovey Mine," other people began to dance as well. Forrestina saw Sarah and Carl swaying together—Sarah caught her eye and gave her a naughty wink—and even Lucy and Joseph joined the group of people dancing, though Joseph's mouth was set in a grim line. He hadn't liked Max on sight and was apparently determined to keep on disliking him. No matter; Forrestina was giddy with joy. In order to keep their talented tight-rope walker, Ringling had given Max a job as a game barker—kiddie games, like throwing a baseball at milk bottles or hurling dull-tipped darts at balloons tacked to the wall. It was a step down from what he was used to, but Forrestina's admirable salary more than enough made up the difference.

"Besides," Max had reasoned, when Forrestina broached the subject, "if it gets to be too much, I can always sneak away and do a little independent broad-tossing offsite." He stopped Forrestina's protest with a raised palm. "Not one word," he said, his tone cold. "You don't ever tell me what I can or cannot do. I will not have a woman bossing me around—even if she makes more money than me." He leaned forward, his dark eyes close to her own. "Do you understand me?"

Forrestina closed her mouth at once. She'd learned through painful experience not to make Max mad; his few flashes of temper were often punctuated by a slap or a hair-pull—*but*, she told herself, *it's never anything major, and he's always so sorry afterwards.* He'd sometimes even cry when begging for forgiveness. Now in his arms, listening to him sing words of love, she broomed the dark cobwebs of worry and doubt out of the corners of her mind. She thought with sudden painful longing of Tilly and her favorite, oft-repeated saying: "Don't borrow trouble," an admonition against worrying about what tomorrow might bring. No, Forrestina had no intention of borrowing anything. If trouble came, she would just have to own it.

Chapter Ten

The Circus Years, 1912

FORRESTINA SAT ON THE EDGE of her platform worrying, her feet dangling down into space. Yesterday during practice she'd fallen five times into the net, and while falling when she was trying out something new wasn't uncommon, she hadn't been working on anything new. No, yesterday she'd just been warming up, getting her "sea legs" (as Lucy called it) by walking from end to end on the rope. Suddenly, without warning, black dots began to float in front of her eyes and the world started to spin. That happened over and over, ending each time with an unplanned tumble off the rope. She'd never had problems with dizziness before, and she was frightened. Had she somehow lost her ability to walk the rope? What if she became dizzy and fell during a show? She would hate for the net to have to be put in place during a performance—it took away from the thrill of danger—but if she kept falling, Joseph would insist. First he'd sneer and remind her that she was weak and unprofessional, of course, and brag to her that he and Lucy had never used a net even once during a show, but the shaming would be just for his own pleasure. She'd still have to have the net because one thing that Ringling tried to avoid was splattering their patrons with the brains and blood of their performers. It was just smart business.

She sat on her platform, gripping the wood with her hands and gazing up into the air, trying to find her nerve again. Anxiousness was making her sick to her stomach; she didn't want to have to go back to being a ballet girl. Not only would she miss the beauty and challenge of tightrope-walking, she'd also miss the pay. Aerialists were the cream of the crop in the circus world, and her salary was now an astonishing fifteen dollars a week. Not that she had much to show for it—Max had expensive habits. He liked to take her and her earnings to whichever gambling event was popular in whatever town they happened to be in: cock fights in Missouri, boxing in Illinois, horse racing in Kentucky, dog fights in Oklahoma, and they lost more than they won. For a man who made his trade in gambling, he was pretty terrible at it.

Whenever she suggested that he should perhaps stop spending all of their (her) earnings, he became nasty, shouting at her and accusing her of trying to hen-peck him to death. It was easier to keep silent and try to hide a few dollars here and there in Sarah's tent—dear Sarah, who took the bills from her, sighing and frowning but never saying a word, simply tucking the money into the bottom of her own trunk. Forrestina was saving for a rainy day, and lately the rain had turned into a typhoon. Max was getting into fights with both circus folks and customers, and Mr. Stone had informed him that if he did not shape up and behave himself with more decorum, he would have to leave with or without his wife. Forrestina was an asset, yes, but no one was worth that much trouble.

Max's response had been to stalk out and set up his Three-Card Monte table at the leech circus behind Ringling. Forrestina found him there later with his arm around a brassy blond woman with huge breasts and bright red lipstick—she was, Max told Forrestina, slurring his words as he swallowed more gin, going to be his new shill for the season. The woman eyed Forrestina with frank hostility, and Forrestina walked away from them both knowing that if Max hadn't slept with her already, he would certainly do so soon. Trudging back to her tent at Ringling, she realized that she didn't care. All the fight had gone out of her lately, and the only thing that brought her comfort was the satisfaction she felt when she was able to find a few dollars more to hide away in Sarah's trunk. One more temper-fueled skirmish and Max would be gone, and she'd decided that she wasn't going with him—she would stay with her Ringling family, where she was safe, and where any bruises she got were from her honest work and not from the cruel fists of a man who'd duped her into believing he loved her.

Lucy pulled her out of the dark cavern of her thoughts, calling to her from far below. "Are you going to sit up there forever or what, Lollo? I noticed you haven't been doing so hot lately. Come down here so I can look at you."

Reluctantly Forrestina obeyed, opting to climb down the ladder instead of falling into the net. Once she reached the bottom, she caught the dubious expression on Lucy's face. "You took the long way down," Lucy commented. "Hm." She leaned forward, peering closely at Forrestina, then touched the younger woman's forehead with the back of her hand. "No fever," she said. "So what's wrong with you, eh? Is it physical, or is it that no-good man of yours? I don't know why you don't send him down the road. Joseph would be happy to toss him away for you." She chuckled in that deep-throated way of hers. "He'd toss 'Old Broad Tosser' right down the road, all right."

It was an old refrain. After the first few months of Forrestina's marriage, all the Ringling folk had collectively decided that they hated Max as much as they hated an empty tent on show night. He'd turned mean even when he wasn't drunk, screaming profanities at Forrestina in public and knocking her around in private, and he was shifty, tricking quite a few of them out of big portions of their paychecks with his cards. Worst of all, he didn't even try to hide his infidelities, something that made the Ringling men draw defensively around Forrestina and the women to mutter curses at his manhood when he swaggered by. The members of the Ringling circus family weren't always known for keeping to the straight and narrow—their wild natures were what had attracted them to the circus in the first place, after all—but they were loyal, territorial, and fiercely protective of their own, like wolves in a pack. Forrestina was *theirs*, and they circled Max with slitted eyes, waiting for their chance to tear him apart— or at least chase him away.

"It's not Max," Forrestina told Lucy. "I'm just feeling a little off. Maybe it's a bout of swimmer's ear—I swam in that little creek up the road a couple of days ago, trying to cool off, and it still feels like I may have some water trapped in my left ear."

"Well, go find some rubbing alcohol to dry it up. Nets are put away tomorrow, unless you think you need it for the show."

"I won't need it," Forrestina said. "I'll be fine." To prove her statement, she climbed quickly up the ladder to the top of the pole and then, without letting herself think about it, walked briskly from one side of the rope to the other. She never even wobbled. Relieved, she began to practice in earnest, and by the time she was done for the day, she felt mainly like her old self again. It was probably just nerves, she told herself—even the most experienced aerialist suffered those from time to time.

The next night, as she sat in the dressing tent adjusting her filmy leaf-green costume and attaching sparkling pins to her hair, she noticed Sarah peeking in at her. Surprised, she cried, "Sarah, what are you doing in here? Aren't you supposed to be worshipping a golden calf right now?" (Mr. Wilson was still on a "lascivious scenes from ancient Biblical times" kick—Sarah surmised that it was to get back at his too-religious mother and his suffocating upbringing. His Bible stories were a heck of a lot racier than Forrestina remembered from childhood, that was for sure.)

Sarah took a pin from Forrestina's hair and readjusted it so that it would show better. "We are on break—the elephants are making their rounds right now. Jody doesn't like to bring them out when we're doing our thing—says the rowdy fans make them nervous, and no one likes a nervous pachyderm. Besides, they poop an awful lot, and it's hard to lose yourself in dance when you're worried you may end up knee-deep in elephant dung." She leaned over and wrapped her slender arms around Forrestina's neck. "Are you feeling okay?" she asked.

Forrestina turned and looked into her friend's face. She was startled to see that Sarah's lip was trembling and her eyes were brimming with tears. She disentangled herself from Sarah's grip, stood, and then reached out to hug her properly. "Hey, what's all this?" she asked. "I'm fine."

Sarah gripped her tightly for a few moments, then pulled away, wiping tears from her cheeks. "I've had a bad feeling all day," she said. She fidgeted with a corner of her faux leopard-skin cape. "A real bad feeling." Abruptly she blurted out, "Forrestina, don't go out on the wire tonight. Say you're sick."

"What are you talking about?" Forrestina said. "Of course I'm going out. I have to."

"Please, Tina," Sarah said. She gripped Forrestina's arm so hard, Forrestina gasped with the pain of it. "I stopped by Rose's tent and got a reading on you, just to double-check. She laid out the cards and then got real upset. She said that something terrible was on the horizon." Sarah squeezed Forrestina's arm again, even harder, her fingertips like iron. "Tina, she drew the Death card. She said I should try to talk you out of performing tonight— and you know she wouldn't do that if she wasn't really afraid."

Forrestina resisted an urge to cross herself and instead pulled her arm free, rubbing her bruised flesh. "Nonsense," she replied, not liking the tremble she heard in her own voice. "You know Rose is full of bunk most of the time. Honestly, Sarah," she said, forcing a laugh. "You of all people should not be fooled by a circus gypsy's 'predictions.' She's a con woman; I think her people are from right here in Kansas. Hardly the gypsy capital of the world!"

"Not when it comes to us, she's not," Sarah said stubbornly. "If it's one of the family, she tells the truth—even if the truth is that she doesn't know the future. I've never seen her so shaken as she was when she read the cards today, Tina. I think she really saw something."

"She can't read my fortune if I'm not there," Forrestina said firmly. "I didn't cut the deck. So maybe YOU are the one who isn't meant to perform tonight." She waved her hand at her friend. "Now shoo. I've got to finish getting ready." As Sarah turned to go, her beautiful face a perfect mask of wretchedness, Forrestina reached out and caught her sleeve. "Don't worry," she said gently. "Really. I will be extra-careful, I promise."

The misery on Sarah's face didn't clear. Wordlessly, she left the tent, and

Forrestina watched her go, trying to lose the sense of dread that Sarah had left behind her like a heavy sweet funereal-floral perfume.

Forrestina heard a loud *thump*, a cry, and then Max saying, "Damn it, Sarah! Stay outta my way!" Her husband came into the tent, smoothing his disheveled hair back. "That friend of yours is a clumsy cow," he complained. "She smacked into me going full speed, almost knocked us both for a loop." He leaned over Forrestina, not looking at her at all but checking himself in her mirror, stroking his thin mustache into place around his full lips. "She didn't even apologize," he finished, incredulous.

"She was upset."

"Really? About what? *Boy* trouble? Hard to imagine a looker like her ever having any trouble getting a man. What a figure!" He whistled low, then put his hands on Forrestina's bare shoulders, knotting his fingers into her flesh. She shrugged him off.

"Aw, darlin', don't be that way," Max said. He reached around to cup her breast with his left hand, and she pushed him away.

"Stop it," she said. "Anyone could come in and see you."

"So let 'em," Max said, nuzzling her neck. "You're my wife. I can do whatever I want with you, whenever I want to." He squeezed harder and her breast began to throb painfully.

"Max," she said. "Really. Stop. I have to finish getting ready. And that hurts. Besides," she said, forcing a smile, "if I don't get on the rope, I don't get paid."

Those were the magic words. Max sighed and released her. He slouched over to the corner of the tent, where he watched her as she finished twisting crystals into her hair and rouging her cheeks so that they would not look dead-white under the spotlights. She fought sudden waves of nausea—this was the worst case of nerves she'd experienced since her first show. Was it because of Sarah's dire prediction? Or was it being around Max?

"You look like a painted whore," Max said sullenly. "I hate you with all that junk on your face."

Stung, she retorted, "You would know about whores. You keep company with enough of them." In a flash, he was on her, his face twisted in rage, his fist raised. She closed her eyes, anticipating the blow, but before it landed, Joseph's deep voice bellowed, "ENOUGH!" Forrestina opened her eyes and saw Max go tumbling across the room. Lucy, clucking something dire and wicked-sounding in Russian and casting Max an equally wicked look, gathered Forrestina up and ushered her to the Big Top's entrance. "Come, Lollo," she said. "It's time to perform." She beckoned her husband. "Joseph. Leave the trash on the floor. Come."

"Drunken idiot," Joseph spat before joining the women at the show door. Lucy squeezed Forrestina's shaking hand. "Put it out of your mind, child," she said. "Concentrate on the show. After, we will figure out what to do with Mr. So-and-So in there."

"Throw him back in the gutter where he belongs is what we will do," Joseph said, clenching and unclenching his fist. "I'm serious, *Lollo-kolyuchka*. It's enough. What happens when he breaks your arm or your leg? What's the point of all our training then, eh?"

Lucy glared up at her husband. "Joseph, enough," she hissed. "Later." She gathered Forrestina's face in her tiny hands and looked at her intently. "You must only think of the rope now. If you are distracted, you will fall. Take some deep breaths."

Forrestina, her entire body trembling, obeyed, pulling air in through her nose, closing her eyes, and then pushing the air back out slowly through rounded lips. She repeated this a few more times and felt her heartbeat slow. To clear her mind, she used a trick she often had to employ before a show. She packed all thoughts of Max into a tiny square box and hid them in a dark, empty corner of her mind. She knew she would have to unpack that box later, but for now, they would stay there while she concentrated on her performance. She extended her hands, palms down. They were steady. She nodded at Lucy and Joseph. "I'm fine now," she said. "Thank you."

"Just in time," Lucy said. "Here comes your story." Forrestina heard Bob Mack begin her fairy-tale, and she stepped out of the darkness and into the light. Smiling radiantly at the roaring, faceless crowd, waving to them with both arms, she turned back to the tent opening and blew a kiss to her watching friends. Lucy, using two hands, blew a kiss back. Behind them, Forrestina spotted Max watching too, his arms across his chest, his expression murderous. The box in her mind opened a crack and a few unwelcome thoughts slithered out, grotesque, with too many legs and fanged teeth. All of her calm disappeared as she began to climb the steel pole on shaky legs. Her physical eyes were fixed on the platform above her, but with something like terror, her mental eyes watched those crawling thoughts tumbling towards her.

Once she reached her platform, the cheering crowd hushed. All was dark, save for the circle of light trained on her. "Get it together, Forrestina. Do your damn job," she whispered fiercely to herself, and then, as she had often said to herself as a child, "I dare you." She drew in another deep breath, then placed her foot on the wire. She took a few steps, wobbled just a bit. The crowd sucked in their collective breath and then let it out in a *whoosh* of relief like wind rushing down a corridor as she found her balance. She did a forward handstand, letting her body bend over until she righted herself again with a snap, then she flipped backwards onto the wire. Every time she was right-side up again, the applause was thunderous. She relaxed as she began to feel the familiar rhythm take hold. The crawling dark thoughts were chased back into their box, and she was empty again, focused on letting her body bend and stretch and move. Lucy was right; after the performance, she would have to figure out what she was going to do about Max, but for now, her breathing and movements and the wire beneath her feet were all that mattered.

She finished her final flip and landed safely on the wooden platform and then, as she always did, she took a few dainty steps back out onto the wire to take her bows. The applause and cheers from below were deafening. As she bent low, her arms extended to her side in a modified curtsey, she realized that the wire was suddenly hard for her to see, a wavy line that seemed to be moving rapidly from side to side. Cold sweat pearled her forehead. As she lifted her body upright, she felt herself first sway, and then fall. Time slowed, and she stepped outside herself, watching as her own slim bright figure floated down gently, a feather drifting through the black air. She heard screams in the distance and wondered idly who they were for.

Just before she hit the cushioned emergency rescue mat that, unbeknownst to her, Sarah had bullied Bob into positioning under the wire once the tent had grown dark, she thought, *So Gypsy Rose really can read cards. Huh.* Time sped back up, and she felt the sudden excruciating jolt of her body hitting a hard surface much too fast. There was a tearing, ripping sensation deep inside her stomach, and then, mercifully, she felt nothing at all.

CHAPTER ELEVEN

Fayetteville, 1972

"AFTER I WOKE UP, I discovered I had lost everything," Forrestina said. "No job, no husband, and no baby."

Betty looked up from her notebook, her pen in the air. "Wait—a baby?" she said. Dread's icy fingers slipped up her spine, and she dropped her pen into her lap. "What baby?"

Forrestina sighed, an exhaled leaking of sorrow that to Betty seemed as if it were coming from the deepest part of the elderly woman. "I was pregnant," Forrestina said. "That's where the dizziness was coming from. Doctor told me after I woke up that it was a boy." She rubbed her dry eyes with gnarled fingers. "I was never able to have another. When I fell, it damaged my insides and they had to take out my uterus to stop the bleeding."

Betty covered her mouth. "A hysterectomy?" she asked. The word tasted like dry aspirin on her tongue, bitter and unkind.

Forrestina nodded, her eyes far away. "Yep. My only child, my boy, dead at three months." She squinted fiercely, and Betty couldn't tell if she was blinking away tears or hardening her heart. Forrestina turned to regard her, her expression cold, defensive. "I suppose you're wondering why I got on the wire if I was pregnant. Probably think I deserved it for being so careless."

Betty shook her head, hurt that Forrestina would think her so callous. "Of course not," she said quietly. "No one deserves that. Besides, I assume you didn't even know."

Forrestina continued to glare at Betty suspiciously for a moment more, then her face softened. "That's right," she said. "I didn't know. I hadn't had my monthlies for a while, but I was never very regular, and I was so naïve that it never occurred to me that I might be pregnant."

"It's very common for athletes, especially underweight athletes like gymnasts, to have irregular periods," Betty said, desperately trying to find something comforting to say. She hesitated a moment, then dared to reach over and place her hand on Forrestina's balled-up fist. "Ms. Campbell, I know it wasn't your fault," Betty said gently. "Please; you mustn't blame yourself."

Forrestina sighed deeply again, opening her hand, turning her palm over and giving Betty's hand a squeeze before moving it away. "I appreciate that," she said. "It's nice of you to say. It's not true, of course—it *was* my fault; I was the fool who fell off the wire and went crashing into the ground—but it was an accident. If I had known, I probably wouldn't have risked it." She shrugged. "Or maybe I would have kept right on working as long as I could. We didn't like to let anything interfere with our work—we all had contracts to fulfill, after all. Still, I am sure that if I had known, I at least would've used the net, no matter how bad it made me feel." Another big sigh. "Can't change the past, so there's no point in grieving over it too much, I reckon."

"Do you want to stop for the day?" Betty asked. Half of her wanted Forrestina to say "yes" so she could run out to her car and let herself have a good cry over what she'd just been told, but the other half—the *reporter* half—wanted to keep digging this story out. It occurred to her also that leaving Forrestina now in this silent, grim room alone with all her unearthed painful thoughts and the ghost of a lost child would be unthinkably cruel.

"Nah, I'm okay," Forrestina said. She lifted her hat and raked her fingers through her hair. "Let's keep going. We gotta get past this part sometime. It may as well be today."

"Right," Betty said, straightening up, squelching her feelings down. "So you said no husband and no job? What happened?"

Forrestina looked at Betty sideways. "What do you think happened?" she replied. "I was in the hospital, unconscious for a week. After I woke up, Ringling produced my contract, which said I was obligated to perform and that if I failed in my duties to the circus, my contract was null and void. Because I was pretty broken up—my right arm was busted, I had a fractured rib, and of course, there were my lady problems—they figured I wouldn't be back on the wire any time soon, if ever. Once someone falls like that, she has a hard time finding her nerve again. In fact, they probably wouldn't have wanted me even if I was able to perform. My fall in front of all of those people was real bad publicity." She blew a puff of air out between wrinkled lips. "Whoo. I was unconscious, of course, but I can imagine the tap-dancing Bob Mack must've executed to calm the crowd and make them think everything was all right, even when he pretty much figured I was lying there deader'n a doornail." Her forehead creased. "I worried for a long time about all the children in the crowd watching me, how scared and confused they must've been. I hope I didn't cause them nightmares. I still feel bad about that."

Typical Forrestina, Betty thought. There she'd been, fighting for her life, her only chance at motherhood having slipped from her, and she was still worrying over the effect her accident might have on a bunch of strange children in the crowd. She sat back in her chair. She was beginning to get angry. "So Ringling fired you just like that? Where were their hearts?"

Forrestina waved her hand impatiently. "They were running a business, girl. I knew the risks, and I didn't hold any hard feelings toward them. Everybody was surely sorry—when I woke up, my room was filled with flowers and cards from my circus family, including from the Mr. Ringlings themselves. Sarah told me later that Mrs. Hayes stayed by my side during those first few nights, just daring the nurses to try and run her out. 'She's one of my girls,' she kept telling them, even though I hadn't technically been one for years, 'and I'll not leave her.'" Forrestina laughed. "It's a pure mystery of life to find out that those whose hearts you think are the hardest wind up being the kindest."

Betty gazed at Forrestina, armored in her men's overalls and coarse talk, and smiled, remembering Murray's stories of Forrestina's legendary crankiness and compassion.

Forrestina continued. "Even Mr. Stone, whose job it was to fire me, tried to make it as painless as possible. He paid my hospital bill—something he didn't have to do—and made sure that my owed pay was secured and slipped under my pillow where Max couldn't find it. That was the kindest thing he could've done, saving my money from my husband."

Betty shifted in her chair. "So tell me how Max reacted," she said. She had a hunch she knew the answer but needed to hear Forrestina say it.

Forrestina shrugged her thin shoulders. "Once he realized that he was now married to a woman who would no longer be bringing in the money, who was banged up and defective and would never have kids . . . well." She leaned over and busied herself with rubbing at a spot on her boot that Betty could not see. She said, "He hooked up with one of the hoochie-coochie girls from the latest grafter circus and took off—just slunk off into the night. Left behind a note that simply said, *Sorry, Darlin'. You know I'm no good. You're better off without me.*" She twisted her lips in a bitter smile. "Can you beat that? I mean, he was *right*, of course, but what a pantywaist thing to do."

"Jerk," Betty hissed. She was finding it very hard to stay impartial.

Forrestina grinned. "Exactly," she said. "I never heard from the son-of-a-bitch again. After I did a little crying over him—not too much, mind, but it seemed like *some* crying was in order—I counted up the wad of cash Mr. Stone had tucked under my pillow—fifty dollars plus the thirty-seven I had hidden in Sarah's trunk—and decided Max's leaving was good riddance. That man liked to have bled me dry with his gambling and his drinking. And of course, there was his forever roving eye." She shook her head, then pointed a crooked index finger at Betty, witch-like. "Learn from me," she ordered severely, narrowing her eyes. "You stay away from the dark, handsome ones. They may make your heart flutter and your knees weak and set your pants on fire, but they ain't worth it."

Betty laughed and thought of Steve, who she'd been dating for over a year now. He was the furthest thing there was from dark and dangerous, a tall, thin, studious young man who was all knees and elbows. He came from a nice middle-class family and was studying to be a lawyer. Betty found his clumsiness and old-fashioned politeness charming, though she had to admit, he could sometimes be a tad boring. Still, after hearing Forrestina's story, Betty decided maybe stable and boring weren't the worst attributes a man could have. She flipped a page on her notebook and said, "What about Sarah? And Lucy and Joseph? Did they have any say into what happened to you?" She still thought it was supremely unfair that Forrestina, a headliner for Ringling Brothers Circus for so many years, would just be left like that. After all, she'd probably made the circus ten times the amount it would've cost to help her mend.

Forrestina shook her head. "Shoot, there wasn't a thing they could do," she said. "We all knew the score and we all understood the risks. If you wanted a *safe* job, you stayed away from the circus." Betty furrowed her brow, causing Forrestina to reach out and pat her arm. "It's all right, honey," she said. "I really don't blame Ringling. They were actually pretty good to me, all told. But like I said, they had a business to run, and my accident happened three weeks before they were scheduled to pack up and move the show to Illinois. They couldn't wait for me."

Forrestina said during the time she was laid up in the hospital, Sarah and Lucy visited every day. By the time Ringling was loaded on the trains and ready to press on, she was up and moving, albeit slowly. Sarah found her a room in a boarding house in town where she could stay while she finished recovering, and a lawyer to finalize her divorce on the grounds of abandonment. With careful planning, the money Mr. Stone and Sarah had hidden would last long enough for Forrestina to figure out what came next.

"Did you never think to contact your parents?" Betty asked. Even if they were furious with her, she was their daughter, after all. Surely they would want to help.

"I would never stoop," Forrestina said. "I made that bed and I was bound to lie in it all by myself." She paused and looked down at her hands for a moment. Betty watched as she fiddled with a simple band of silver inset with turquoise on her middle right finger. "Truth," she said finally. "Lucy did track them down and sent a telegram. They sent back a reply saying thank you for the information but they no longer had a daughter by that name." She stroked her chin absently. "I never expected anything different. My mother was not a forgiving woman." She let out a hard, brittle little laugh that contained no amusement, but the smile she chased it with was glorious. "Damn, Lucy was fit to be tied, though. You shoulda seen her pacing up and down in the hospital room, shaking that bit of paper, cursing my parents in the most marvelous mixture of English, Russian, and what I gather was her own gypsy tongue. She was outraged enough for the both of us." She chuckled. "She was a good friend, old Lucy."

The two women sat in silence for a moment, then Betty asked, as gently as she could, "Can you tell me what your goodbye to Lucy and Sarah was like?"

Forrestina shifted in her chair. "Oh, we were sad, of course, but we kept in touch," she said. "They sent me postcards from every stop, and I wrote letters and had them delivered through Ringling's main office—it's hard to receive letters without a permanent address, you know. Sarah met a nice man a year or so later and quit the circus. He was a preacher, if you can believe it, and she had three young 'uns, became a proper little housewife. She even set up a beauty parlor in her garage, just liked she talked about. We kept up regular letters once we both had addresses and talked on the telephone later on when we had 'em installed. She died twenty years ago—lung cancer." Betty watched as Forrestina touched the sparkling teardrop diamond earring in her right ear. "After she died, her eldest, a sweet gal Sarah insisted on naming 'Tina' after me—isn't that a hoot?—sent me a farewell letter from her mother, written the week before Sarah died."

Forrestina's eyes took on that faraway look people get when they are seeing ghosts moving around in the past. "Sarah was my first true female friend and a sister to take the place of the ones I left behind. She knew me when I was young," she said, her voice low and sad. "That's a treasure you don't realize you've got until it's gone. I tell you, I miss being young and beautiful in somebody's memory, and not just the cranky, creaky bag of bones I am now." She held her hands out and examined the backs of them—they were sun-spotted and thinned by age to tissue paper. She sighed. "Though I may look eighty on the outside, I never feel more than seventeen in here." She tapped her chest with her crooked index finger.

Betty sat quietly. Though she was dying to know what the letter from Sarah said, she knew better than to ask. She recalled her granny once saying that a preacher gives everyone her own sip of wine and her own wafer because some things are too sacred to share. If Forrestina wanted to tell Betty what the letter said, she would. If she didn't, then Betty didn't feel she had any right to know.

After a long while, Forrestina reached over and took a sip of water from the glass perched on the edge of her bed. "I lost track of Lucy and Joseph—as far as I know, they stayed with the show until they could no longer climb the ladder. Of course, they are long dead too, I suppose." She tried to laugh. "Lordy. Old age is a son-of-a-bitch, I tell ya. Everybody you ever knew starts to disappear and you're left standing all alone, thinking, 'What just happened?' Really kicks the breath out of you." She balled her hands into fists and set them on her knees. "Getting old ain't for cowards," she said.

Betty let Forrestina sit for a moment more to collect herself; though she was eager to keep on going, she didn't want to push too hard. It was clear that the telling of this part of her story hurt, and Betty was sorry to be the one causing the pain. After a bit, though, she cleared her throat, and asked in a carefully neutral tone, "So Sarah left you in the care of a . . ." Betty checked her notes from earlier, ". . . Mrs. Crawford in Lawrence, Kansas? How long did you stay there?"

"For about two years," Forrestina said. "After I was able to move around pretty good, Mrs. Crawford helped me find a job at the local drugstore. I worked at the counter—helped customers, tidied the place, filled prescriptions for Dr. Marsh, the pharmacist. I even helped him keep his books—turns out I actually had a pretty good head for figures. I worked there for a while, and then I got a job as a waitress at a diner."

Betty was astonished. Somehow the idea of Forrestina working a "normal" job had never occurred to her. Forrestina chuckled dryly. "Your face," she said. She shook her head ruefully. "Yeah, well, just because I was good at it didn't mean I liked it. Sometimes the sheer boringness of it all made me want to pull my hair out. Dr. Marsh was a kind man, as was Jolene, who owned the diner, and I can never repay Mrs. Crawford for all she did for me. But I was restless. I thought about trying to join up with another circus—a smaller one—but I just didn't have the heart for it anymore."

She grew somber. "My nerve was gone, and oh, how I grieved for that little one I lost, and for all the others I would never have. I knew I could never get up on a wire again. I didn't *deserve* to get up on the wire again." Forrestina covered her eyes with the heels of her palms, a childlike gesture that hurt Betty's heart. Wordlessly, she dug a pack of Kleenex out of her macramé handbag and passed a tissue to the old woman, who accepted it with a small murmur of thanks and wiped her eyes and nose.

"It was summertime that drew me out again and set me on my next course," Forrestina continued, sniffing. "I visited a carnival set up outside of town. It was not as grand as a circus, of course, but it was still a fine place to eat food that was too sweet and greasy, ride some rides, and lose some money on unwinnable games."

Betty smiled, relieved to be out of dangerous territory. "The unwinnable games," she said. "Your rats."

"My rats," Forrestina agreed, smiling back at Betty briefly before a sudden cloud chased it away. "Hon," she said wearily, "I'm tired. We can talk some more another day, if you still want to."

Betty rose, clutching her notebook to her chest. There was obviously so much more to Forrestina's story, but after their long talk today, she seemed deflated and more fragile than when Betty had first come in. Betty began to worry; what if telling her tale did Forrestina more harm than good? She imagined curiosity and conscience as fighters putting on their gloves and starting a ring-fight in her head, but of course, curiosity won. She said, praying that the answer would be "yes," "So, can I come back next week?"

Forrestina grinned the impish grin Betty was learning to love. "Lord Almighty," she said. "If you ain't got nothing else more worthwhile in this world to do than sit and listen to an old lady blabber—" She shrugged, shoving her hands in her overall pockets. "Then by all means, let's do this again. Same time next week. I sure ain't going nowhere."

Overjoyed, Betty thanked her, said a quick goodbye to the still-silent, still-unmoving roommate, and made her way out of the nursing home. That night she stayed up until past midnight organizing and typing her handwritten notes, working hard to capture in print what she'd heard and seen. The next morning, when she presented what she'd written to her boss, Murray nodded in that matter-of-fact way of his and said, "Interesting. Keep digging. This is shaping up to be a nice feature story."

Emboldened and buzzing from the praise, restrained as it was, Betty headed back to the nursing home the next week. This time when she stopped by the sour attendant's desk, the woman said, "Ms. Campbell is not in her room. She said to meet her on the porch out back."

Betty made her way down the dingy hallway, following the black-and-white vinyl squares until she came to the common area. Card tables were set up around the room, and at them Betty noted a sparse population of residents, some listlessly pushing jigsaw puzzle pieces around, others holding dominos up to aged eyes before clicking them down. Some simply sat and stared into space, their wrinkled hands folded neatly on the tabletops before them. Over in the corner, a large television set in a wooden box frame was turned to "The Andy Griffith Show," and Betty saw three old men asleep on the sofa in front of it, each one snoring loudly through slack, open mouths.

Past the tables, two large glass doors opened onto a concrete verandah.

Betty realized that this is what the attendant must've meant by "the porch." She slipped outside and saw that Forrestina was sitting in an aluminum lawn chair, her legs as always sprawled unladylike before her, her eyes closed, her face lifted to the sky like a sunflower. Her old battered brown cowboy hat was on her head, but she had pushed it back, presumably so that she could feel the full effect of the sunshine. Betty grabbed another faded lawn chair and set it next to her.

"I thought this would be nicer," Forrestina said without opening her eyes. "It's such a lovely day. Warm for early March."

Betty agreed; spring in Arkansas was something to be cherished because it took a while to gear up and only stuck around for a minute. After a little bit of lizard-on-a-hot-rock, contented silence, Betty decided it was time to hear a carnival story. "So, Ms. Campbell," she began, uncapping her Bic pen, "let's go back to your rats."

Forrestina grinned and put both her hands behind her head, her fingers interlocked, her face still lifted to the sun. "Cursed critters," she said. "My ugly, mean, old, money-making rats. Lord, how I did love them."

CHAPTER TWELVE

Interlude, 1914

FORRESTINA WANDERED THROUGH the carnival, winding her way back and forth through the rows and rows of booths, taking in the heat and excitement, trying to beat back the old familiar longing to be on the road, to charm rubes out of hard-earned dollars by giving them a little dazzle for their dull lives. As she approached the "Test-Your-Strength" tower, she paused to watch the barker in charge of the game do his thing. He was tall—over six feet, Forrestina guessed—and heavily built, like a lumberjack, and he sported an impressive brushy red-brown beard to boot. In each of his big hands he held the rubber-headed mallets that were used to strike the game's pad, twirling them in slow arcs as if they weighed nothing. Spotting Forrestina, he offered one of the handles to her. "Want to test your strength, little lady?" he asked. "There's a quarter in it for you if you hit hard enough to ring the bell."

A man standing in the small knot of people surrounding the game guffawed. "How can that little bitty thing hit the bell? She's no bigger than a fly. Don't waste your nickel, girl," he advised. He winked at her. "I got a better game for you—it's called 'find the weasel.' It's in my pants. You can play for free."

Forrestina cast a long, measuring look at the rube. He was clean-shaven, ferret-eyed and pale. His navy suit jacket was slung over his shoulder, held there by one hooked finger, and his white shirt-sleeves were rolled up to his biceps. He was the type of guy who would come into her café and argue that a little squeeze of her bottom was an expected side dish to the coffee she poured, and don't even think about him leaving a tip. She hated him on sight. Reaching with her right hand into the small beaded change purse attached by a velvet cord to her left wrist, she pulled out one shiny new nickel. Holding it high for all to see, pinched between thumb and forefinger, she offered it to the huge bear running the game. As he held his giant palm out for her to drop the nickel into, she smiled at him sweetly and leaned forward. "Where's the sweet spot?" she whispered, trying not to move her lips as she did so. "And where's the dummy mallet—the one I can actually swing?"

He stood back and examined her from top to bottom, a slow grin of admiration spreading across his face. She noticed that between his mustache and beard were straight, very white teeth and a pair of rather shapely lips. He handed her the mallet in his left hand. "Let me show you how to lift it and swing," he said loudly. He put one hand beneath her elbow, and with the other lifted the long wooden neck of the mallet, his fingers gripping below where she held the mallet in both of her hands. As he stood close to her, he murmured in her ear, "Upper right corner, just above the pad. Make it look good." He released her and stepped away.

Forrestina let the mallet drop suddenly, her body bending as if the sheer weight was too much for her. She dragged the head of it—in truth it weighed no more than a croquet mallet—through the dirt, and positioned herself in front of the slim rectangular sign that stretched above her some six feet. She gazed upwards; the sign was divided by such scientific strength assessments as "Puny" (at the bottom), "Kid Sister," "Preteen Boy," "Now You're Growing Up," and finally, at the top near the steel bell, "Strong Man—You Win!" She swallowed hard—that bell seemed very far away.

The rube who'd started all of this jeered at her. "Really, what a waste," he called out. "She can't even pick the hammer up." He stepped forward, reaching for the mallet. "Why don't you let me take care of that for you, sweetie?" he asked, his beady eyes glittering like a snake's.

The game-man stepped in. "Back off, Buddy. Her nickel, her swing."

The rube opened his mouth as if to argue, then, his eyes taking in the size of the man in front of him, wisely thought better of it. "Suits me," he shrugged. "I'm happy to watch her make a fool of herself."

Forrestina resisted an urge to use the mallet to smash him in the face. If things worked out the way she hoped, he would get his, and soon. Taking a deep breath, she lifted the hammer over her head, pretending that it took all of her strength to do so, and then let it drop exactly where the game-man had said. As she did, she moved to her right, blocking the view of the spectators just slightly so that they could not see where the blow landed. The black disk inside the glass-casing of the sign shot straight up and smacked the bell with a resounding *ding*, and the crowd—minus one of course—cheered.

The game-man raised his remaining mallet over his head. "Way to go, Miss," he said. "Take a bow." He nodded at the crowd and winked at her. She obeyed, sweeping her arms and skirts out wide, curtseying first right and then left. As she distracted the rubes, she saw the game-man bend down to pick up the light mallet she'd dropped. He deftly tossed it under the low sheeted platform they were standing on, then just as deftly pulled out a different mallet. He straightened, dug into his pocket, and produced a quarter. "Here you go, Missy," he said, handing it to her. She accepted it with a beatific smile.

The game-man addressed the crowd. "So who's next? Who wants to try Jack Campbell's game of strength? Who has the courage to try their skill after this Amazonian creature showed us all how it's to be done?" The crowd laughed, obviously enjoying the joke that the tiny redhead in front of them could be deemed "Amazonian." Forrestina hammed it up, flexing her biceps at them.

"Come on," the man said. "Don't let ol' Jack down. Is there no one in the crowd willing to represent the male of the species?" He pointed to the obnoxious rube from before. "How about you?" he asked. "You sure were saying a lot before. You think you can do as well as this little girl?"

The rube scowled, and his friends standing with him started their taunts. "Come on, Mark," one man said. "You were bragging before about how strong you are. Show us something."

Jack placed his booted foot on a stool that stood nearby. "How 'bout we make it interesting?" he said to Mark. "Fifty to one that you can't hit that bell."

Before Mark could answer, Forrestina held her newly-won quarter up in the air. "Jack, is it?" she asked, addressing the man running the game. He nodded. "I would like to lay a bet. Is that allowed?"

Jack stroked his beard. "It's a free country," he said. "What did you have in mind?"

Forrestina turned to Mark, who was watching her with his washed-out, snaky eyes. "I bet you my two bits to yours that you can't do better than me," she said. The crowd hooted in appreciation of her pluck.

"I'll lay a bet against that," a friend of Mark's said. He pulled out a quarter too. "Mine against yours that Mark will hit that bell in one try."

Other people in the crowd started to pull their money out as well, hollering to join the betting, convinced that if Forrestina could hit the bell, surely a *man* would have no problem. Jack held up his right hand, palm out. "Okay, okay," he said, voice raised to be heard over the clamor. He reached into his back pants pocket and pulled out a small wire-bound notebook and a pencil. He noted down everyone's bet, then said, "Okay, bets are closed. If Mark hits that bell, we divide the winnings between you all. If he doesn't," he shrugged, "then it gets split between me and. . ." he raised an eyebrow at her, and she said, "Forrestina."

"Forrestina? Lovely name for a lovely woman," he commented, scribbling again on his pad of paper. Before handing Mark a mallet, Jack said casually, "I noticed you didn't put any money up against the lady. You need to fork a quarter over, bud."

Flushing, Mark dug into his front pants pocket and pulled out two dimes and a nickel. "Here," he grumbled, shoving the coins towards Jack, who calmly added it to the pile of silver in his hand. He jotted down Mark's name with a flourish.

"Come on, come on," Mark said. "I ain't got all day." He glared at Forrestina. "Get ready to see how a real man handles this game, girl."

"Talk, talk, talk," she retorted, rolling her eyes.

Impassively Jack held out both mallets to Mark. "You wanna pick which one to swing with?" he asked. Mark grabbed for both of them and when Jack let go, he was pulled downwards by the weight, almost falling over. The crowd laughed, and he flushed again. Dropping one of the mallets, he lined himself up and lifted his arms overhead, swinging down as hard as he could on the center of the square black pad, grunting with the effort. The disk inside the glass rose . . . all the way to "Kid Sister."

The crowd of people clapped and jeered, seeming to forget that most of them had just lost money. Everyone knew someone like this jerk, and there was something vastly satisfying about watching him make a fool of himself. Jack put a sympathetic paw on Mark's shoulder. "Aw, brother," he said. "Tough luck." He turned to the crowd. "I think our man here was just warming up. Whaddya say? Shall we call that a practice run and let him try again?"

They all clapped their assent. Mark snarled, "Let me use the other mallet."

Jack handed it to him, and Mark breathed out heavily before raising it overhead with both hands and slamming it down on the black square.

"Kid Sister," the sign informed him again flatly.

Amid the laughter, Forrestina cupped her hands around her mouth and called out, "Why didn't you bring a real man with you to help you out, *Kid Sister?*"

Bellowing with rage, Mark flung the handle of the mallet down. "You stupid broad," he spat out at Forrestina. "There's no way you could've hit that bell." Understanding slowly dawned on his ugly face. "Unless the game is rigged and you're part of it." He raised his fist and took a step forward. "I oughta knock your teeth out." The crowd fell silent as Forrestina dug her heels in and lifted her chin. No matter what, she was not going to flinch away. She'd sooner die. Besides, when living with Max she'd learned how to take a punch.

Before he could unload on her, though, Jack reached over, almost casually, and lifted Mark by the scruff of his neck. "Now you listen to me, buddy," he said in a pleasant, conversational tone. "You apologize to this sweet gal, and then you take your sorry self away from my carnival and don't come back. If I see you here again, I promise you that I will stomp you into a mud hole. Are we clear?" When Mark didn't answer right away, Jack shook him gently, like a cat shaking her naughty kitten. "Are-we-clear?" he asked again.

"Yes," Mark stammered.

"Good," Jack said. He sat Mark back on his feet and gestured in Forrestina's direction. "Well, go ahead," he said.

Mark swallowed hard. "I apologize," he said through grinding teeth, eyes fixed on the ground like a chastened schoolboy.

Forrestina set her hands on her hips and leaned forward. "Mister," she said sweetly, batting her eyelashes, "you and your apology can go straight to the devil." She turned her heel and flounced away, the roars of appreciation from the crowd ringing in her ears. It was a sound she sure missed.

She walked along slowly, not really seeing the bustle of people around her, lost in an old day-dream of cheers in a circus tent. After a few moments, she heard heavy, rapid footsteps coming up behind her. "Hey, Miss! Miss Forrestina with the pretty hair and the pretty name!"

She slowed and turned to see Jack hurrying after her. He was waving two closed fists overhead. "Half of this belongs to you," he panted once he caught up to her. He pushed a pile of coins into her hands.

She considered them for a moment, then shoved them into her skirt pocket. "It was a pleasure doing business with you, Jack," she said, smiling pleasantly at him. "Thanks for keeping that idiot Mark in line." She turned to go, but he caught her hand.

"Wait," he said. Her eyes narrowed as she looked pointedly down at the hand clasping her, and he hastily let go, holding his palms out. "Easy," he said. "I just wanted to ask you which carnival outfit you're with. I thought we were the only ones scheduled for Lawrence this month."

"What makes you think I'm with a carnival?" Forrestina asked, pleased that he'd figured out she wasn't just a run-of-the-mill rube.

"Well, you knew about the sweet spot and you knew about the dummy mallet. Also, you grifted that crowd but good, staggering around and pretending the mallet was almost too heavy to carry." He whistled admiringly. "That was a nice piece of acting, right there."

They started to walk along together at a nice, comfortable pace, Jack shortening his steps to accommodate the difference in their height. He nudged her gently with his elbow. "Come on," he said, "'fess up."

"No carnival," she replied. "Circus."

"No kidding?" Jack said. "Which one?"

"Ringling," Forrestina replied. "Though our circus would've never tolerated cons. But I knew someone who played people easier than a baby plays pat-a-cake, and he taught me all the tricks he knew." She frowned. "Of course, his best one was how to disappear."

"So he wasn't a con man. He was a magician," Jack said.

"Aren't they the same thing?" Forrestina asked. Thinking of Max made her feel tired and suddenly ready to return to her solitary room in Mrs. Crawford's boarding house.

Jack didn't seem ready to let her go, however. "So why did you leave?" he asked. "And what do you do now? Haven't I seen you working at Jolene's Diner? Man, their pies are something else—the butterscotch makes me want to slap my pappy!"

Forrestina laughed uproariously at that. "Shoot, I haven't heard that expression since I was a little tyke in Louisiana," she said. "Before we moved to Missouri."

Jack grinned down at her. "Louisiana, then Missouri, then all around with Ringling, and now here in Kansas. Keep talking and I'll have your life story pieced together in no time."

Forrestina stiffened. She'd sworn off con men, even cheerful, friendly ones like Jack. She moved a step away from him, cleared her throat, then stuck her right hand out for him to shake. "I enjoyed our little trick, Jack," she said, "but I really need to get on home. It was very nice meeting you. Good luck in Lawrence; hope you make your goal before moving on."

Jack regarded her hand for a moment before sighing regretfully and taking it in his own. His strong grip was firm but not painful, and he held her fingers for a moment too long before releasing her. "Bye, Ms. Forrestina," he said. "Thanks for your help. You're quite a gal."

"I'm glad you think so," she said. "Goodbye." She left him and walked away. After a few seconds, she glanced over her shoulder to see if he was watching her go. She just couldn't resist. He was, and when he saw her, he smiled widely and waved. She didn't wave back, just picked up her pace, scolding herself for being an idiot as she went along. The last thing she needed in her life was another handsome man who knew how to tell lies.

Later that night, though, tossing and turning in her lonely twin-sized bed, she was distracted by thoughts of Jack's pecan eyes, his gleaming teeth, the feel of his strong hands on hers, and the way he lifted that rube off his feet as if he weighed nothing. But it wasn't just Jack who disturbed her normally peaceful sleep. She also thought about the way the crowd at the game had responded to her performance and how *good* it had felt to hear their laughter and applause. As she rolled over, punching at her lumpy pillow viciously, trying to get comfortable, she realized that she was tired of staying in one place and bored stiff with playing it safe. She shifted to her back and stared at the white plaster ceiling. She remembered Lucy standing beside her bedside when she was recovering in the hospital. Sarah had secured Forrestina's room at the boarding house, but Lucy was convinced that Forrestina would not need it long. "You have the soul of a gypsy, Lollo," she'd said, patting Forrestina's hand. "You are doomed to forever long to live your life outside the lines. You will recover and then come find us again, yes?" She leaned down and kissed Forrestina's cheek. "It's a curse of love for the open road I give you," she whispered, "because you are of my tribe and I would have you with me." Blinking in the darkness, thinking on those words now, Forrestina felt the old familiar stirrings to be out-and-on pull at her, like the moon tugging at the ocean. As far as curses went, it wasn't so bad.

When Jack showed up at her diner the next day, as she knew he would, Forrestina poured him a cup of black coffee, set a huge slice of butterscotch pie in front of him, its two-inch high meringue quivering and sweating golden beads, and announced, "I just quit my job. So you think I can get a place with your outfit?"

He grinned widely in response and called for an extra fork.

CHAPTER THIRTEEN

The Carnival Years, 1920

"RATS, RATS, COME PLAY WITH my rats," Forrestina sang out to the cheerful, sweaty carnival patrons passing her. As the crowd swept by, she spotted a group of teenage boys. She put her hands on her hips and cocked her head to the side. "Come on, boys," she said, smiling her sweetest smile—at twenty-nine, she was still plenty pretty enough to use her feminine wiles to greatest effect—"won't you try out my game? It's an easy win. Bet a penny on a color, bet a penny on a rat. Win something nice for your sweethearts." She pointed to the cellophane-wrapped stuffed bears, giraffes, and monkeys tacked to the underside of her booth's red-and-white striped awning. They swayed gently in a welcome breeze, nodding to one another behind their plastic shrouds, as if in agreement: *Oh yes, win us! Take us home!* Forrestina batted at the bear, sending it into a wild spin. "Or if you'd rather play a *man's* game," she said, "forget the toys and win some real money." She allowed the dimple in her right cheek to deepen.

The boys, hanging on the edge of fourteen or so and seeming unable to resist the charms of a pretty woman and the chance to win big, slowed and then stopped, moving to Forrestina's booth curiously. She hid a smile of victory. She had them. "That's right, handsome young men," she crooned. "Step out of that hot sun, at least. It's nice and cool in my shade." She winked at them, and they all laughed, jostling each other with their elbows, clearly pleased to be referred to as "men."

"So how does the game work?" asked one of the boys, a short, muscular kid wearing his shirtsleeves rolled to his elbows. Forrestina stepped back so they could see the inside of her booth. A large square box was set into the center of a huge round ring, the top flat, the bottom disappearing out of sight towards the ground. The ring was surrounded by clear glass and joined together by glue. On the square's face were eight circles of different colors: red, green, blue, yellow, orange, purple, black, and pink. On the outside of the booth, running down the front and left side, were two low counters, under which crimson satin hung to the ground. The counters were each divided into ten sections; in every section, the wood was painted with eight small circles that mimicked the colored circles on the box inside the booth.

"Have a seat, boys." Forrestina indicated the tall three-legged wooden stools set alongside the outer edges of the counter. She slipped through a top-to-ground slit in the crimson fabric that fully covered two sides of her booth, creating side and back "walls." She stooped down and produced a wire cage. The boys leaned forward eagerly to have a look.

"Say, what's that?" one of the boys asked, pushing the brim of his baseball cap back a little so he could see better. "Are those *rats*?"

Indeed they were. Forrestina reached in and pulled out one of the rats—the white one she called Peter. He was good-sized—nine inches long, not counting his tail—with pink, nervous eyes and quivering whiskers. He was her most docile rat, so he got the privilege of being the first to meet the customers; no one wanted to see blood right off the bat. She'd leave Judas, her biggest and meanest rat, until last, whereupon he would most definitely bite her and she would most definitely bleed. If he weren't trained so well, she'd be tempted to wring his stupid little neck.

She held Peter up, murmuring soothing words to him as he wriggled in her hand. "The game is easy," she told the boys. "In front of you is your game card, as it were. You set your penny on the color of the circle that you think one of my rats will run into and then I spin my Wheel of Chance to determine which color pays the biggest. Of course, you also have to bet on which *rat* will go into which hole—I have three rats, this white one, a grey, and a black. White pays for one—double or nothing. Grey pays for two, and black, well, he's our champion. He's a stubborn cuss, but if luck is with you, that rat pays five to one. So whaddya say, boys?" She set Peter down in front of them, let them stroke his soft fur for a moment. "Want to try your luck?"

Three of the boys decided they absolutely did. Forrestina slipped Peter back into the cage and walked over to a chalkboard set up on a tall easel against the back of the booth. After the boys put their pennies down on colors, she asked them to bet on their rat, writing down both the number of their booth section and the color they selected, and spun the big red-and-white wheel standing next to the chalkboard. Two of the boys had bet Peter on different colors, but the muscular, athletic-looking kid, clearly their leader, decided to chance on Judas. Forrestina grabbed the squirming Peter and Judas out of the cage. Judas twisted and bestowed his usual nip on her; after all these years he apparently still did not believe this to be a dignified life for a rat. She set them down in the ring and stood back to let them do their thing.

The boys cheered their rats on: "Come on, Whitey. To the green hole! No, the other way, stupid mouse! The *green* one!"

"That's it, boy. Get away from that nasty green circle. Move on over to the purple one!" "Black rat, go to yellow! To YELLOW, I say!"

The rats ambled around the square sniffing, their pointed pink noses twitching. Finally Peter disappeared into the purple hole—cheers from the boy who'd just won back his penny and one more, groans from the boy who'd lost. Judas scrabbled around for another few seconds. He paused at yellow for a moment, turned his head to stare at Forrestina with his blackberry-seed eyes, then reversed course and shot down the red hole.

More groans as the teens clapped the biggest loser on the back. Forrestina collected the coins from the boards, handed two back to the winner, and said to the other two, "Hard luck, fellas. Want to try again?"

They did, as did two of their other friends and three men who had stopped to watch. From then on business continued to be brisk all day, and around Forrestina's booth the sound of good-natured moans and hurrahs of winners and losers was punctuated by Forrestina's encouraging banter. Finally, when the rides shut down at ten o'clock and lights all over the carnival began going out, Forrestina took one more round of bets and collected her winnings. She thanked her patsies, extracting promises from them that she would see them again tomorrow, and pulled the booth's canvas coverings down. She secured the canvas walls with nylon cords tied to the four tall wooden stakes that supported the booth and washed her blackboard clean with the damp rag sitting in a bucket on the ground. Finished with the tidying up, she allowed herself a rest on the small squat stool set in the corner. Her scarred hands were covered in fresh bites; she would need to wash and disinfect the wounds as soon as she was back in her caravan. She opened the cage and tipped it over, letting the rats run freely around in the scrabbly grass that passed for her floor, throwing them bits of carrot she kept in her pocket. She eyed Judas, who tucked his treat into his cheek and stared back at her contemplatively.

"Good work today, devil's spawn," she said. She reached down and ran the tip of a finger along his sleek back, making sure to keep well away from his razor teeth. "You didn't slip up once." For all his orneriness, Judas made her a lot of money, but that was not the only reason he was her favorite. While he was well-trained to watch for her tapping fingers so he could know which holes to avoid, he had his own mind when he wasn't working, and Forrestina respected that. She figured his bites were his way of saying that he knew his job and would do it, but only because he had no reason not to. She rubbed the top of his head again. "You surely are a right bastard," she said affectionately, handing him another piece of carrot. He took it from her delicately in his paws and stored it in his other cheek.

She heard the rustling of canvas being freed, and the curtained door to her booth opened. A burly, brown-bearded man stepped in. He peered over the table at her. "Who's a bastard?" he growled. He walked over and sat down in the grass beside her, careful not to crush her rats. "Shoo, you pests," he said, pulling his battered leather farm hat from his head and flapping it at them. Peter and Paul, the grey rat, scurried away from him, squeaking annoyance at the intrusion, but Judas stood his ground, his teeth bared, the carrots in his cheeks making him appear to be smiling widely and cartoonishly. Forrestina scooped him up and set him out of harm's way. Jack did not tolerate his insolence like she did, and Judas was likely to get flung across the booth if he snapped at her now.

Jack reached out and tugged at her hands, turning them over. "Good Lord, Forrestina," he said, gently touching one of her scars with his thick forefinger.

She pulled away. "They look worse than they feel, Jack," she said. "Don't fret yourself." Seeing darkness gather on his bushy eyebrows as his eyes tracked the black rat, she said, "He gets nervous performing, is all. Besides, he never misses; I had fifty people bet on him today—*fifty*! All wins for me and not a penny out on him!"

Jack still looked unconvinced, so to distract him she stood up from her stool and deposited herself sideways into his lap. He grunted in surprise, then put his arms around her, cradling her as if she were a child. In terms of size, she may as well have been—Jack was a brute of a man, barrel-broad in the chest, with a belly that was pure muscle. Once, when he was drunk, Forrestina had seen him fight three men at once and whip the tar out of every one of them, roaring like a wounded bull all the while as his hammer-like fists rained blows on their heads. When he'd awoken from his alcohol-fueled stupor later, he'd looked around sadly at the busted-up bar and equally busted-up men and swore to stay off the bottle. "I don't want to be a dumb drunk who just cracks heads. That were my Pa; it ain't me," he said.

And most of the time, he kept his pledge, sometimes saying, "I guess I oughta thank President Wilson and his infernal Prohibition for my new teetotaler ways." He'd then be forced to duck, laughing, to escape Forrestina's swiping fist—he knew she despised Woodrow Wilson and his nose-in-everybody's-business policies. She firmly believed that Americans should be free to make their own decisions—good *and* bad—and resented a government that treated its citizens like children by telling them what they could and could not do. Besides, on a more practical, less personal level, rubes were a heck of a lot harder to fleece when they were sober. Wilson and his Prohibition could go jump in a pond for all Forrestina cared; she wanted Jack sober, but by his own choice. She figured it would stick better that way. Sober Jack was stolid and dependable, quiet and intelligent, the opposite of selfish Max, and Forrestina had fallen easily in love with the careful way he treated her, as if she were made of spun sugar. The outside world might believe that she was tough and independent, but she was really very fragile; her heart, unlike her bones, was still broken—not for Max, but for her unborn child—and she'd been amazed and grateful when Jack recognized that almost immediately without her having to say a word.

For six years now, she'd been with the carnival and with Jack, living with him in their shared caravan, wintering in rustic campgrounds when the carnival season was through, training her rats and tricking rubes in the spring and summer. It was a good enough life—not perfect, of course, often rough and uncomfortable and uncertain—but still, she didn't believe in exasperating God with ingratitude. Just enough was still enough.

Pulling herself out of Jack's lap, she gathered her rats up and popped them back into their cage. She picked it up by the handle. "Come on, Jack," she said. "Let's call it a day, shall we?"

He hauled himself up and took the cage from her. "Last week of the season," he said. "The summers just seem to go by faster and faster." They walked through the carnival, murmuring greetings to the people they knew as they passed by, watching as the electric lights continued to wink out one by one and were replaced by the softer lights in the grassy hay field where the caravans were parked and the tents set up. A small campfire had been lit, and several of the carnies were sitting on fold-up chairs, eating supper from tin plates and chatting companionably about the day's wins and losses. Overhead, the pre-midnight moon was half-closed, and it glimmered hard and bright, like the white of a witch's eye.

Jack handed Forrestina the rat cage. "I'll be up in a minute. I have to go speak to Lou," he said. Lou was the traveling show's wrestling attraction; for a dime you could test your strength against him, see if you could pin him down to the mat and win the odds. Of course, no one *ever* won the odds. He was tricky because he was a small man—no more than five foot six—but he was quick as a rattler and strong as a rhino. Forrestina had seen him flip and pin men twice his size with no more fuss than as if he were flipping a child.

Lou the Strong was part of the Bixby Traveling Carnival "wonders" tent. Along with him, the carnival featured Mela, the toddler-simple, pin-headed daughter of Mr. Bixby; Valentino, the sword-swallower; another, even hairier Jack called "Jack the Wolf Boy;" and Brian, the tattooed man, who wore the stories of ancient Greece on his body and recounted those stories to listening crowds, pointing to his flesh illustrations as he did so. The carnival also boasted pony rides for the kids and delicious portable food: sizzling hot dogs and hamburgers, pink and blue "fairy floss" that was spun in a metal bowl before being wrapped around a newspaper cone and handed to happy customers, hot buttered popcorn and tart lemonade, and sticky, tooth-ruining toffee apples. There were all sorts of games, from easy-to-win kiddie games like Go-Fish and Pick-a-Duck, to more "skill" oriented (and fixed) betting games, including hers and Jack's. For a travelling show, theirs was pretty small, but Forrestina and Jack stayed because the owner left them alone to their own devices. He was far too busy taking gentle care of his poor tiny-headed, tiny-brained daughter, the only thing left of the beloved wife who had died giving birth to her, to worry about what the rest of them were doing. He was good at finding towns, renting fields, and advertising, and in return, he took a ten percent cut of all the carnival profits. Forrestina thought they were lucky—it was nice not to have someone enforcing a bunch of rules, and the folks in the show got along fairly well, rarely fighting and mostly looking out for each other. Like all misfits, they seemed to have a tacit awareness that it was them versus the rubes, people they disdained for their sheer naïve idiocy, yet whose money and attention they couldn't live without. Of course, the rubes felt the same about them, treating them like trash and thieves yet unable to stop themselves from coming back night after night. "Like mating frogs drawn to a well that has a snake curled in the bottom of it," Forrestina told Jack.

Periodically a separate "flesh tent" would join them for a season or two, but the owner of the hoochie-coochie burlesque kept his girls separate from the rest of them, camping his fleet of caravans in a rented field a half mile away. The gossip among the Bixby folk was that the girls took rubes back to their caravans for extra cash, something that the normally hands-off Hans Bixby flat-out refused to allow in his regular group, so they were forced to set up away from the rest of the carnival workers. That was more than fine with Forrestina; she had not forgotten the floozy who had run off with Max. (Though now she freely admitted the tart had done her a favor. Knowing Max the way she did, she could almost—*almost*—pity the woman.) Still and all, she didn't trust the vapid half-dressed creatures of the burlesque; after all, a woman whose sole job was to paint her face, shake her tush, and spread her legs probably had no scruples when it came to respecting another woman's private property. Forrestina planned on keeping her Jack far away from the burlesque Brendas—fool me once, as the old saying went.

Forrestina set her rat cage down near the caravan's wooden steps, in a grassy area where the rats could do their business with no extra clean up needed. She covered the cage with a light cotton sheet, leaving about two inches open at the bottom for extra air, then walked over to where their caravan's horses were staked. "Hey, boys," she said, fishing in her pocket for more carrots. She opened her hand and let the grey-speckled Medi nuzzle the carrot from her palm, his prickly muzzle warm. She stroked his head between his perked ears, then fed some carrots to the other horse, Ocre. He was rust-colored, like Jack, with a black mane, and he blew warm air on her palms as he carefully retrieved his treat from her. A pair of gentler horses she'd never known, always a nice break after a day spent dealing with Judas and his single-minded, independent hatred.

She patted them both on their cheeks. "Good night, Medi-Ocre," she said to them. Their names were a joke Jack had thought up. After hearing all the horses named "Champion" and "Prince" and "King" he'd come across when going from town to town, he proudly said of his horses, these two sturdy, patient brothers, "These boys ain't champions or royalty. They're just average. Hell, they're mediocre, at best—and mediocre is about right for me!" Forrestina loved this story but hoped Jack didn't feel the same way about her—she liked to imagine she was at least one step above mediocre.

She stopped by the rain barrel next to their caravan and dipped some water out with a shallow metal ladle. Grabbing a sliver of lye soap from where it sat on the caravan's large spoked wheel, she washed her hands, using the ladle to rinse. She took special care with the bite marks that dotted her skin, wincing at the sting as soap met open flesh. She wiped her hands on a flannel cloth resting next to the soap, then made her way back to the door and climbed the three steps into her caravan. Fumbling a bit in the dark, she fired up a couple of kerosene lamps, watching them flare and hiss before she adjusted them to the correct light she needed. She reached into the wooden cupboard and pulled out a tin of pork and beans, opened it with a crank-handled opener, and dumped the beans into a long-handled saucepan. Jack could claim that she was a mediocre cook, she supposed, and she couldn't fault him for it. He never seemed to mind what she slapped down in front of him, though, and she was sure as heck not going to get fancy with food if she didn't have to. Cooking had always bored her—what was the point of all that fuss for something that would be gone in a moment, leaving behind only more work in the washing up? She could think of a dozen better things to do with her time. Besides, she really liked pork and beans.

Firing up the kerosene-powered, camp-sized cook stove, she heated the beans, adding a squirt of catsup and a handful of brown sugar before slicing some extra salt pork into the pot. As the beans began to bubble, she pulled a loaf of brown bread out of the tin bread box on the caravan's tiny wooden counter, sliced a few pieces, and spread pale oleo on thickly with a butter knife. She filled two tin plates with beans, added the bread slices on the side, and then carefully made her way back outside. Sitting on the top step of the caravan, she set Jack's supper on the step below her and picked up her spoon, blowing on the hot beans before taking a bite. They were sweet and salty and perfect, and she closed her eyes, savoring the simple joy of simple flavors.

"By the look on your face, you must be thinking of me," Jack said, interrupting her reveries. He picked up his plate and sat down just below her, his shoulder at her knees. He shoveled some beans into his mouth and then took a huge bite of bread.

"You keep believing that," Forrestina replied, nudging him softly with her knee. She took another bite, chewed, and then said, "So what did you and Lou talk about?"

"Oh you know, making plans," Jack said. He scraped up the last of his supper with his spoon, wiped his mouth and beard with the back of his hand, and belched in satisfaction. "Pardon me," he said. He leaned his head on Forrestina's knee. After a quiet moment, he asked casually, "So, Red, what do you think about us buying a little piece of land by the White River in Arkansas?"

"Arkansas? Whatever for?" Forrestina said, setting her plate down.

"Well, we ain't going to carnival forever, are we?" Jack said. "Besides, the property I'm thinking of would be a perfect place to winter every year. It's out of the way, easy to clear, and we can rent spots for other traveling show folks to winter in too. It's close enough to the river for washing and far enough out of town so folks won't bother us."

"And why would folks want to bother us, Jack?" Forrestina asked, keeping her tone even. "Jack? Far enough for what?"

Jack sighed. "Lou thinks a little moonshine operation set back in the woods won't hurt nobody," he said. He stroked his beard with one hand. "I told him you wouldn't like it, but he promised to keep his outfit far on the outskirts, away from the living area, and he agreed to do no selling on the property. The land belongs to a cousin of his, so he can get us a good price. He'd buy it himself, 'cept he ain't got the money for it." Jack took her hand and looked up at her. In the darkness, his eyes were black smudges in his face. "Honey, I won't take a drop. I swear. Besides," he said, his sudden white grin piercing the shadows, "a moonshine still on land you own would let you thumb your nose at that Yankee skunk President Wilson, wouldn't it?"

Forrestina sat silent, worrying over everything Jack had just said. It was true that they'd been pooling and saving their money for a while now with an eye to investing in something for the future, and a piece of property where they could winter meant Jack wasn't ready to leave the travelling life just yet. And while she hated drinking on principle because of what it did to a man, making moonshine way out in the sticks wasn't really that risky a proposition—they wouldn't be Al Capone by any stretch of the imagination. As for Jack and his promise. . . She raked her fingers through her hair, thinking. So far, he'd shown great restraint around booze despite having plenty of opportunities. Besides, he was a grown man, not her child, and she would just have to hope for the best. She patted his head lightly, then wound her fingers into his hair. "Well, hell," she sighed. "I guess it's my patriotic duty as an American to stand up against that over-reaching buffoon. So let's do it."

Jack hooted and extracted himself from her fingers. He stood, picking up both their plates and heading over to the rain barrel to do the washing up. "I'll tell Lou we can do it tomorrow. Thanks, Red," he said. "You're still quite a gal."

"And don't you forget it," she called after him. Later, pressed close to him on their tiny shared bed along the back wall of the caravan, she counted her blessings and said her prayers as she did every night, but sleep stayed away as worry gnawed at her like Judas sharpening his teeth on the wires of his cage. Purchasing land, laying down roots—starting a moonshine business, for Pete's sake. . .! *Here I go*, she thought. *Buying that old trouble again.* She just hoped that this time the price wouldn't be so dear.

CHAPTER FOURTEEN

Postcard
To Mrs. Sarah Clarke
487 Brown Street
Darlington, IN

September 17, 1921

Dear Sarah,

As per the photo on the front, greetings from the White River in Arkansas! I was happy to hear that your little Tina is growing strong and sturdy—has she her mother's good looks as well as height? Pass along my regards to Christopher; Jack sends the same to you. He and I are now land barons (ha), 75 acres on the river. We set up a camp for carnival folk to winter at. Always a good time, as you can imagine. If you ever need a break from the domestic life, I can surely find a space for you! You can even help me fix my hair—it's an ever-tangled mess as always. I would love to cut it, but Jack likes it long, and you know how we girls like to keep our men happy, ha-ha. Seriously though, I long to see you, if time and circumstance ever permits, and camping is fun for the whole family.

With Love and Ever Yours,

Forrestina

CHAPTER FIFTEEN

The River Years, 1927

FORRESTINA LEFT JOHNNY'S HARDWARE in Mountain Home, Arkansas, and climbed into her Model T Runabout pickup truck, the squat square bed filled with supplies for the camp. She and Jack had bought the truck two years ago, and from the first moment her hands touched the steering wheel, she'd taken to driving like a toddler takes to pudding. Flying down the dirt roads and young highways at a mind-boggling top speed of forty miles per hour, Forrestina felt that old familiar rush of danger and joy she'd only ever experienced on the wire. Today as she pulled out of town and onto the rough-cut Highway 68, she jammed her foot down on the gas pedal and careened down the road, the curls that had escaped from her heavy braid blowing wildly around her face in the wind. As was her habit when she was feeling particularly joyful, she began to count her blessings out loud. She had money under her mattress (literally—she and Jack distrusted banks so they opted to sock their money away in various hidey-holes), an imperfect man whom she loved anyway, a four-month stint on the road with the carnival, and a place of her own that she could call home at the end of her summer travels. Why, she was even crazy about their current president, Mr. Calvin Coolidge, a solemn, limited-government man who led the country with thrift and then just let everyone *be*. Yes indeed, 1927 had been a good year thus far.

As she buzzed along the highway, inhaling the sharp clean smells of the Ozarks in October, she admired the cacophony of colors all around her.

Blazing shades of red, orange, and yellow replaced the bright summer green of the trees, as if a child had tripped and spilled his box of paints over the hills. The sunlight had gone from fierce to gentle, and Forrestina began to sing loudly, with abandon: *"Make believe you are glad when you're sorry, sunshine will follow the rain. When things go wrong, it won't be long, soon they'll be right again."* She turned the truck off the highway and onto the dirt road that led to her camp, then made a left into an area set off from the highway. She slowed and then yanked the clutch to "park" in front of a small square building. It was low of roof, its concrete-blocked walls painted a dazzling, pristine white. Two sparkling-clean, sizable picture windows were set into the walls on either side of the screened door, and "White River Grocery and Gas" was painted in three-feet tall red letters directly onto the building, the words stretched boldly above the window frames and the door. To the right of the building, a lone gas pump, painted the same cherry-red as the store's name and round-topped like a lollipop, stood ready for business.

As she climbed from the truck, Jack stepped out of the grocery store, the bells attached to the door jingling wildly. "About time," he said grumpily, walking over to the truck and grabbing two cardboard boxes of food out of the truck's bed. "I need to be out clearing brush, not minding the store."

Forrestina bit back a sharp retort—"clearing the brush" had lately come to mean drinking Lou's moonshine. Despite his good intentions and Forrestina's hopes, Jack's dry days had ended when it became easier to find illegal hooch. Still, she was in too good a mood today to pick a fight. She gathered three brown-paper grocery bags in her arms and carried them into the store. She set them down on a low wooden counter that stretched for eight feet near the back of the store and held the massively heavy iron cash register. She called to Jack, who'd gone out and come back in with another three bags, "Are the spots filled?"

Jack set his bags next to the others. He reached in, pulled out a jar of catsup and examined it, turning it in his big hands before putting it back down.

"Yeah," he said. "Almost a full house. Our carnies, of course, and a couple of new groups from Jones Brothers' Travelling Circus. You ever hear of them?"

Forrestina had. "Calling themselves a circus is a joke," she snorted. "They have one clown—a hateful old wretch named Calypso Charlie—a couple of tired old horses they run around a ring, and I think a monkey in a cage." She began unloading the groceries from the bags and carrying them to the four sets of wheeled metal shelves in the store. "Though I seem to remember that their fortune teller, Madame Mystic, is actually pretty good. She's about the only honest one of the bunch, if you can believe it." She arranged a jar of mustard so that its label was facing forward, then walked back over to where Jack was leaning against the counter watching her. "You best keep an eye on them," she advised. "I'm sure they're not above helping themselves to whatever they find laying around—even if they have to pick a few locks to help with the finding."

Jack pulled the lower lapels of the heavy green-and-black plaid work jacket he wore over his overalls open and showed Forrestina a pistol in a short leather holster strapped high on his left hip. "They best keep an eye on *me*," he said. "Ain't nobody going to steal from Jack Campbell and live to enjoy it."

"Lord, Jack," Forrestina said, exasperated. "Why do you need to wear a gun? It looks to me like you're just asking for trouble."

Jack let his coat drop back over the gun. "If everybody plays nice, then the gun stays where it is." He rummaged through the bags, found a Baby Ruth candy bar, and peeled the wrapper back. He stuffed half of it in his mouth. "You know that we can't run the business we do and not have a little muscle behind it."

Forrestina didn't mind muscles so much; fighting was a regular part of the rough and tumble life they lived. It was guns in the hands of hot-tempered men—especially hot-tempered *drunk* men—that worried her. "Well, just be careful," she sighed. She knew she may as well tell the river to keep its feet dry.

"Will do," Jack replied, swallowing the rest of his candy and waving his old hat over his shoulder at her as he left. A moment later, she heard the truck roar into life. She walked to one of the windows and watched Jack tear down the road, leaving behind billows of red dust. She found that her good mood had gone with him. Disconsolately she surveyed the work in front of her. She wanted to be driving hell-for-leather down the road too, but somebody had to get the store in order, and that someone was her. "Blessings, Forrestina," she reminded herself aloud. "You have a store that makes money and a pot to piss in." She marched to the front of the shop and grabbed a bag, then set about re-stocking the shelves, which mainly consisted of camping staples; since her clientele were chiefly carnival folk wintering at their grounds, she didn't need to keep much variety in stock. She had canned goods, of course, like pork-n-beans and Spam, and necessaries like coffee, tea, sugar, and bread. In the small ice-box she kept cheese, milk, butter, and stuff for sandwiches, like rolls of ham or smoked bologna, ready to be sliced. Forrestina also kept a good supply of candy for the carnie kids. It was common knowledge among the wildly-free children of the carnivals that "Ms. Red," as they called her, would never ask them to pay; she would, in fact, scold them if they even dared try.

In addition to food, Forrestina made sure to lay in necessary toiletries like soap, toothpowder, kerosene for lamps, matches, and cartons of cigarettes in varying brands (Camel being the most popular by far because it was the cheapest). Unlike most carnies she knew, Forrestina had never taken to smoking. She hated the way it burned her throat and made her cough, and the taste it left over was foul, like licking a rained-on fire-pit. Just thinking of it made her wince. She sifted through the glass jar on the counter and selected a grape-flavored lollipop. She shucked it of its cellophane wrapper and popped it into her mouth, dousing the memory of cigarettes with pure sugar. She returned to stocking supplies, sucking on the candy, taking inventory as she went.

Once finished with that task, she checked the cash in the till, totting up the amounts minus the cash taken out for replenishments. The till was three dollars short. Frowning, she checked her addition again and then heaved a sigh. Her figures were right. That was three dollars she'd never see again; by now the money would be deep in Lou's pocket as Jack grandly passed around mason jars of the strip-the-paint-off-the-barn moonshine Lou made in his makeshift distillery. He was mighty generous when he was in his cups, but how could she complain? The ever-dwindling candy supply was proof that they both had their weaknesses.

The bells over the door jangled and Amos Turner, proprietor of the Turner Family Travelling Circus, strode in, immaculately dressed in tails as always. Looking at him with his hair carefully oiled and combed, his moustache thin and spidery along his lips, his somewhat frayed tails brushed free of dust, Forrestina had to hide a smile. He was a pompous, dandy jackass, that was for sure, but even jackasses needed to eat, and Amos was harmless enough. With him, Forrestina saw, was Ruby, who Amos had stolen from another show to work as the Turner Family Circus's lone exotic dancer. She was also his personal bed-warmer. Ruby was a pleasingly plump dumpling of a girl, curved and padded in all the right places, blond and pink-cheeked. Like a lot of the flappers of her day, she was free-spirited, good-natured, and seemed as cheerfully simple as the day was long.

"Afternoon, Mr. Turner," Forrestina said. "Ms. Ruby."

Ruby flashed a dimple at her. "Good afternoon, Red," she replied, her voice high and kittenish. She was dressed in a straight-lined, long-sleeved frock with a white Peter Pan collar. The waist of the chestnut-brown dress was well below her hips, the hem set sensibly halfway between her knees and her ankles. She wasn't wearing a hat, and her hair was bobbed short and crimped in charming waves. She always saved the sexy for her show, and that was one reason Forrestina had liked her almost immediately.

Amos nodded at Forrestina. "Hello, Ms. Red," he said. Forrestina wondered, not for the first time, if anyone knew her real name. When they'd first moved out here, Jack started calling their winter quarters "Red's White River," and then, impressed by his own inadvertently clever wordplay, started referring to her as "White River Red." The name was eventually shortened to just "Red," and now that was all anyone ever called her. Forrestina would've preferred Lucy's nickname for her—"Lollo"—but no one had asked her what she wanted. Carnies loved to give nicknames to each other, and they were rarely nice, so she was just grateful that she wasn't called Fat Joe or One-Eyed Dean or Rat-Faced Mike.

Amos picked up a wire basket that was set inside the doorway. While he shopped, Ruby wandered up to the counter and leaned on it with her left elbow, her chin resting in her hand. She drummed the blood-red varnished fingernails of her right hand on the wood absent-mindedly. "So how goes it?" she asked. "Jack still working with Lou?"

Forrestina warmed to the sympathy she saw in Ruby's bright, ice-blue eyes. "It's okay," she said. She lowered her voice. "It's not so bad during the season. It's just that winters are so long and Jack gets bored easily, you know?" She shrugged. "In terms of money, the moonshine's not a bad little racket, so I guess I can't complain."

"Ain't that the truth," Ruby said. "You two seem to be doing pretty good for yourselves—got a nice piece of property on the river, got this here store, got that nifty pick-up truck. You just make sure your name is on all the deeds too, you hear?" She laughed, full-throated and surprisingly bitter, and Forrestina suddenly remembered that despite her childish, doll-like appearance, Ruby was no infant in the trees—she was a hoochie coochie girl through and through. Ruby set a penny piece down on the counter and pulled a cherry lollipop from the jar on the counter.

Forrestina pushed the coin back at her. "The candy is free for your company," she said. "I'm starving for a little female gossip." She gestured at Amos with her head. "How are things with you and Prince Charming there?" she asked. "He treating you okay? Not making you do extra work for the rubes, is he?"

Ruby shrugged. "He's fine," she said, tapping her front teeth gently with her candy. "Right now he only asks me to do extra work for *him*." She turned and watched Amos as he checked his purchases against the list he held clutched in his fist. "I ain't got no complaints so far. He's clean and decent and he doesn't hit me—three things I sure couldn't say about my last boss, Maestro DeLay—you remember him? His show was almost all girls—hoochies, fortune tellers, contortionists—and he used us like his own personal harem and rented us out like whores in a whorehouse." She curled her lip, forked the two fingers of her right hand, and said menacingly, "May he die poor, alone, and without a working penis." Forrestina recognized the curse and grinned broadly; Ruby had clearly picked up some gypsy ways from her former workmates. She took Ruby's left hand in her own, and they both pretended to spit on the ground in unison, saying "Amen" to seal the curse.

Forrestina knew Maestro DeLay, all right; when he'd shown up wanting to winter at their place a couple of years back, she'd put her foot down with Jack and demanded that he say no. Not only had she despised the small dark man with the thick Greek accent and eyes that crawled over her like dirty fingers, she wasn't crazy about the slatterns who accompanied him. Individually they were all right, but as a group they were dangerous. Tilly had always said that a rabbit knows a fox track same as a hound, and Forrestina was damned if that passel of vixens was going to spend several months in her warren, cozying up to her old dog. She told Jack to send them on their way, and despite his best efforts to argue for the poor little lambs all alone in the big, wide world with no place to lay their weary heads, she'd remained unmoved. "Stingy" and "uncompassionate" were not traits anyone had ever been able to lay at her door, and she was determined that "stupid" wouldn't be, either. So Jack had reluctantly turned Maestro, his money, and his women down. As the flashy caravan went off to find friendlier accommodations, leaving the scent of cheap perfume in its wake, Forrestina ignored Jack glowering beside her and waved them on, a satisfied smile on her face.

She noticed that Ruby was staring at her expectantly and realized the girl must've asked her a question. "I'm sorry," she said. "I was wool-gathering. What did you say?"

"I asked you if you're planning on hitting the circuit again in the summer, now that you have the store and all," Ruby answered.

"Oh, you know me—I've got itchy feet," Forrestina said. It was a question she'd been thinking about for a while. Jack had mentioned opening the campground and the store up for summer tourists while the carnies were off earning their wages, but Forrestina still hated the idea of staying in one place for too long. Rambling was in her bones. She liked to see different parts of America, liked the towns they passed through and the towns they set down in for a weekend or a week. She enjoyed the carnival family—the quiet conversations around the shared campfire, the dramatic squabbles between folk that were quick to flare up and just as quick to die down, and the sense of belonging to a group she'd chosen for herself. She also liked "roughing it," enjoyed the feeling of living close to the land and being self-sufficient. Too much comfort for too long made her uneasy—she didn't want to get soft. She'd never lived in a place that had electric lights—there was electricity in the grocery store to keep the ice box running, but the winter camp still relied on fire and kerosene for light and heat. When it got chilly, Forrestina and Jack, along with the other carnies, disappeared into their various traveling vehicles and piled on the blankets, huddling body to body for warmth. The biggest luxuries Forrestina had grown used to were the two outhouses Jack had set up on the edge of the camp and the hand-pump for water in the center of camp. The water came straight from a line he'd connected to the river, so they had to boil it before drinking, but it was still a darn sight easier than hauling buckets.

Forrestina glanced down at her hands, scarred from the bites of her aggravated rats and rough from chopping wood. There were certainly easier ways to make a living—being a secretary, for example, or a shop girl, or a waitress—but she preferred her life to theirs.

"You look like the cat what got the cream," Ruby said.

Forrestina smiled. "I suppose I am at that," she said, and the two women rested in companionable silence.

Amos strode over and plonked a loaf of white bread, a jar of mayonnaise, two cans of beans, and a box of cornflakes on the counter. "Gimme half a pound of bologna, thick sliced, a half-pound of American cheese, thin sliced, and a pint of milk," he said. He glanced over his list. "Oh, and you got eggs?"

Forrestina counted out twelve fresh eggs she'd gotten from a local farmer and placed them carefully in a cardboard carton. She put Amos's other items in a brown paper bag and tallied up the damage. Amos handed her his money, she made change, and he lifted the bags in his arms. "Come on, honey," he said to Ruby. "Let's go get ourselves settled in for the night. It's supposed to get cold."

"Not with me around," Ruby said, batting her eyes at him and then winking at Forrestina. Amos shook his head and grinned. "A lady, she ain't," he said, not without affection. "Good afternoon to you, Ms. Red. And thanks."

Ruby hopped off the stool she'd been perched on. "Bye, Red," she trilled as she followed her man out the door. "I'll see you around the fire."

"Bye, y'all," Forrestina said. She hoped the pair wouldn't spend the *entire* winter season "keeping warm;" she really did enjoy Ruby's company. Looking down at her wristwatch, she noted that it was four-thirty and decided to close up for the day. If anyone wanted anything, they could always track her down at the site, and she'd be happy to go get them whatever they needed.

After pulling on her outdoor jacket, she locked the shop door, checked to make sure the gas pump was off, and stood for a moment, looking down the dirt road that led to the site. Jack would come for her soon—he was usually back with the truck around five o'clock—but today she wanted to walk. It was only a two-mile trek to the campground, and by the time she got there, the world would still be more dusk than dark. As she walked along, she enjoyed the solitude, listening to the crunch of her sensible flat-heeled shoes on the gravel road and nothing else. Amos had been right—it was already beginning to get cold. She didn't mind, though; her jacket was warm, and the hat she'd pulled over her long hair would keep the heat in her head. She thought fondly of Tilly and how she'd always claimed that most of a person's body heat escaped through the crown of his head. As a result, she'd been religiously fanatic about the girls going nowhere without hats in the fall, bonnets in the spring and summer, and knit caps when it turned cold, and Forrestina still hardly went anywhere without having a hat close at hand. "God, I miss that wise old woman," she said out loud, realizing as she said the words that she meant them as a prayer. She was not particularly religious, but she didn't understand how people who didn't believe in God got through life. Who did they turn to when times were bad or thank when times were good? She had to believe that someone smarter than her was up there, making sure things down here didn't get too out of hand.

She turned onto the narrow spit of path that served as their road to the campground. The numerous dirt potholes were filled with milky tea-colored water after yesterday's fitful rain, and she resisted a sudden urge to go splashing in them. Despite the joy puddle-jumping might bring her, cold, wet socks turned into cold, wet feet, and she still had a mile to go.

Instead, she began to address God again, her hands in her pockets. "Let everyone back home be okay, huh? Just keep them safe," she said, lifting her face. She squinted up at a sliver of late sunshine cutting through the trees, the bands of soft light striping her face. She wondered how the girls had turned out. They were both grown women now: Beatrice would be thirty-two and Genevieve almost thirty. How was it possible? In her mind, they were forever children, and she pictured them as she'd last seen them—Bea, a rather suspicious, mousey-featured girl with drab brown mousey hair to match, and Genny, sweet-faced and rosy and plump, her hair like strawberries strained through gold.

And Petey, like her, would be forty in a few years—*forty*! She couldn't fathom it. He was probably married with a passel of kind, rowdy kids, all watched over and flourishing under the beaming sunshine of their Grandma Tilly—if she were still alive. Unexpected tears formed in Forrestina's eyes, surprising her. She hardly ever cried, but here, alone in God's nature, she thought, *Why not?* and let lose. The tears rolled down her face unimpeded, soaking their heat in tracks down the slopes of her cheeks, gathering for a moment on the edge of her chin before dropping off to pool in her clavicle, like sadness's explorers charting their own crooked course. She even allowed herself just a tiny moment to wonder after her parents—her father and his timid smile, her impatient, ever-moving mother. Her heart squeezed painfully, and she slammed the door of emotion shut, locking it up tightly. Wiping the dampness from her cheeks with her left hand and swiping at her moist nose, she looked up at the tree-tops again and murmured quickly, "Please bless Mama and Papa as well, amen."

Of course, as always her pleas were met with silence (a fact she was grateful for—she'd have toppled into the mud-puddles if God had spoken up), but she knew she'd been heard, and after her good cry and long prayer, she felt scooped out, clean and calm.

She stepped into the campground holding on to some much-needed peace and looked around, her hands on her hips, shyly pleased as always by this little homestead she and Jack had created together. The sign announcing their campground was a big rectangular plank nailed to an oak tree. On it, Jack had painted "Red's White River Campground. 25 cents per night. Weekly and monthly rates available" in blocky white letters. Past the sign were twenty spaces cleared for campsites: ten on the left side of the road nearest the river, and ten on the right, closer to the woods and the two outhouses. Each site had been scraped bare of scrub brush, and she and Jack had carefully set small circles of smooth river stones down for fires. A black iron grate, six bars wide and three feet long, was laid across each fire-pit. The grates were strong enough to hold a frying pan or a pot, and melded to the side, hanging over the pit, was a thick hook for coffee pots.

Along with groceries and gas, Forrestina and Jack also sold firewood, which they stacked in neat bundles next to their own site. Every fall,

Forrestina and Jack tromped into the woods and chopped down trees with their axes and long saw. Forrestina worked as hard as Jack, feeling her muscles strengthen with every blow to the unforgiving hardwood. They took turns splitting, using an iron wedge driven into the logs by a heavy mallet—one of Jack's old "test your strength" mallets, as a matter of fact—and carried armfuls of wood back to their caravan to be stacked, greener wood in the back, last year's cured and dried wood moved up to the front. Since the campground was open in the chilly fall and downright cold winter, the firewood was a nice extra little source of income for them.

Their gaily painted red-and-yellow caravan was situated on top of the sloping hill and was the first thing people saw upon entering the campground. In the very center of the campsite, where the road curved and then turned back on itself to form an exit as well as an entrance, Jack had cleared a larger space for a big, crackling community bonfire. They set long, split logs out as seats all around the fire, and many nights found most, if not all, of the campers seated on those logs, drinking coffee and smoking, telling stories, singing songs, staring dreamily at the orange sparks that leapt up into the dark Ozark sky. If there wasn't a bonfire spot in heaven, well, Forrestina didn't think she wanted to go there after all.

When she reached the occupied part of the campground, she spotted Jack and Lou sitting on one of those logs, their heads together. She felt a pang of unease; it was fair to say Lou was not a positive influence on Jack, so whatever they were talking about so intently was likely not good. She walked over and said to them casually, "Hey, boys. Got my wood all sold yet?"

They jumped apart, guilty as dogs digging in the flowerbeds. "Hey, Red," Lou said, his nervous grin plumping up his chubby cheeks. After abandoning his carnival work, Lou had let himself go, eating too much, sampling his moonshine too often, and getting fat in the process. Forrestina thought the formerly wiry strong man was now a dead ringer for Oliver Hardy. He wasn't near as jovial, though, and Jack was certainly no Stan Laurel. "Hey, yourself," she said back to him. Lou glanced anxiously at Jack, who grunted but said nothing. Forrestina sat down in the newly-opened space between the two men.

"So what are you two cooking up?" she asked, looking sternly first at one man and then the other. "You may as well come clean with it so I can start the hollering."

"Shoot, Red, there's no need for hollering," Lou said, trying to cover his apprehension with a laugh. For a man who'd once made his living fighting, he was surprisingly timid, and he seemed particularly scared of Forrestina and her fiery temper.

Forrestina narrowed her eyes at him and watched as he swallowed hard. "Well," he began haltingly, "you know how good the moonshine business is going, right?"

Forrestina nodded, keeping her eyes fixed on him, pinning him like a bug on a needle. She still felt a mite uneasy about the illegal still, but honestly, she could hardly spit in the woods in Arkansas and not hit somebody's moonshine operation. Rather than stopping the public from drinking, prohibition had merely created more entrepreneurs, stealthy distillers, and law men who were more than happy to look the other way for a few bucks payoff a month and a bottle of the spirits now and again. "Yeah, it's going all right," she said cautiously, waiting for the other shoe to drop.

"It's going more than all right," Lou exclaimed. He reached frantically into an inner pocket in his jacket and pulled out a wad of bills. He thrust them towards her face. "Lookie here, Red," he said. "This is just this month's takings!"

She ignored the money and turned her body from him. "Okay," she said to Jack, who was busy studying the dusky sky. "Business is good. So?"

"So the hardest part about the moonshine business is delivering to customers," Jack drawled, dropping his gaze to meet hers. "It's also the riskiest part—if we sell out in the open, we may come across a cop who's not part of the deal and then it's off to the pokey for us. If we *don't* deliver in a more public area, we end up not selling as much—no one wants to drive out all this way just for a few bottles of hooch."

"You've got this nice, big piece of property, here, see?" Lou interjected eagerly. "Whole parts of it that aren't even used up. Parts that could be cleared to boost your firewood business." His eyes in the darkening gloom of a fall twilight had all but disappeared in the cinnamon-bun folds of his face.

Forrestina realized with a jolt what they were planning. "You want to build a dance-hall," she said dully.

"We want to build a dance-hall," Jack agreed, his tone neutral. Forrestina figured he must be saving his energy for the coming squabble when they were alone, and she was good goshdarned if she'd hold her tongue like a meek kitten. If he wanted a fight, he'd get one right now.

"No," she said.

Lou blinked slowly, stupidly. "No?" He looked at Jack, bewildered. "No, Jack?"

Jack set his hands on his knees and hitched himself up ponderously, then he casually reached down and dragged Forrestina to her feet by one arm. She tried to pull away but he held her fast, his steely grip burrowing into her flesh. "Lou," he said, "you will have to excuse us, please. Red and I need to have a private conversation."

Lou jumped to his feet, in his haste almost falling over the log he'd been sitting on. "Sure, sure," he said. "No problem. I've got some stuff I need to talk to my corn man about." He hurried off, casting a quick worried glance behind him as his short legs moved him rapidly away.

Forrestina wrenched her arm from Jack's hand, and this time he let her go. "What the hell, Jack?" she asked, furious. "I'm all for making a few bucks, but I only put up with the moonshine business because it's a way to pay off our land. You told me once we were in the clear on our debt, the still would be closed— we'd put our money into making this a real community for the wintering carnival and circus folks, with enough left over so we could shut down and run our games in the summer. Now you want to make the liquor business *permanent?*" She balled her fist. She wanted to punch Jack in the nose, see him bleed. How could he not see that a dance hall was another chain to bind her to one spot?

Jack leaned over her and said quietly, in a menacing tone he'd never used on her before, "Keep it down, Red. Let's go for a walk down by the river, then you can yowl and screech to your heart's content." He strode in the direction of the water without looking back to see if she was following. Shaking with rage, she stomped after him. Jack kept his long pace and she had to trot to keep up, panting with the effort, neither one of them speaking.

Finally, once they were well clear of the campsite, Jack stopped and turned to face her, his hands shoved in his pants pockets. "Now," he said, "before you commence your hollering, let me explain some things to you. Prohibition is on its way out. People are tired of sneaking around trying to find a place to drink, and while he himself doesn't imbibe, our good president Coolidge doesn't cotton much to telling free Americans what they can and cannot pour down their throats. In the big cities, the cops and politicians are tired of watching the mob bosses get rich off liquor and not being able to stop them. Everybody can see that this no-drinking thing hasn't worked—nothing was fixed by banning liquor, and some things were made much worse."

He rubbed his bristly beard, the rusty-brown now threaded with streaks of grey. Being three years shy of fifty was starting to show on his face. "I know you're not crazy about how rowdy folks get when they're drinking, but for Pete's sake, Red, you've lived the circus and carnival life for a long time— you know this is how it is with us." His voice dropped, becoming gentle and a little wistful. "I heard someone say once that carnies are the ghost people, drifting in and out of this world, breaking rules and owning our damnation with a tip of the hat and a greasy grin. This here is our ghost kingdom, and now me and you have a chance to reign over a little corner of it."

Forrestina struggled to answer him. She understood what he was saying but he didn't know about Max, about what Max had done. She'd never told him. Oh, he knew that she'd been married, of course, and that she'd lost a baby and could never have any more, but those were just facts she'd related to him as if she were talking about the capital of Iowa or the outrageous cost of coffee. He didn't know about Max's drinking and whoring and cruelty—in truth, he had his own past he didn't ever discuss, and they were happy to just let those old parts of their lives lie. What was done, was done—the past didn't matter. Now she saw that she'd been fooling herself. An aching, rotten tooth ignored would eventually stop hurting—for a while. But left long enough that rotten tooth would flare up and take over a person's head with pain until it was dealt with. The throb of worry that Jack would turn into Max was becoming more and more intense, and Forrestina didn't think she could bear the pain if the worry turned into reality.

"Look," Jack said, his voice still gentle. He held out a hand to her, and after a hard minute, she took it. "I know you've got doubts. But honey, this is our chance to make hay while the sun is shining. Who knows what tomorrow will bring?" He drew her to him, folding her in his big embrace. "We'll be careful. We'll start small—just a little sugar shack on the upper part of our property, where that thicket is close and hard to see." He sighed pensively. "With our store and our dance-hall and our camp, we can put money back and think about building a *real* house." Forrestina lifted her head and looked up at him, startled. He laughed. "Yeah, ol' Jack is getting tired of the road," he said. "I'm ready to stay in one place for a while, and Arkansas suits me fine. What do you think? Are you ready to make an honest man outta me?"

A line from Charles Dickens's *A Christmas Carol* suddenly floated into her mind: "I wear the chain I forged in life. I made it link by link, and yard by yard; I girded it on of my own free will, and of my own free will I wore it." *My own free will,* she thought. *Chains forged by love.* She shoved Jack away. "Get stuffed, Jack Campbell," she said, bending over to close her fingers around a lump of river mud. "Ain't no woman in her right mind going to marry you."

"Thank God you're not in your right mind then," Jack said, laughing, dodging the clod of dirt suddenly hurtling towards his head.

They were married a few days later in a small, unofficial ceremony held at the campsite. The wedding was officiated by a carnie named Holy Mike who claimed to be a real minister when he wasn't fleecing rubes at cards. Forrestina had her doubts about how holy he was—she'd seen many a female traipsing in and out of his caravan every night—and as to whether or not he was an ordained minister, she just didn't care. As far as she was concerned, a bond between a man and a woman was something they promised each other and their God—it didn't matter a hoot to her whether or not it was deemed "legal" by the State of Arkansas. Forrestina and Jack's carnival family, along with the newcomers from Amos's stable (Ruby had been joined by Margie and Kitty, two more girls stolen away from Maestro), clapped wildly and cheered when Jack kissed his bride and then announced to them all, "This here is Mrs. Forrestina 'White River Red' Campbell, folks—and ain't she the prettiest gal you've ever seen?"

After their boisterous agreement, most of the carnies spent the rest of the night sampling Lou's latest batch of moonshine for free, going rapidly from noisy drunks to passed-out drunks. As Forrestina picked her way around the bodies of her friends sprawled out on the wooden picnic tables Jack had set up around the camping area, she smiled. It was as fine a wedding as any.

A week later they began construction on the dance hall, Jack driving over to the lumber yard and coming home with loads of building material in the pick-up, Forrestina busy keeping the shop going. She told Jack she wanted to come by and see the progress, but he wouldn't hear of it. "Wait until it's done," he said. "I want it to be a surprise."

"For goodness sake, Jack," said Forrestina, exasperated. She hated surprises and he knew it. After a couple of months, however, Jack popped into the shop, flipped the cardboard "Open" sign in the front door over to "Closed," and said, "Lock 'er up, Red. It's time for the grand reveal."

Forrestina didn't need to be told twice. Once she'd resigned herself to the idea of a dance hall, she'd actually started to look forward to it. She imagined most of the folk there would be carnies and circus people, and she did love a good party, even if she didn't drink. This, she hoped, would be like a good party every night. She followed Jack outside, pausing to lock the store door before hopping into the truck. They took off towards camp and then continued past the campground on a new, roughly hewn road for about a mile, winding their way at an angle down closer to the river. Forrestina glimpsed a new clearing in what had previously been a densely forested thicket, and she soon spied a metal splash of tin roofing shining through the trees.

Jack reached his big hand over and covered her face above her nose. "Don't peek," he said.

Obediently she closed her eyes, and after a few minutes she felt the truck jerk to a stop. Keeping her eyes squeezed shut, she heard Jack open his door and then hurry around to open hers, all the while hollering, "Keep 'em closed, now. Don't you look!" He took her elbow and carefully guided her out of the truck, led her forward a few steps, then turned her slightly to the left. "Okay," he said, "go ahead. Open 'em up."

Forrestina blinked against the sudden light. As her vision cleared, she saw that she was standing a few feet from a rectangular, almost barn-like building, wood-planked walls left in their natural unvarnished, knotted state, a bright-green corrugated angled tin roof set high and proud from the walls. The building blended in with the trees around it, a nice little hidey-hole in the woods. There were two short steps that led up to the small porch, which stretched along the front of the building and was protected by a waist-high wooden rail. The front door had been painted a bright cornflower blue. Forrestina turned to smile at Jack, who was grinning from ear to ear. "The door is blue," she exclaimed. "You *do* listen to me when I talk sometimes."

Jack nodded. "Well, of course I do, woman," he said. "You told me blue doors are lucky, and I figured we need all the luck we can get." He pointed up. "But you haven't even noticed the best part," he said.

Forrestina's eyes tracked his finger. When she saw what he was so gleeful about, she socked him hard in the arm.

"Jack, you damn rascal," she cried. He started to guffaw, rubbing his sore arm, and after a minute, she began laughing too. Above the door, a long plank, painted white, bore the name of the dance hall: "White River Red's Pleasure Palace."

"'Pleasure Palace,' indeed," she said. "Honestly, Jack—it sounds like a whore-house."

Jack slipped an arm around her waist. "Then allow me to be the first to call you 'Madam,' Madam," he said. "Come on—I can't wait for you to see the inside."

Together they climbed the steps. Inside, the building was cavernous and empty, a wooden floor stretching out before them, just waiting for dancers to fill it. Along the sides of the hall, ten round wooden tables had been set up— five on each side—and metal folding chairs were tucked around them. White cotton tablecloths were set on the tables, along with pint mason jars holding thick short candles. Kerosene lamps had been strung high on the long side walls, and at the very end of the hall stood an upraised wooden stage. Jack led Forrestina to it. "This here is where the band can play," he said proudly.

"What band?"

"Any band who wants to, I guess."

Forrestina liked this—many carnies were very musical, carrying their drums and trumpets and guitars and fiddles with them everywhere they went. Music seemed to flow wherever they were; it would be good to have somewhere for the various talents to join up and share their songs. And many of them could sing, too—why, Ruby had the sweet voice of a song-bird. Forrestina wandered along the stage and then down the steps to the bar set up on the left. It was a long box, open on the back side that joined the wall. It had a shiny varnished wooden counter, which was stacked with clean glasses and bowls for peanuts. Forrestina opened the squat hinged square door on the short right side of the box and entered the open space. She squatted down to examine the interior of the bar—tall bottles of moonshine were set into the built-in shelves. It looked to her like it was all Lou's hooch, which was probably for the best—not having to involve another alcohol provider was safest. She straightened back up and saw Jack watching her, waiting for a reaction. She slipped out from behind the bar and walked over to him, hands on her hips, her lips pursed.

"Well," Jack asked, a mite anxiously, "what do you think?"

She leapt up and threw her arms around his broad neck, kissing him full on the mouth. "It's grand, Jack. You and the boys did a great job."

Jack pulled her tighter to him. "I'm glad you like it," he said. He began to hum and sway, and suddenly Forrestina found herself being spun around the dance floor. They twirled about wildly for several minutes, with only Jack's humming for music. Finally, out of breath, Forrestina pulled away and stumbled over to one of the seats, where she collapsed, laughing.

"Enough," she said, holding up a hand. "I'm not as young as I once was." She eyed Jack, whose forehead and cheeks above his beard were red from exertion. "Come to think of it, neither are you, old man."

Jack pulled out one of the chairs next to her and plonked himself down. "I *am* old," he said. He waggled his bushy eyebrows at her. "That's why I married me a woman eleven years my junior. So she can change my old-man diapers when need be."

"I'll just knock you in the head and roll you into that river," Forrestina said. "Put you out of your misery."

After catching her breath, she stood up and wandered around the room, taking it all in. *What a strange ride, life*, she thought. Here she was, a formerly good Catholic woman who didn't enjoy drinking, and there her name was above the door of an illegal bar. She turned to Jack and held out both hands to him. He took them, and she tugged at him, driving her heels in with the effort of pulling him upright. "Come on, then," she said. "Let's commence offering some pleasure in this here palace of mine."

CHAPTER SIXTEEN

Fayetteville, 1972

"SO JACK WAS GOOD TO YOU?" Betty asked. It was a purely subjective, not entirely professional question, she knew, but the truth was she'd stopped seeing Forrestina as just a news story a long time ago. The weeks flew by, and when Betty wasn't sitting with her new acquaintance, she was thinking of her. She found herself impatiently hurrying through her other assignments at the paper—Little League reports, shop openings, festival details, and of course, obituaries—so that she could pore over her notes. Forrestina was a difficult person to read—on the one hand very open and direct, answering Betty's questions without hesitation or diplomacy, yet on the other hand, Betty sensed she held a lot back—the *emotion* behind her stories. If Betty got too close to a particularly painful subject, Forrestina's face closed up like a Slinky on the bottom of the stairs. Anything to do with Max or the baby she'd lost she'd relate in flat tones, as if she were merely reciting "The Rime of the Ancient Mariner." Now, when Betty asked her question about Jack, she saw the curled wires that had been cheerfully extending recoil suddenly, and she knew they were in choppy waters again. When Forrestina didn't answer for a full twenty seconds, Betty prompted softly, "Ms. Campbell?"

She'd been studying her hands intently, but when she looked up, Betty was startled by the tears in her eyes. Betty reached out to her tentatively and was relieved that she let her place her hands on the again balled-up fists, which lay knotted in her denim lap.

"Ms. Forrestina, we don't have to talk about this right now if you don't want," Betty said. She knew that letting her off the hook now might be a colossal mistake—if she struck while Forrestina was so obviously vulnerable, she might get a rare glimpse past that armadillo shell of hers, but purposefully hurting her was out of the question. Betty had realized that the story had ceased to be as important as the person. There was no question that she was smitten by this old feisty gal. She was all the things Betty had always longed to be but was not yet. Betty liked to imagine herself as a modern woman, a career gal, a mild feminist, but she knew deep down that she was not brave enough to be a true pioneer; convention and timidity always stopped her short. It had taken far too long for her to work up the courage to demand a better gig at the paper, and even now, she let Murray pile work on her that he'd never expect from her male colleagues. She'd endured the butt-pats and the "honeys" from fellow male reporters, not wanting to make a fuss or be seen as a hysterical female, all the while gritting her teeth, convincing herself that they meant no harm, that it was just the way they were. "Boys will be boys," as the old cliché went . . . so why did putting up with those boys always make her feel so small and helpless?

After spending more and more time with Forrestina, Betty began to change her mind on what she was willing to put up with. The next time Don, the paper's sportswriter, smacked her tush as she passed by, Betty channeled her inner-Forrestina. In as cold and carrying a voice as she could muster, she said, "Don, if you touch any part of me ever again, you will be pulling back bloody stumps." She lifted her voice and looked around the room. "And that goes for all you other putzes in this office." Her heart was pounding—she'd always hated confrontation—but she made herself lean right down into Don's former-high-school-football-champ face and say, "Do you understand me, you Neanderthal? Hands. Off."

The clattering of typewriters suddenly ceased. All eyes turned towards them as Don pulled away from Betty like she was a blazing torch. "Geez, lighten up, Betty," he stammered, a flush taking over his face.

"I mean it," Betty told him. "Treat me as if I was your sister. That is, unless you are in the habit of grabbing her butt, too." That brought on laughter around the room. As Betty walked back to her cubicle, her chin lifted and her head held high, she glimpsed her boss watching her from his doorway. He gave her a solemn nod, and Betty nodded back, feeling as if she'd gained a tiny inch of the respect she'd been desperately clawing for. She couldn't wait to share her triumph with Forrestina, giddy in anticipation of the praise she knew would be heaped on her for standing up for herself. Yet when she next met Forrestina and asked her about Jack, the old woman began to blink back tears, and Betty forgot her tale of victory.

Forrestina answered her question slowly. "Was Jack good to me?" Her voice became mournful and lost, like a fairy-tale foundling in a forest, and it occurred to Betty that maybe she didn't want to see the bare pads of her hero's feet of clay, after all. She rose hurriedly, but before she could take the coward's way out, Forrestina turned her hands over so that they were gripping Betty's tightly, and the young woman sat back down.

"What you need to know about Jack is this," Forrestina said, in that quiet, dreadful voice, "he didn't know how to love me when the drink completely took him over, and I didn't know how to love him enough to bring him back from the drink." Up went the rim of her hat as her restless fingers raked at her hair. She gazed beyond Betty, her eyes distant, searching for a past Betty could not see. "Are you sure you want this?" she asked. "It's a long, sour tale with no happy ending, little Betty."

Betty sensed the past Forrestina had been fearfully looking for over Betty's shoulder move forward, impatient to take shape, and knew that there was only one answer she could give; she'd walked in the shadows with Forrestina before and there was no turning back. Steeling herself, she extracted her hands and flipped her notebook back open. "I'm ready," she said, gripping her pen so tightly that her fingers turned a bloodless white. "Go ahead."

CHAPTER SEVENTEEN

The River Years, 1935

AS FORRESTINA SWEPT UP THE BEER bottles and cigarette butts strewn on the wooden floor of White River Red's (mercifully she'd talked Jack into dropping the "Pleasure Palace" part), a sudden drowsy breeze, fragrant with the smell of the honeysuckle that grew in great tangles in the woods along the bank, drifted across the White River, bringing with it some much-needed relief from the oppressive June heat. She stopped for a moment to appreciate the air, lifting the coiled braid of hair she wore down her back, letting the coolness kiss her neck. It had been a busy evening, as usual; since the dissolution of Prohibition, their bar was packed almost every night. Lou had long since broken down his still and moved on; now that liquor was legal again, people wanted to drink more than corn whiskey. It didn't seem to matter that the country was in what the newspapers called "The Great Depression"—the folks who came out to White River Red's bar always managed to find money for a drink and a dance or two, and the reason for that was simple: most of their regular custom was still carnie and circus folk, who, because of their suspicion of banks, hadn't been affected at all by the crash on Wall Street. Forrestina herself had never put a single dime in a bank account, choosing instead to hide her money at home in a locked metal box hidden beneath her sweaters in a low wooden chest-of-drawers.

She'd worried that the Depression might hurt the carnival business (and in turn, hurt her own), but so far it hadn't. She supposed people needed an escape from their fears, and the hope of scoring big on a gamble, or watching half-naked girls in a tent, or even stuffing their faces with carnival junk-food, was a temporary antidote for the bleakness of real life. After a visit to the carnival, many of those same rubes found themselves at her bar, drinking what was left of their money, washing their problems and worries away in a flood of amber spirits. While Forrestina welcomed them all, carnie or rube (in this economy, how could she not?), too many strangers made her uneasy. She was looking forward to the winter season, when the campground would be filled with familiar faces again and the rubes would stay safely tucked away in their own homes in town.

She stood in the doorway and leaned against her broom, listening to the cacophony of sound that is nighttime in the South. Katydids and crickets screeched at each other, so high-pitched, they made a body's eyes water, and frogs from the river chirred their unearthly laughter. Somewhere close by, an amorous whippoorwill pleaded into the dark, trying to entice a mate. Forrestina thought that those poets who wrote about the peace and quiet of the night must be Yankees, because nocturnal silence did not exist where she lived, even when all creatures of the human variety were fast asleep.

She too longed to be asleep in her bed, but somebody had to clean up this mess—Jack had sampled a few too many types of drink in their bar as usual and was passed out below the stage, his back against the wooden steps, his shaggy head thrown back as he snored like a buzz-saw. Forrestina sighed. His drinking had gotten worse, and with it, his temper. As she'd feared, her sweet, gentle, funny bear of a man was a mean drunk. Of *course* he was; mean drunks were her lot in life, it seemed. God help her. *God helps those who help themselves*, her mother's smug voice said in her mind. It occurred to her that maybe it was time for her to help herself out the door, hit the road with her rats, work a circuit up towards Illinois so she could see Sarah more. Instead of being the one left, she could be the one leaving this time.

"Ms. Red?" Her thoughts were interrupted by a tentative male voice calling to her from the darkness outside. It was Theo Johnson, a slender, meek-mannered young townie who'd lately taken to hanging out at their dance hall on a regular basis. He was much too green for their place—hell, he wasn't twenty if he was a day—but his wife, a loud-mouthed, trashy, bleach-blond gal fifteen years his senior, dragged him there with her. Night after night, the graceless Mrs. Johnson would set Theo in the corner with a beer and then ignore him for the rest of the evening while she danced with every man in the place who'd have her. She was shameless, pressing herself against her partners, laughing loudly as she shimmied and slid, her butt squeezed into skin-tight skirts and looking every bit like two fat slabs of pork-back stuffed in sausage casings. And all the while, Theo just watched her sadly, his one beer lasting him all night.

Lately Forrestina had noticed that Mrs. Johnson spent a lot of time wiggling at Jack, and Jack was happy to oblige her, spinning her around the room, pulling her close, his big hands agreeably taking her up on what she was offering. There'd been a time when such a sight would've made Forrestina gnash her teeth with rage, and she would've come roaring across the floor, ready to slap cheeks and pull hair, but that time had long passed. Now she just felt tired—too tired to fight, too tired to care. About Jack anyway.

She found herself sympathizing with Theo, though, whose miserable expression she'd glimpsed while he watched her man rubbing himself all over Theo's woman. She recognized his misery, knew it as well as she knew her own face, and she hurt for him. He was so damned young. She wanted to tell him to just leave—leave the bar, leave his wife, get out and start again, make better choices the next time—but who was she to give such advice? All her troubles had been caused by her misjudged taste in men.

"Theo?" she answered him now, stepping out onto the porch. "What are you doing back here? Bar is closed."

"I know," Theo replied. He moved into the wide band of light pouring through the bar's open door, and Forrestina could see his defined Adam's apple bob as he swallowed hard. Obviously something was weighing heavy on his mind. After a minute he looked up, the light hitting the reflections of his round glasses and giving him tiny yellow moons for eyes. "I wondered if my Mitzy," he stopped, swallowed again. "I wondered if Jack and Mitzy. . ." He pulled his newsboy cap from his head and twisted it in his hands. "Well, you see, I left early, you know, and Mitzy's still not home." He dropped his gaze, the twin moons on his face disappearing. "I'm just worried about her, is all," he said to the dusty ground.

Forrestina knew full well the agony of lying in an empty marital bed, tossing and turning, imagining the worst, and the worst not always being the death of the beloved. Gently she said, "I don't know where Mitzy is, Theo, but she's not with Jack. He's inside alone, sleeping it off. You can check for yourself if you want."

"Oh, that's okay," Theo said hurriedly, holding his palms out to her. "I don't need to—if you say so, I believe you. I'm sorry I bothered you—you must think me such a dope."

"Not at all," Forrestina said. "I think you're a good man who's anxious about his wife. I'm sure she'll be home soon—heck, she's probably there already. You should just go on and get some rest."

He nodded, the two yellow moons bobbing up and down on his cheeks. "Sure," he said. Without another word, he turned and melted into the noisy dark.

Forrestina stood on the porch, watching the space where he'd been for a long time, and when Jack woke at noon the next day, she was waiting. She jabbed her finger in his face. "I want you to leave Mitzy Johnson alone," she said.

Jack groaned, using the wall to pull himself to standing. He rubbed his head. "Satan's bells, woman," he growled. "Lower your voice. My head is pounding stakes."

"Good!" Forrestina shouted. She moved her finger from his face to jab at his chest. "Serves you right, you no-good, philandering drunk. What do you think you're doing, carrying on the way you do? You're an old fool if you think Mitzy is interested in anything but free drinks from you."

Jack brushed her finger away. "Go to hell, Red," he said wearily. "You're the one who pushed me out of our bed, so don't be complaining when others welcome me into theirs. A man's got needs."

155

"Oh, right," she retorted. "This is all my fault." She shook her head in disgust. "It doesn't have anything to do with your mistress, Gin."

"Yeah, yeah," Jack muttered, flapping one big hand at her. "Change the dang record, will ya?" He pushed himself off the wall with effort, then stumbled out of the bar, wincing and holding his left palm up to block the slab of white-hot sunlight assaulting his face. As he staggered away, he called over his shoulder, "And Red, I've told you before: you ain't my mother. If you don't like me the way I am now, you can just skedaddle on down the road."

Okay, then, Forrestina thought, *God helps those who help themselves*. Jack would have to cough up her share of the bar and store when she left, though—she sure as heck wasn't going back out on the road empty-handed. Since Jack spent most of his time now either drunk or hungover, the lion's share of the work in running the store, the camp, and the infernal bar had fallen to her, and she was damned if she wasn't taking what was owed her when she left.

She and Jack avoided each other all day, but that night, Jack made a point of seeking Mitzy out. He'd been drinking steadily for hours and was good and sauced. "Beat it, shrimp," he said to Theo as he pushed the younger man out of his way roughly. "I feel like dancing with your wife." He took a swig of beer in the bottle he held in one hand, then wrapped his other arm around Mitzy's bare shoulders. "Red told me to leave you alone," he slurred, leaning into her face confidingly. "But she can't boss me because I'm a man." He straightened up and shouted in Forrestina's direction, "Hear that, Red? I'm a man!" He turned back to Mitzy. "I'm a man," he repeated dully.

"You sure are, honey," Mitzy soothed, smiling at him broadly, showing a mouthful of long yellow teeth streaked with the fuchsia lipstick she wore on her thin lips.

Forrestina ignored them both, busying herself behind the counter, washing the sticky wood with a pale yellow sponge, refilling peanut bowls. Jack gestured at Theo with the beer bottle and said, "I'm not like this pipsqueak you're married to, Mitzy." He bent over and now put his florid face in Theo's. "Hear me,

Pipsqueak? I said I'm gonna dance with your wife now. You got a problem with that?"

Theo flushed and studied the tips of his mirror-shiny black leather shoes. He didn't say a word.

"I didn't think so," Jack scoffed. He thrust his half-empty bottle forward. "Hold my drink," he told Theo, then led Mitzy to the dance floor.

As soon as Jack and Mitzy started dancing, Forrestina left the bar and walked over to where Theo stood. He was watching the pair in bleak silence, still obediently clutching Jack's beer bottle. She took it gently from his hand, replacing it wordlessly with a shot glass brimming with whisky. He stared at the glass blankly, as if wondering how it had gotten there, then looked up at her, his dull brown eyes pools of despair.

"Go on, drink up," Forrestina said. "You need it."

He considered the glass for a moment, then knocked the alcohol back with one swallow. Immediately his face turned rhubarb pink and he began to cough and sputter.

Jack, who'd been keeping an eye on them, crowed loudly, raising his voice so that he could be heard throughout the bar, "Ha! What a surprise that candy-ass Teddy can't hold his liquor. Red, you shoulda given him a glass of milk."

In Jack's arms, Mitzy giggled in that crow-caw, grating way she had. "He is a baby," she said. "Poor *little* Theo." As she emphasized the word "little," she held her index finger and thumb apart about an inch.

"Little, huh," Jack asked. He let go of Mitzy and held his arms out wide, his closed fingers pointed forward, his palms facing each other. "That ain't a problem you'll find with old Jack," he said, and Mitzy threw her head back, cackling.

In a quavering voice, Theo said, "Mitzy, I think it's time we went home now, don't you?" Forrestina could tell he was trying hard to be brave, and all at once she pictured what he must've looked like as a small boy, squaring his shoulders, clenching his fists, his hair slicked down and parted carefully in the middle. This was a man who knew something about being bullied, all right.

Jack put his arms back around Mitzy and moved his hands to her fat bottom. "Mitzy ain't going nowhere, *The-o-dore*," he said. "Are you, honey?" He squeezed hard, causing Mitzy to purr out some cat-in-heat assent.

Theo blanched, and Forrestina was suddenly very afraid he would start to cry. If he did that, Jack would never let him leave without a beating—he'd be on the young man like a crocodile scenting blood. "For God's sake, Jack, knock it off," she said. She glanced at Theo, whose face had started to crumple, then back at the stumbling pair in front of her. She had to deflect Jack's attention, and fast. She strode forward to Mitzy, who was taller than her by a good four inches, and said, "Mitzy, kindly remove your flabby rear from my husband's hand." Before the woman could respond, Forrestina reached up and grabbed a handful of brassy, over-sprayed hair. She pulled straight down, and Mitzy stooped over, hollering, "Ow! Ow! Turn loose!"

Forrestina ignored her squawks, tugging her along by her hair until they reached the front door, which had been propped open to let in some fresh air. Many of the people inside the bar, who'd stopped dancing and talking when Forrestina grabbed Mitzy, followed behind, enjoying the spectacle. Once outside, Forrestina deftly freed herself from Mitzy's hair and shoved at the woman's forehead with the heel of her palm, causing Mitzy to stumble down the stairs backwards. Mitzy lost her balance on the last step, pin-wheeling her arms desperately, then she fell on her bottom into the dirt.

Forrestina dusted her palms together. "There," she said, satisfied. "Good riddance to bad rubbish."

Mitzy sat in the dirt yowling like a screech-frog, her legs stuck out in front of her. A few patrons—mainly women, Forrestina noted—applauded, calling, "Atta girl, Red. You showed that floozy who's boss." She nodded her thanks to them, then as she turned to go back into the bar, she was startled by a crashing noise. She pushed past several people just in time to see Jack pick

Theo up and throw him against the wall. The slight man's glasses were broken and hung at an angle on his nose, which was bleeding profusely. Jack punched him in the gut and then the side, and Forrestina heard a sickening crunch that could only be a rib or two breaking.

She ran forward and threw herself in front of Theo, stopping Jack mid-punch. "You son-of-a-bitch!" she yelled at him, furious. "You want to hit him again, you gotta do it through me. Look at you, big man, picking on someone half your size! Impress us all, why don't you? Hit a woman now—maybe we can find a toddler for you to smack around next, and a puppy for you to kick for good measure!"

Jack stood with his right fist cocked back. "Get out of the way, Red," he snarled. "You've already shamed me enough. Why do you care so much about this little twerp, huh? You running around on me with him? You plan on getting rid of old Jack and setting up house with a little boy you can boss around? By God, he's going to get what's coming to him, and then I'll deal with you." His eyes, bloodshot with whiskey, were as wild and dangerous as a rabid wolf's. *He just might kill him,* she thought, horror like acid creeping into her throat. *He might beat the kid to death.*

She reached her arms out towards her husband. "Jack, come on. Think about what you're doing," she said, trying desperately to calm him down. "You've said your piece. You've made your point. Why don't you go on home and sleep it off?"

Jack stared at her for a moment, his eyes still bleary with drink and rage, then he dropped his hand. He half-turned away, and Forrestina let out the breath she'd been holding.

"It's okay, Theo," she said to the trembling, bleeding man sprawled on the floor behind her, and before she could say anything else, Jack turned back, quick as a rattler, and crashed his fist into her face. She heard, more than felt, her nose break, and a warm gush of sudden blood coated her lips and chin, bringing with it the taste of old pennies. Explosions of blue, white, and red, firecrackers of pain, took over her eyesight, and she crumpled to her knees. Distantly she heard screams and Jack thundering incomprehensibly like a Spanish bull. She groped a hand out to him and her fingers snagged the pistol he wore slung around his waist. She pulled it free of its holster, shaking her head, trying to clear her vision. It felt as if she were swimming with her eyes open through muddy red waters. She dropped the gun and heard it clatter as it hit the ground and slid away.

Jack punched her again, this time hitting her square in her stomach. She doubled over, unable to catch her breath, then fell to the floor. From this position, she could see that Theo was also still on the ground, scrabbling along behind Jack on his hands and knees. He reached for the pistol she'd dropped, grabbed it, then stood, holding it with the barrel pointed at Jack. His hands were shaking. She opened her mouth to shout—what, exactly? Stop? Watch out? Shoot him? Jack caught her expression and turned to see the quivering man with the gun. He staggered a few steps forward as Theo backed up. Jack wiped his hand across his mouth. "What are you going to do with that, Pansy?" he asked, eyes glinting. He reached forward and Theo leveled the gun at him. Jack laughed. "Boy, put that thing down," he said. He sounded unconcerned, almost pleasant, as if he were giving a kindly piece of fatherly advice. "You're going to shoot your own fool foot off. Give it here, now."

Theo, pale-faced and still trembling, continued to hold the gun out, his finger on the trigger. He flicked his gaze down to where Forrestina lay curled up in a ball. Their eyes locked for a moment, and Forrestina knew that either Jack or this poor, bullied, sensitive kid was going to die tonight. Which one of them it should be was clear. She mouthed the word "safety" at him. Theo stared at her blankly for a moment, then understanding lit up his eyes. He clicked the safety latch off with his thumb.

Jack growled, "You little sissy, I'm going to beat your head into a pulp and feed your body to the river bass." He charged, and Theo closed his eyes and pulled the trigger. Jack's body stopped its forward motion. He swayed, taking a few unsteady steps. A small dark hole in his forehead began first to smoke, and then to bleed. He went down without a word, crashing forward onto the floor like a giant oak. The back of his head was a splayed mess of blood and bone and brains, a spongey open flower of tissue.

Theo dropped the gun and sat down hard on his butt, his legs crossed in front of him, swami-style. Forrestina got to her feet unsteadily, still doubled up from the punch to her gut. She tottered over to where Theo was slumped. Tears were rolling down his thin cheeks, and he wouldn't look at her.

"It's all right," she told him. "It's all right, Theo." She picked the gun up from the floor beside him. "Shush, now." She stashed the gun in her skirt pocket, then looked around at the cluster of people all silently watching her. She pointed at Amos, who was standing on the edge of the crowd. "Amos," she said, "would you please go on out to the highway and grab the sheriff? Tell him that Jack has been shot by Theo Johnson, but that it was with Jack's own gun and it was in self-defense." She regarded the others with a steely gaze. "That's how I saw it, anyway. Anyone see anything different?"

She turned and looked pointedly at Mitzy, who'd come back in when she'd heard the shot and was sobbing noisily in the doorway. Mitzy sniffed and shook her head, her eyes cast down, and Forrestina relaxed. Mitzy was a whore, for sure, but she wasn't a fool. With Jack dead, what good would it do her to lose Theo to jail?

"Okay, then," Forrestina said. "Go on, Amos."

Amos nodded. "I'll be back as soon as I can rouse Sheriff Joe," he said. His eyes drifted to the huge collapsed figure of Jack. Blood pillowed the big man's face-down head. "Are you sure you're all right, Red? You want to come with me?" He looked at a rube standing on the sidelines and said, "Cover that up, will ya, buddy?"

"Sure thing," the rube, whose name was Brian, said. He tugged a white cloth from the nearest table and flung it over the body, where it settled in slow drifts, turning what once had been Jack into a cotton mountain on the floor.

"I'm okay, Amos," Forrestina said. She looked around the room. "Some of you need to give a statement to the Sheriff, corroborate my story, but not all of you. If any of you would rather not chat with the police, feel free to scram. Nobody's going to remember you were here."

That started a small stampede, with several people hurrying out the door—including, Forrestina noted sourly, Theo's cowardly wife, Mitzy. Soon only a half dozen people remained, including Ruby, who took Forrestina by the hand and led her to one of the metal folding chairs. Ruby found a bottle of whisky and two shot glasses and sat down at the table, pouring a finger of alcohol into each glass. She pushed one over to Forrestina. "Drink this, Red," she said. Automatically Forrestina shook her head, and Ruby said, "Oh, come on. I know you don't normally drink, but honey, this is one of those times that was *made* for drinking. Consider it medicine for your nerves." She thrust the glass forcefully into Forrestina's hand, and after a moment, Forrestina relented, throwing the drink back and gasping as she slammed the glass back onto the table.

Ruby smiled and refilled it. "Atta girl," she said. She lifted her own glass in a salute and downed the drink much more expertly. She set her glass down and reached over, gingerly touching Forrestina's face with her fingertips. "Good lord," she said. "Jack sure did a number on you, girl."

Forrestina winced and pulled away, not able to look at the hulk on the ground which had once been her husband. She supposed she should cry, but so far the tears hadn't even threatened to flow. Idly, she wondered why; Jack had been a mean old bastard when the drink was on him, to be sure, but he'd never hit her before, and it hadn't all been bad times. She closed her eyes and thought of a summer long ago when Jack had surprised her by picking a whole armful of Queen Anne's Lace, weeds to most people, and sticking them in empty mayonnaise jars all around their caravan. He'd gotten ahold of some powdered dye and filled the jars with colored water, and in just a few hours, those stately white wildflowers became splashes of the rainbow, nodding their now pink, blue, yellow, green, and violet heads regally in the breeze. Forrestina smiled, remembering how she'd laughed with pure delight when she opened the door and saw them, and how Jack's nut-brown eyes shone like new coins at the sound of her joy.

She squeezed the lids of her eyes tighter, trying to will some tears, but still nothing came. Giving up, she opened her eyes and spotted Theo still slumped on the floor, his head buried on his forearms, which he had propped on his upturned knees. A more miserable character she'd never seen. "Theo," she called. He wouldn't look up, so she sighed and said again, louder, more forcefully, "Theo! Attend to me, dang it!" This time he lifted his face and she saw tears running in steady streams down his cheeks. It seemed he was crying enough for the both of them. She leaned forward, one hand on the table, the other resting on her knee. In a kinder tone, she said, "Thank you."

Theo stared at her, dull-eyed and uncomprehending. She said it again. "I mean it—thank you. You defended yourself and tried to protect me. You're a hero, in my book."

"A hero?" Theo repeated slowly, his voice faint, wondering. His brow creased, as if he was trying to puzzle out what those two small words might mean.

Ruby glanced at Forrestina then took up the thread, moving from the table to kneel down beside the still-sniffling young man. She placed a hand on his shoulder. "Red's right, Theo," she said. "You and Red were the only ones in this whole place brave enough to stand up to old Jack." She swiveled around a little on her heel and addressed the half-dozen silent watchers who'd chosen to remain. "Ain't that right?" she called to them. "We all saw Jack beating the tar out of Theo, and he liked to kill Red." She pointed at Forrestina. "Just look at the state of her face! He said he was going to kill Theo, too. We all heard him say it, and ain't nobody here who doubts he meant it, right?"

"And that's what we're all going to tell the Sheriff, too," Forrestina said. She narrowed her eyes and let her gaze touch every face, one after the other, marking them, letting them know that she'd seen them and would remember.

She was rewarded by nods all around. Not a one of them there had any particular care for Jack; he'd lost most of his real friends long ago due to his bad temper and his too-easy fists. The people who'd stayed behind tonight were firmly on Forrestina's side, happy to finally be of some service to their Red, who'd they always liked a lot more than they'd liked Jack, and for good reason: she was good-natured, hard-working, and generous with both her resources and her smiles. Many of them had come back to their caravans or cabins at one point or another to find that she'd left a stack of wood or a bag of groceries for them when times were lean. If they could pay back her kindness in some small way, they were happy to do it.

Just then a paddy wagon came careening up the dirt road, blue lights flashing and sirens blaring. A moment later, Sheriff Joe, a rotund, sweaty little man, rolled in through the bar doors. He surveyed the crowd, resting his hand theatrically on the gun at his hip. "Okay, folks," he bellowed, "now what in the hell has happened here? Amos said something about Jack being killed?"

"Right over there, Sheriff," Ruby said from her place on the ground next to Theo, pointing.

Joe frowned. He strode over to the tablecloth-shrouded Jack, lifted a corner, and then hurriedly dropped it back, his pallor a sudden sickly pea-green shade. He took a deep breath, turning his back on the corpse deliberately. "Where's Red?" he asked.

Forrestina stood up from her chair and walked over. She smoothed her skirt with one hand, extending the other to Joe pleasantly. Courtesy caused him to take it and shake it before he remembered that he was here investigating a possible murder, not a tea party. He pulled away.

"So, Red," he said, clearing his throat, "why don't you tell me what happened? Amos said it was Theo what killed Jack?"

Theo, still sitting on the floor with his hands to his head, let out a pitiful groan, and Joe jumped back, half-pulling his gun from its holster. Forrestina stopped him with a gentle hand on his shoulder. "I think we've had enough guns for one night, Sheriff," she said quietly. She beckoned Joe to sit down at one of the tables and said to Ruby, "Ruby, dear, would you pour the Sheriff a cup of coffee? I keep some hot in a thermos under the bar for when someone needs help sobering up."

"Sure, Red," Ruby said, nodding. She gave Theo one more pat on his shoulder and then stood and ducked behind the bar. A few minutes later she returned with two steaming mugs, which she set in front of Joe and Forrestina.

"Thank you," Forrestina said. She took a long deliberate sip, and Joe, watching her closely, followed suit. He swallowed his coffee and then said, "Damn, Red. Did Jack do that to your face?"

She nodded. "You know his temper," she said.

Joe sighed. "I surely do," he said. "You know, I figured it was just a matter of time before either Jack killed someone or got himself killed." He took another sip of his coffee and then said apologetically, "Truth be told, I half expected it to be you, Red, one way or the other." His normally cheerful face drew in clouds. "It weren't right for him to hit a woman," he muttered. "It just weren't. 'Specially not a good woman like you." He smiled at her almost shyly. "I ain't never forgot how you kept me from breaking my old lady's heart that night, you know," he said. Forrestina returned his smile, remembering the time Joe had come in to the bar to celebrate his promotion to sheriff, and how later she'd guided him to their old empty caravan (which they'd moved to another site) to sleep it off so he wouldn't kill himself driving home to his new wife. "Our secret," she'd told him the next day, when he came wincing out of the caravan, shame-faced. She'd handed him a plate of bacon and eggs, a strong cup of coffee, and kept her promise.

"I appreciate that," Forrestina said now. She set her mug down. "I'll tell you all that happened, and you can ask these folks the truth of it—they witnessed the whole sorry affair." With that, she began her recitation of the night's events, leaving out the part where Jack had been antagonizing Theo by groping the younger man's wife. She figured that little tidbit gave Theo a less noble motive for the killing—plus Joe would want to talk to Mitzy, and she didn't trust that rattlesnake not to sell her own husband down the river. Forrestina finished her tale by saying, "I'm no expert in the law, of course, but to me and everybody here who saw it, it was a clear case of self-defense."

She touched her swollen eye and Joe cringed, the clouds on his face turning towards thunder. "I'm absolutely certain that Jack wanted to kill Theo, and once he'd done that, he would've probably finished the job he'd started on me," she said. She lowered her voice, and Joe had to lean in so he could hear her better. "Theo saved my life as well as his own," she whispered, allowing her voice to tremble slightly. It was the only lie she told that night, and she told it without hesitation: despite the beating, she never really believed that Jack would kill her. However, he certainly would've killed Theo, of that she had no doubt. To her, Theo's life, still stretched before him with promise, was worth more than hers and Jack's put together, so she didn't see the harm in adding a little something to strengthen the chance that he'd get to live that life.

Joe responded as she knew he would. He was, after all, a kind man with a soft heart, totally unsuited for his job, and he was clearly outraged that big, strong Jack would hit a helpless woman, so tiny in comparison to him. He patted her arm. "I am sorry, Ms. Red," he said. "What a mess. You deserved better." He turned to address the knot of people standing around. "You all corroborate what Red here has said?" he asked. "Theo did this in self-defense of himself and to save Red?"

Ruby spoke up, her voice clear and strong. "That's right, Sheriff," she said. "Jack was going to kill Red, and when Theo tried to stop him, he tried to kill Theo too. The kid didn't have a choice. That Jack was a vicious brute sometimes."

Joe stood and hitched his pants up under his ponderous belly. "Theo," he said to the man sitting hunched over on the floor, "I'm going to have to ask you to come along with me and give a statement at the jail-house. I don't figure the DA will want to keep you, but we have to dot them i's and cross them t's, you know." He gestured to a couple of men in the group. "Y'all help me load Jack into the back of the wagon," he said.

After Jack's body was stashed respectfully away, Joe helped Theo into the passenger seat of his car. Forrestina and the others followed behind. Through the open window, Theo turned to Forrestina, his eyes puffy with tears. "I'm so sorry, Ms. Red. So sorry," he murmured, over and over. She reached in and hugged his neck tight, then whispered in his ear, "You quit that bawling. You didn't do anything wrong. Make sure you tell them that and only that when you get to the station." She kissed him gently on the top of his head and said, still in a whisper, "You're a good man, Theo, and you don't deserve any grief over this. You sure don't deserve to spend your life in jail for a no-good dog like Jack. So knock it off. You want me to forgive you, you do what I say and tell them it was self-defense." She released him and he nodded, not looking at her.

As she watched them drive away, Forrestina thought with a pang that the sweet boy Theo had been just a few hours ago was most likely gone. He'd killed a human being, and that would change him forever, just as sure as death had changed Jack. "Damn-hell life," she muttered. Wearily she shooed the last remaining malingerers out of the door of the bar, thanking them for their help with the Sheriff, promising to let them know if she needed anything. She kissed Ruby, who was last, on the cheek, thanking her too, then turned and went alone into the bar, locking the door behind her. She snuffed out the lights and sat in the darkness near the bloody spot where Jack had died, and was relieved when the tears finally came pouring out of her. She railed aloud at the unfairness of it all, mourning the man Jack had not been for a long time, mourning her tarnished dreams. She beat at her chest, wailing, pulled at her hair, wept until her eyes were as dry as marbles and her throat was raw. Finally she just sat, exhausted, empty, her head drooping down, strands of her hair hanging in her face. She remained that way for the rest of the night, staring mutely at the dark spot on the floor. When dawn finally came knocking at the windows with its streaks of hopeful sunlight, she stood mechanically, rolled up her sleeves, and found a mop and a bucket. She began to clean up last night's mess, scrubbing the floor until it gleamed wetly in the early morning light, all traces of blood washed away. It was a new day and she still had a bar to run—*her* bar.

It was her dang name over the dang door, after all.

Chapter Eighteen

A Note inside a Package
To Mrs. Forrestina Bradley Campbell
White River Campsite
Arkansas

June 28, 1935

My dearest Forrestina,

I was so sorry to hear about your troubles and of the unfortunate passing of Jack. I know it is wrong to speak ill of the dead, so I will resist. I know that you told me in your telegram that you did not want me coming down because of my little ones, but I will jump on a train in a minute and make my way to your river, if that is what you need. My heart hurts for you, my sweet, sweet friend. I wanted so desperately to send something to you that would bring you comfort and let you know that you are loved, so I am sending my diamond earrings, which once belonged to my mother and grandmother, two women who also deserved more than they got. Wear them and know that like diamonds, you are a treasure that shines. You are in my prayers and in the prayers of my husband's whole congregation. That's a lot of folks talking to God about you, my dear. I hope you feel it.

Love and Wishes for a Brighter Future,

Sarah

CHAPTER NINETEEN

THREE AND A HALF MONTHS AFTER Forrestina planted Jack in the ground, a jury acquitted Theodore Martin Johnson of all charges, and he moved back north where he'd originally hailed from. He didn't take Mitzy with him. Where that trashy piece of bad luck ended up, Forrestina neither knew nor cared—Mrs. Johnson-that-was simply melted away like dirty snow, amen and hallelujah. For her part, Forrestina was wearily relieved when the trial was finally done; she was mighty tired of having to go into town to give her testimony over and over. Now it was all finished, she could finally try to get on with living. These last few months had hardened, fossilized her, her once delicate heart now encased in a thick protective bark, and she welcomed it. Not feeling anything was an asset, especially at the bar, which was more popular than ever. Having stepped into the realm of infamy, White River Red's was now the rough kind of place where a person may or may not get stabbed if he looked at someone the wrong way (and, the gossips reminded their listeners in breathless wonder, don't forget that one guy who was actually *killed*, right over there!). As a result of Jack's undignified death, the bar was filled night after night with people who wanted to walk on the wild side.

Forrestina didn't mind the nosy whispers and felt more than up to the job of maintaining peace. She carried Jack's pistol in the pocket of whatever skirt she was wearing each night, its heavy, deadly weight a reminder and strange comfort. It was as if Jack—the old Jack she'd loved—was still around to take care of her. He'd always insisted that she know how to load and shoot the thing, saying "This here is a harsh life I've asked you to live with me. I need to know you can take care of yourself if I'm not around." He would lead her out back in the woods and give her different targets to shoot at—a knot in a tree-trunk, a bit of paper nailed to a branch, a row of empty beer bottles set on a log, gleaming amber-brown in the sunlight. She remembered being so proud when she overheard him bragging to someone once that his old lady was a dead-eye every bit as good as Miss Annie Oakley. She wasn't, of course, but she was a pretty decent shot.

And of course, the gun was nice in case she needed to dissuade an overly-ambitious wooer. Now that she was a widow without Jack's menacing hulk shadowing her, she could hardly take a step without some man trying to convince her that he was the one who would love her (and her money) forever. It wasn't just the money they wanted, she had to admit to herself; she knew she was still attractive. Her hair was as apple red as ever, not faded or grey, and hard work had kept her lithe and slender. Though she was able to shrug the advances of her hopeful (usually drunk) would-be paramours off easily, she decided it wouldn't hurt to be extra careful in the way she presented herself to the public. Never one for flashy clothes anyway, she made sure to wear plain, sensible blouses and skirts and stolid, comfortable shoes. She left the sexy to her female patrons and worked on blending into the background like furniture, a wholly utilitarian servant-boss. She did allow herself two pieces of vanity, though: bright red Maybelline lipstick, which always made her feel like a glamorous movie star no matter how drab her dress, and Sarah's sparkling earrings, which she wore every day. She usually fashioned her hair in a bun or a pulled-back braid just so that she could catch a glimpse of her earrings shimmering in the dim windows of the bar. Seeing them brought her comfort, as Sarah had hoped they would—sparks of light in the darkness, just like her Sarah.

One night, late in September, after she'd chased the last drunk out the door with a broom and turned down the lights, she paused for a moment before turning to her nightly clean-up chores. Slipping out of her shoes, she sighed at the pure pleasure of freed feet. It was a hot, sticky, Indian-summer night, and she felt as if she might boil to death in the bar. She lifted her skirt up and pulled her stockings off, hopping from one foot to the other as she freed herself from the itchy nylons. She stuffed them into one of the deep pockets on her skirt and wandered out to the porch. The gift of an unexpected breeze cooled her bare skin, bringing with it the promise of fall. Sighing, she perched on the wide porch rail, pulling her knees to her chest like a girl, her skirt skimming her shins. There wasn't much more she asked for in life now—just a little peace, bare feet, and some cool air.

A rustling in the woods caught her attention. "Hello?" she called out into the night.

She didn't expect an answer and got none—the bar had been closed for an hour, after all. It was no doubt a possum or armadillo, those snuffling creatures who shunned the day and conducted their business at night. Just like her.

She padded back into the bar, her feet sticking to the floorboards where the more rowdy customers had slopped their drinks. She began throwing bottles and caps into the big plastic barrel she used as a trash can, then swept cigarette butts out the propped-open front door and into the dirt yard. She decided she would wait until tomorrow to mop the floors; right now, she was beat. She picked the metal cashbox up by its rectangular handle, patted her front pocket where the gun was stashed, and walked outside. On the porch, she slipped her shoes back on and locked the bar door, then made her way along the dark path that led a half a mile through the woods to the house that Jack had built to replace their caravan. A fixed-to-a-foundation, honest-to-God house—yet another anchor she hadn't ever asked for or wanted, but here she was.

As she moved deeper into the woods, her mind already fixed on tomorrow's tasks, she heard the sharp snap of a twig to her left. She stopped, listening hard, her startled heart thumping wildly. Nothing else stirred, and so she began to walk on, chiding herself for being so silly. She'd traversed this little dirt path a hundred times in the dark—and now that Jack was dead, almost always alone. "It's just a critter," she told herself sternly. "Stop being a ninny. What, girl, you believe in haunts now?" She raised her voice and said, "Jack, if that's you, why don't you do me a favor and go mop the floor? I'll call you an angel instead of a devil." She started to whistle defiantly until another snap and rustle too loud to be an armadillo caused her to turn. Her blood froze. A tall dark figure was easing itself out from behind the trees.

"Who is that?" she demanded.

The figure, no ghost, moved quickly. It grabbed at her, hauling her from the path and dragging her deeper into the woods. She dropped the cashbox and opened her mouth to scream, and a rough hand clamped over her face. "Shut up, you tramp," a man's deep voice said in her ear. His breath was hot on her face and stank of booze. She was pushed onto the ground, and she landed on her hands and knees, gasping as rocks scraped at the flesh of her palms. Her mind was scrabbling as she tried to make sense of what was happening, but horror trapped her into a neat web of inertia. The man, panting, lifted her skirt above her waist and frantically yanked at her undergarments, trying to pull them down with one hand while keeping the other plunged into her hair, tugging at it and making her eyes sting.

Suddenly what was about to happen to her if she didn't stop it broke through her sludgy thoughts like a heavy rock piercing through the ice of frozen midnight waters. Desperately she twisted, trying to get free, and then screamed as thick hanks of her hair were pulled out by the roots. She drove her elbow backwards as hard as she could and heard the man grunt in pain. He loosened his grip slightly and she tore herself free. She scrambled forward, still on her hands and knees. She found her feet, began to first stumble and then run.

The man, tangled up in the trousers he'd pulled down to his knees, cursed loudly. "You slut," he roared. "Get back here!"

As she ran, she could hear the man crashing through the underbrush behind her. Blind panic caused her to forget where she was. Her foot caught on a root curving up through the ground and she fell again, crying in pain as she felt her ankle twist a little. Sobbing, she scooted to the nearest tree and sat with her back against the rough bark. Close—too close—she heard the man croon, "I'm going to find you, Red, and when I do, we will finish what we started. Come on out now." She pressed her hands over her mouth to quiet her breathing, praying desperately that he would walk on by.

"I can hear your heart beating," he said in a terrible sing-song voice. "Poor little frightened rabbit." He came into view, a little ahead of her and to her left, and she watched him pause for a moment, his head lifted as if he were a deer testing the odors on the wind. She flattened herself against the trunk, but he turned suddenly and was on her, dragging her away from the tree. She struggled under his hands, and he punched her full in the face. In a nightmare replay of her last night with Jack, she heard a crack, saw stars, and tasted copper in the back of her throat.

The man threw her on the ground again, this time facing him, and in the sudden stream of moonlight breaking through the branches above, Forrestina saw his face and recognized him. He was a rube who'd been in the bar every night for the last month. He was much younger than her, probably only twenty or twenty-five years old, a wiry, serious-faced man who drank steadily through the night, not speaking to anyone, his eyes fixed on her as she went about her business. She'd been a little nervous under his dark gaze, but flattered, too—she'd figured her time for catching a *young* man's eye was over. What a fool she'd been to mistake that look for admiration; it was, she realized now, the same look a lion fixes on a zebra.

The man, his knees on either side of her hips, his pants still undone, began again to tug at her clothes, this time tearing at the fabric covering her breasts, and Forrestina remembered what she should have thought of first: the gun, still heavy in the right front pocket of her skirt. She was afraid to reach for it, though, afraid of what would happen if she failed. Lucy's voice suddenly filled her head: *"Panic makes you fall, so think of your breathing, Lollo. Slow and still. One breath in, one breath out, blocking out everything else."*

Forrestina blew silently through rounded lips, and slowly, slowly, trying to ignore what the man on top of her was doing, she inched her hand down along the side of her thigh and into her pocket. Her fingertips touched the cold metal of the gun's handle, and she resisted jerking it out. If he sensed what she was doing, he'd swat the gun out of her hand before she had time to cock it. *Slow*, she told herself. *Slow.*

The man had her blouse open now and was busy trying to figure out the complicated cage around her torso, cursing as he fumbled with the stays. She felt a quick flash of gratitude that she'd never taken to those newfangled brassieres, choosing her old habit of wearing corsets instead. He was making progress, though; she needed to distract him so she could get the gun free. "You don't have to be so rough," she said, reaching out to touch him, forcing the fingers on one hand to unclench, flatten, stroke. "I will be good." She was gritting her teeth so hard, her jaw ached. Startled, the man stopped ripping at her clothes, and then he moved against her. "Well, that's nice," he murmured, low. He leaned over and kissed her roughly on the mouth, and she fought the urge to vomit.

"You know, Red," he panted, sitting back so that she would have more room to touch him, "I have discovered that in this world if you want something, you just have to take it. So I decided a few weeks ago that I was going to take you." He eyed her and smiled a skeleton's grin, cold and empty of life. "And while this is *very* nice, it doesn't matter if you're a good girl or not. I'm gonna have you, and then I'm gonna kill you. Wanna know how?" He leaned forward and put his hands around her throat, his fingers at first barely exerting pressure on her skin. "With your little neck, you'll be dead in a minute. After you're dead, I'll mosey back and retrieve that cashbox you dropped, then hop a train and disappear into the night." He moved his lips to her ears. "I'm real good at disappearing," he said, tightening his fingers.

It's now or never, Forrestina thought. She grasped the man's testicles, then squeezed as hard as she could, feeling the muscles in her forearm jump.

She was fiercely glad that all her wood-splitting had made her hands strong. The man released her, hollering in pain as he tried to pull free, and she squeezed harder, twisting before letting him go. He fell sideways off of her, gasping, and she got to her knees, pulling the gun from her pocket. She cocked the hammer back with her thumb, and he lunged at her, screaming like an animal. She shot him, his squawk of surprise almost lost in the deafening crash of the gunshot. Even in the darkness, she could see the spreading stain of blood on his chest.

She got to her feet and walked over to where he lay flat on his back. He was dead, his eyes wide in frozen shock and disbelief. She knelt down on one knee next to him and said, "Pretty good disappearing act, all right. You should join the circus." She spat in his face and then sat back, the adrenaline draining from her body causing her to shake. She sank into the dirt and sat there, feeling more alone than she'd ever felt in her life. Would she never have peace? Was this constant struggle really the price she would have to pay, over and over, for the life she'd chosen for herself? If so, it was too steep a cost.

Eventually, she stood up and wearily began to walk, limping a little. Everything hurt, from her beaten face to her bare, torn feet, which had slipped out of her shoes when she made her desperate escape attempt. She turned a corner and saw the White River before her, a wide ribbon of tarnished silver. She headed straight for it and stepped into the water. She knelt in the shallows, gasping a little at the cold, and used her cupped palm to scoop water up, scrubbing fiercely at her lips and chest, trying to get the crawling feeling of the man's mouth and hands off of her skin. She picked up a smooth river rock and scoured the hand that had touched his groin until it was raw and bleeding. Finally she sat back on the shore, her hands stretched out behind her, propping her up. The night, which had moved into the blackness of the earliest morning hours, felt close and watchful, and Forrestina was blankly pleased to see chips of stars pushing through the straggling clouds. She felt sleepy and scooped-out, like a Jack O' Lantern, hollow and stringy, and she wondered if her face had frozen into a grotesque smile. She needed to get up and get moving, though. Morning was just around the corner, and this night still had dark work left in it.

She slowly got to her feet. It was hard to walk because her legs had gone to sleep. She stamped and cried out as a thousand heated pinpricks woke her muscles up. She stood for a moment, looking around, marking where she was and where she'd come from. To make sure she wouldn't forget, she ripped a sleeve off of her torn blouse. She walked to a tree at the shoreline adjacent to where the man she'd killed lay and tied the scrap of red fabric to a skinny twig. She was wide awake now and thinking of Jack's recent death and Theo's long trial. She didn't have the strength to go through all that again—and this time, it was *her* who'd done the killing. With no witnesses. Worse than the fear of prison and trials, she would have to tell people what that bastard in the woods had tried to do to her. The thought of reliving that moment made her want to throw up. Thoughtfully she gazed at the woods, so far from anything and anyone, and then she looked back at the deep, slow-moving section of a very large, very long river. Her attacker had said he was good at disappearing, and if, as she suspected, she'd not been his first victim, he was probably telling the truth.

She would need help moving the body, though.

She picked her way back to camp, and when she finally spotted the dim outline of her one-story house sitting dark and silent in the distance, she felt dizzy with relief. She pushed open her front screen door, which she usually left unlocked. That was one thing tonight's events would change forever. She pulled her torn blouse off and dropped it in the metal trash can in the kitchen, then did the same with her skirt.

She rummaged around in the back of her bedroom closet and found an old pair of overalls that had once belonged to Jack. She used them as gardening clothes, the ragged bottoms of the legs fringed with denim strings where she'd cut them off so they wouldn't drag the ground when she walked.

She slipped on a faded apple-green cotton blouse and then drew the overalls up, snapping the hooks of the straps to the one-pocketed bib. She pulled two pairs of soft socks and her black rubber wellingtons onto her throbbing feet. She would need to tend to her cuts soon before they became infected, but that task would have to wait. She put a couple of aspirins in her mouth, wincing at the bitter taste, and swallowed them dry. Before leaving her house again, she searched for the old cotton sheet she used to cover the floors when she was painting. It was wadded up in the utility closet, and she slipped it under her arm before stepping back outside.

She crept away from the house and walked along the outskirts of the camp, trying not to make any sound. Luckily the end-of-the-season crowd slept long and hard—working and traveling all summer had exhausted the carnies, who'd slowly been making their way back to the White River Campground for their winter break. She made her way up to Amos and Ruby's bullet-shaped silver camper trailer, now unhooked from their Bentley Sedan. (Ruby claimed that Amos loved that car more than her, and Forrestina half-believed her, though it was clear that he was also pretty crazy about Ruby.) She was relieved to see that tonight the car was gone and remembered that Amos was out scouting, looking around for the best spot to set up next season. He would be away for at least a week, and he'd left Ruby behind to look out for Forrestina; after the incident with Jack, he worried about her and told her so. Despite her initial impression that he was a pretentious fool, Amos had turned out to be a pretty good guy. It was true what Tilly had always said: it wasn't fair to judge a book by its cover— or by its greasy, carefully combed hair, in this case.

Taking a deep breath, Forrestina stood on the low metal step and knocked softly. After a moment of silence, she opened the door. "Ruby," she whispered into the dark closeness of the trailer. She stepped in and said, a little louder this time, "Ruby?"

She could make out stirrings in the bedroom area of the trailer. She tiptoed forward through the tiny kitchen aisle and found Ruby in a tangle of sheets, her blond hair, cut in the latest short, chin-skimming style, sticking up at odd angles instead of smoothed in the careful waves she normally wore.

"Red?" Ruby said, sitting up and rubbing her eyes as Forrestina sank down next to her on the bed. "Red, what's going on? What time is it?" She reached over and lit the small battery-operated lantern set on a ridge of the camper that served as her bedside table. She peered at Forrestina and gasped. "Red, what happened? Who did that?" She reached out and brushed the hair away from Forrestina's forehead. "Honey, your poor face," she cried.

Forrestina felt her swollen eye cautiously. "Yeah, he took at me pretty bad," she said. "But believe me, Ruby, it could have been much worse." Tears threatened, and she shook her head, fighting them. She thought she was done with crying for the night, but being here, safe at camp and sitting with someone who cared for her, made her want to start the waterworks again. *Stop it*, she told herself. She needed to get a grip; she didn't have time for bawling right now.

"Who is 'he,' Red?" Though it was hard to see clearly through only one good eye, Forrestina could tell Ruby was looking her over, trying to assess the full damage. She placed a gentle hand on Forrestina's arm. "Did the whoreson hurt you . . . in other ways?" she asked, a hard edge on her question, and Forrestina thought, not for the first time, about Ruby's experiences in the flesh circus. Forrestina had figured out long ago that Ruby's dimpled simpleton shtick was just an act, and she knew that underneath Ruby's vacuous smile was the clever brain of a compassionate, rational, tough-as-steel woman. It's why Forrestina had come to her for help.

She shook her head. "He tried but I stopped him," she said. She knotted her fingers together in her lap, her head lowered, her heart beating fast. "Ruby, I killed him."

"Good," Ruby said, her response cold and immediate. "Shot him with that old gun of Jack's, I hope."

Forrestina nodded and shifted on the bed. She reached for her friend's hand. It was unfair, dragging Ruby into yet another mess, but she didn't have a choice. There was no way she was going to the police, and there was no one else around she trusted. "Ruby, I'm going to ask you for the biggest favor I've ever asked anyone in my life."

"Anything, Red," Ruby said without hesitation, and Forrestina loved her for it.

"He attacked me, pulled my clothes to pieces and was just about to—" she worried at the pinky nail of Ruby's hand for a moment "—well, *you* know, and so I got my gun out of my pocket just in time and I shot him point-blank in the heart. I think he was dead before he hit the ground, it was that fast."

Ruby squeezed her hand. "You did the right thing, Doll. Who knows that he wouldn't have killed you after he'd finished. Animals like that make up their own rules. I'll be glad to tell the Sheriff so."

Forrestina glanced up. "That's just the thing, Ruby," she said. "I don't think I can take any more of the police looking me over and getting in my business." She stopped, unable to go on. How could she ask Ruby to help with this? It was too much.

Ruby sat silently for a couple of minutes, then gently tugged herself free from her friend's hand. She pushed the covers of her bed back. "Well, then, we'll just have to dump the body," she said, almost cheerfully, as if she were proposing a picnic instead of an illegal burial. "You wait outside for a minute— there's hardly room in here for me to turn around—and I'll get changed." She stood on her knees on the bed and pressed her cheek to Forrestina's, hugging her tightly. "It's going to be all right, Red," she said. "I promise."

Forrestina nodded, too overwhelmed to speak, then made her way quietly back out of the trailer. She peered anxiously at the sky while she waited—was it beginning to lighten a little bit? She had no idea what time it was. Her mother had often said that it was always darkest before the dawn, a saying that made no sense to Forrestina when she was a child. In fact, once she'd actually stayed up all night to check, watching sleepily as darkness faded to light, and the shift from night to morning had been a slow progression of shades dropping away bit by bit. Now she found herself checking the night sky, waiting for the inky dark to explode into sunshine. They needed to get their work done before the campground woke up.

Right on cue, Ruby stepped out of the trailer, tying her hair back in a filmy nylon scarf. She was wearing an old black skirt—better to hide stains, she explained—and a dull brown blouse. Like Forrestina, she wore rubber wellingtons on her feet. "Come on," she whispered. "We'd better hurry."

Forrestina led her through the campsite and back into the woods. They passed the bar, and then Forrestina made a sharp right turn and headed towards the river. Once they were on the bank, she walked along the edge of the tree line, looking for her blouse sleeve. She finally spotted the bit of rag fluttering in a spirited breeze, and called to Ruby, "This way!" They were farther away from the bar than she'd first thought, and that was good. The deeper they were in the woods, the less likely anyone would notice anything amiss.

They walked about a hundred yards from the bank and almost tripped over the body, a dark, hulking shadow hidden on the forest floor. They both stood gazing at him for a moment, then Ruby said, "Okay, then. How we going to do this? You got a shovel?"

Forrestina shook her head and pulled out the wadded-up sheet. "I thought we could flip him over onto this and pull him down to the river," she said. "It's not very far. Once we're there, we can fill his pockets with stones and roll him into that deep spot in the water. He should settle on the bottom for a good long while, and then the current will eventually move him downstream." She spread the sheet out on the ground next to the body. "It's lucky that the bar and camp are both upstream—even if he does finally wash up, he'll likely be far away from us."

"That's a good plan," Ruby said. She moved so that she was standing at the head of the dead man, her left foot planted on the top edge of the sheet. She reached down and took hold of both of his arms and, bending her knees and setting her heels in deep, managed to flip him to his side.

"Quick," she panted, "you get behind him and shove him over."

Forrestina knelt behind the body and placed her hands flat against him, one near his shoulders, the other low, near his rear. His back was a sticky mess. She shoved with all of her strength while Ruby pulled, and they managed to roll the body onto the edge of the sheet. He was now face down, so Ruby had to pull him over by the shoulders while Forrestina pushed him high on the chest and near his stomach. He rolled again and landed square in the middle of their makeshift cloth travois. They each grabbed a corner and began to pull, gasping with the effort. "Dear Baby Jesus," Ruby huffed, "so *this* is what they mean by 'dead weight!'"

Forrestina laughed at that, and Ruby joined her, giggling. It was slow going, and they had to stop often to rest their arms, but finally they made it to the river's edge. They scurried around, looking for the heaviest rocks they could find, and began to fill the man's patched trouser pockets with stones. Ruby had the good idea to unbutton what was left of his shirt and fill it and his chest cavity with rocks, too. Forrestina felt a little green during that process, but Ruby took it all in stride, happily shoving rocks into the cavernous hole in the man's body.

"Did you know that I used to want to be a nurse?" she chirped as she worked at her grisly task, her hands gloved in blood and gore. "Blood and stuff never bothered me one bit. I was actually fascinated by it all." She finished stuffing the corpse's shirt and chest and then used a long strip of torn sheet to bind the rocks in place. "Of course, my family never had any money, so I had to drop out of school when I was ten and get a job. Still, I always thought I would've been pretty good at it." She sat back and surveyed her handiwork. "Okay," she said, satisfied. "I think he's ready for Davy Jones's locker."

"That's at the bottom of the ocean, goose," Forrestina said fondly. She desperately wanted to tell Ruby how much she admired her—how she was in awe of Ruby's bravery and cool-headed efficiency—but she just couldn't. Sharing how she felt had never been easy for her. Instead, she rose, and she and Ruby pulled the body into the water.

As the river hit their waists, they both sucked in their breath together—the water was freezing. They walked the body in deeper and deeper, fighting to keep him from sinking right away, gripping his slippery torso tightly in their arms. Finally, when they were about fifty yards from the bank and the water was well past their chests, Forrestina felt her toes slip over the edge of the deep drop-off she'd been looking for. She told Ruby to stop, then they both let go at the same time, watching as the man Forrestina had saved herself from sank out of sight. They hurried back up to the bank, too cold and intent on getting out of the freezing water to speak. They sat on the rocks next to each other, watching as bubbles swirled and broke on the surface where the body had been. Finally, that stopped too. The sun overtook the last grayness of the night and filled the sky with its soft lemon glow.

"It's going to be a beautiful day," Ruby commented, her face lifted, her eyes fixed on the pale morning sky.

"It surely is," Forrestina replied. She took Ruby's hand, and they sat there together for a long time like a pair of contented turtles, warming themselves as the rocks beneath them began to heat under the sun. In front of them, the White River continued its slow, quiet stirrings and kept all its secrets safe.

CHAPTER TWENTY

Fayetteville, 1972

BETTY EXHALED LOUDLY AND slumped back in her chair. She felt as if she'd just run a marathon, her heart was beating that fast. "And you never got caught?"

"Nope." Forrestina reached over to the little green metal patio table they were sitting next to and took a long swallow of her sweet iced tea, then set her glass back down. Her hands, as always, were steady; Betty had noticed she wasn't afflicted by the shakes that often came with aging, and the terrible story she'd just told did not show itself in trembling. She obviously felt no remorse about the killing, and Betty was glad.

"Ruby and I went back to the house to clean up. After we got the blood and mud off our skin, I made her get the scissors from the kitchen drawer and cut my hair to above my shoulders, straight across, just like I wear it now. She didn't want to—argued with me something fierce, but I insisted." She tugged at the ragged ends of her bobbed hair self-consciously and uttered a short, rueful laugh. "A'course the lady who does our hair here doesn't have the beauty skills Ruby had." She pulled a section of hair across her face, over her nose so she could examine it. "I admit that I cried something awful, seeing my poor red hair laying there in a pile at my feet. Isn't that a silly thing to cry over? Pure vanity." She snorted and let her hair drop from her fingers. "But that night I made up my mind that I had to stop looking and acting so gosh-darn lady-like. I needed to be seen as a boss, not a woman."

Betty stayed silent. She wondered if the real reason for her change was that Forrestina didn't feel safe looking desirable to men anymore. Dull anger at the unfairness of it all throbbed in Betty's forehead like a pulse as it occurred to her that bastard had not only taken away Forrestina's sense of security in the world, he'd made her think that her soft femininity was to blame. If he wasn't already crumbled fish food, Betty thought she would've liked to cheerfully hunt the monster down and shoot him all over again herself.

Forrestina continued. "The next day I drove into town to a store that sold men's clothing, and I bought me four pairs of the smallest men's overalls I could find. I still had to hem the cuffs some so they wouldn't trip me up. I bought a bunch of flannel shirts, too, some boy-sized work boots, and this hat, and that's what I wore around the camp and the bar from then on. By the time I sold the bar, I was so comfortable in my ways, I just kept it up. Shoot, after that night, I was done trying to be pretty."

Betty thought about the corsets she'd spied hanging in Forrestina's open closet door once, those tiny, ancient fabric cages of torture that a nurse told her Forrestina strapped herself into every morning before pulling her overalls on, and noted that as she talked to Betty now, she was fiddling with her diamond earrings. It was clear that despite her claims to the contrary, Forrestina hadn't given up *all* her female vanity, and this evidence that the would-be rapist hadn't been able to completely steal that from her cheered Betty up immensely.

"So you going to turn me in?" Forrestina asked casually, staring straight ahead at the squat, square green of the only grass in the place—a 1950s-era, tract-house patch of lawn that served as the "courtyard" at the Oaks.

"Of course not," Betty snapped, hurt that she would even ask. Did Forrestina think she was a snitch? Then she remembered, not for the first time, that she was supposed to be a reporter, and reporters should, well, *report*. Betty softened her tone. "I don't think you did anything wrong, Ms. Campbell—" Forrestina glared at Betty, who quickly amended her words, "—Ms. *Forrestina*.

Ruby was right—it was self-defense. Disposing of the body was probably not the best idea; had you gotten caught, that would've made you seem guilty, but since you didn't. . . ." Betty shrugged.

"Let the dead bury the dead, huh?" Forrestina said. "Book of Luke, chapter 9, verse 60." At Betty's look of surprise, she cackled. "Didn't think I was the Bible-reading type, did you? Shoot, I've read the Good Book from cover to cover. I try to read at least one chapter every night. Always have, ever since me and Jack first bought the campsite." She stood up, joints popping and creaking. "Lord, I'm tired of sitting," she said. "Let's you and me take a few turns around our spacious gardens here."

Betty stood up as well and stretched, her hands on her lower back. She was glad to be up and moving; as she'd listened to Forrestina's story, every muscle in her body had remained tensed, and now they were sore and bunched-feeling. Betty set her pad and paper down on the patio table, hoping that whatever tale Forrestina told her next, she would be able to remember long enough to write down. Forrestina surprised her again by shyly slipping her arm through Betty's own. They started to slowly stroll around the square yard like two ladies in a Jane Austen novel. Betty squinted down at Forrestina, with her ratty old hat on her head and her clomping boots, and bit back a laugh—what would Ms. Austen make of this decidedly ungenteel woman? Betty decided Austen would probably love her—Lizzie Bennet in overalls. After all, they had the same spirit. The sun, which had been bright and fiercely hot that morning, had burned itself down like a candle flame and was starting to sink lower in the sky, but the day was still too warm for comfort. Betty wished for a breeze, but the stingy construction of the buildings around the courtyard all but doused that hope.

Forrestina interrupted her thoughts. "I got a nicer story. Let me tell you about a fine preaching man I once knew." She nodded at a pair of elderly women, who were sitting on lawn chairs in the sparse shade of the striped canvas awning extending from the buildings around the courtyard. "Hello, Mabel, Rose," she called to them. They were playing gin rummy on the table set between them, and one of the ladies waved a wizened hand in response and chirped back, "Hey there, Forrestina. Hot enough for you?"

"Ain't it just, though," Forrestina replied. She picked up the thread of her story. "So that first fall when we bought the campsite, we were pretty full up with our own carnival folk and those from the other carnivals we got to know. The season was just winding down, and people were excited to try us out. Pretty soon we had just one site left open and were thinking about using it to set up an extra bonfire spot. Before we could start loading it up with wood, though, a pair of black horses came riding in on a Thursday afternoon, pulling a black carriage. There weren't any decorations on the horse, so I knew right away that it wasn't a circus or carnie wagon." She shook her head, smiling at her shoes. "Carnie and circus folks are a gaudy bunch, I admit, and they loved to braid bright ribbons in their horses' manes and attach all manner of pom-poms and jingling bells to their bridles." She grinned up at Betty. "You should've seen how fancy I made Medi and Ocre."

Betty thought there was nothing in the world at that moment she wanted more than to admire Forrestina's gaily decorated, long-suffering horses, and she told her so.

"They surely were a sight to behold," Forrestina said fondly. She walked a few steps, lost in the silence of memory, then cleared her throat and continued. "There was no writing or anything on the flat sides of the carriage, either. A tall, thin man sat on the bench of the carriage, driving the horses. He wore a black suit and a black stove-top hat and looked all the world like death riding into our midst. In fact, Gypsy Sue took one look at him, hooked her fingers in protection of the evil eye, lifted her volumes of colored petticoats up, and ran away on her fat little legs. She wouldn't go near him the whole time he was there, said if he looked at her, he would know all her sins and she would surely turn to stone."

Forrestina laughed and shook her head. "She was a crazy broad, but good at telling fortunes, and really good with healing herbs and teas. She was our camp's version of a doctor, and I don't think any real doctor could've done any better taking care of our bands' little scrapes and pains. Where do you think medicine came from, anyway? From the herbs and plants of the earth, and the women who knew how to use them."

"Right, but tell me about that man in black," Betty said. She didn't have time for Forrestina to wander off track and begin telling her the history of natural medicine, though she had no doubt Forrestina probably knew it—she'd never met such a wealth of random knowledge. If Forrestina heard or read something once, she seemed to squirrel it away in her brain in case she needed it in the future. Saying that she was sharp was like saying the war in Vietnam was a bit of a skirmish—words couldn't possibly encapsulate the bigger truth.

"Right," Forrestina said, then grinned her impish grin. "Move along, old woman. Miles to go before you sleep. I got it."

Betty started to protest, then shut up. Why bother? Forrestina had her dead to rights.

"The thin man in black rode over to the empty site as if he'd known all along exactly where it was, his back straight as an iron rod. He pulled the reins, not speaking, and when the horses stopped, he climbed down and turned to me and Jack—like most of the other folk at the campground, save Gypsy Sue, we'd followed him in. He lifted his hat and bowed low from the waist, then returned the hat to his head." She chuckled, "Lord, I felt like I'd fallen into a Charles Dickens novel. I kept expecting a little orphan boy to pop out of that wagon, begging for more gruel."

Betty smiled, as always charmed by Forrestina's effortless apt allusions. In just this afternoon, she'd heard Forrestina quote the Bible and Robert Frost, and now she spoke of Dickens. And she'd said she'd never even gotten past the ninth grade in school. Wonderful, winsome Forrestina Campbell—what a treasure trove of surprises she was turning out to be.

Forrestina continued her story. "Jack cleared his throat and stepped forward, his hand extended. I'd never seen him nervous before, but I saw sweat popping out all over his big forehead that day. 'How do,' he said to the stranger. 'I'm the owner of this establishment. I suppose you are wanting to set down for a night or two?'

"The man regarded Jack's hand for just a second, then took it and shook it. Jack said later that his grip was strong, an admirable quality in a man that other men respect. 'I am the Reverend Jacob Nells,' he said. 'I have a tent revival scheduled for this coming weekend in town, and I need a place to rest that's away from the townsfolk between sermons. There are always kind offers from the hosting congregation to stay in their homes, of course, but I need my own quiet space so that the Spirit of the Lord can renew my words." Forrestina smiled. "Later on, the Reverend told me what he *really* needed was a place to get away from all the holy spinsters. An unmarried preacher is catnip to their species, apparently."

Betty laughed at that and watched Forrestina's eyes dance with pleasure. She was ever the performer, and if she couldn't walk a rope or run a game anymore, she obviously relished the fact that she could still entertain with a story.

"So the Reverend paid Jack seventy-five cents for four nights, and an extra nickel for a bundle of firewood, and then he disappeared into his carriage. We left him alone that first night, since it was obvious that this was what he wanted. The next day, he left early, taking his carriage along, and didn't return until around nine o'clock that night. He sat out on the log we'd pulled up as a seat for him by his fire-pit, and read quietly by firelight from his big, black, leather-bound Bible, eating tuna cold from the can and sipping coffee from a tin cup. The next morning, he and his carriage got going early again and didn't return until late afternoon. The carnies had been out late too, it being the weekend and prime pickings for them, so everybody was pretty tired out. Still, I was surprised at how respectfully muted they were while he was there—normally they didn't give two figs for what others thought of them, especially *religious* others, but Reverend Nells had a way about him that made people stay quiet. Stern, but not mean."

Forrestina rubbed the scars on her hands. "Jack and I were still running our games then too, taking turns watching over the store and campsite and working the carnival, and after a day of being nipped by that crabby Judas—"

"Hang on," Betty interrupted. "Judas was still alive?"

"Well, not the *original* Judas," Forrestina laughed. "By this time I was on my fifth, each one meaner 'n the last. I don't know why I kept picking such damn ugly-tempered rats. I think the devil was in each and every one. Still, the mean ones were the cleverest—something that is true about rats *and* men. You can have that one for free." She nudged at Betty with her sharp elbow.

"Duly noted," Betty said, and she nodded in pleased satisfaction.

"So," Forrestina continued, "I was curious about that preacher while he was with us. I'd never minded the religious like some people in our profession did—our priest back home was a kind man who was scared to death of my mother, and though I didn't go to Mass very often since leaving home, I always knew I was welcome if I wanted to go. It was pretty hard to find many Catholic churches in Arkansas at that time, though. Reverend Nells was Protestant and severe-looking, but he lived his faith; I saw him carrying water more than once for some of the burlesque girls at our site."

She caught Betty's expression and wagged her finger. "And *not* for the reasons you think, Missy, so wipe that smile off your face. No, he was more like Jesus ministering to the adulterous woman. He was respectful and proper, but he didn't act like he was better than anyone. He was good with the little ones, too—when the carnie kids ran rampage through his camp, whooping and carrying on like they did, he never once spoke sharply to them. He even joined in on a quick game of tag once, chasing those dirty-faced urchins around, his coat off, his long thin legs stretched out like a spider's, letting the littlest ones catch him again and again. I liked him, and I decided to get up and go to his last sermon before he moved on.

"That Sunday morning, I dressed in my simplest navy-blue skirt set—I even wore a pair of white kid gloves, can you beat that?—and made my way out to where the revival tent was set up. There was a crowd, let me tell you— plain-faced women in their special-day hats, men in their faded Sunday best, girls and boys in clothes they were obviously not comfortable in, worrying at shoes they didn't want on their feet—and there at the front, on a little wooden stage, was Reverend Nells.

"I took a seat on one of the hard, wooden pews near the back just about the time the singing started. There was a blue-haired lady banging determinedly away on a slightly out-of-tune piano, which had been set next to the stage, and the people in the tent sang those old hymns like they were performing for God Himself." She smiled a little wistfully. "I suppose they were, at that. I didn't know the words to the songs, of course—Baptists and Catholics don't sing the same hymns, as a general rule—but listening to those simple folks worshipping their God . . . well, what they lacked in musical ability, they surely made up for in passion. I couldn't help but feel that this little patch of dirt in Arkansas had somehow become . . . holy. You know?"

She seemed to catch herself being what she called "sappy" and laughed self-consciously. "Well, mercy. Look at me, waxing all poetical."

Betty squeezed her hand and stayed silent. She knew exactly how Forrestina felt—her family had been regulars at Grace Baptist Church before Betty was even born, and there were plenty of times when she imagined God sitting in the pews, singing His own praise with the congregation.

"So the Reverend stood up—he'd stayed seated on a little metal chair, nodding his head in time with the songs, clapping along but not singing, his eyes closed as if in prayer. As soon as he rose, though, the crowd fell silent, and you could feel the electricity of anticipation in the place."

Betty filed "electricity of anticipation" away in her mind to use as a direct quote—Forrestina always acted self-deprecating about her education and manners, but she was amazingly eloquent, using phrases or words that, as a writer, Betty admired and was even a little jealous of.

"Reverend Nells opened his mouth and boy, he started to *preach*. His voice was strong and loud, and he knew just when to soften his tones and then boom out for emphasis—he would've made a great carnival barker. 'My fellow sojourners on this earth,' he began, 'I stand before you a sinner, condemned by my sin to burn in the eternal fires of hell.' He swept his gaze over the crowd, and it was like he was looking into every single person's soul and seeing all their secret sins. When his eyes lit on me, I felt my stomach drop like a rock thrown in the river, and I wanted to hide my face with my hands. I knew later what the prophet Isaiah meant when he said, 'Woe is me, for I am a man of unclean lips.' Yessiree, I did.

"Reverend Nells surprised me with his next words, though. He said, 'But I won't be roasting in those fires. No, sir. I am redeemed by a holy and gracious God. A God who made me, knows me, and crazily enough, not only loves me—he *likes* me, too.'

"He shook his head, as if he himself couldn't believe what he was saying. 'And he loves you, too, my wayward brothers and sisters,' he said, again turning that piercing gaze on us all. This time, though, his eyes were warm, and my fear turned to hope.

"Reverend Nells held his worn-out Bible in his right hand like a shield, unopened. 'Let me tell you what the prophet Zephaniah had to say about God,' he said, still not opening the Bible but quoting words he'd obviously read so many times, they were now a part of him. 'The Lord your God is with you. He is mighty to save. He will take great delight in you, He will quiet you with his love.' Rev. Nells held his arms out. 'When's the last time you felt as if someone was delighted in you, not because of what you'd done but because of who you were? Who here has a troubled mind that needs quieting? Your gracious Father in heaven wants to soothe your soul with his ever-constant love. And that's not even my favorite part.' He set his Bible down on the chair behind him and rubbed his big hands together gleefully, his sudden chickenpox grin wide, and we responded in kind, grinning back eagerly, straining on the edge of our seats to hear what he had to say next. The Bible says that 'He will rejoice over you with singing. *Singing*!' He clapped his hands like a child. 'Can you beat that?' he asked. 'Your God loves you so much and is so pleased with what he has made in you, he can't help breaking into song when he thinks of you!' Rev. Nells threw his head back and sang loudly in his deep, rich bass, 'Blessed be the name, blessed be the name, blessed be the name of the Lord.'

"The crowd burst into applause, joining him in song, and Reverend Nells nodded, still smiling. I clapped too, tears running down my cheeks. Thoughts of my mother and father, who had held their love attached to the price of my behavior, was set against the idea of all that unconditional, approving love, and I felt like hugging somebody's neck for pure joy." Forrestina pushed her hat back and scratched her forehead, bemused. "Would you believe I actually did? I looked over at the little old lady sitting next to me, who was probably a hundred if she was a day, and she looked back at me, and we just threw our arms around each other, laughing and crying. After a moment, Rev. Nells raised his hands, palms out, and the audience quieted down. 'I see that God has got ahold of some of you,' he said. 'Now don't deny him your part. Turn to him. Talk to him. Tell him your hurts and your sorrows, ask for forgiveness, and let him heal your broken hearts. Give that chorus of angels who rejoices when a sinner comes to God a reason to *sing*.'

Forrestina closed her eyes, trusting Betty to lead her along as she plumbed the mines of memory. "The Reverend preached on for two hours straight—I've never seen such stamina—but no one seemed to notice or mind. The time just flew by. Finally he finished, swabbing at his sweat-shiny forehead with his big white hankie, and he made his 'invitation,' was what he called it. Half the crowd rushed forward to be saved, or I guess re-saved, though to my understanding, once you've been redeemed once, that's all it takes. Some people just like to hedge their bets, I guess.

"I didn't go forward physically, though inside a big part of me did. I had a little talk with God all by myself, and I was sure He heard me there in my pew just fine. I sat for a long time with my eyes closed, listening as people filtered out of the tent. When I finally opened them, everyone had gone except the Reverend. He was watching me with that solemn, kind expression of his.

He walked over and said, 'May I sit, Miss Forrestina?' I replied yes, of course, and he settled next to me. He didn't talk at first, just sat staring down at the Bible in his hands, then he said, 'I tell you that in the same way, there will be more joy in heaven over one sinner who repents than over ninety-nine righteous ones who have no need of repentance.' He stroked the still-closed cover of his Bible and then handed it to me. It seemed to pain him to do so. 'Miss Forrestina,' he said, 'this here has been my constant companion for over thirty-five years. I got it when I was just a young man starting out with a burning need to share God's word. And today, I heard God tell me as clear as I am now talking to you that I needed to give my friend over to someone who would soon have great need of it.' He turned and looked at me, and the expression on his face was such a mixture of pity and sorrow, it scared me a little. If I had been Gypsy Sue, I would've run from the place screaming. Instead, I took the book from him and held it to my chest. I still remember that it felt warm from his hands.

"'Read it every night,' he said. 'Read it even when you don't understand it. Read it when you don't want to hear what it's got to say—*especially* when you don't want to hear what it's got to say.' He looked me deep in the eyes and said, 'Pay attention to the verses that talk about God's love. Because he does love you, Miss Forrestina. Never doubt that.'

"He stood up, and I did too. 'I'm heading on now,' he said. 'Someone from the church that hosted me is coming to clear away the tent.' He reached out and put his hand on my shoulder. 'God bless you, Miss Forrestina,' he said. 'I want you to know that you are now officially on my daily prayer list.'

"He walked out of the tent and I listened to him climb into the carriage and gee-up the horses. When I walked outside too, he was just a cloud of dust going down the road. I was still floating on the waters of God's love and wasn't in any hurry to get back to the campsite, so I found me a place further up the river and sat there reading through my Bible until supper time." She crooked her head and looked into the flat blue sky. "On that terrible night by the river, when I was in the deepest pit of my despair, I thought maybe I'd brought all my troubles upon myself because of my sinful ways. I had myself convinced that God must be mad at me, and that I deserved all the pain and suffering I'd endured. Then a verse from Rev. Nells's Bible suddenly came to me, as clear as day. It was a promise about God never leaving or forsaking me. I swear, it was if the Lord hisself was there, reminding me that he'd been there all along—it was him who made me remember the gun. He'd given me the strength to fight, and he warn't mad at me at all." She turned and smiled broadly at Betty. "I remembered again Rev. Nells saying God loved me, and I knew it to be true, and I was plum ashamed that I'd forgotten. Right then I determined to quit feeling sorry for myself."

Forrestina and Betty had walked around the courtyard at least fifteen times by the end of her story, and Betty could tell she was getting tired. "Why don't we go back to your room?" Betty suggested. Forrestina agreed immediately. Once Forrestina was settled in her easy-chair, Betty started to take her leave, promising she'd be back next week. She wanted to get to her car and scribble down the story she'd just been told, but before she could get out the door, Forrestina stopped her.

"Let me show you something," she said. "Before you go."

Betty sat down on the edge of Forrestina's bed and watched her walk over and open the top drawer on her two-drawer nightstand. She pulled out a large black leather-bound book and passed it to Betty. It was a Bible, the leather cracked, the edges worn soft. When Betty opened it, she saw that the margins of the onion-skin pages were covered in notes, and that one out of every three or so verses were highlighted in yellow or underlined in red, blue, or black ink. Some of the notes were exclamations—*You don't say!* or *Wow!* or *True!* Others were more fierce, questioning—*So what does that mean? Make up your mind!* Betty realized with a start that she was holding in her hands a lifetime of faith. *Talk about holy patches of dirt*, she thought, and shivered with the enormity of it.

After a moment, Forrestina took the Bible from Betty and set it reverently back in its place. She closed the drawer. "Okay, then," she said. "Get out of here. I'll see you next week."

"Next week," Betty agreed. She left, mind swirling with all she had heard that day of pain, and love, and fear—and grace.

Oh, what grace.

The next week, when she knocked on Forrestina's door and pushed it open, she found the old woman pacing the room.

"Oh, good," Forrestina said, rushing over and giving her an unexpected hug. "You're here. After you left, I was feeling terrible about telling you all my stories of bad men who done me wrong—I swanny, I must sound like a hokey country song—so I couldn't hardly wait for you to come back so I could tell you about the one man in my life who never once let me down. The love of my life."

She pointed to the chair opposite her. "Sit," she said, and Betty obeyed.

Chapter Twenty-One

Springdale, 1951

FORRESTINA STOOD OUTSIDE HER new home, blinking at the sun that perched atop the pointed roof. She still couldn't believe she'd gone and done it—sold her bar and set up house inside the limits of an honest-to-God city. A *small* city, to be sure—at the last census, Springdale only boasted a population of 3,319 people—but still, technically a city. She was now officially "a townie." "I can hear you laughing your fool head off, Jack," she muttered to her dead husband, whom she often spoke to when no one else was around. He'd been a good husband longer than he'd been bad, after all, and he'd paid for the bad. She didn't hold anything against him anymore.

The house was a modest one-story, two bedrooms and a bathroom complete with a sink and a tub (the toilet was in the rough-planked shack outhouse out back). The clapboard wooden siding was painted white, faded and chipped in spots, but the trim was still bright, a cheerful, Christmas-tree green. The house was set a ways back from the dirt road that passed as "Chestnut Street," with a broad expanse of green lawn in the front and a cracked sidewalk leading from the metal gate to her front stoop. Besides the house, she owned the twenty-five acres of scraggly, dirt-pocked land that stretched out behind the screened-in back porch. And owned she did—she owed not a penny because a man from Mississippi had recently inherited the property from his mother when she died, and he'd offered Forrestina a straight trade of his property for hers with a thousand dollars cash to round it off. She was suddenly, to her surprise, not too badly off. With careful saving, she could live on the money for a couple of years—three, if she was very frugal. Of course, she didn't plan on just sitting around, doing nothing. She'd been working since she was fifteen, so why would she stop now?

Forrestina walked onto the front porch and reached up, feeling along the top of the door's wide trim until her fingers touched cool metal. The key to the front door was right where the man from Mississippi had promised to leave it. She opened the screen door, wincing at its rusty-throated protest, then turned the key in the lock. She stepped inside the house and turned in a slow circle, saying aloud, "What do you think, Jack? Not too shabby, huh?" She was eager to take another tour of her new place, which she'd only seen once before, and that in haste.

The front door opened into a short hallway; to the left was the living room, with its red-bricked fireplace and hearth and wood-paneled walls; to the right, one of the bedrooms. Back further was the kitchen, bright with sunshine because of the large window that faced the back yard. In the kitchen was a sherbet-green porcelain gas cook-stove, trimmed in white, and a metal sink with actual running water. Life in the modern age away from the campground was a marvel, Forrestina thought as she turned the tap on and off and watched the water gush from the iron spigots. She wandered to the back of the house, which was taken up by the master bedroom, wallpapered in a delicate pink rose pattern set against a cream background, and the bathroom, with its big tub on clawed feet and deep porcelain sink. Running water in there, too; goodness gracious.

Moving through the house slowly, taking it all in, Forrestina made her way to the door off of the kitchen and walked out onto the screened-in porch. This was her favorite room, with its encircling screened windows that stretched from hip-level to roof, allowing breezes in but shutting out bugs. She unfolded a metal chair—Mr. Mississippi had abandoned a lot of little odds and ends of his mother's that would not fit in his truck—and sat down, thinking about how quickly this had all come to pass. She hadn't even considered selling up until two months ago, when the man from Mississippi came in, leaned over the bar, and announced he'd like to take her establishment off her hands. As if the bar was some sort of imposition, a burden that he was graciously freeing her from. The funny thing was, as he spoke the words, darned if she didn't suddenly *feel* like it was a burden, and one she was ready to be rid of. Forrestina told him yes before she had time to talk herself out of it.

Truth be told, she was tired. For most of her life, she'd worked with one goal in mind: to make others happy. In the circus, she danced her wire for the crowds to hear their gasps and laughter and applause. Working the carnivals, she took money in and gave money out, reveling in the smiles on the rubes' faces and the delight of the little ones who watched her rats scamper around their ring. And early on, running the bar gave her a chance to bring some cheer as she poured drinks, offered advice, and made jokes with the men and women who came in seeking a break from their mundane lives. In the last few years, though, she'd started to grow weary of people who only cheered up when they were drunk. Most of her closest friends had given up the carnie life and moved away; after Amos returned from the war, he and Ruby had married, and they were now settled in California, and Red found herself missing intimate conversations with sober people.

Indeed, while some barflies cheered up with a drink or two in them, others became more bitter and angry the drunker they got, and their misery, Forrestina soon discovered, was infectious, like tuberculosis. As she listened to the nightly litany of human horror and pain, she started thinking again about Max and the baby, and bad Jack, and then her parents and her sisters; about Petey and Tilly, Sarah and Lucy and Joseph, and soon the sheer weight of her own loss threatened to drag her down into dark, murky places she'd thought she'd left behind. When the man from Mississippi handed her a way out, it was a life-preserver that she grabbed at gratefully. She agreed at once to sell, and in two weeks she left the bar and her old life behind, taking with her a few household items, her rocks, and her carnival junk, which included her "Wheel of Chance," with its red and black numbers, the canvas from her carnival tent, and a crank-operated organ mounted to a small wheeled barrow. The organ had been a payment from a Spanish carnie called One-Eye Garcia, who'd wintered at her campsite ten years back. One-Eye had a dancing monkey he'd named "Don" after a book about a crazy man who fought windmills, and though the carnie and the monkey had long since disappeared from her life, she still liked to listen to the scratchy, dramatic operas the old organ croaked out when she turned the handle. Besides, living through the Depression had trained her not to throw anything away.

On the morning she left the campsite for good, she set her big rat cage on the truck seat next to her before setting off. Though she hadn't run a real carnival game in years, she still kept rats out of habit and the vague notion that they provided her a financial escape hatch if she ever needed one. She poked a finger through the wire and scratched grey Paul, the tenth of that name, on his back. He sat there, blinking at her, while the latest Judas bared his ugly yellow teeth. "Come on, boys," she said to them. "Let's see what the world has in store for us next." They didn't argue; their world was the same no matter where she moved them: cage and wheel, food and water. She wished the rest of her own life could be that simple.

Now, sitting on her back porch and watching the pat of buttery sun melt into the tree line, Forrestina felt a hopeful contentedness sweep over her. She was sixty years old—officially on her way to elderly—and despite her past troubles, she was doing all right. She had a roof over her head, some money in her pocket, and tomorrow her greatest treasure was set to be delivered. She eyed the drooping clothesline out back and decided that one of her first tasks would be to restring it so she could hang out her sheets. There wasn't anything nicer than falling asleep on air-dried sheets that smelled of sunshine and nature, as far as she was concerned. Plus, her laundry needs were soon going to be doubled.

She stood and headed for the kitchen. Too tired to cook, she decided on a simple supper of bread-and-margarine sandwiches, wolfing them down in a few quick bites. She rinsed the butter knife, setting it on a tea-towel to dry, then stumbled to bed, shucking off her overalls and flannel shirt, deftly untying her corset strings and sighing with the pleasure that always came from her nightly unbinding. She pulled an old cotton nightdress over her head, then crawled in between the crisp sheets she'd already tucked around the queen-sized mattress, another leftover from the previous tenant. She was asleep almost before her head hit the pillow.

CHAPTER TWENTY-TWO

BRIGHT AND EARLY THE NEXT MORNING, Forrestina worked on setting up the house. After unpacking stacks of cardboard boxes, she broke them down and stacked them neatly in the shed out back. She had no plans to move anytime soon, but habits of the transient ran deep, and it was better to be prepared. She swept and mopped all the floors in the house, first opening the windows so they would dry quickly. Once finished with that, she sat down at her wooden kitchen table to make a list of things to buy in town. As she'd noted the evening before, she needed a new plastic clothes line—the four lines now stretched six feet long between two crucifix-style iron poles were saggy and cracked, covered in a black mold that would stain her clothes. She would get the new line at the hardware store and then pick up a few groceries at the local supermarket. She decided to drive; though she'd always enjoyed a nice walk, she lived right on the outskirts of Springdale, about five miles from downtown, and it was too far to carry a bunch of bags if she didn't have to. She wasn't as young as she once had been, after all.

She stripped off her grubby work clothes and pulled on a pair of clean overalls, her best blue-and-white checked flannel shirt, and her work boots. She washed her face in the cold water of the bathroom sink, then yanked a comb through her short red hair. She paused long enough to slip Sarah's earrings into the tiny pinpricked holes of her lobes, turning her head first one way and then the other, watching herself in the mirror as she fastened the delicate gold backs to the posts, then, jamming her worn leather hat onto her head, she grabbed her car keys from the low, slim table in the hallway, locked the front door, and set out for town in her old pickup.

At the Safeway supermarket, she walked around, pushing a wheeled wire basket, its bockety front wheel thumping grievously. The store was brightly lit and filled to capacity with all manner of foodstuffs, much grander than her simple grocery store at the campground had been. She threw another loaf of bread in her basket—the one at home was half gone already, and she went through bread fast—and a package of hamburger buns. Consulting her list, ticking off items as she went, she added four tins of Spam, pickles, mayonnaise, creamy peanut butter, some bananas, and a pot of apple-butter to the basket, then made her way to the refrigerated section. There she grabbed a pint of milk, a tub of margarine, a brick of sharp cheddar cheese, and a pint of chocolate ice cream. After a moment's consideration, she added a pint of strawberry and vanilla; someone she knew would enjoy the treat of all three flavors at once. She moved to the back of the store, where the butcher was set up, and asked him to grind her a pound of beef. Her favorite food was cheeseburgers, and she couldn't wait to try frying one on her new gas stove. She wondered if the meat would taste different without the familiar seasoning of smoke from a wood stove.

She watched the butcher at his work, the slab of beef coming out of the grinder like fat strings of thick red yarn onto the sheet of white butcher paper. He finished grinding out a mound of meat, set it on the scale for show (it was a perfect pound), and closed it up in the paper, finishing the job with a square of cream masking tape to keep it closed.

"You're new here," the butcher said, setting the package on top of the glass counter. He squinted behind a pair of round glasses. "Are you? You seem familiar to me somehow."

"Well, kind of new," Forrestina said. "I just moved into the old LaFoy place, but I used to work around here some, many years ago."

The butcher, a man twenty-five years or more younger than her, leaned forward, his big hands splayed on the counter. He examined her face, puzzled, and Forrestina tilted her head, holding his gaze, waiting to see if he could figure it out. He slapped the heel of his hand to his forehead. "I *do* remember you," he exclaimed. "You used to work at the carnival that came through every summer. You were the rat lady!" He cupped his hands along the sides of his mouth and hollered, "Rats, rats, come play with my rats." He dropped his hands and shook his head, "Boy, I lost a lot of money at your game." He wiped his grimy right hand on his gore-stained apron and stuck it out. "Tom Bellows."

She shook his hand without hesitation, not minding one bit that it was not, strictly speaking, clean. Years of the gypsy life had driven any squeamishness about germs out of her. "Forrestina Campbell," she replied. "Pleased to meet you, Tom."

"Forrestina Campbell . . ." Tom said musingly. "That don't sound right. Didn't they used to call you 'White River Red'?"

She sighed. New home, fresh start, old name. Ah, well. "Yep," she said, "that they did. And still do."

"No kidding," Tom said delightedly. "White River Red, here at my butcher counter." Grinning, he put his fisted hands on his hips and regarded her. "So you bought the old LaFoy place. It needs some work, don't it?"

"It's a little rough around the edges," Forrestina admitted. "But I'm pretty handy. Plus I've got help on the way."

"Well, good," Tom said. "Listen, if you need extra help, holler at me. I got a twelve-year-old boy who is always looking to make a little baseball-card money."

"I will keep that in mind," Forrestina said. "Many hands do make light work." She picked up her package of hamburger meat and placed it in the basket, then set a pre-wrapped tube of bologna next to it. As she turned to leave, Tom said, "You have yourself a nice day now, Ms. Campbell."

"Thank you. You too, Mr. Bellows," she said over her shoulder as she pushed her cart down the aisle.

"It's Tom," he called out after her.

She was absurdly pleased—the first person she'd met here was roundly jovial and kind, surely a good sign. Maybe being a townie wasn't going to be so bad after all. She made her way to the front counter and began unloading her basket, plonking the food items down next to the cash register. The shop clerk, a thin, dour-looking middle-aged man with sallow yellow skin, rang her purchases up, punching in the numbers with his long index finger.

"Two dollars and twenty-five cents," he grunted.

Forrestina dug into her pockets and pulled out three crumpled dollar bills. She smoothed them out on the counter, then handed them to the clerk, who punched a few more buttons, slapped the bills into their space in the drawer, and handed her three quarters in change. He put her groceries in four paper sacks and handed them to her wordlessly. After she took the bags from him, he pointedly returned to organizing the products on the shelf behind him.

"You have a nice day, too," Forrestina said to his back, then she marched with her bags to her truck. Okay, so one for two in her new town; in other words, normal. She drove a few blocks to Ace's Hardware, where she found an affable conglomeration of men standing around yapping. They were polite enough, but too busy with their own gossip to pay her much mind, which was fine with her. She bought her clothesline, then decided to drive around so that she could see what else the town did and did not have. As she drove past the barber shop, the beauty shop, and First National Bank, she began to scheme ways to make money. As luck would have it, her new property boasted several peach trees, and they were loaded with fruit. She could sell the peaches along the road out of the back of her pick-up. There was also a huge wild blackberry thicket all along her fence. Though a thorny business, picking blackberries was not a problem for her because of her tough, scarred hands. Besides, she loved to can blackberry jam, and a good slice of warm, bubbling blackberry cobbler underneath a scoop of vanilla ice cream was one of life's pure pleasures.

Along with the peaches and blackberries, summer crops, her property also had a good strand of trees in the back twelve acres, and she was still good at chopping wood. She couldn't fell the trees by herself, of course, but carnies were always looking for winter work, and she'd made it known before leaving camp that she would be looking for some help when the carnival season ended. After the wood was cut and split, she'd be able to sell bundles of firewood out of her pickup, saving as much money as possible so that when winter came she could hibernate like a cozy old bear.

And there were her rocks, too. A few years back, while driving through a town called West Fork, she'd spotted huge chunks of glassy rocks stacked atop a low stone wall. The colors, opaque pearly white, cobalt blue, pale sea-green, and a deep, ruby red, were so dazzling that she had to pull her car over so she could get a better look. The rocks sparked opal-gold wherever the sun hit them, and gazing in wonder, Forrestina pictured the fairy-tale dwarves who must've freed them from their deep gem caverns, hi-hoeing them merrily up to the world of light.

She found the owner of the rocks inside a hut behind the wall, an ancient stooped woman who herself could've stepped from a fairy-story, one that featured candy houses. After a quick negotiation on price, Forrestina bought as many rocks as her pick-up would hold. The old lady, certainly not a witch—well, *probably* not a witch—was happy to find someone as excited about her treasures as she was. She held Forrestina spellbound for an afternoon as she told her all about each type of rock and where Forrestina could find more. From then on, whenever she could, Forrestina bought all manner of quartz crystals, slag glass, and obsidian, every one glimmering like a magic spell. She displayed them everywhere: atop posts around the White River Campsite, in straight lines along the outside of her gas and grocery store, and on the ends of the bar at White River Red's. When she moved, she took her glassy pieces of rainbow with her, and after unloading them, realized she had more than enough to set out and sell at a modest mark-up. She'd share the splendor she'd discovered, just as the old woman had shared with her.

After her trip to town, Forrestina returned home, put her groceries away, and fixed the clothesline, snipping out the old cords with a heavy pair of scissors and restringing it with new ones. Next, she rolled her aluminum washtub, with its metal scrubbing grate, off the back porch and into the yard. She began filling the tub with water, using the black rubber hose she'd attached to the spigot coming out from the side of the house. She still couldn't get over all this ready water—no hauling, no boil-purifying—it was a wondrous time to be alive, indeed.

She washed her other three pairs of overalls, three of her shirts, and a pile of socks and undergarments, including one of her two corsets (the other she was currently wearing under her overalls). Despite her outer appearance, she was still a woman, after all, and going without a corset was akin to going around stark naked. She didn't believe in brassieres—how on earth did they keep everything in place? She didn't think they could, and she was damned if she would go about her business jiggling all over the place. No sir, she'd keep to her sturdy, dependable (*and complicated—don't forget complicated,* a voice whispered in her mind before she pushed it away) corsets. Let the modern woman flop free; she still had her standards.

She opened the valve on the back of the tub and drained the soapy water, watching as it swept a line of black ants down the gutter in a gushing river of white foam. She refilled the tub with clear water and rinsed everything, drained the tub again, then began to wring the clothes vigorously, plopping them wetly into a waiting straw basket. She proceeded to hang her clothes up on the new line, pleased at the amount of good sunshine they would receive for most of the day. She'd lay money down that a woman had dictated where to set the clothesline; while men certainly had their uses, they weren't particularly astute in domestic matters like where the sun would shine longest in a yard.

After she finished hanging her washing, she went into the kitchen and made herself a sandwich for lunch, slathering mayo and mustard on two slices of white bread and frying up a thick piece of bologna she'd cut from the long tube sitting in the ice-box. To the sandwich, she added a thick slice of Vidalia onion—her favorite because of its almost sugar-like sweetness—and a piece of the sharp cheddar cheese she'd bought that morning. She took her sandwich outside to the front porch and sat on the steps so she could enjoy her food in the fresh air. The bologna was wonderfully salty. As she chewed, she eyed the natural-stone wall that ran along the front of her yard. It was a perfect place to set her rocks.

After a moment, she noticed a cloud of red dirt heading towards her on the road, then watched as a dark green, rust-spotted car rolled up to the gate and stopped. The passenger door flew open, and a blond-headed man put one foot on the ground and then swung his other leg out wide. He waved at her, grinning, his face alight, and began an awkward rapid step-swing, step-swing towards her.

"Well, if it isn't my own Rocket George," Forrestina exclaimed, jumping to her feet and brushing the crumbs from her palms. She trotted forward, beaming, her arms open wide. The man caught her in an embrace and hugged her fiercely, lifting her off the ground.

"Hi, Ms. Red," the man said happily. "I haven't seen you in for-*ever*. He turned her loose and Forrestina stood back, gazing at him, her hands on her hips.

"Well, boy, you are a sight for sore eyes," Forrestina said. "I've been missing your handsome face." She didn't mention that they'd only been apart for one day. To the sweet-faced man standing in front of her, a day was a lifetime.

"Rocket" George Brooks blushed and shifted his stance to better balance on his left leg. For the right, he wore a wooden prosthesis. He'd lost that leg ten years ago working on a mechanical rocket ride in a carnival in Springfield, Missouri. He'd been under the machine, checking the cables to figure out why it was going too fast, when another carnie, seeing a line of children and wondering why the ride wasn't on, hit the switch. George's leg, the only part of him not completely under the ride, was cut off as neat as you please just under the knee.

Forrestina had met George shortly after the accident. He'd come in with his carnival troupe from Oklahoma to rent some campsites, and once they were all settled, some of them had made their way to White River Red's Bar and Dance Hall. George had refused to drink anything but Coca-Cola—said he'd promised his mama he would never touch a drop, and he never had. Plus, he told her as she took his order, he hated the smell. It was "yucky." She'd smiled at him and agreed. As he sat there, minding his own business and sipping his Coke out of the bottle, a couple of townie thugs, dumb-ox drunks, started to heckle him.

"Hey Stumpy!" they called. "Why don't you get up and show us a few dance moves?" Their laughs were the high-pitched yips of coyotes. "Stumpy! You lose anything else besides that leg?"

Forrestina watched the young man's fingers tighten on the bottle, but he said nothing. He was a big, sturdy fellow, and even with his missing leg looked like he could probably beat the tar out of any man who challenged him. He studiously ignored the teasing, but when his bright blue eyes caught hers, Forrestina saw that they were swimming with tears, and she realized with a pang that he would not be defending himself—he was what Tilly called "a little slow." Watching him try so hard not to cry, she began to throb with rage, as she always did when faced with cruelty aimed at innocents.

She untied her bar apron and folded it deliberately, setting it on the counter. "Charlie, I think this place may be too crowded tonight," she said casually to Charlie Bill, one of the carnie regulars she paid to help her pour drinks and keep the peace now that Jack was gone.

Charlie set his beer bottle on the wooden bar and stood up from one of the tall three-legged stools. "Lead the way, Boss," he said. He interlaced his fingers and bent his wrists up, cracking his knuckles loudly.

"Stay here and just watch for my cue," Forrestina said. She walked over alone to the crippled boy's table, holding a green-glass bottle. "Hey there, handsome," she said kindly. "I brought you another Coke—on the house." She set the bottle down, then pulled out a chair opposite him and sat down.

He looked up at her, still blinking back tears. Even though he was in no way feminine, Forrestina thought he was extraordinarily pretty, with golden hair that fell in fetching curls over his forehead, turquoise eyes, and a strong, chiseled jaw. His skin was deeply tanned—probably from working outdoors most of his life—and his torso and arms were strong and muscular.

He accepted the drink. "Thank you, Missus," he said.

"*Thank you, Missus*," one of the rube townies mimicked in a high falsetto. The other two laughed, and emboldened, the first rube hollered out, "Hey Red, why you wasting time on that cripple?" He stumbled forward a bit. "I bet you still got a woman's body under those overalls. How 'bout you leave the cripple alone and you let me show you what a *whole* man can do for you?" He grabbed his crotch and leered at her.

The young man sitting across from her leapt up, his left hand on the table for balance, his right curled into a fist. "You ought not to say things like that to a lady," he said to the rube through gritted teeth. "It ain't right."

Forrestina reached out her hand and gently tugged him back into his seat. "It's okay, honey," she said. "Don't mind them. They're fools."

"It ain't okay," the boy said miserably. He swatted at the knee above the empty space where his limb had once been whole. "Stupid rocket ride," he said. "If my leg was still here, I'd lick 'em for saying such things to you."

"I know you would," Forrestina soothed. She put her hand over his for a moment. "I'm going to teach you something, sweetheart. You watch me. Pay attention, now." She stood and sashayed over to the rube with the big mouth. Behind him, she saw Charlie tense as he waited for her signal.

"Well, well," she said. "So you got something to show me, do you, big boy?" She reached out a teasing hand and rested it on the rube's chest. He was lanky and oily and stank of booze and sweat. She moved her hand from his chest to his shoulder, as if she wanted to dance. "Like to make fun of the less fortunate, do you, you waste of matter?" Her tone, teasing and playful, didn't match her words, and the idiot thug's face twisted in confusion as he tried to figure out how to react. The regular patrons of the bar had stopped talking and were watching in gleeful expectation. They knew that when Red used her sweet, girlie voice, somebody was going to end up spitting out blood—and usually a few teeth.

The drunk townie put his arm around Forrestina, grabbing her by the waist and pulling her close. His breathing was so rank with liquor that it would catch fire if a match was lit near his mouth. "Come on, forget the cripple," he murmured. "Let's you and me go out back for a minute."

"About a minute is fifty seconds longer than you'd last, I'm sure," Forrestina said. "Would you even get your pants off in time, I wonder?" She cocked her head and looked at him coyly. "You *know* that if you finish before you get it in, it don't count. Right, Mr. Quick-Draw McGraw?" She pushed away from him. "Shoot. You're probably technically still a virgin," she sneered.

The bar erupted in laughter. The townie flushed a deep brick-red and let go of Forrestina's waist. He lifted his arm, his elbow cocked at an angle across his upper body. His palm faced his opposite shoulder, the fingers of his hand closed as he prepared to backhand her across the face. In one smooth movement, Forrestina kneed him in the groin, so hard she felt her knee connect with his pelvis bone. He screamed and sank to all fours before doubling up into a fetal position. He moaned and rolled, and the two other townies rushed towards her. She flicked her eyes at Charlie, and he moved forward, grabbing one man by the neck and throwing him across the room. The other man swung at Forrestina, and she side-stepped him easily, throwing him off balance. As he stumbled past her, she pulled her gun from her pocket and cocked it, holding it to his temple.

"I want you, on behalf of your stupid friends, to apologize to that young man over there," she said pleasantly, as if she were suggesting he take a nice

Sunday stroll. "And then I want you all to take your trashy townie asses out of my bar. If I see any of you again, I swear to God I will put a bullet in your head, though I doubt there's a brain between the three of you to hit. I don't reckon any of you would be missed."

The townie with the gun to his head swallowed hard. "Yes, ma'am," he said. He was clearly brighter than his friends. He addressed the young crippled man. "I'm sorry for what we said," he stammered. "It wasn't nice. You can't help your leg."

"Good boy," Forrestina said. She inched the gun away from his temple and used it to gesture to the door. "Now get out."

He didn't need to be asked twice. He scurried away, and as the crowd of people watching jeered, Forrestina called to them, "Who wants to take the rest of the trash out?" Several carnies rushed forward, waving their hands, shouting, "Me! Me!" One group hustled the rube who Charlie had tossed across the room out the door, shoving, pushing, calling him names. Another group helped Charlie pick up the still groaning groin-injured man and hefted him outside. Forrestina heard a heavy *thud* as they threw him unceremoniously off of the porch and onto the hard-packed dirt of the path. "A round on the house," she hollered, and was cheered yet again. "Charlie, set 'em up." She sat back down at the table with the young man. "What's your name?" she asked him.

"George. George Brooks," he answered, and then, proudly, "Guess what? I'm nineteen."

"Really? Why, you're a real grown-up," Forrestina said. She extended her hand. "Well, George Brooks, I'm Forrestina. People in here call me 'Red.'"

"Forrestina is a pretty name, but it's hard to say," George said, taking her hand and shaking it. He smiled at her shyly. "And you're a pretty lady. You have neat polka-dotted eyes." He squinted up at the rafters. "My name is not pretty. It's just George—real plain." He sighed. "George is better than the other things people call me, though," he said sadly.

Forrestina could imagine. "Well," she said slowly. "It's been my experience that the more you fight something, the more it seems to set in. If you act like you don't mind, it loses its power to hurt you." That was a lie, but it was the best she had to offer him.

George chewed on a thumbnail, thinking. "Sticks and stones may break my bones, but words will never hurt me," he said. He turned a wide smile on her, and it was like being bathed in sunshine. "That's what my momma said when kids were mean to me." The sunshine on his face suddenly winked out, and his eyes clouded again with tears. "I miss my momma," he said sorrowfully. "I loved her a whole bunch, and she loved me." Forrestina patted him on the arm, not saying anything, and after a moment the rainclouds in George's eyes passed as quickly as they'd appeared. Picking up the thread of their conversation again, he said, "Being called Stumpy ain't as bad as being called stupid, but it still ain't nice."

Forrestina thought for a moment, and then said, "I've got an idea. How about we come up with a new nickname—one you like? Maybe start calling you 'Rocket George' after the ride that took your leg? It's a good, respectable carnie name, and if it sticks, maybe some of the other, meaner names won't. Whaddya say?"

George furrowed his brow, thinking it over. "Rocket George," he said slowly, musingly. Suddenly he beamed, and Forrestina again felt like sunshine was pouring out at her. *Of course his momma had loved him,* she thought. She didn't imagine anyone who spent longer than five minutes with him could resist loving him.

"I like it!" George said. "I know lots of carnival folks with those kinds of names—Baby-Face Brewster, Two-Step Sally, Gypsy Sue. I'll fit right in. Besides, it's a heck of a lot better than Stumpy." His gorgeous blue-green eyes danced with excitement.

"Then let's try this again," Forrestina said. She extended her hand. "I'm very pleased to meet you, Rocket George," she said. "My name is Forrestina Campbell, but you can call me 'Red'."

George shook her hand, grinning. "Pleased to meetcha, Ms. Red," he said.

They watched the happy patrons of the bar together in companionable silence for a few minutes, then George said, "Ms. Red?"

"Hmm?"

"You told me to watch you for a lesson when you threw those mean guys out. Was the lesson that I should get a gun?"

Forrestina felt cold. The last thing this innocent man-child needed was a gun. "No," she said. "You don't need a gun. I only carry one because I'm so small—if I was a great big fellow like you, I wouldn't need it either." She pointed at Charlie, who'd finished pouring drinks and was now back on his stool, sipping his beer and keeping an eye on the crowd. She said, "The lesson I wanted you to learn is that if you're going to pick a fight, make sure you've got friends to back you up. Preferably friends who are bigger than you." She reached across the table and took George's face in her hands. "It's good to make as many friends as you can so that you'll always have people around when you need them. As the Good Book says, 'Two are better than one, because they have a good return for their labor. If either of them falls down, one can help the other up. But pity anyone who falls and has no one to help them up.'"

"Will you be my friend, Ms. Red?" George asked bashfully. "Sometimes I do fall down, and I'd sure like you to be around to pick me up."

Forrestina kissed him on the forehead, then let go of his cheeks. "Of course I will," she said. She looked at his happy face, open and utterly free from beguilement, and had another idea. "Say, George," she said, "what are your plans, now that you can't work the rides anymore? They got something else for you to do?"

George frowned. "They say they're trying to find something for me, but it's hard. I'm not smart enough to run the games—I'm bad at counting—and I can't move fast enough now to fix the machines. Which is too bad, because I'm good with machines." He sighed miserably.

"Well," Forrestina said, "now that the bar is so busy, I need a little help. Do you think you might want to work for me? I can give you room and board and fifteen dollars a week. Does that sound fair to you?"

George clapped his hands. "Does it?" he exclaimed. "Yes, Ma'am!" He looked around the room eagerly. "I can sweep and clean up. And if you need anything fixed, I can do it. I can chop wood and split it, and I can throw old bottles away. I can do about anything but cook." His smiled widened, showing perfect teeth. "My little sister used to say I would burn water trying to boil it. She was silly—how do you burn water?"

"How indeed?" Forrestina said, laughing. "All right then, you stick around until closing tonight and clear up the trash, and I'll talk to your carnie manager about your contract and wages." She eyed his shortened leg. "And you better let me handle the sweeping."

George said, "Okay, but when I get fitted for my new leg, I'm gonna take over that part of the cleaning too."

"Fair enough," Forrestina said. "For now, you help Charlie keep an eye on things for me." She left him sitting in his chair grinning at the crowd of people who would soon get to know him and love him. She wasn't sure what had come over her. While it was true that she could use a little janitorial help, hiring a simple, crippled boy and taking responsibility for him based on nothing more than a sudden whim was rash, even for her. Still, she'd meant what she'd said about people needing as many friends as they could get, and befriending this sweet-natured boy felt like the right thing to do. Besides, she'd always had a soft spot for strays.

That night she set George up in her and Jack's old caravan, which was still parked next to her house, and the next morning he sat at her kitchen table, happily shoveling hotcakes into his mouth as fast as she could flip them on the griddle. From then on, he took all of his meals at her house, and on nights when the bar was not open, spent his evenings until bedtime with her, too, telling her stories he'd heard in the bar and around the camp and listening intently as she read aloud to him from her stack of books. Like her, his favorite was her old battered copy of *Treasure Island*. He was slavishly devoted to her, hopping behind her wherever she went, asking questions and offering advice in a non-stop chatter that would grate on most people but to her lonely ears was a delicious waterfall of words. She was ever patient with him, and he turned out to be a hard worker, just as he'd promised he would be. He took over cleaning the bar after closing, and when he was fitted with his new prosthetic leg, he was indeed able to help with the wood cutting and stacking. He also kept her old truck running better than it ever had before. Reading was hard for him, and math was, as he'd said "too ugly mean to understand," but he had a real gift when it came to machinery.

Ten years later, when the man from Mississippi offered to swap his place for hers, Forrestina sat George down for a talk. "George," she said, "I'm selling out, but that doesn't mean you have to leave. You can stay here and work for the Mississippi man—I've already spoken to him about it, and he said he'd be happy to have such a good worker on hand to show him the ropes." She kept her tone light so as not to alarm him, but inside, her heart was breaking. She couldn't imagine life without her sweet-natured Rocket George.

George shook his head slowly. "No, Ma'am," he said. "I'm not staying if you're leaving. What was it that pretty lady in the Bible said to her dead husband's ma?" (In addition to classic novels, Forrestina regularly read stories out of the Bible to George, and he remembered them all with uncanny clarity.) "Wherever you go, I gotta go?"

It was close enough. Forrestina hid a smile, and said, "Her name was Ruth. But George," she shoved her hands in her overall pockets, "I can't pay you like I used to. I will have to figure out a new way to make money. Plus I don't think there is a separate house on the property. You'd have to sleep in the spare bedroom."

"What do I care about that?" George asked carelessly. "I'm at your house most days anyway, and I'd work for you for free. You're my best friend." He frowned as a new thought occurred to him. "Unless you don't want me around." He got to his feet, his eyes beginning to well up at the very idea.

Forrestina stood as well and wrapped her arms around him in a hug. Her head reached just below his shoulder. "Don't be silly," she said into his chest. "I always want my pal close by."

That settled it: Forrestina left first to set up the house, and a day later George arrived with another load of her stuff from the campground. After climbing out of the car, he stiffly ran around checking out the house and yard, hollering compliments about every little thing he saw as he went. "Look at this yard!" "Oh wow—an apple tree!" "Red, have you seen the chicken coop? Can we have chickens? Please say we can have chickens—I love scrambled eggs. With cheese on top!"

Forrestina turned to speak to the driver of the car, Mac the Marvel, a carnie sword swallower. "Thanks for bringing my boy up, Mac," she said.

"Anytime, Red," he replied. They stood together and watched George hop-dragging himself from corner to corner of the yard and in and out of the house, a whirlwind of excitement. "You sure about this—him being underfoot in your house all the time?"

"Of course I'm sure," she said, a little peevishly. "George is more help than trouble."

"Oh, I know," Mac agreed. "I'm sorry. I meant no offense."

"You're forgiven," Forrestina said, nudging him with her shoulder. She gestured at Mac's car. "We'd better get the rest of my stuff unloaded, huh?" She put her hands around her mouth and hollered, "George! Get over here and give us a hand, will ya?"

George obeyed at once. Together the three of them emptied the car of its contents, piling everything up on the front porch. Forrestina made a jug of sweet lemonade, and after drinking two tall glasses, Mac said, "Well, I'd best be on my way." He stuck out his hand for George to shake and said, "You be careful, Rocket George. And watch out for our Red."

"Oh, I will, Mac," George said solemnly, pumping Mac's hand up and down. "Nothing will happen to Ms. Red while I'm around."

"Good," Mac said. He looked at Forrestina. "Bye, Red," he said. "I guess I'll be seeing you the next time you get a hankering to visit the carnival. Next year, that is." He sighed forlornly.

Forrestina knew that sigh; every carnie felt a deep sense of loss mixed with relief at the end of the summer season. "You come out and visit us anytime," she said. She walked Mac to his car, then waved as she watched him speed off down the road.

She turned back towards her house and surveyed it, thinking that once her horses arrived, her place would be complete. A few years ago, she'd bought three ponies too old for long bouts of service off a carnie who was less sentimental. The ponies had taken to biting the children when they were sick of being ridden, and their owner had made the mistake of mentioning the words "glue factory" in Forrestina's hearing. She'd hollered and cussed and wheedled until, just looking for some peace, the shell-shocked man agreed to sell them to her at a sinfully low price. With love and patience, Forrestina had nursed the ponies back to healthy coats and better attitudes; they even accepted small children on their backs again, as long as it was for no more than a couple of hours at a time. Mr. Mississippi had arranged for them to be delivered to her house as part of the final sale terms.

Forrestina looked at the pile of junk on her porch and groaned. She still had a lot of work to do, but it was happy work, making a home, arranging her things, building plans for the future. And now her George was here to help her, there was no way she could be lonely. She pushed aside some boxes so she could get inside her house. "George," she called out the back door to the golden-haired man hopping up and down stiffly on one leg as he tried to pick peaches from the nearest tree, "what do you want for dinner?" She already knew the answer: fried Spam on white bread with mayo—that's what George would eat every night of his life if given the chance. She waited, heard his shouted answer, and then, smiling, began to slice up the pink canned meat.

CHAPTER TWENTY-THREE

Springdale, 1955

"HOLD ON GIRLS, LET ME ASK."

Forrestina looked up from where she was setting a fence post along the side of her front yard, George standing next to her, ready to drive the post into the hole he'd dug. Near the gate, a tidy woman was trying to corral her three children—all dark-curled girls—as they ran shouting along the gated wall that spanned the front of the yard. The top of the wall was lined with Forrestina's crystal quartz rocks, and they sparkled in the sunlight, painting the grey stones with rose and blue and green light. Forrestina wiped her sweaty forehead with a red kerchief and stuffed it into her front overall pocket, then walked over to the gate.

The woman said to her, "Oh goodness, I'm so sorry to bother you. You're obviously busy. It's just that the girls and I pass your place every day on our way in to town—we live over that direction a half-mile," she gestured down the road, "and the girls beg me every time to stop so they can look at your rocks. Today I just couldn't resist." She clasped a yellow vinyl rectangular handbag in two neatly gloved hands. "They are beautiful."

"It's no bother at all," Forrestina said. She opened the gate, pulling it wide so that it would stay open, and stepped through. Kneeling, she said softly to the smallest girl, an apple-cheeked tot of about four, "Hey, what's your name?"

The little girl stuck her index finger between her rosy lips and regarded Forrestina solemnly. The eldest girl, who looked to be about eight, answered for her, saying, "Her name is Margaret. We call her Meg."

Forrestina said, "Hello, Meg." She squinted up at the older girl. "And what's your name?"

The girl replied, "I'm Hannah, and that is my other sister, Emily." Emily, busy racing from one end of the wall to the next, paused long enough to flash them a smile at hearing her name, then she tore off again.

"Well, I'm very pleased to meet you all," Forrestina said. "My name is—"

"Red," Meg said suddenly around her submerged index finger. She removed it, glistening with slobber, and pointed at Forrestina's hair beneath her hat.

Forrestina chuckled. "That's right, honey," she said. "My hair is red, and so is my name." She offered her hand to the little girl, who accepted it, and they walked slowly along the wall hand-in-hand. They stopped at the biggest rock Forrestina owned, a giant cylindrical clear quartz crystal. "Do you girls want to see some magic?" she asked.

Meg nodded and Hannah answered, "Yes, Ma'am. Please." Forrestina liked her polite manners and sent an approving smile to her watching mother, who'd joined them and seemed as curious as her daughters to see what would happen. Even Emily had stopped running for a moment. Forrestina looked up at the sky, gauged the sun's path, and adjusted the crystal on the wall. It caught the light and flooded the stone and ground in front of them in a rainbow prism of color. Forrestina took Meg's two hands and moved them so that they made a cup, then held them in the refracted light. The little girl squealed in delight as her hands striped yellow, green, blue, violet, and orange. Forrestina smiled. "Look at you, Meg," she said. "You caught a rainbow."

The other two girls immediately thrust their cupped hands in the light too, exclaiming with pleasure. Forrestina watched them, pleased, and then glanced over at their mother. She was amused by the look of longing on the woman's face. Forrestina elbowed her. "Go on, Mom," she said. "You catch one too."

The woman hesitated for half a second, then laughed. She joined her girls, stretching her hands out, making rainbow sleeves on her bare arms. George, who'd stopped working to see what trick Forrestina was going to do, caught Forrestina's eye and she winked at him. He winked back.

Still laughing, the woman said to Forrestina, "Thank you so much, Miss . . ."

Forrestina said, "You can call me Red."

"I'm Sherry Thatcher," the woman said. "I'm so pleased to meet you." She looked up at Forrestina's house and said, "You've done a lot of work on this place—I remember how awfully bare and patchy the yard was. Now it's so green—and the flowers you've planted! Those peony bushes are lovely!"

Forrestina said, "Thank you. Would you like to come in for a glass of lemonade? We could drink it on the back porch, and then your girls could meet my monkey."

"Monkey?" Hannah and Emily trilled in unison. They began tugging on the flounced skirt of their mother's red-and-white polka-dot dress. "Please, Mommy? Please?"

Sherry said, "We'd love to. But we don't want to keep you from your work—you looked busy when we pulled up." She eyed George curiously.

"Naw, it's no trouble," Forrestina said. "We were about to take a break anyway." She hollered at George, "George, come over here and meet Mrs. Thatcher and her girls."

He obliged. "Pleased to meet you," he said to Sherry in his open, frank manner, sticking out his big hand for her to shake. "Your dress is polka-dots like Red's eyes."

Forrestina patted his back and said, "That's right, George." To Sherry, she said, "This here is my boy, Rocket George. He helps me out and takes care of me—makes sure I eat my oatmeal every day."

George threw his head back and laughed uproariously at that. "Go on," he said, shoving Forrestina playfully. He grinned at Sherry. "She hates oatmeal," he confided. "Tells me it tastes like wallpaper paste and feels like it has fingernail clippings in it."

"Ew," Emily cried, wrinkling her freckled nose. "I hate oatmeal too," she told Forrestina. "But Momma makes me eat it." She turned to her mother and asked accusingly, "Momma, do you feed me fingernail clippings?"

"Heavens to Betsy," Sherry groaned theatrically. "Now I will never be able to get my girls to eat oatmeal ever again."

"Don't you worry about it, Missus." George said. He beckoned the girls with a finger. "I can show you who DOES love oats," he said. "Maybe you want to be like them." He walked them around the side of the house, and Forrestina said to Sherry, "You can go ahead with them—I'll fix our glasses and then meet you all on the back porch."

Sherry obeyed, and Forrestina headed into the house. She poured sweet lemonade into six slender glasses that were patterned with bright fruits in primary colors. She set the glasses on a metal tray and carried them to the table on the back porch. Outside, George, demonstrating his usual uncanny knack for soothing animals and children, was introducing the girls to her three ponies. He dipped his hand in the cloth oat bag and put some first in Hannah's hand, and then in Emily's, showing them how to hold their palms flat so that the ponies would take the food without accidently catching fingers. Forrestina walked back into the kitchen and stacked a dozen fresh baked chocolate-chip cookies on a plate, then took the plate and some napkins back out to the porch. She called through the screen, "Why don't you girls wash your hands—you too, George—and then come get some refreshments? Afterwards George can saddle up the ponies and y'all can take a ride."

The girls cheered and tumbled after George, who led them to the water spigot attached to the back side of the house. Next to the spigot was a concrete block, and on the block sat a bar of Ivory soap, which Forrestina and George both used to wash their hands after a hard day's work so as not to dirty up door handles. George turned the spigot on full blast, and the girls squealed as drops of water splashed out onto their arms, legs, and faces.

"Girls, try not to get soaked through and through," Sherry called. She walked up the four steps onto the back porch and took a seat. "Lord, I wouldn't mind getting a little splash myself," she said, fanning her pink face with her pocketbook. "Is it ever going to cool down, do you think?"

"Not for a while," Forrestina said. She pushed one of the glasses towards Sherry, who took it and drank half immediately.

"Ah, that hits the spot," Sherry said, smacking her lips. She watched George, who was carefully applying soap to her girls' hands and encouraging them to "rub, scrub, scrub" the lather in. "Your son is a sweet young man," she said.

Forrestina replied, "Well, he's not actually my son—and he's not so young, though he looks and acts it. He's thirty-two—older than you, I bet. For some reason, his brain stopped aging past about nine years old." She smiled. "Which happens to be my favorite age for a boy, as it were."

"Is he related to you?" Sherry asked.

"In the way all we carnival folks are related, I guess. But we don't share any blood ties, if that's what you're asking. He just came along at a time when he needed me, and I guess he'll stay until he doesn't anymore." Outside, George had finished rinsing all eight hands, including his own, and was shepherding the girls towards the house, swing-dragging his fake leg as he went. "Truth be told," Forrestina said, "I've since discovered I need him as much as he needs me. I can't fathom what I'd do without him."

"Sounds like y'all are lucky to have each other, then," Sherry said gently. She stood when the girls clattered up the steps, and directed them to their seats as Forrestina handed out lemonade and cookies. After a few contented minutes, Emily said, through a mouthful of crumbs, "Ms. Red, thank you for showing us the rainbows and horses, but didn't you say something about a monkey?"

"Oh, I did!" Forrestina exclaimed. "If you all are finished, I'll introduce you to her."

The girls crammed the rest of their cookies in their mouths over the protests of their mother to "slow down and act like ladies" and drained their lemonade glasses. Forrestina led them back outside to the shed she'd turned into a makeshift barn. Inside the shed was a large cage, iron-barred on the top and all four sides. In the cage, a lawnmower-tire swing hung on a rope. A plastic tub of water was set in one corner, and in the other sat a square plywood box with a round hole cut out into the side. Reclining on top of the tire, her feet in the air, her body stretched upside down, was a small golden-yellow female baboon. When she heard Forrestina say, "How's my girl?" she twisted her neck sideways and regarded them all with bright amber eyes. Forrestina unlatched the bolt that kept the cage closed and said, "Come on out."

The baboon allowed herself to drop to the ground, landing on her feet. She strolled out of the cage, completely unimpressed by her sudden freedom, and waited patiently for Forrestina to clip the metal clasp of a leash to the blue dog collar around her neck. When Forrestina said, "Up!" she sprang lightly onto Forrestina's back. The girls responded with applause.

"She's so pretty," Meg said, inching closer. "What's her name? Can I pet her?"

Forrestina stooped down, balancing on one knee so that the baboon was level with the little girl. "Her name is Cleopatra, but we just call her Cleo, and if you give her this bit of banana, she'll be your friend forever." She handed Meg a quarter of a banana still in its peel. The little girl cautiously held the fruit out, and quick as a flash, Cleo reached forward with her long-fingered, slender paws and grabbed the banana away. Cleo peeped her thanks and began peeling the banana delicately.

"Oh, she's so cute," the other two girls chorused. Forrestina handed them each the rest of the banana and allowed them to feed Cleo, who jumped off her back and sat in the grass, placidly accepting the gifts from her newest fans. Sherry, who'd walked over with them, said, "Mercy, she's tiny—I always thought baboons were huge. Where did you get her?"

Forrestina plopped down and sat cross-legged in the grass. Sherry joined her, leaning back on straight arms, her legs out in front of her, her ankles crossed in a lady-like manner. Forrestina told Sherry that Cleo had been given to her shortly after she moved to her house in Springdale. Cleo's owner, a carnival worker but a stranger to Forrestina, had decided to pack up and move back home to whatever god-forsaken foreign country he came from—Forrestina could never remember where—Libya? Liberia? Laos? Hearing about how Forrestina had rescued the old ponies, he'd showed up at her place in the hopes that she would buy the monkey off of him. "If you do not," he told her sadly, his dark almond eyes filling with crocodilian tears, "I will have to take her into the woods and shoot her. I cannot turn an African baboon loose in an Arkansan forest."

Forrestina peered into the iron-barred cage at the small orange-gold baboon, whose liquid amber eyes were sad, like her owner's. The man opened the cage door and beckoned her, calling her by name. She shyly moved forward, her quick eyes darting from the man to Forrestina. He reached in and clipped a leash to the collar around her neck and then handed it to Forrestina. "You just say 'up' to her," he said.

Forrestina held the leash slack and said softly, "Up, Cleo." Quick as a flash, the monkey darted out of the cage and leapt into her arms and then climbed onto her back, her leather paws so light, Forrestina hardly felt her weight at all. Forrestina turned her head to look at the baboon, and Cleo cocked her own head, peering into Forrestina's face, chittering, and Forrestina was lost. "How big will she get?" she asked. "What do I feed her? How is she with children?"

Cleo's owner smiled, showing long teeth in his olive-skinned face. "First we need to discuss payment. Cleo is a well-trained exotic animal. She doesn't come cheap."

Forrestina handed the leash back to him and said, "To him, Cleo." Cleo obeyed, leaping from Forrestina's back to her owner's in one smooth move. Forrestina said, "Get off my property, you shyster."

"No, no," the man said, his palms out in supplication, his face creased in distress. "I will make you a good deal. Just give me enough to be on my way. Twenty-five dollars."

Forrestina snorted. "I thought you were going to shoot her." She stroked her chin. "I'll give you five."

"Ten," the man pleaded, holding both hands up, the fingers spread wide. "Ten and I will throw in the cage and all her belongings."

Forrestina said, "Seven and a half. Take it or leave it."

The man sighed dramatically but smiled. "You have made me poor, but no matter. What care I for money when I know my darling Cleo will be cared for?" He handed the leash back to her, and she dug the money out from the leather pouch she wore tied inside her overalls. She laid a five, two ones, and two quarters in his waiting palm, and he made the money disappear into his coat pocket.

"Now to answer your question," he said. "Cleo is a Guinea baboon, from the western part of Africa, or so I'm told. She's already full-grown—she is small for her species, about thirty pounds, I'd say."

"How old is she?" Forrestina asked, softly stroking the baboon's head. Cleo closed her eyes in pleasure.

"I don't really know. She's a mature adult—between fifteen to twenty years, I'd say."

"Hold on." Sherry interrupted Forrestina's story. "Twenty? How long do baboons live?"

"That's what I asked," Forrestina said. "The man said baboons can live up to thirty-five or forty years—can you beat that? They're not like dogs or rats."

"Wow," Hannah interjected. The older girl had left her two energetic sisters, who were being led around the yard on the back of the ponies by George, and she now inched closer to the adults, listening with rapt attention. Forrestina remembered being that age, loving when Mother had friends over so that she could creep in on the grown-up conversations, listening to their gentle gossip, watching her mother relax, laugh, shock, and be shocked. If she was still enough, they wouldn't notice her for a while, and she could take mental notes on how women talked to each other and about each other.

"That's right," Forrestina said to Hannah. She patted the ground by her knee, and Hannah moved to sit next to her. She continued her story. "So the baboon's owner left Cleo with me, and she joined my strange little family. She's okay with George because he's so much like a kid, but she's partial to other women." She included Hannah in that classification with a warm smile and was rewarded by the girl's beam of pride. Cleo, who'd been chasing the younger girls and gently smacking at their bare legs with her paws, got tired and wandered back to Forrestina. She climbed into her owner's lap, laying her head in the crook of Forrestina's arm, turning her neck so she could fix her eyes imploringly on Hannah. Of course the little girl couldn't resist her charms and reached over to scratch her on the neck. In a few minutes, Cleo was asleep, each inhale accompanied by a soft snore and each exhale a rumbling purr from her chest.

Sherry glanced down at the silver round-faced wristwatch on her slender arm. "Goodness, look at the time," she said. "I had no idea that we'd been here so long." She jumped up and brushed grass from the back of her dress. "Come on, Hannah. We need to get home and fix Daddy's supper. Emily! Meg! Time to go!" Hannah gave Cleo one more pat before following her mother. Forrestina pulled herself up with a small grunt, still holding Cleo like a baby, and set the sleeping baboon back in her cage. George lifted Meg and Emily down from their saddles, and then he and Forrestina walked the family to their car.

"Thank you for showing us the ponies, Mr. George," Emily said, remembering her manners. Meg expressed her thanks by hugging his leg, and he grinned in response.

"And thank *you* for letting us spend the afternoon with you," Sherry told Forrestina. "The girls and I haven't had such a nice outing in I-don't-know-how-long."

"You're welcome anytime," Forrestina told her. After the girls and Sherry were situated in the car, Sherry started the engine. Before she drove off,

Forrestina set her hands on the open window of the front passenger side and said, "I mean it, now." She looked in the backseat at the happily worn-out children. "All of you girls are welcome anytime. George and I are here most days, unless we're out selling stuff, and we're always glad for company."

"We'll be back," Sherry promised. Forrestina stepped away, and she and George waved as the car backed out and headed down the road. Sherry honked her horn once and disappeared in a cloud of dust. Forrestina and George stood watching the little cloud in silence. Forrestina suddenly felt inexplicably sorry for herself. She hadn't realized how much she'd missed the company of children. She glanced at George's glum face and figured he was feeling the same way; after all, bringing happiness to kids had once been their stock-and-trade. After a moment, she heaved a big sigh. "Come on, George," she said. "Those fence posts ain't going to set themselves."

"I reckon not," he said sadly. They returned to their work, each wrapped in their silent thoughts, then George, who never stayed blue long, said, "They were fun, weren't they, Red? And the momma said they'd be back." He lifted a post and dropped it into its hole. "I bet they will, and when they do, I'll teach them your funny song." He began to sing the song Forrestina had taught him about mares and does eating oats, and listening to him, Forrestina's funk began to lift. She was sure George was right—they'd be back. As George finished his song— "a kid'll eat ivy too, wouldn't you?"—she hooked her arm through his and said, "Let's go unsaddle the ponies, and then after supper, we'll go into town and get us some ice-cream cones at the Dairy Queen. What do you say?"

Of course, his reply was a resounding, "Yes."

CHAPTER TWENTY-FOUR

THE NEXT WEEK SHERRY AND HER daughters were back, and they brought with them another woman and her two girls. A few days later, a new carload of visitors arrived, and pretty soon, George and Forrestina were showing off their small menagerie daily, giving pony rides and parading Cleo and the rat brothers around for all to see. Forrestina, a big believer in the necessity of refreshments and not wanting to be caught unawares, stayed up nights baking cookies and squeezing lemons for lemonade. Her generosity paid off: the ladies who stopped by her house with their children turned out to be good for business—they often left with newly purchased crystals for the kids (Forrestina kept a quantity of smaller, more affordable rocks for sale), a bushel or two of peaches, and a dozen brown eggs from Forrestina's busily-laying broody hens.

"See, George," Forrestina said one night as she counted out coins and dollar bills, lining them up in her metal cash box and stashing them under the loose floorboard in the sitting room that served as her bank, "carnies and circus folk attract children like milk attracts cookies. Luckily those children are always attached to their moms, and those moms have got money to burn, it seems." She set the floorboard down with a bang and leaned back on her heels, her hands on her splayed knees. "Though I would show the kiddies our treasures even if their mothers weren't buying stuff."

She noticed George was frowning fiercely out the dark window, obviously not listening to her. "Hey Bub, what's wrong?" she asked.

George turned his frown towards her. "I'm worrying about something, Red."

Forrestina stood and walked over to where he was slouched against the kitchen table. At that angle, she was able to reach up and sling an arm around his neck. "Well," she said, "tell ol' Red what it is and let's see if we can't figure out a solution together."

George laid his cheek down on the hand she rested just below his collarbone. "You know that batch of folks that came near the end today—that busted-up hillbilly truck filled with those raggedy kids?"

Forrestina did remember—there seemed to be about fifty of them all piled into the back of the truck bed, though there were probably no more than seven. Seven rambunctious boys and girls, and one very tired, thread-paper worn mother. The kids had bolted out of the truck before it had even skidded to a stop and started running in ten different directions all at once, shrieking wildly.

"Yeah. What about them?" Forrestina asked, removing her arm from George. It had started to ache at that awkward angle.

George dropped his head and sniffed miserably. She could see that he was struggling to speak, which was not normal for him.

"George, hey, it's all right," she said. "What is it?"

"I don't want to get them in trouble," he muttered to his shoes. "Two of them done something bad and I saw it but I don't want you to be mad at them."

"Tell me what they did, George," Forrestina said, now very curious.

George swallowed, then looked at her, his green-blue eyes wide in anguish. "They filled their pockets with peaches and didn't pay for them. And they stole four eggs. They STOLE, Red—and stealing is bad, ain't it? Folks who steal go straight to hell is what my preacher told us when I was a little boy." His face crumpled and Forrestina saw with some alarm that he was about to start one of his noisy, long blubbers. "They's just kids. Poor things is hungry—I heard the littlest one say they hadn't had anything in the house to eat for three days. Their daddy done run off on them again, is what she said."

Forrestina recalled with a pang how the cookies she'd carried out to them had disappeared down their throats with hardly a chew. If George had heard right, that was the first thing they'd eaten in days. If she'd only known, she would have insisted on fixing them all a big supper.

She patted George's arm. "Don't you fret, now," she told him. "God is not going to punish those kids. I would've given them the peaches and eggs and more if I'd known they were in a bad way. So really, it wasn't stealing if I would've given it to them anyway. See?"

George chewed on his lower lip and the raindrop tears abated from his eyes. *Storm averted*, Forrestina thought to herself, relieved. *Now what to do about the poor family?* She couldn't bear to think of them going to bed with hollow bellies.

"Did you happen to hear what their last name was, George? Think real hard. If we know their name, maybe we can find them and help them out." It was a long-shot—George was not very good at remembering things short-term—but this time he said, without hesitation, "Their last name was Ruby. I remember because one of them yelled at the other, 'John Ruby, you get back here,' and it made me think of that pretty Ruby we used to know back at your bar, and then I thought it was funny that they had a first name for a last—and a *girl's* name, at that."

Forrestina was impressed. "Good work, George," she said. "You would make a dandy Sherlock Holmes with an ear for details like that."

George chuckled, pleased by the compliment—lately they'd moved away from Robert Louis Stevenson and his pirates, and now Forrestina was reading the great works of Sir Arthur Conan Doyle aloud to George at night. Forrestina said, "Tomorrow we'll head up to the Safeway store and buy some groceries, and then we'll ask Tom the butcher if he knows where the Rubys live." She swatted him gently on the shoulder. "Now you get to bed; we've got a big day ahead of us."

Early the next morning, George and Forrestina drove to the grocery store and loaded a wheeled shopping cart with five loaves of bread, three gallons of milk, three jars of peanut butter, four bags of potato chips, apples, three boxes of cornflakes, a pound of sugar, a pound of flour, two cans of Crisco shortening, and four packages of assorted chocolate and vanilla crème sandwich cookies. As an afterthought, Forrestina grabbed a package of uninflated party balloons.

Next they made their way to the butcher's station in the store. Tom was still as cheerful and friendly as the first time Forrestina had met him. "Well, hello there, Ms. Campbell," he said. He winked at George. "And there's my old pal, Rocket George. You been a big help to Ms. Campbell?" he asked.

George nodded vigorously. "Yes sir, Mr. Tom," he said. "She says she couldn't do without me."

"And I can't," Forrestina said. "But we ain't here for idle chit-chat. I got a big order for you, Tom, and time's a'wastin." She pushed a scrap of yellow notebook paper at him across the counter. On it, she'd written "3 lbs. thick-sliced bologna, 3 lbs. ground round, 2 lbs. bacon, 4 packages beef hot dogs."

Tom picked up the list and studied it for a moment. "Ma'am, you do have lovely penmanship," he remarked, not for the first time. Forrestina grunted in reply. Mother had insisted that her girls learn all the etiquette she thought they would need as proper little debutantes, and a fine hand for invitations and thank-you notes was a must. Forrestina had found it to be a useless skill in the real world and resented the hours she'd been forced to practice it. Learning how to fix a stopped-up sink—now *that* was a useful skill.

Tom finished reading the note and looked up. "This is an awful lot of meat, Ms. Campbell. You throwing a party? Or have you got yourself one of those new deep freezers to fill up?"

"My business is my business, Tom Bellows," Forrestina snapped at him peevishly. "Now get to slicing and grinding."

"Don't worry, Tom. She don't mean to be cranky. That's just how she talks sometimes," George said comfortingly in a very loud whisper that could be heard by everyone around. Forrestina snorted but didn't respond.

"Thanks, George," Tom said in the same loud, theatrical whisper, then catching the black look Forrestina shot him, rapidly sliced a thick piece of bologna and held it up for her approval. She nodded, and he sliced up the rest quickly, wrapping it in white butcher paper and setting it on the counter, followed by the ground round, the bacon, and the hot dogs. Forrestina put the meat in her cart, then, feeling sorry for her gruff tone, said, "Thank you, Tom. That's just perfect." She leaned an elbow up on the curved glass surface of the counter. "Say, you think you could help me out?"

"I'll sure try," Tom said.

"You know where I could find a family named Ruby? Small, thin, worn-out looking momma, about a hundred scrawny kids?"

Tom produced the chewed nub of a pencil from behind his ear and flipped the scrap of paper she'd used to write out her meat order over to the blank side. "Sure I do," he said, sketching out a map. "They live about ten miles outta town towards Fayetteville, down in Rabbit Holler." He went over the directions he'd written on the paper with her, and then, as Forrestina thanked him and tucked the paper into the front pocket of her bib overalls, he said, "What do you want them for? They ain't causing trouble, are they?"

"Now what kind of trouble could that weary woman and her precious clan do?" Forrestina asked.

Tom squinted at her, not sure if she was teasing him or not. "None, I guess," he said. "It's their Pa. Mean old drunk—spends most of his time down at the Black Hawk." He scratched his head. "Though come to think of it, I heard something about him taking off and leaving poor Mrs. Ruby to fend for herself." He eyed Forrestina's full cart, his gaze settling on the balloons. "What did you say you were going to do with all this food again?"

George opened his mouth to tattle, and Forrestina shoved him with her cart, causing him to totter a little on his one good leg. "I didn't," she replied shortly. "Have a nice day, Tom."

"You too," he said to her retreating back. She was halfway down the aisle when she heard him holler, "You're a good woman, Mrs. Campbell."

"Gosh-darn fool," she muttered.

George eyed her curiously. "Tom? No, I think he's nice," he said.

"Well, of course he's nice," Forrestina admitted grudgingly. "Nosy—but nice."

After paying for the groceries and loading them into the back of the pick-up, Forrestina made her way to the Ruby house, making George read the directions to her for practice as they went along. Soon they were bumping down a rough, red-dirt road. They drove up to a forlorn-looking, dilapidated shack, and Forrestina parked next to the short sidewalk leading to the sagging porch. Dandelions poked their fierce yellow heads up through the cracks in the sidewalk and waved spiky arms, warning trespassers away. Forrestina gazed at the shack in wonder. "How do you suppose they all fit in that house?" she asked.

George, pragmatic as always, shrugged and said, "If that's all they got, I guess they make do."

"I guess you're right," Forrestina agreed. She pulled her beat-up old hat from her head and ran her hands through her hair. "So now we gotta figure out how to get *these* groceries," pointing towards the back of the truck, "onto *that* porch," pointing up to the house, "without getting caught."

"Is it time for a stealth mission?" George asked. He rubbed his hands together gleefully.

"It is," Forrestina said, thinking about the first time she'd done something like this a few years ago. She'd gone in to the First National Bank in Springdale and asked the manager, Mr. Sherman, for a small loan—it had been a wet spring, and she needed some quick cash to replace the leaking roof on her house. She had no bank account there (or anywhere else, for that matter, since she still didn't trust banks, especially not since the Crash), but Mr. Sherman remembered her fondly from her carnival years and made her a loan of a hundred dollars from the cash drawer in his office. After a successful month of peach sales, she came in to pay him back with interest, counting out the bills from the wad of cash stashed in her leather pouch, and she overheard him speaking on the phone. He was talking to someone in a sorry, quiet tone about a family who'd come on hard times and were about to have their gas shut off. When he hung up, Forrestina, unashamed at having been eavesdropping, demanded to know who the family was and why *he* was being called about it.

"I'm a deacon at the Second Baptist Church here, and I get benevolence calls," Mr. Sherman explained. "I try to find a little bit of extra church money to help people when I can. It's too bad, though—we've had a lot of calls lately and our fund is dry."

"Give me their names," Forrestina insisted. "I had a good month, as you can see, and I want to help out." When Mr. Sherman hesitated, she said, "Look, just cause I don't go to your church, it don't mean I don't know my Christian obligations. Gimme that name."

Mr. Sherman agreed to her request. He wrote the family's name and address down on the back of a blank deposit slip, and Forrestina went straight out to the gas company to pay the family's bill for that month and lay a deposit down for the second. It felt good, being able to help her neighbors again. Pretty soon, she got in the habit of stopping into the bank every month or so to see if there was anyone else who needed bills paid or food bought. Her one demand, to the gas company AND to Mr. Sherman, was that they were not to reveal her name to the people she helped. "It pisses me off when people thank me for just being decent," she said fiercely. From then on, whenever Mr. Sherman gave her the name of a hungry family, she'd take George at night to the house and make him stand guard while she snuck the food onto the front porch. After dropping off the bags and boxes of food, she'd ring the doorbell and then dash back to the car, speeding away before the door opened. She and George had started calling these nightly benevolence calls their "stealth missions," and he loved them.

Now at the Rubys' house, they both sat in the car, looking at the shack together. She could hear the shouts of children in the back yard. There was no way she wouldn't get caught if she tried to leave the bags on the porch right now. "Lemme see your watch," she said to George, who obediently thrust his right wrist at her. It was a fine old timepiece, gold-faced, with an oiled leather black band. George had told her it'd belonged to his father, who'd died when George was just a boy.

"Before she died, my momma give it to me and said I should sell it," he'd said, "but I just couldn't bear to. Even though I can't never figure out how to read the dad-gum thing."

Forrestina had tried to teach him to tell time on the watch, but the concept of dashes representing numbers was just too baffling for him. Still, that didn't stop him from wearing it every day all the same, and Forrestina, with her impractical diamond earrings, understood.

"It's only half-past ten," Forrestina said. "We need to get these groceries home and in the icebox, but now that we know how to get here, we can find it in the dark. We'll come back later."

George nodded placidly and began whistling "Ten Little Fishes" to himself.

At eight o'clock that night, they stole back down the turn-off to the Ruby house. Forrestina cut her headlights and engine and coasted in, silent as a shark. About fifty feet from the house, she pulled over. The lights inside were all off as the shack slept with the occupants inside it. Forrestina wasn't surprised—she bet Mrs. Ruby tried to get her brood in bed as early as possible. Sleep was undoubtedly the only time she had any peace all day.

Forrestina whispered to George, "You ready? Can you do this quietly?" He was usually pretty graceful despite his wooden leg, but now he was sleepy, and when he got sleepy, he sometimes got clumsy.

He yawned wide and said, "Yep. Stealthy as she goes." Forrestina smiled; ever since she'd taught him the word "stealth," George used it as often as he could: the chickens were stealthy, Cleo was stealthy—even the sun creeping in over the curtains did so with stealth, as far as George was concerned.

"Okay, then," she said. "Let's go."

The pair of them inched their car doors open and left them open. They made their way to the back of the pick-up, hunkering down, and she grabbed two sacks of groceries, while George picked up four. As they crept up to the gate, Forrestina stopped and listened. She'd forgotten to check and see if there was a dog. Cautiously she moved forward, George behind her, and after a few steps, she relaxed. If the Rubys had a watch-dog, it was terrible at its job. She motioned for George to stay at the bottom of the sagging wooden stairs to the porch— there was no way to keep his fake leg from clomping. She tiptoed up to the front door and set her bags next to it, then went down and got the bags from George, two at a time, and carried them up too. She nodded at him, and he rushed back to the car, getting himself in and putting his hand on his door handle.

Taking a deep breath, Forrestina lifted her knuckle to the door, and then banged on it as loud as she could. She took off running, leaping down the stairs and bolting towards the car as George slammed his door shut. Yellow light illuminated her path. She threw herself into the car, started the engine, and took off, yanking her door shut on the go. George had his nose pressed to his window and reported, "The momma found the bags!" He turned to Forrestina and raised his fists in victory. "We did it!"

Forrestina drove a half-mile then took a side road to set her back towards her own home. She imagined the Rubys' late-night feast and smiled. "Another successful secret mission complete, Agent Rocket George," she said.

The only reply she got in return was a soft snore; stealthy George had fallen fast asleep.

CHAPTER TWENTY-FIVE

Fayetteville, 1972

WHILE WRITING DOWN FORRESTINA'S own words was Betty's primary form of research, she'd also been busy tracking down as many outside leads as she could. Everybody older than forty seemed to have a story about White River Red, and most were more than happy to share them. Betty sat on dozens of front porches, sipping sweet iced tea, drank gallons of black coffee while eating fresh baked fruit pies in living rooms, and dropped salty Planters peanuts into her icy Coca-Cola bottles in beauty parlors, scribbling on her note pad between sips and bites. "This story is going to cause me to balloon fifty pounds before it is over," she complained to Steve, sucking in her stomach to fasten the belt on her polyester skirt.

He reached over and squeezed her rump appreciatively. "Never mind," he said. "I like a woman with a little meat on her bones."

Betty laughed and slapped him away. "Hands to yourself, Mister," she told him. "You gotta buy the cow if you want the milk."

Steve grinned and lifted Betty's left hand, which, as of three days ago, now sported a half-carat diamond engagement ring. "I get the milk on credit, right?" he said.

"You'll get the goods when you say, 'I do.' And all sales are final," Betty told him, before kissing him deeply.

Back at work, Murray asked Betty how things were progressing on the story, and she fobbed him off by replying, "Fine. It's going to be a dandy."

She knew he was anxious to get her back full time on obits, but Betty was just as determined to stay off. Forrestina's story was the only one she was interested in telling. Before he could ask any more questions, Betty ducked down out of sight into her "office"—one of the ten three-walled partitions in the open room that was supposed to afford her a sense of privacy, though the noise of phones ringing, typewriters clacking, and loud voices discussing work and personal stories negated any sense of being alone. As she sifted through the stacks of notes on her desk, a woman peeked her head over the top of the corkboard cubicle wall. "Miss McLaughlin?" she asked uncertainly.

"Yes?" Betty replied, looking up from her electric typewriter at a tidy woman in her early thirties, slim, with a puffy cloud of light brown hair that was styled in a dated 1960s bouffant. The woman stepped around the wall into Betty's workspace. "My dad told me you were looking for stories about White River Red and suggested I contact you," she said. "Do you have a minute?"

Betty was already up and reaching for her leather fringed jacket. Most of the people she'd spoken to so far about Forrestina were older, but this woman would've been a child when she knew Forrestina, and Betty was eager to get a fresh perspective from a different generation. "Absolutely, Miss. . .?"

"Please call me Jo. Jo March," the woman said. Seeing the expression on Betty's face, she laughed and said, "Yes, my mother knew what she was doing when she named me. She loved *Little Women*. Goodness, the teasing I endured as a child!" She pushed the bridge of her square-lensed glasses up on her nose a little. "Truth be told, I never minded that much. I was always secretly proud to be named after a heroine who knew her own mind."

"Well, Jo March, can we go to the diner across the street to talk?" Betty asked. "It's so crowded and noisy here at the newspaper office."

Jo agreed at once. As they left, Betty called out to Don, who'd stayed well away from her ever since he'd been publicly shamed, "Don, I'm going to lunch if anyone asks."

"Okay," he said, not even glancing up from the copy he was working on.

Betty remembered that the Fayetteville Purple Bulldogs had experienced a very narrow win against the Springdale Bulldogs last weekend, and she figured Don was busy crafting a bitterly acerbic response. He took town pride very seriously.

Betty pushed the glass main door of the newspaper office open, and together she and Jo walked down the steps that led to the outside. Across the street, the women settled in a back booth at *The Blue Plate Special*, sliding across the baby-blue vinyl seats to face one another across the table. After placing their orders with Cheryl, the waitress who greeted Betty by name, Betty opened her notebook and took out her pen, poised for action.

"So, Miss March—sorry—Jo," Betty said, "tell me your White River Red story."

Jo took a sip of the coffee Cheryl had set down. "When I first met Red at school during the annual Forrestina Campbell Day, she was tending to an old nag of a pony who was not feeling up to being clambered on by fifty children," she began. She smiled at the memory. "She was so gentle with that poor old horse. The other kids were busy playing the games she'd brought and taking turns riding the other two ponies, but I just wanted to sit with her and the sick horse—I loved animals. While we sat there together, quietly stroking the pony's mane, we soon got to talking about all kinds of animals and the care of them. She talked to me like I was a grown up, not like I was a little kid, you know? She was the first adult to speak to me that way, like we were equals and I had something interesting to say. I never forgot how good that talk made me feel."

"How old were you?" Betty asked.

"I was eight," Jo said. She took another sip of coffee. "When it was time for school to be over, Red said to me, 'You're a nice young lady, Jo, and seem to have a way with God's lesser creatures. You ever think about being a veterinarian when you grow up?' I hadn't of course—all the grown ladies I knew were housewives and mothers. I thought that's what I had to be too, and

I said so. Red said, 'Honey, you can be whatever God gifted you to be. If you want to tend a house and raise a family, why you do it—it's a noble calling. But if you want to do something different, then you do that.' She shook my hand and said, 'If you *do* decide to become a vet, I'll count on you to come out and help me with my critters.' When I went home and told my mother about that conversation, she surprised me by saying, 'Well, Ms. Red is right. You want to go to school to be an animal doctor, your dad and I will be happy to help.' You could've knocked me over with a feather!"

"So did you become a veterinarian?" Betty asked.

Jo shook her head. "No," she said. "But I did go to college—got a degree in pharmacology. I'm the head pharmacist at Miller's Drugstore in Chouteau."

Betty was surprised; Chouteau was a town in Oklahoma between Springdale and Tulsa, almost a two-hour drive. Miss March had come quite a ways to tell her story. Betty scribbled down a couple of notes and then said, "So tell me about this Forrestina Campbell Day. No one has mentioned it to me so far."

Jo beamed. "Oh, it was wonderful," she said. "Every year in May, Red would show up at our school, Jaybird Elementary, with her horse trailer and pick-up. She put on a little carnival just for us, and everything was free—the pony rides, the rat games, the balloons, and the blackberry shortcake."

"*Blackberry* shortcake?" Betty said. "I've never heard of blackberry shortcake before—just strawberry."

Jo said, "Well, it was because Red hated strawberries—she grew and sold them but refused to eat them because she said they made her itch—so she and that Rocket George who lived with her picked wild blackberries all over Northwest Arkansas and Northeast Oklahoma, canning jars and jars of the stuff and sealing it with paraffin. When it was school carnival time, she'd bring dozens of those jars of blackberries, along with stacks of light angel food cakes and freshly-made, sweet whipped cream, and she'd get the cooks to make up bowls of the dessert for us all. It was the best thing I'd ever tasted." She closed her eyes for a moment and sighed wistfully. "Blackberry shortcake—a White River Red specialty, tart and sweet and original, just like her."

Cheryl arrived back at the booth, balancing two heavy white ceramic plates of food. She set them down in front of Betty and Jo, checked to make sure they were all right, then left them to their talking. She was accustomed to the reporters from the newspaper office using this as their unofficial interview room, and Betty knew she wouldn't bother the women again until they called for the check. Betty took a big bite from her cheeseburger. It was cooked exactly the way she liked it—crispy well-done. Jo picked daintily at her Cobb salad. "I remember when I could eat like that and still stay skinny," she said. "Ah, the joys of youth and metabolism. Enjoy it."

Betty wiped the grease of the burger from her lips with the paper napkin she'd pulled from the metal dispenser on the table. "I'm afraid it's catching up with me already," she said. "I'm going to have to diet like crazy to fit into my wedding dress."

"Oh, you're getting married?" Jo said. "Congratulations! When's the big day?"

"January first," Betty said. "New Year, new life." She dipped a French fry in catsup. "So back to your story. Forrestina came every year to your elementary school for a carnival. How did the teachers feel about that?"

"Oh, I think they loved it," Jo said. "It was an entire day they didn't have to teach, after all—a little vacation for them, too. Red and George took care of everything—the setting up, the cleaning up, the cost—and they always included everyone at the school. We kids sure got a hoot out of watching Mr. Jackson, our principal, betting on the rats and Miss Shelly poking bananas at that baboon Red loved so much." Jo shook her head. "Poor Red—when that monkey died, it just about did her in." She took a bite of her salad and said, "Did you know she wanted to have it stuffed?" She shuddered a little. "The idea of that baboon with its long teeth and glass amber eyes watching you wherever you went . . . ghastly. Thank God it didn't work out."

"Why didn't it work out?" Betty asked. Forrestina hadn't gotten around to telling her about the death of Cleo yet.

"Well, the story around school was that she found the monkey—what was its name?"

"Cleo," Betty replied.

"That's right—Cleo. Cleo got sick after getting into some rat poison Red put out in the shed. Ironic, right? Red liked trained rats in a cage but not in her shed. After Cleo died, Red was hysterical, sad and feeling guilty all at once. She loaded the dead baboon up in a big Styrofoam cooler she kept in the shed—gracious, she had *everything* in that shed—put it in her pick-up bed, and drove hell-for-leather to the Piggly Wiggly. She packed the monkey in ice right there in the parking lot and then headed for Tulsa, where she'd found a man who said he would stuff it for her. Not quite to Locust Grove, on a stretch that was pretty deserted, her truck blew a tire, and as usual, Red didn't have a spare. She was always giving her spares away to poor folks who had need of them.

"Red stood on the side of the road all day, trying to flag down help, but back then the highway to Tulsa could be pretty lonely. It was the middle of July, hot as the Devil's breath, and by the time a farmer stopped, the ice had all melted and poor old Cleo had started to turn. Red ended up taking Cleo back home and burying her in the back pasture, where she had quite a pet cemetery by that point. Red was always taking in wounded animals and trying to fix them up—raccoons, possums, once, a tiny baby skunk who waddled after her like a dog—and when the animals eventually died, she stuck them in her pet cemetery, putting up wooden crosses that bore their names, the date they died, and some silly epitaph she or George came up with. Not surprisingly, Cleo got a BIG grave marker, with the words, 'Beloved Cleopatra: Of All Pharaoh's Wives, You Were the Furriest.'"

Betty threw back her head and roared with laughter, and Jo joined in. "Yep," she said, wiping merry tears from her eyes, "Red was something else." She reached across the table and took Betty's hand. "I'm so glad you're writing a story about her," she said. "She was an amazing person. Fearless, with a heart of gold." She leaned her chin in her hands, elbows on the table. "A school friend of mine who lives in West Fork visited Red a couple years back and said she caught Red sitting on her porch, crying her eyes out because she was missing George. By that time she'd lost everything." She sighed. "It doesn't seem fair that someone who gave so much to so many ended up with nothing. But that was Red—she never saved for her own rainy day tomorrow if she could help someone with their showers today."

Full of misgiving, Betty made a note to ask Forrestina about George during her next visit. She looked at her wristwatch and motioned to Cheryl for the check. Betty said, "I've really got to get back to work—I've got a deadline today. But Jo, I sure do appreciate you talking to me."

The women walked back to the office together chatting, then Betty thanked her again and headed into the office. She was deep in typing that day's conversation when Murray's head appeared above her wall.

"Betty, my office. Now, please."

Betty stopped typing and replied, "Right away, Boss" to the back of his head; he'd already started walking back to his own office. Betty scanned the last line she'd written, scribbled down the next hook on a piece of paper, and stood. Through the big window that faced out on the cubicles, she could see Murray settling himself in at his desk.

She walked over and knocked on the half-open door, and he beckoned her in with his hand. Betty entered the room and saw that as usual there was nowhere for her to sit, so she just stood at his desk, waiting, her hands folded in front of her. She felt like a school girl in the principal's office. Finally Murray wrote a few notes on whatever it was he was reading, capped his pen, and set it down. He looked up. "So, Betty," he said, "I need a serious update on the White River Red story."

"Well, sir," Betty said, "I've been getting quite the tales from her and about her. Enough to write a book."

Murray looked at Betty severely over the top of his glasses. He said nothing, so Betty kept on talking. "The things she has lived through—my word, you wouldn't believe how—"

"When will you have something ready for print?" Murray interrupted. "We've been short-handed on our basic reporting because you've been spending so much time either talking to the old bird or working on her story." He leaned back in his chair and set his head in his interlaced hands behind him. "I need something soon—short copy for a lifestyle piece. Nothing more. This isn't a serial, and it is *not*" he sat up and pointed a long finger at her "a *book*. So you'd better get to editing what you've got."

Betty flushed. Honestly, she had no idea how she was going to condense all that Forrestina had told her, but she'd been working at the newspaper long enough to know that most of it would end up on the chopping block. Reluctantly she said, "Can you give me one more week? I have a meeting with Forrestina again in a few days and there are some loose ends that need to be tied up." The idea of not talking with Forrestina weekly made her miserable, but she'd known the day would come when she'd have to finish this story.

"One week," Murray said. "And remember: People like to read happy, folksy tales while they're relaxing on Sundays."

Betty was alarmed—she would not have called Forrestina's story a happy one by any stretch. Murray must've seen something on her face, because he said. "Happy, Betty. I don't want some tragic sad-sack tale, you got it? White River Red's name makes people reminisce with a smile—I don't want anything that will change that."

Betty nodded, despondent, knowing that most of what she'd written would have to be re-done and that facts would have to be glossed over. *Such is the life of a reporter*, she thought glumly. As she headed back to her desk, ready to ball up what had taken her all morning to write, Betty realized that Forrestina would probably take Murray's side if asked. She'd want the truth to have a cheerful face painted on it; her whole life had been spent trying to make people forget their troubles. Resigned, Betty rolled a fresh sheet of paper into her cream-colored Eldorado typewriter and started Forrestina's story anew.

By the time she was ready to leave for the day, Betty had her frame, but she still needed an ending. She pulled the last paper out of the typewriter's roller and set it on the short stack of already-typed papers, then tugged a clear plastic cover over the Eldorado to keep the dust out. She was more than ready to go home; she was tired and a little sad, and she was looking forward to seeing her fiancée's kind, open face. In the morning she would call the nursing home and confirm her appointment, but tonight she was planning on eating a good meal (Steve was a terrific cook), drink a glass of good wine, and hopefully get a good night's sleep. She thought of Forrestina once telling her that this here life was all she got, so she'd better make the best of it. Betty intended to take her wise advice.

A few days later, she interviewed Forrestina back in her room. As usual, Ethel the roommate was lying curled on her side, eyes open, lost in whatever interior world she roamed. Forrestina was propped up in her chair, a lilac and lettuce-green knitted afghan wrapped around her thin shoulders. She'd been sick lately, one of the home's nurses told Betty when she'd arrived, and today Forrestina looked every minute of her eighty years, drawn and hollow-cheeked. Betty noticed she clutched a white kerchief in her hand, and every once in a while she'd raise it to her mouth and hack a cough into it as they talked.

"Ms. Forrestina, I've got most of the stuff I need for our story," Betty said, trying to cover her concern by sounding cheerful. "You're almost rid of me and all my pesky questions."

Forrestina cocked her head like a bird, not fooled one bit. "Shoot, you know you're no bother," she said. "I'll miss your visits, girl. I surely will."

"I can still come and see you, even when the story is done," Betty said, and at that moment, she meant it. Forrestina just nodded her head wearily in response. Something else was different about her, other than the tiredness, and

Betty puzzled over it for a few minutes before she figured it out. "Ms. Forrestina, you're not wearing your earrings," she exclaimed. Betty had never once seen her without them, and most everyone she'd talked to always mentioned Red and her diamond ear-bobs—it was as much a part of her regular costume as her overalls, boots, and hat.

Forrestina reached up and touched her bare lobes. "I sent them Priority Mail to Tina, Sarah's girl," she said. "I don't want this place selling them to pay my bill when I pop off. They need to be back in Sarah's family."

Betty forced a laugh. "Pop off—honestly. You're as fit as a fiddle, Ms. Forrestina."

She was rewarded with a wry, weak half-smile. After a few minutes of silence, Betty said, "Hey, I spoke to a young woman who told me about the Forrestina Campbell Day carnivals you held at her school. She said you inspired her to go to college."

"Did I?" Forrestina asked listlessly. "Well, how do you like that?" She fell silent again. This was the first time Betty had to drag conversation from Forrestina; she could tell that the old woman was really not feeling very well, and Betty was worried. Still she pressed on—she had to get a few things locked down, if not for the paper, then for her own sense of closure. Betty cleared her throat. "She said that one time a friend of hers came to visit you and you were crying about George. I wondered what happened to him. Do you think you're up to telling that story?"

"Of course I am," Forrestina snapped. "I'm not senile yet, am I?" Seeing Betty's hurt expression, she reached over to pat Betty's arm. "I'm sorry, hon," she said. "All these ghosts we've stirred up have been keeping me awake at night, stealing my sleep. Lucy always said that the dead are just waiting around to hear what we have to say about them, and that once we start talking, they push in because it's the only way they get to live again, through our memories." She lifted her chin and shook her fist in the air. "Did you hear that, you crazy old gypsy bird? I'm talking about you. Enjoy!"

Cold dread made Betty's skin retract. "You're not talking about George, are you? Please tell me he's not dead," she whispered.

"Oh, no," Forrestina said. "Why, I got a letter from him just last week." She waved her hand towards her nightstand. "Right there on top of my Bible—grab that and have a look."

Betty exhaled in relief and obeyed, pulling a half-sheet of yellow construction paper out of an envelope. The return address was Ohio. On the yellow paper, George had written with a purple crayon in a child-like scrawl, *"Dear Red, I am fine. Sister takes good care of me, tho she still does not lik to eat spam sand witches as much as we do. She makes good peach pi so it is ok. I hope you are fine. I miss you. Don't forget me. Your pal ever, Rocket George. P.S. I love Sister but you are still my best friend."*

Betty swallowed the stone-sized lump in her throat, blinking hard at the tears that had started in her eyes. She took a long time replacing the letter, struggling to get control of herself, before sitting back down in her chair. She pushed a lock of hair behind her ear, swiping at her eye with her pinky finger as she did so, wiping a tell-tale drop of water away with it. "So George has a sister," she said briskly.

Forrestina handed Betty a hanky with a wry smile. "Mary Brooks—sweetest gal I've ever met," she said. "Sometimes when I'm being selfish and feeling sorry for myself, I wish she weren't so sweet. Then I would've had an excuse to turn her away. But no, that girl was all the good I ever wanted for my George. She showed up at my place in West Fork about ten years ago."

"You left Springdale?" Betty asked. "Any particular reason why?"

Forrestina snorted. "More people started to move in and cramp my style. Lots of hoity-toity folk complaining about my place, saying I need to clean it up, talking about how trashy it looked outside." She glared at Betty. "I had a use for every single thing I saved, and if I didn't need it at that particular moment, I might sometime in the future. You wouldn't believe what people just throw away."

Betty thought of her grandpa's description of "Red's junk-yard," as he called it when she'd asked him to tell her his stories about Forrestina, and bit back a smile.

"So I finally got tired of the fussing, packed up my stuff, and moved to West Fork, where there weren't as many people to stick their noses into my business. Traded my place for one up there in the woods. Turned out to be a bad move—I didn't have so much hassle, true, but the firewood-selling business wasn't great. Most people up there cut their own wood. Plus the house I traded was worth a lot more than the one I ended up with." She shrugged. "Live and learn, I reckon.

"So one day, George and I were sitting down to a late supper, and we heard this knock on the door. George said, 'I'll get it,' and when he opened the door, I heard him say in this wondering voice, 'Momma? Momma! I thought you was dead!'

"A soft female voice, tender as a turtledove's, said, 'George, it's your sister, Mary. Lord God, George. Is it really you?' I stood up from the table and when I walked over to the doorway, there was a woman in her early to mid-thirties wrapping her arms tight around my boy. He was goggling at her, his arms trapped to his sides by her hug. 'How can you be Mary?' he asked scornfully. 'You're too old.'

"Mary laughed, and God almighty, that laugh was bird-song and starlight. She said, 'Georgie, I grew up. You did too!'

"He stared at her for a long time, struggling to make sense of it all, then his frown broke apart into the biggest smile I'd ever seen. He cried, 'Mary! My own baby sister,' and started hugging her back so hard that she gasped and said, still laughing, 'Easy, George! You're gonna squeeze me half to death!'

"He turned around and saw me watching. He dragged the woman in by her hand. 'Red!' he said. 'You'll never believe it. This here is my kid sister, Mary. I ain't seen her since we was kids!' He beamed at her. 'Look at how old she is!'

"The woman, as blond and pretty as her brother, stepped forward shyly. 'Pleased to meet you, Mrs. Campbell,' she said. 'I can't thank you enough for taking care of my brother all these years.' She turned a glowing face to him. It was as if she didn't want to take her eyes off him, like if she did, he might disappear into mist. 'I've been looking for him so long; I can't believe I finally found him.'"

"How *did* she find him?" Betty asked, her mouth agape.

Forrestina said, "Well, you see, she was younger than George by six years. When their momma died, George was seventeen and Mary was just eleven. An aunt in Ohio took Mary in, but George was expected to fend for himself—at that time, a seventeen-year-old was pretty much considered an adult, and George was just slow, not physically handicapped. He found a job with the carnival and then Mary lost track of him. She told me about how she cried and cried when George hugged her goodbye; he was her favorite person in the world, she said, and she missed him every day. She finished school, went to secretarial college, and started working at a lawyer's office. She never married and saved every dime she made to buy a house with two bedrooms; she said her plan was always to find her beloved older brother and bring him to live with her.

"After several years, she quit her first job and started working for a criminal lawyer. He was a good man—a good boss—and they became friends as well as colleagues. When she told him about George, he put her in touch with a private detective he sometimes used for his cases. She hired the detective, but he had a devil of a time tracking George down because of George's job with the carnival—there had been a fire or something, and the carnival's records were all gone. After much effort, he dug up the name of someone from George's last gig who remembered George. The old carnie told the detective about my campsite, the detective called the man from Mississippi who'd bought my place, and that man told him where George and I were living. The morning the detective passed my address on to Mary, she didn't wait one minute—she jumped in her car and drove ten hours straight, only stopping for gas and to pee. And finally there she stood in my living room, big as life and ready to take away my heart, and damn it, I couldn't even begrudge her for it."

Forrestina sighed. "Of course, there was no way I was going to stop George from leaving with her. You shoulda seen them—their faces were twin fountains of elation whenever they looked at each other. Mary joined us for supper that night, and George held onto her hand the whole time. He just wouldn't turn loose, and she didn't seem to want him to. She stayed the night, and then the next morning we packed up George's belongings in a couple of cardboard boxes and I saw them on their way. I made her take what money I had left—told her it was George's back pay. I wanted to help them out as much as I could."

Forrestina pulled the afghan closer around her shoulders. "Gracious, it was so *quiet* around the house without George jabbering every minute of every day. But Mary's arrival was a blessing. I'd started slowing down, and I had begun to worry about what would happen to George once I was too feeble to function properly. I didn't want to saddle him with the responsibility of taking care of me—he could hardly take care of himself." She smiled wistfully. "They didn't abandon me, though. They've been out to visit a few times, and she's real good about calling every two weeks to check on me. She always lets George talk on the phone as long as he likes, and those calls make my day, though I do worry about her long-distance phone bills. And George writes me every week or so. He's so happy. My boy." She sighed and sank into another silence, and Betty let her be, scribbling details in her notebook. After a quiet while, Betty noticed Forrestina's breathing had become deeper, and she looked up to see that the old woman was fast asleep, her head tilted back slightly, her wrinkled lips pursing soft puffs of air out as she exhaled. She looked to Betty like she was about a thousand years old. Betty slipped her pad of paper and pen into her purse, then leaned over and adjusted Forrestina's afghan. She stirred and opened her eyes blearily.

"Ms. Forrestina?" Betty said softly. "I'm gonna head out now, let you get some rest."

Forrestina reached over and took Betty's hand, squeezing it. "I think you can call me Red now, honey," she said. She closed her eyes and fell back asleep. Betty kissed her forehead lightly, something she would never have dared to do while Forrestina was awake, and tiptoed out of the room, closing the door behind her.

When Betty got back to the office, there was a note on her desk from Murray that said "*Check back issues—info on WRR.*" Even though it was almost quitting time, Betty headed down to the basement that was designated as the newspaper's archive room and found a notice of auction from October, 1971, sitting on the top of a file cabinet. The ad read: "*Auction: Estate of 'White River Red'—Forrestina Campbell. Declared Incompetent, Sale Ordered by the Washington County Probate Court.*"

Incompetent. Betty stared at that hateful word for a long time. Though she knew it was just a legal term used so that Forrestina could be moved into the state-run nursing home, it made her furious. There was nothing incompetent about Forrestina Campbell—circus queen, rat lady, barmaid, kind, generous, funny, brave White River Red. *Where were* those *descriptions*? Betty wondered.

Betty skimmed through the inventory of items for sale, and as she read, fascinated, images of Red's stories began to take shape. Among the usual household junk, the auction listed an organ grinder that "*still worked and played several opera tunes,*" pony ride equipment, various carnival tents and poles, cases of stuffed animals such as rats, raccoons, pigeons, and "*quartz glass of all shapes and colors!*" Betty turned the page and caught her breath. There, in grainy newspaper black-and-white, was a picture captioned "*Carnival 'Wheel of Chance.'*" Forrestina's rat wheel. Betty touched the picture with a fingertip, jealous of the stranger who'd ended up carrying it away. Did he know how very lucky he was to possess such a treasure? Could he sense, even a little, the wheel's importance when he bid on it?

Betty replaced the newspaper in its file and left the archive room. The building was dark—it'd grown late while Betty was reading, and everyone had left for the day. She gathered up her notes, locked the door behind her, and headed home to write her article. As per Murray's instructions, she would make it short and sunny and filled with only half-truths, but Betty no longer minded. Forrestina's real story, was, like her rat wheel, something sacred hidden in the ordinary, and like the wheel's new owner, Betty was lucky to have it. When the article came out on Sunday, Betty took two copies, still warm from the press, to the nursing home. One she gave to Sue, as promised, and the other she presented with a flourish to Red. "Here you are," she said, dropping the paper, opened to Forrestina's page, into the elderly woman's lap. "You're officially famous."

Forrestina, still weak and a little distant, managed a small smile. "Well, hot dog," she said. She looked down briefly, then handed the paper back to Betty. "Would you sit down and read it to me, honey?" she asked. Betty obliged, and when she'd finished, Forrestina applauded lightly. "You're a hell of a writer, girl," she said. "Thank you for making me sound so good."

"You're welcome," Betty said, and she leaned over and hugged her frail friend. She was a little deflated—it was hard to celebrate when Red seemed so minimized. "And thank *you*," she said. "For telling me your story—all of your story. I'll never forget it."

Forrestina smiled, and for just a moment, her spark was back. "You make sure that boy of yours treats you right," she said. She pointed at Betty's engagement ring. "Don't you take any guff from him."

Betty laughed. "Why don't you line him out for me at the wedding?" she asked. "We'd love for you to attend."

Forrestina tugged at her hat, looking pleased. "Well, I thank you for the invite," she said. "And if I'm feeling better, I promise I'll try and make it." Unbeknownst to them both, she would not be able to keep her promise; a bout of pneumonia would land her in the hospital for three weeks at the end of December and into the New Year.

After a few minutes of small talk, Betty left and headed back to the office to pick up a few more copies of the paper. On her desk was another note from Murray: *Congrats on the piece—it was good. Come Monday, I've got another feature for you to start working on. —M.*

She sat at her desk, reading over her story one more time. Murray was right—it was pretty darn good.

CHAPTER TWENTY-SIX

Fayetteville, 1973

RED DIED IN AUGUST OF 1973. The cause of death, according to the official coroner's report, was heart failure, but the romantic side of Betty wondered if Red had really died of a broken heart—being cooped up in that depressing nursing home must've been torture for her. Betty heard about Forrestina's death from Murray Jackson; by then, Betty had married Steve and they'd moved up to Tulsa, Oklahoma, where Steve had gotten a job at a respectable law firm. Betty briefly considered trying to get a job at a newspaper in Tulsa but abandoned the idea when she discovered she was pregnant—the morning sickness was something awful, lasting not just mornings, but afternoons and nights as well, and with Steve's job, she didn't have to work if she didn't want to. Right now, anyway, she felt like she had enough on her plate.

The call came while Betty was reading a recipe for Chop Suey, which she'd planned to try for supper that night; because she was four months along and finally over the worst of the sickness, she was actually interested in food again. Betty picked up the receiver of the phone, and before she could speak, she heard the familiar voice of her former boss. He said, not bothering to identify himself first, "Hey Bets, how you doing?"

"I'm okay, Murray. What's going on?" Betty replied.

"Just thought you'd want to know that White River Red died three nights ago. Funeral's in two days. Graveside service."

The blood rushed from Betty's head, and she sank down in a nearby easy-chair, gripping the phone's handle tightly. Dimly she heard Murray say, "Betty? You okay?"

Of course *I'm not okay*, Betty wanted to shout. *Red is dead but the world is still spinning.* It was like hearing Old Faithful had dried up, or the Grand Canyon had filled with water—Red was supposed to be a monument Betty could visit whenever she wanted. She was supposed to be around to meet Betty's son or daughter. She finally managed to say, through numb lips, "Yeah. Fine. Where?"

Murray gave her the name of the cemetery and the time of the funeral. Betty thanked him, but before she hung up, a terrible thought struck her. "Murray," she said, "do you know if the home called Rocket George and his sister with the news?"

"I doubt it," Murray said. "That place puts in little effort when it comes to funerals—gotta keep costs low. The only reason I found out was because Mark, our morgue tipster, was the one who collected her body, and he thought I'd be interested because of your story. I got some details to pass to the obit department—I made sure that it went out this morning—and she didn't list a next-of-kin."

"Well, thanks," Betty said again, then hung up. She ached with sorrow right down to her toes, and when she thought of the difficult phone call she would have to make to George's sister (Betty had kept her number in her pile of White River Red notes), she ached even more.

When Steve came home, he found Betty still sitting in the chair, holding the phone, day having turned its corner into dark, her eyes swollen from tears. Mary's weeping and George's confused, anguished bellowing still rang in her ears. She'd never heard such grief. Silently, Betty's good man gathered her up in his arms and held her as she cried like a child. When she told him she wanted to go to the funeral alone, he didn't argue.

On the day of the funeral, Betty rose early, dressed in a simple sleeveless black shift dress that accommodated her expanding girth, and drove the two hours from Tulsa to Friendship Cemetery in Springdale, Arkansas. Red had purchased herself a plot there many years ago when she still had cash in her pocket—Betty remembered her story about how she'd bought the plot as a favor for a struggling funeral salesman. She'd felt sorry for him, she'd said. As Betty stepped into the quiet, dignified little cemetery where Forrestina was laid to rest, she was happy that Red's generosity had finally paid her back. The State of Arkansas had shelled out for the simple pine box Forrestina was buried in, but there were no casket flowers and no tombstone; if she'd died without that funeral plot, she'd likely have been cremated, her ashes disposed of privately. It was too awful for Betty to think about.

As she looked around, Betty was astonished by the number of people at Red's funeral—at least sixty, all crowded around the mound of freshly turned dirt. She recognized many faces, people she'd interviewed for her article, including Jo March. Jo spotted Betty and waved, sadness dulling her normally friendly smile. She was speaking to a strikingly tall, beautiful woman whose sheet of string-straight black hair fell to her waist. The woman turned her head, and Betty recognized the diamond earrings flashing in her lobes. Betty realized she must be Tina, the daughter of Sarah's who shared Red's name. Betty felt the same sense of wonder she'd experienced when looking at the picture of Red's rat wheel, like a kid who sees her fairy tale stories coming to life.

The preacher conducting the sermon kept the service short and sincere, focusing his message on Red's compassionate generosity. "May we all take the lessons of Red's life and find our own ways to help others, to give all that we can, to show our love in our actions," he said at the end. He closed in prayer, asking that God be merciful on this beloved daughter of His, and Betty wept freely as she thought of the earthly parents who'd chosen not to know the masterpiece they'd had a part in creating. What fools they'd been.

Once the preacher was finished, Betty made her way through the crowd, saying hello to people she knew, answering questions about her impending motherhood, agreeing that yes, the funeral service had been nice. Jo hugged her fiercely, then introduced her to Tina. "I started to call in and check on Red every couple of months after she sent my mother's earrings to me," Tina told Betty, "and I happened to call the morning she died. I knew I had to come to the funeral—my mother loved her so much—so I booked a flight right away."

After a few minutes, Betty worked her way over to the preacher and thanked him for his sermon. She found out that he had been, like Jo, another one of Red's Jaybird Elementary kids, and that he'd requested the job and refused payment. Betty took herself off to the side and watched as many people knelt, whispered quiet words to Red, and laid flowers on her grave. Betty still held the bouquet she'd brought; she was waiting for the crowd to leave before she placed them on Forrestina's grave. Rather than the traditional funeral lilies, Betty had chosen flowers that were riotous in color—a huge yellow sunflower, orange Black-Eyed Susans, white daisies, purple cornflowers, pink foxgloves, all tied up with an apple-red bow. Carnie colors, in other words.

Finally, when everyone had left, Betty stepped over to the grave. She leaned down, sifting through the cards attached to the bouquets blanketing the mound of dirt, reading the names and the heartfelt "thank-yous." *Red would be so mad*, she thought, smiling. Still, who could find fault with those tiny rectangles of thanks? Looking at all the notes, it was clear to Betty that Red had been loved. A large wreath of pink roses with a plastic blue-and-red toy rocket tied to it caught her eye, and she realized that though Mary and George had not been able to fly down from Ohio on such short notice, they'd managed to order a very special remembrance to be put on Red's grave. Betty stooped, kneeling in the dirt, and laid her own offering under the simple metal post that served as Red's grave-marker. "*Forrestina Bradley Campbell*," the white paper under Plexiglas on the rectangular marker read, the letters starkly, impassively black. "*Born April 15, 1891. Died August 19, 1973.*" It was pitiful in its cruel brevity, but Betty knew that didn't matter. The crowd at Red's funeral had been testament enough to her life.

"Rats, rats, come play with my rats," Betty whispered. She stood and brushed the dirt from her knees. "I'll see you around, Ms. Forrestina," she said, gazing down at the grave. She needed to say Forrestina's name aloud, just in case. In the buzzing of that hot, late-summer afternoon, a sudden delicious breeze lifted the sweaty hair from her forehead, and Betty felt the stirrings of Red and all her Peters, Pauls, and Judases, summoned, and listening carefully.

AUTHOR'S NOTE

This book is a complicated mish-mash of truth (as far as memories and stories told can ever be true) and imagination, a fictional work heavily influenced by a few facts. Some of the characters were real—Forrestina "White River Red" Campbell was real, "Big Broad Tosser" Keyes was real (though I christened him with the first name, "Max"), and Jack Campbell was real—but most of the other characters as they are written are not. The few solid facts I included were gathered from various places: from my grandparents, who told me their stories, from the people who shared their remembrances at a Shiloh Museum's featured event about White River Red in Springdale, and from a seven-page booklet titled *White River Red: A Legend in Her Own Time,* written by local historian and storyteller, the late Phillip Steele. Mr. Steele, a faithful curator of the tales of the Ozarks, conducted hours of interviews and compiled his notes into a brief history of Forrestina's life, and I am forever grateful for the insight I gleaned from his tiny but wonderful biography.

A note about Forrestina's grave: Seven years after her death, a group of local folks decided that Forrestina had gone without a proper headstone long enough, and through their efforts, raised enough money to buy her a large, rose-red granite stone. It was erected in 1981, and upon it is engraved the symbols of Forrestina's colorful life: a merry-go-round, a big top, an elephant, a rose—and of course, a rat. The inscription reads:

"White River Red"
Forrestina Bradley Campbell
April 15, 1891 – Aug. 19, 1973
A Legend in Her Own Time.
Erected in Her Memory By Friends, 1981

As Red once told George, it's good to have friends.

—Becky Marietta, June 27, 2017

ACKNOWLEDGEMENTS

This book of mine began with the gleam of an eye and a few stories told on front porches. For the stories and the gleam that turned into a blaze, I am grateful to my grandpas, Fred D. Stamps and Ira Lewis, who I called Pa and Chief. I miss them.

As I mentioned in the author's note, I am indebted to Phillip Steele for his short biography about Forrestina and for his steadfast chronicling of Arkansas history. I am also grateful to Shiloh Museum for hosting the talk that allowed me to visit with so many folks who remembered the real White River Red. If, dear reader, you're ever in Springdale, Arkansas, you should drop by the museum—you might even get to see Red's Wheel of Chance!

Big, hearty, thank you hulloos to my beta readers, Molly Martin and my mom, Sandra Lewis, who both laughed and cried in exactly the right places, and Amanda Himes, gentle friend and English pro. You all saw this book in its very rough infant stage and you still had kind things to say about it. Asante sana.

Thank you to all my writing mentors. To Dr. Jeff Conine, who taught me how to be honest in my writing, who faithfully and uncomplainingly read everything I sent him, and who never let me cheat, thank you for all that AND for being my friend these many years. I believe I owe you lunch. Thanks also to Dr. Jackie Wilcox and Professor Susan Semrow, who probably never realized how much their encouraging words about my writing gave me courage. And thank you to my dad, Richard Lewis, my writing hero who gave me this talent and has always encouraged me to use it.

Thank you to my precious friend, Lori McLaughlin Kauffman, who was always my best reader. Her laugh was the wind chime of my soul, and I miss her every day. She was and continues to be my favorite muse.

Thanks, too, to my other super pals, the "Aunties," the "Impenetrables": Shannon Clayberg, Trisha Lynn, Jenna Scates, and my sister, Sara Toombs. You lassies laugh with me, boogie with me, get mad at who I want you to get mad at, clap for me when I need it the most, and keep me sane, and I love you for it. Let's keep growing old and sassy together, shall we?

Thank you, thank you to my fantastic editor, Jennifer Haskin, for her sharp eye and ever-cheerful, ever-helpful suggestions. My book is better because of her. Big thanks as well to all the excellent folks at TouchPoint Press. I appreciate y'all, every one.

And finally, thank you to my husband, Casey Marietta, who whooped and danced me around the room when I discovered my book was going to be published. His unwavering belief in my abilities, however enhanced and distorted by love, is what keeps me going in this life. I love you, Doll-Boy.

Made in the USA
Coppell, TX
20 April 2021